The Ink Stain

Also by Meg and Tom Keneally

The Soldier's Curse
The Unmourned
The Power Game

Meg and Tom
KENEALLY

The Ink Stain

THE
MONSARRAT
SERIES

VINTAGE BOOKS
Australia

A Vintage Australia book
Published by Penguin Random House Australia Pty Ltd
Level 3, 100 Pacific Highway, North Sydney NSW 2060
penguin.com.au

Penguin
Random House
Australia

First published by Vintage Australia in 2019

Copyright © Margaret Keneally and The Serpentine Publishing Company 2019

The moral right of the authors has been asserted.

All rights reserved. No part of this publication may be reproduced, published, performed in public or communicated to the public in any form or by any means without prior written permission from Penguin Random House Australia Pty Ltd or its authorised licensees.

Addresses for the Penguin Random House group of companies can be found at global.penguinrandomhouse.com/offices.

A catalogue record for this book is available from the National Library of Australia

ISBN 978 0 14379 030 3

Cover image courtesy of Shutterstock
Cover design by Christabella Designs
Typeset in 12.5/15.5 Adobe Caslon Pro by Midland Typesetters, Australia
Printed in Australia by Griffin Press, an accredited ISO AS/NZS 14001:2004 Environmental Management System printer

MIX
Paper from
responsible sources
FSC® C009448

For Jane Hall Keneally
Descendant of an early newspaper hero of New South Wales
And to the memory of Dr John Keneally

From the Sydney Chronicle

March 1826

Yet those who condemn the ticket-of-leave man for what they see as his unwillingness to put the full weight of his shoulder to the colonial wheel need ask themselves: why should he?

A man who has served his sentence should be able to expect freedom, yet those with a ticket of leave cannot truly be called free. They are unable to travel where their fancy takes them. They are unable to apply such skills as they have in districts where these skills are needed, if such districts fall outside the boundaries to which they have been confined. They are, of course, unable to return home.

I have noted more than once that those who lament the attitudes of many with tickets of leave are loath to acknowledge any industry on their part, and would likely ignore the greatest displays of virtue, as long as they can persist in the damaging notion that criminals are created by nature, and cannot escape their destiny. When their self-appointed betters view them thus, it is remarkable they are willing to make even the smallest of contributions to colonial society.

Yet, ticket-of-leave men do make contributions, to their own credit and to the shame of their detractors.

One such man labours in Parramatta's Government House, as clerk to the governor's private secretary. By all accounts in possession of a fine intellect, Hugh Llewelyn Monsarrat once used his gifts to impersonate a barrister. For this, he was justly punished. Now, he bends his intelligence to the task of identifying the colony's most nefarious murderers, ensuring they can no longer ply their gruesome trade.

Such a man is usually shunned in the church and the street by his so-called betters. In the case of Mr Monsarrat, some of those betters would not be alive without him.

Prologue

Sydney Gaol
March 1826

'What's it for this time, Mr Hallward? Trespassing again?'

As the chief warden of Sydney's George Street Gaol, it was a question Frank Gleeson rarely needed to ask – he did not get many return visitors.

'No, Frank. Trespassing was last time – at the church, remember? We're back to criminal libel now.'

The prison stones gave Hallward's deep voice a rumbling, ominous sound. The place had better acoustics than St Paul's Cathedral. Frank should know – he'd heard enough moans bounce off the walls in his time as warden. He found it interesting that here, where the primary walls of the vast colonial penal system were made of water and wilderness, the stones still reproduced some of the echo, bulk and menace of a prison in the British counties.

Hallward, though, was an unusual prisoner. He was not a moaner. He was too busy writing. He was also one of Frank's more frequent guests.

Frank was not above providing some additional comforts in exchange for a fee. He considered himself a practical warden. To those who robbed in the dead of night or forced themselves on women or stabbed rusty daggers into their friends, he gave nuggetty bread and brackish water and the occasional kick in the ribs. But to those who had done no more than stab a piece of paper with a pen – well, no harm in being lenient. Especially when they could pay.

They all, though, paid more than Hallward. Not that he knew it. Frank wanted to keep Hallward writing, so he charged him just enough to cover expenses, and let the man believe he was being genially swindled. At this remove from the British Parliament, the governor had the power of a king. There was no voting here, even for landowners; no boroughs, even rotten ones. The only voice people like Frank had came out of the mouths of people like Hallward.

'Two shillings, then,' said Frank.

Hallward looked up from the desk, which was covered in neat stacks of paper. Probably the finest item ever seen in this cell, the desk stood like a fantastical island in the middle of the grey ooze, the bare splintered boards, and the high, barred and grimed windows. During Hallward's first few incarcerations he had paid handsomely to rent a desk, and Frank had procured him a new one each time. Now Frank kept just this one in a storeroom, knowing it would be needed again before long.

'Price has gone up,' said Hallward.

'Risk has gone up. And the cost of bread. You know this yourself, champion of the common man that you are.'

Hallward chuckled, shaking his head. 'I cannot fault your enterprising nature, Frank. Although many might charge more. As you say, the risk . . .'

'Is worth it. Not all of us have friends in Government House. We need someone to speak for us.'

'I don't believe I've any friends at Government House either. The look on that charlatan Duchamp's face when he poked his head into my cell could've curdled milk.'

'I wish I could have given you some warning, but he arrived unannounced.'

'The question is, why. But a question for another day. All right then. As soon as I'm out. You know I'm good for it. Peter – the new copyboy, you've not met him – will be here to collect all this while I'm in court.'

'And it will be in tomorrow's paper?'

'If I'm allowed to continue writing it,' Hallward said.

'Is it something that might land you back in here?'

'Or ensure I'll never be back here again. Can't tell you this time, Frank, sorry.'

'You can trust me, though! You told me about the break-in story, the one you fought the duel over, and I didn't breathe a word.'

'I know, I know. But this one – I can feel the heat coming off it. It will cut that bastard Darling's administration from neck to crotch. The information in these pages, Frank, is far more dangerous than any musket ball. I would not want to put you at undue risk.'

Frank looked nervously around and peered out the door to make sure Crowdy wasn't listening. His deputy warden, a self-righteous man, was prone to eavesdropping. It would be a great risk to refer to the governor in such crass terms around Crowdy, even for an inveterate upsetter of applecarts like Hallward.

Crowdy couldn't have heard, though, because Frank saw him now, walking down the long hallway towards the cell.

'Time, is it?' said Frank, when Crowdy arrived. 'Already?'

'According to the clock it is. You cannot argue with a clock,' said Crowdy.

Frank shook his head. 'I'm getting as bad as the inmates. They constantly moan that time loses meaning here. But they say it drags, not gallops, and the sun wasn't yet in the corner of the yard when I came in.'

'Well, no matter where the sun is, the cart's here,' said Crowdy. He looked at the desk, then at some chicken bones on a plate on the floor – the remains of Hallward's most recent meal – and scowled. 'Criminals are criminals,' he said to Frank, 'whatever weapon they use to commit their crime.'

'I'll sheath my weapon for now,' said Hallward. He made a great show of stacking his papers, fastidiously smoothing their edges and risking a glance at Frank as he placed them in a drawer.

'More sedition?' Crowdy asked.

'Not a bit of it. Letters to my parents. A few final demands to advertisers who have been less than prompt with their payments – the patent tonic people are the worst.'

Crowdy stepped forward, holding out a hand from which manacles dangled.

'Surely not necessary, in this case,' said Frank.

'His Excellency was willing to chain soldiers who had fought for Britain,' said Crowdy. 'Don't think he'd approve of leaving this one with his hands free.'

Hallward shrugged, putting his hands out for the manacles. 'Must follow processes. Like a good soldier.'

Crowdy placed a rough hand on Hallward's shoulder and shoved him towards the door. 'You coming?' Crowdy asked Frank.

'In a minute. This one's wily, so I'll search the cell for contraband.'

Crowdy nodded, propelled Hallward through the cell door. When a prisoner's hands were bound, Crowdy liked to make their owners move so fast that they risked tripping with no way to break their fall.

Frank waited for Crowdy's and Hallward's footsteps to recede, withdrew the papers from the desk drawer and stuffed them in his shirt. He would have to think of a pretext to stay behind and send Crowdy to guard Hallward in his place. Hallward had entrusted him with the documents in good faith, and when it came to faith, a career of speaking for the downtrodden – not to mention two shillings a day – bought a lot of it.

By the time Frank got outside, Crowdy was unlocking the prison cart. He was having a little trouble with the padlock given that he still had one hand on Hallward's arm, although the prisoner was showing no signs of wishing to flee. Frank guessed that he did not want to provide entertainment for the inhabitants of the buildings that overlooked the prison yard.

'You think he's going to grow wings?' Frank asked Crowdy. 'Give it here.'

He had to admit that even with both hands, wrestling the padlock into submission was no easy task. The blasted thing was becoming increasingly disagreeable in protest at being rained on and infiltrated by the salty ocean breeze.

If Frank had managed to open the door a few seconds earlier, it might not have happened.

The *crack* of the shot, the shock of the disturbed air, sent Frank stumbling backwards to the ground. His skull connected with a rock. He shook his head to clear the encroaching fog, rubbed his eyes, and put his hand down into a puddle – odd, as it hadn't rained for a week.

Odd, too, that the puddle was bright red, and even odder that this liquid was flowing from the ruined forehead of Henry Hallward. His hands, free or not, would have been useless in breaking this particular fall.

~·~

Frank was not the only one who stumbled at the shot. A boy, skirting the outer wall of the prison, jumped and landed awkwardly on a turned ankle. He leaned against the wall for a moment, listening to his breath gradually slow, looking at the sky as he often did when disturbed. The sky, at least, was free.

Between him and the blue was the open attic window of one of the taller houses that fringed the gaol. The window slowly began to close, but not before the boy saw a glint.

Others, he knew, thought of metal in terms of jewellery or finely wrought iron. But his short life in The Rocks had taught him that it more often took the form of a knife, or a gun.

By the time it occurred to him that someone would have to be there to close the window, and might have seen him in the process, he was already running.

Chapter 1

Sydney
April 1826

Hannah Mulrooney didn't trust the woman. Her clothes were far too pristine. They lacked the discreet patches on the black skirts Hannah habitually wore, each tiny stitch a testament to hard work. If you judged this woman by her clothes, she'd never done anything more arduous than lift a fan on a hot day. The buttoned-up blue jacket, the fussy little lace collar, the brooch at the neck – why in the name of God use a brooch when you had perfectly good buttons? – spoke of a woman whose greatest challenge was which cut of meat to tell the cook to order. But the most galling part was her shooting Hannah poisonous looks from the mirror in the boarding house parlour.

'Must I really come?' Hannah asked. 'People talk in front of servants as though they were coat stands. They might not be as loose-lipped in front of ... whatever I am now.'

Hugh Llewelyn Monsarrat lowered his newspaper and sighed. 'Housekeepers usually don't get invited to garden parties at Government House – and the Sydney version of it, no less.

You will learn nothing if you stay here. Few victims of crime touch me as does the case of Hallward, since only enemies of the truth could have wished him dead. I need you and your talent for observation to give him peace.'

Hannah threw Monsarrat a quick smile, took an angry glance in the mirror and looked around the parlour. This place was irritating her, with its fussy little lace doilies and vases that held no flowers. As soon as she and Mr Monsarrat had arrived at the boarding house she had bustled into the kitchen, looking around for the kettle in order to start the journey towards a restorative cup of tea.

'Do you always make yourself at home in other people's kitchens?' The voice was high-pitched and nasal, the irritating monotone of a housefly.

Hannah had turned to see a prim-looking woman with a long nose and pinched lips standing in the kitchen doorway.

'Ah, you must be Miss Douglas. Thank you for letting us some rooms at such short notice.'

'You are permitted in the parlour and your rooms. Not in here,' Miss Douglas said.

'Of course. I would never cross a boundary in another woman's kitchen. So, you will be making us tea, then?'

'No,' Miss Douglas had said.

Hannah felt she had more than enough justification to be in a foul mood. 'I'm trussed and I'm trapped,' she said. 'I will do it – for you, Mr Monsarrat. And for the man who was slain. But don't ask me to be happy about *how* I have to do it!' She walked to the armchair where he was sitting, his long legs stretched out and impeding her progress. She reached for the waist of her skirt, frowned, and used a word she had previously heard only from the lips of certain soldiers and the rougher convicts.

Monsarrat was wise enough not to remark on it. 'I've just thought of another advantage of this situation,' he said. 'I can mewl or wail or be irretrievably stupid, or any of the other many crimes you accuse me of, without the risk of a thrashing from your cleaning cloth.'

'I'll find something else,' said Hannah. 'Maybe a fan – never saw the point of them until now. Yet while I am forced to transform myself, you sit there reading the paper.'

Monsarrat folded the *Colonial Flyer* and placed it on the table. 'Research, dear lady. And the only paper available to me, as it happens. The *Sydney Chronicle* has temporarily ceased operations, as you well know. More's the pity. Henry Hallward was one of the few willing to challenge the governor.'

'The governor you work for,' said Hannah.

'Doesn't mean I agree with him. With his assumption that the colony is his to carve up and give away. With his view that former convicts are only good for building roads, and producing an ongoing supply of labourers. I wonder sometimes if I'm a coward for not speaking as Hallward does – well, did.'

'You're no coward,' Hannah said. 'Yours might be a quieter bravery, but that's all to the good. There are some of us who would prefer you to stay alive.'

Hannah suspected Monsarrat was more distressed by Hallward's murder than he let on. He had told her of the *Chronicle*'s story about him while bundling her onto a packet to Sydney, the same vessel they had stepped off at Parramatta only a few days previously. She hated travelling by water but recognised it was preferable – barely – to the undulating road, which by many accounts was lined with more bushrangers than trees. She had fancied at the time that she had seen a shadow cross his face. The paper had been a favourite of his since Hallward had thundered against an editorial written by one of his own reporters. Hallward was known for allowing a range of views onto his pages, and if he disagreed with them, he preferred to publicly castigate the articles' authors than prevent their publication in the first place. When a hapless journalist had accused a convict, Grace O'Leary, of murder on no more evidence than her involvement in a riot, Hallward had written the following day, 'If justified action against tyranny proves that one is also guilty of any murder which happens to occur in one's vicinity, every person of courage should be locked up.'

'I can't fault his argument,' Monsarrat had said at the time. Hannah had smiled. She suspected Monsarrat was thinking more of Grace's eyes than Hallward's rhetorical prowess. For Monsarrat, a man who planted the thoughts of others on paper but was not allowed to express his own, a man shunned by both the lags and the gentry, the paper had assumed all the significance of a talisman. 'Not an easy thing to do: go against the common assumption that those of us with convictions on our records are cancers in the civic body,' he had said as they set off for Sydney.

'Hard enough to defend a creature such as yourself, Mr Monsarrat,' Hannah had said.

Hannah was also worried that the emphatic end to Hallward's life would deter others from criticising the new governor, a man with all the power of a potentate, in an administration where a powerful few decided on lives and deaths. She felt the murder as keenly as Mr Monsarrat did, perhaps more. If Mr Monsarrat needed someone to speak for him, she – a woman, a former convict and, of course, one of those lawless Irish who couldn't be trusted – might as well be mute.

Now, though, she was not fretting about the death of a newspaperman. Twenty letters from Hannah to her son, Padraig, had been dispatched into the country's arid interior, where as far as she knew he was droving. They had yet to provoke a response. Still she kept writing, trying not to scold him for his silence, while hoping it was for reasons which deserved scolding – the carelessness of a young man, the impulse to find something more entertaining to do than write to his mother. But she did not want to be away from home should a missive arrive as repayment for all her scribbling.

Mr Monsarrat tossed the paper onto a side table and unfolded his long frame from the chair. 'I should get ready,' he said. 'If I can make myself half as presentable as you, I'll be delighted.'

Monsarrat was obliged to solve all the crimes his superior chose to place in front of him. His freedom depended on his usefulness. He would have bent all of his efforts towards doing so, anyway – beguiled, perhaps, by the possibility of adding even a thin layer of justice to the strata of unfairness which characterised this place every bit as much as the striped sandstone of its cliffs.

He didn't know why Henry Hallward had been killed. But if it was for his writing, perhaps even for his opinions on ticket-of-leave convicts, Monsarrat felt he would fully deserve to be haunted by the man if he was unable to find his killer. Still, while Mrs Mulrooney waited for letters which never came, tried not to think about what her son's silence might mean, Monsarrat was chasing his own shadow. He hoped, soon, he would be given time to do so. Ralph Eveleigh, the governor's private secretary in Parramatta, had seemed sympathetic – though not sympathetic enough to allow Monsarrat time to unpack properly after his return from Van Diemen's Land.

'Embarrassing, really,' Eveleigh had said, after fetching Monsarrat from the tiny clerk's office and sitting him down in the private secretary's more spacious rooms. 'Shot from on high. Damn thing happened on government property – the shot was fired into the prison, no less, while the fellow was crossing the yard, being taken for trial. Place is supposed to protect the outside world from its inmates, but people tend to get nervous about its ability to do so when it can't protect its inmates from the outside world.' Eveleigh drew a newspaper from a stack on his desk and flicked it across the polished surface so that it landed in Monsarrat's lap. The masthead, in impossibly ornate Gothic script, was the *Sydney Chronicle*. 'Not my favourite, I have to say.' Eveleigh glanced at Monsarrat. 'Hallward does occasionally get things right – the utility of ticket-of-leave men, for example – but he is not very, well, measured.'

For Eveleigh, who set great store by being measured, this was a tremendous indictment.

'You are under no obligation to read it, I suppose,' said Monsarrat.

'Don't be ridiculous, man, of course I am. Especially now. It might have escaped your attention in Van Diemen's Land, but our new governor is not the most popular of men.'

Monsarrat had read enough, heard enough over the past few months to know this was true. Ralph Darling's two immediate predecessors had been progressives who seemed to believe convicts were not irreparably tarnished, that they still retained some humanity. Governor Darling thought those before him had been far too lenient, and he had set about a vigorous program of correction.

'I need to know what people are saying, you see,' Eveleigh said. 'The weak-minded seem unable to distinguish facts from the opinions of a newspaper editor, so those opinions might as well be facts. At least I'll have some blessed relief from the *Chronicle*, though.'

'Oh? Is it shutting down?'

'Not yet, although it's not out of the question. At present there is no one to edit it. Because its editor found himself in the rather unfortunate position of lying in a prison yard with a lead ball in his brain.'

Monsarrat knew, then, that any pleas for a delay in his dispatch to Sydney would be ignored. His value to Eveleigh lay in his discretion, and in the fact that an investigation by him was less likely to draw attention than if a constable was trampling around. It was why Eveleigh dispatched Monsarrat to deal with the more sensitive cases. And it was now obvious that this one was more sensitive than most.

'You're to assist the governor's new private secretary in Sydney, Colonel Edward Duchamp,' Eveleigh told Monsarrat.

'Ah. Good. It will be helpful to have the support of such a highly placed official.'

'I wouldn't rely on it, Monsarrat. Fellow served with the governor – he's a former colonel of engineers. Duchamp believes that because he and the governor perspired together in Mauritius, he owns the man.'

'Still, if he has requested me, he can hardly obstruct me.'

'The thing is, he hasn't exactly requested you. A case of this nature . . . well, if it's not handled well, I wouldn't rule out a riot or two. It's not really in my power to insist, but I did everything I could. Told him that London was watching. That the administration needed to be seen to pursue this particular killer. That failing to do so would see any unrest laid at his door.'

Eveleigh riffled through the papers on his desk, extracted one and handed it to Monsarrat.

'I have the honour to inform you . . .' – it started, as most official letters did, even if the writer went on to inform the reader that they had the intelligence of a toadstool – '. . . that I will accept your subordinate, and given the praise you have heaped on him, I anticipate he will bring this matter to a speedy conclusion. As you know, Sydney contains many more capable men than Parramatta, some of whom will be disappointed they have not been given carriage of this matter. Should your man fail it will have serious consequences – for him and, more especially, for you.'

Monsarrat handed back the letter. 'Is he threatening you, sir?'

'Oh, probably. He most certainly does not like me. I wrote to him when he first arrived a few months ago – you wouldn't be aware of this, as I decided to do it personally rather than dictate it to you. I told him how things were done. Helpful information, I'd have thought.'

'And he ignored you?'

'Worse. Duchamp wrote back to tell me he'd be thankful if I could keep my opinions to myself. Said the governor wants to, what was the word ... ah, yes, *rejuvenate* his staff. And he has some thoughts on what needs to be done.'

'You don't think –'

'That if you fail, he will use it as a pretext to oust me? Yes, that's precisely what I think, and he will probably throw every obstacle he can into your path. I may have been foolish, and will deny it should you ever remind me I spoke those words. But I believe Duchamp stopped resisting because he saw an opportunity to undermine me while claiming he had done everything he could to identify the murderer. So catch this rogue, will you, Monsarrat? There's a good man.'

Monsarrat had wanted to refuse, to beg for more time to search for Grace O'Leary, a woman who had nearly lost her life for a crime she didn't commit, who had made herself a target by helping those whom others believed did not deserve help. He missed her amber-flecked eyes, and he hoped her hair had grown back after the last time he'd seen her – her scalp raw from a punitive haircut, with just a few downy patches. She had been sent away to a mysterious location by the vindictive Reverend Bulmer while Monsarrat was in Van Diemen's Land.

He knew, though, that such a request would not only be refused but would also irritate Eveleigh. Not only, it seemed, did Eveleigh's job depend on Monsarrat's usefulness, but so did Monsarrat's ticket of leave. If he failed to deprive this murderer of his freedom, Monsarrat could well lose his own.

Chapter 2

Mrs Mulrooney still seemed to be in a funk during their coach ride to Sydney's Government House. 'If I'm not your servant, how do we explain my presence?' she asked.

'Perhaps we say you're my mother,' said Monsarrat, a statement he would never have dared to make if she had access to her cleaning cloth.

'Nonsense, who'd believe a word of that? I'm far too young.'

'Very well, then – my aunt.'

'Your *young* aunt, Mr Monsarrat. A good ten or fifteen years younger than your Irish mother who married a tall Englishman, God rest her.'

'In that case, you had better get used to referring to me as Hugh.'

He earned a sharp sidelong glance.

A little over half a year ago, shortly after they had been tumbled into Parramatta after solving the murder of the commandant's wife in Port Macquarie, Monsarrat had invited Mrs Mulrooney to call him by his first name. She had rejected the idea immediately – she could, she said, trust a Mr Monsarrat, but a Hugh might get up to all sorts of trouble. There was no reciprocal offer for him to call her Hannah.

'And I suppose I shall have to refer to you as Auntie,' he said, fighting to repress a small smile.

'If you must, Mr Mon – Hugh. But I wish to note the sacrifice I am making in the service of this investigation.'

'Dear lady, I have noted all of your sacrifices. There have been many, and far more consequential ones than calling me by my first name.'

'Hmph. So, this fellow. Shot in a gaol that is supposed to be secure.'

'Yes. And, of course, we're to find out how and by whom.'

'Eejit of a man, you've forgotten the most important question.'

'Ah. Which is?'

'The question that will lead us to the how and the who. You've forgotten the why.'

It had fallen to the *Colonial Flyer*, now the only functioning newspaper in Sydney, to report on Hallward's death, with none of the rhetorical flourish usually employed by the report's subject. Monsarrat had read the story several times. He took it out of his breast pocket now, glanced at it as the carriage traversed the bumpy Sydney road.

Henry Hallward, it said, was shot by 'person or persons unknown'.

'The motivation for the crime cannot be guessed at, and there exists the possibility that Mr Hallward was not the intended target.'

Though in a yard populated by two obscure wardens and a man whose writing (or ranting, depending on one's perspective) had angered some of the colony's most powerful people, Monsarrat knew whom he would bet on as the target.

Strange, he thought, that there were no post-mortem niceties, no praise for a man who, even if a competitor, was no longer a threat. His musings were interrupted by Mrs Mulrooney. 'Get your long nose out of that thing,' she said. 'We're here.'

Monsarrat had imagined porticos and columns, and perhaps stone blocks more regal than the rendered brick of Parramatta's Government House; it was painted with faint lines which only fooled the eye from a distance that the structure was made of sturdier stuff.

No porticos, though, and no columns: the governor's residence was a simple, if large, two-storey house in the middle of a green expanse. A red-coated guard on the door looked down over a sloping lawn past native cabbage trees and nostalgic roses, with luxuriant ferns hiding the muddy banks of the Tank Stream, which watered Sydney Cove.

The windmills on a ridge to the east seemed set there not to provide flour, but as sentinels over the white-capped blue of the harbour, twins to the small stone fort that squatted on the cove's eastern arm. Warehouses had claimed the foreshore with such confidence that one would think they had been there for centuries rather than a brace of decades; those belonging to merchant families of grand pedigree – traders in tea, skins and sandalwood – battled for space with those belonging to time-served convict traders. The ships that fed the warehouses carried everything from skins to silk into the harbour, and were being loaded with fleece, sandalwood, flax and seal hides for the return journey, while the rough men who had clubbed the seals had been absorbed into a variety of public houses and shebeens.

The current occupant of Sydney's Government House would never have frequented such establishments.

The King's most remote representative, the governor, was currently on Norfolk Island, in hopes of reopening one of the most brutal stations in the empire there. So Duchamp, his private secretary, was for the moment arguably the most powerful person in Sydney. Judging by the silks and jewels draped over the women at the garden party, the silver-topped canes and gold-threaded waistcoats of the men, Sydney's elite knew it.

They didn't, though, know Monsarrat, so most of them chose to ignore him and his companion.

A footman showed them across an empty reception room, its doors opening onto a broad terrace with steps spilling down to a meticulously trimmed lawn dotted with precise splashes of colour from symmetrical flowerbeds. The footman cleared his throat, then raised his voice. 'Mr Hugh Monsarrat, and Mrs...' He looked to Monsarrat for guidance.

'Mrs Hannah Mulrooney,' she said quickly.

Monsarrat shot her a warning glance and berated himself for forgetting to give her a pseudonym. If former convicts were objects of suspicion, Irish ones were even more so.

As the footman completed the introduction, most of the guests did not pause in their conversation. Some glanced quickly towards the newcomers and just as quickly away. In his black coat and plain waistcoat, Monsarrat realised he probably looked far more like a servant than his companion.

There was one man dressed as soberly as him – black coat, black cravat, but with an incongruously fine silver horseshoe pin shining against it. He was standing to the side of a group, straight-backed and long-nosed, perhaps in his forties but with a sneering cast to his face which looked as though it had been in place since childhood. His eyes rested on Monsarrat for longer than was strictly polite.

He stood on the fringes of a group which was being regaled by a much younger man – the kind of conversation with much hawing and backslapping. The younger fellow broke it off after a few moments and ambled up the steps towards Monsarrat and Mrs Mulrooney. He could have benefited from the parasols deployed by some of the women: although he was surely no older than Monsarrat, his wispy hair was thinning and the sun was reddening the bald patch on top of his head. The red coat that marked him as an officer must surely have been trapping enough heat to redden the rest of him. He had a glittering ceremonial sword at his waist, banging against his thigh as he walked, although Monsarrat couldn't imagine what he'd need it for besides cutting cake.

'You're the fellow from upriver,' the man said when he reached them. 'Eveleigh's pet convict.'

A shadow was permanently crouched in a dark recess of Monsarrat's mind, where he always tried to keep it. On the occasions when it unfolded itself, it urged him to acts that were satisfying and just – but, ultimately, dangerous. The man's insult called the shadow to alertness; it whispered that Monsarrat might care to strike him with his best roundhouse.

Monsarrat ignored it and bowed. 'Indeed. And may I present my aunt.'

'Ah, we weren't expecting . . . but of course you are welcome, madam.' The man took Mrs Mulrooney's hand and bowed over it. 'We will find you a suitable diversion.'

'I'm sorry for the intrusion, and none of the fault is with my nephew,' Mrs Mulrooney said. Monsarrat noticed she was flattening out her Irish cadence. 'I suffer from a nervous complaint, you see, and my physician felt a change of scenery might be beneficial. I do assure you my nephew has covered my travel expenses – we are not imposing on the Crown.'

Monsarrat knew she would like to do a lot more to the Crown than impose on it. He risked a grateful glance in her direction, before turning attentively back to the man. 'I presume I have the honour of addressing Colonel Edward Duchamp.'

'Hm,' said Duchamp, turning as a shadow fell across the back of his sunburned neck. It was cast by the tall man who had been staring at Monsarrat.

'Ah,' said Duchamp, clapping the man on the shoulder in a friendly gesture which was not returned. 'May I introduce Albert Bancroft, one of the colony's most successful pastoralists – not sure how: he's more often here than on his property. Still, takes more assigned convicts off my hands than anyone else. Lord knows what he does with them.'

'Work them. Flog them. What else is to be done? They are lower than the treacherous natives who make the life of the pastoral squatter such a trial,' said Bancroft.

'Bertie,' said Duchamp, 'this is Mr Monsarrat. The man from Parramatta, you remember.'

Bancroft stared at Monsarrat, turning his head a little from side to side as though trying to get a better view. Monsarrat had the uncomfortable feeling he was being assessed in terms of how he'd look behind a plough.

'A ticket-of-leave man,' said Bancroft.

'Yes, sir.'

'Done quite well, haven't you?'

'I do my best, Mr Bancroft,' said Monsarrat.

'Well, pleasant a morning as it is, I fear you and I must seek shelter from it in my study, Mr Monsarrat,' said Duchamp. 'You must excuse us, Bertie.' He turned, searching the crowd, and his eyes fixed on a slight young woman in rose silk. 'Henrietta!'

The woman quickly bobbed to a young soldier she had been conversing with, although his side of the discussion seemed to consist of gazing at her. She lifted her skirts and ran towards them at a most unladylike speed. 'Yes, Eddie?' she said indulgently, like an adult interrupted in a task by a beloved yet slightly annoying child.

'Not that name here, thank you,' Duchamp hissed, in what he clearly thought was a whisper. 'Henrietta, this is Mrs Mulrooney. Madam, may I present my sister. She will, I am sure, have no objection to looking after you while your nephew and I discuss certain matters.'

'No objection at all,' said Henrietta, taking Mrs Mulrooney's arm and patting her hand as she guided her into the throng. Mrs Mulrooney glanced quickly back over her shoulder to

Monsarrat. He was reasonably certain that if she could speak, she would remind him again of her sacrifices.

He looked around the garden, at the well-dressed and well-connected guests. He was not investigating a street robbery. One of the killers could be here, an intimate of Duchamp. Perhaps Duchamp didn't know, or perhaps his insistence on meeting during a party was a test of some kind.

Before he and Duchamp could move away, the footman announced another guest. 'Mr Alexander Hawley,' he called, stepping aside to admit a rotund man who shone with sweat as though he had been glazed and fired in a kiln.

Hawley scuttled over to Duchamp. 'Colonel, I am most delighted to be here. I must say, the previous administration never thought to include those who toil on their behalf.'

Duchamp frowned for a moment, before a practised smile settled on his face. 'It is my very great pleasure, Mr ... Mr Hawley. And how are you faring in your current ... occupation?'

'I'm chief clerk now. Colonial Secretary's Office, as you know, of course.' Hawley stood straighter, thrusting his chest out as though he had just been crowned king.

'Good man,' said Duchamp distractedly.

Hawley turned to Monsarrat. 'An unusual name,' said Hawley as the two shook hands. 'But one I've come across before – let me think ... aha, yes! You spent some time in Port Macquarie, I believe?'

'Yes. I was clerk to the commandant there. How on earth did you know?'

'I am something of a connoisseur of fine handwriting. There is lamentably little of it about these days. I always enjoyed receiving letters from the north, and all because of your hand.'

'That is most gratifying,' said Monsarrat, bowing. 'Thank you.'

'I am delighted you could join us today,' said Duchamp to Hawley. 'Please do make yourself at home. However, I'm afraid Mr Monsarrat and I have some business to discuss.'

'Of course,' said Hawley. 'Well, Mr Monsarrat, you must have risen in the world indeed, if you are having private meetings with the governor's secretary.'

Duchamp ushered Monsarrat through a drawing room studded with spindly, ornate chairs and tables, the sunlight coming in through the tall windows doing its best to brighten the room despite the wallpaper, dyed with a dark green pigment which, Monsarrat knew, had toxic properties. 'My sister probably invited that Hawley fellow,' Duchamp said as he led Monsarrat to an arched door at the end of the room. 'She likes collecting people.'

He looked around. 'Jardine!'

The red-coated officer who had been guarding the empty entrance hall when Monsarrat arrived was now standing at the door they were approaching, holding himself immobile as a tree stump. He reanimated and walked towards them.

'Mr Monsarrat, this is my assistant, Lieutenant Jardine,' said the colonel. 'Jardine, you will join us. I do hope this matter will not detain us too long, as I must return to my guests. But Mr Monsarrat, if you are half the investigator that Eveleigh claims, there are certain things you need to know.'

Jardine moved to the door and opened it, saluting as Monsarrat followed Duchamp into another darkly papered room – red this time, and dominated by a large, polished desk crouched at its centre in front of a coronation portrait of the King.

'Truly, Henry Hallward was the most awful man,' Duchamp said, taking off his sword and handing it to Jardine before settling himself behind the desk.

Monsarrat tried not to stare at the colonel's three crystal ink wells, paragons of their type and, to him, beautiful. His eyes, instead, followed the sword's progress.

Duchamp noticed. 'A trifle overdone for a party, I grant you,' he said. 'But symbolism, tradition – they are what separates us from ... well, others.'

'From people like Hallward?' said Monsarrat.

'Quite – we build, he tears down,' Duchamp said, with the portrait of the King, who had his own ceremonial sword, glaring over his shoulder. 'I saw him the day before he died. I like to inspect our fine institutions unannounced, you see. He was lying on his bench, all feigned innocence. A rabble-rouser, and so common, the son of convicts. You can ask anyone. Jardine – you agree, of course.'

'My views are immaterial, sir,' Jardine said. 'Murder is murder and a crime against the Crown, no matter how distasteful the victim.'

Duchamp glanced at Jardine, perhaps expecting a fuller endorsement, but the soldier had resumed staring at the opposite wall and did not seem inclined to elaborate, which was just as well as Duchamp didn't give him time. 'I was inspecting some troops when it happened. Jardine brought me the news,' he said.

Jardine, who had resumed his tree-stump impersonation while standing to the side of Duchamp's desk, quirked an eyebrow upwards. An involuntary tic, perhaps, but odd in a man who held the rest of his body so still. Broad-shouldered and lacking the broken capillaries that netted his commanding officer's face, he seemed far too robust for an administrative role. Monsarrat could imagine him on horseback swinging a sword around above his head, not at a desk blotting ink.

'I see,' said Monsarrat. 'So, shot in the gaol yard. From outside?'

'Yes, although from which building is unclear. Neither of the wardens saw it – just a noise and then he was on the ground.'

'What time did this happen?'

'Around ten, I believe. They'd just brought in the cart to take him to court,' said Duchamp.

'Have the constables started an investigation?'

'No. I'd just leave it to them if it weren't for the fact that Hallward was shot in Crown custody. And the rumours are spreading, too – whispers that he was shot on the orders of some of those he has attacked. Slander, of course. Once these things take hold, though, they can be hard to uproot, and some among the less educated and more gullible believe them no matter what proof they are given to the contrary. Best to disprove them conclusively before they become rusted on, eh? For the sake of the colony's stability. You shouldn't have to look far – the man made enemies in the gutter as well as in the finest drawing rooms.'

'Oh? Man of the people, I thought,' said Monsarrat. 'A hero to those in the gutter, presumably.'

'Mr Monsarrat, Hallward had the soul of a brawler. He was also, I hear, a fixture at some of the less refined establishments in Sydney. Those where a dispute over a game of dice can draw blood. A far more fruitful line of enquiry than looking at the targets of his printed ravings. A line I would like you to pursue. There are gentlemen – a few outside in the garden at this very moment, in fact – who have felt the sharpness of Hallward's pen. Some whose livelihoods have been put at risk by his ramblings. Such things must be put to rest. Do not think this malice has escaped the notice of the Secretary for the Colonies in London.'

'I see. I had best get started. I want to interview the wardens – those who were present when he was shot. And examine the location, of course.'

'Well, as to that, perhaps hold off for a day or two. There's a little unrest at the moment. The guards are still distressed, you see.'

'The murder weapon, then.'

'As Mr Hallward was shot, I think we can safely assume it was a gun,' said Duchamp, smiling in self-congratulation at his own wit.

'Quite. But what sort?'

'Oh, a rifle I should imagine. Plenty of them around.'

'Perhaps, then, if I speak to the doctor who examined the body? I presume there *was* an examination?'

'Oh yes. But Dr Merrick – he's a busy man. He has asked me to send his apologies. There will be a written report in due course, but he is not available for interviews.'

I wonder, thought Monsarrat, if Ralph Eveleigh expected Duchamp's attempts at obstruction to be so shamelessly obvious.

'And the body itself?' he asked.

'In the graveyard at St James' Church,' said Duchamp. 'Where, I suspect, he is far more welcome dead than he ever was alive. His libel was not restricted to secular powers.'

'He angered the clergy?' asked Monsarrat.

'He angered a great many people. If I need to tell you who, Eveleigh has sent the wrong man.'

Monsarrat was used to being asked to solve murders instantly. He was also used to cooperation, or at least the semblance of it.

'Well,' he said, 'you have told me how important it is to put rumours to rest. I'll see if I can discover who owns the property from which the shot was taken. Go through the records in the Colonial Secretary's Office, see who owns it.'

'Oh yes, we're very thorough here in Sydney, Mr Monsarrat. But I really must ask you not to bother the Colonial Secretary. Most inappropriate.'

'May I ask, then, where you suggest I start?'

'I have no intention of doing your job for you, Mr Monsarrat, for I am far too busy with my own. And I'll thank you not to dawdle on your way out – my guests wouldn't appreciate a crow such as yourself at the feast.'

***

Hannah knew that Henrietta was just trying to be kind. But if the girl patted her hand one more time, as though she was a dotard who needed to be kept compliant, Hannah would jump onto a table, yell *Erin go bragh* at the top of her voice, and run.

After twenty minutes, during which Henrietta showed Hannah a polished grand piano on the veranda and insisted she admire the rosebushes, the woman's prattling showed little sign of slowing. She did not even pause to eat, seemingly reluctant to consume any of the tiny cakes set out on the table. Henrietta was verging on emaciated, nearly as thin as some of the women Hannah had met in Parramatta's Female Factory, and it seemed an insult for her to shun food that would have sent a convict into raptures.

The flow of words about dresses and the theatre and horse riding and walks through the new Botanic Gardens slowed, though, when another young woman approached. She was older than Henrietta, perhaps in her late twenties. Her clothes had none of the froth of Henrietta's gown: a dark blue visiting dress, a lace collar. Her hair was not sprouting feathers or studded with jewels, unlike many of the heads here. Her face was angular and well proportioned; she had the smooth skin of someone who had spent much of her life under a gentler sun than this. But her face was drawn, her eyes slightly sunken.

She said, 'Miss Duchamp, is this party to celebrate the passing of Mr Hallward or to mourn the death of free speech?'

A shadow rippled across Henrietta's face for a moment. 'A man's death is nothing to celebrate, Miss Albrecht.'

The woman paused, looking at Henrietta. 'No,' she said quietly. 'No, indeed.' Her voice was clipped. Hannah thought she heard a slight accent, and she saw a tightness around the woman's jaw, a clench of anger quickly smoothed over. Perhaps the woman felt Hannah's eyes on her; she started as though shaken from a reverie. 'And you are?'

'Miss Albrecht, please,' said Henrietta, 'I admire your directness, but perhaps a few more niceties?'

'Although,' said Hannah, 'it does save time.' She turned to Miss Albrecht and smiled. 'I am Hannah Mulrooney.'

The woman inclined her head. 'Carolina Albrecht. I have not heard of you, Mrs Mulrooney.'

'No. I am newly arrived from Parramatta.'

'And why are you here?'

'Perhaps our new friend is weary of such questions,' said Henrietta. 'You know yourself, Miss Albrecht, how wearing such scrutiny can be for a newcomer.'

'I don't mind a bit,' said Hannah.

Henrietta pursed her lips. Hannah risked aiming a small smile at Carolina, whose mouth quirked.

'In any case,' said Henrietta, 'I'm sure Miss Albrecht has some preparations to make.'

'Yes, I do have some business to attend to.'

As Carolina made her way towards the terrace, Hannah noticed that others parted to let her pass, whispering to each other as she did so. She seemed in no hurry to climb the steps, perhaps oblivious to the eyes on her back, or perhaps enjoying them. She went to the piano and trailed a finger along its shining top, as a servant rang a small bell to get the attention of the guests. Carolina perched herself on the edge of the brocade stool before the piano. Perhaps she would pound the keys in frustration – Hannah would sympathise.

'Ladies and gentlemen,' the footman said, 'may I present Miss Carolina Albrecht.'

Judging by the din of the applause that followed, several people had been looking forward to this. When Carolina started playing, Hannah realised why. The performance was perfect, at least as far as she could tell – recital music had not been much of a feature in her life as a convict and then a housekeeper. It was more than that, though; instead of simply depressing the ivory keys, Carolina seemed to be coaxing music out of the reticent mechanism of the piano, notes running together in a way that was almost hypnotic.

Henrietta was one of the few who did not seem rapt. She leaned over to Hannah and whispered in her ear, a gesture that seemed shockingly intimate from a young woman who had probably been schooled in etiquette before learning less important subjects like reading. 'I did not think she would come.'

'Who on earth is she?'

'Quite a good little pianist, as it happens, but the manners of a navvy – I suppose she puts all of her finer feelings into her music. She is a friend of – well, of his.'

'His?'

'Hallward. An awfully common man, dreadfully irresponsible, but those who liked him seemed to do so with some fervour.'

'You must have been shocked to hear of the shooting, common man or not,' said Hannah.

'Oh, yes. I was at the Female School of Industry when it happened. The place trains lower-class girls to be servants, and just as well, good servants are the devil to find, here. One of the girls raced in with the news. It caused most unladylike wailing – he was something of a hero to those people. But Miss Albrecht – I thought she might be too distressed to play.'

'Perhaps she is, but hiding it well,' said Hannah. 'Some have that skill.'

A man spoke behind them. 'You seem engrossed in the performance, Miss Duchamp.' His voice was deep and bore the accent of northern England. Henrietta turned, startled, but released her breath when she saw who had spoken, narrowing her eyes at the man for a moment before her practised smile reappeared.

The man smiled back benignly. In a town where the rich and the commissioned were clean-shaven, and many convicts wore their sentences in the form of beards, this man seemed uncertain as to where he belonged. His moustache was as carefully tended as the flowerbeds, running down the sides of his mouth and then up towards his ears.

'Mr Mobbs, I wasn't expecting you today,' Henrietta said, and turned away.

'Will you not introduce me to your friend?'

Henrietta turned to Hannah. 'Mrs Mulrooney, may I present Mr Gerald Mobbs, proprietor of the *Colonial Flyer*.'

Mobbs smiled and bowed.

'I am so sorry,' Hannah said to him. 'You must be distressed by the loss of your fellow newspaperman.'

'Dreadful business. And we don't want people to get into the habit of shooting editors.' He turned towards the piano. 'She was very tight with Hallward,' he said. 'Makes you wonder why she's here.'

And that, thought Hannah, was no doubt a very good question indeed.

Duchamp had dismissed Monsarrat and Jardine at the same time, as though they were indistinguishable irritants. As they left, the colonel bent over his notes with all the avidity of a man avoiding a garden party.

'A busy man,' said Monsarrat to Jardine.

'Yes, particularly with the governor away.'

'So I imagine he will not take kindly to interruptions should I need to seek permission for anything.'

'You may rely on me, Mr Monsarrat,' said Jardine.

'Is there hope, then, of talking to the doctor or the wardens?'

Jardine held up a hand. 'I wouldn't push on those two. We'll see what can be done in due course. There are, though, other avenues you might pursue as you wait. The editor of the *Colonial Flyer*, Mr Gerald Mobbs.'

'You think he might have had something to do with the murder?' Monsarrat asked.

'Not a bit of it. But he was among Mr Hallward's most frequent critics, together with certain members of the clergy. Now, shall we fetch your aunt?'

'That's helpful of you, Lieutenant.'

'I have been commanded to assist you, Mr Monsarrat, and I take commands from my superior very seriously. As I do breaches of the King's peace and his laws. Killing is one thing on the gallows or the battlefield. But when a hidden person fires on an unarmed man, the coward deserves to feel the full force of the law.'

Hannah squinted at the cramped print. Why did it have to be so small? Why couldn't they just add a few more pages, and then witter on as much as they liked about livestock prices and who had married whom?

'Paper costs money,' said Monsarrat, when she voiced her complaint.

'So do rugs. And we will have to replace that one if you don't stop pacing.'

They had returned to their lodgings for a restorative pot of tea, of which both felt the need if they were to face the afternoon. Miss Douglas was out, so Hannah had the run of the kitchen. And as a guest, she felt justified in slicing off slivers of bread and cheese she had found in the pantry, wrapping them in oilcloth and handing them to Mr Monsarrat, with stern instructions to eat them over the rest of the day. As it was, the man was in danger of falling between the planks of a dock.

After another dozen or so circuits around the room, Monsarrat stopped by the mantelpiece and slapped his palm on it. 'What is he playing at?'

'Duchamp? You don't really need me to answer that, do you?'

'No. No, it was rhetorical.'

Hannah withdrew a little notebook from her pocket, with a pencil stub wedged between pages that were covered in lists of words. 'Spell that, please.'

'Dear lady, I admire your commitment to broadening your vocabulary, but I'm not sure we have time for it just now.'

'You had better hurry up, then.'

He sighed, stopped pacing and spelled the word. 'It means I don't want an answer. I was asking for effect.'

'Ridiculous reason to ask a question. Mr Eveleigh did warn you the colonel would make it difficult.'

'There's a difference between difficult and impossible. Before you decide to whack me, yes, I am well aware my usefulness as an investigator would not be possible were it not for you. But that reputation will be shredded before too long if things keep going as they are, despite your perspicacity.'

Hannah held the pencil up again, but a rare look of irritation from Monsarrat made her lower it.

'You don't think Duchamp's involved in some way, do you?' she asked.

'Well, he certainly has no reason to mourn Mr Hallward's passing,' said Monsarrat. 'But if he was involved, surely he would have been better off ensuring that the investigation was given to someone he trusts – he could ultimately find a scapegoat or announce that it's not possible to solve the crime.'

'One of those wrinkles, isn't it?' said Hannah. She detested it when facts refused to fit neatly with one another, and there was always a reason why they didn't.

'It's a wrinkle we will have to set aside, for now. Here, what do you think of this?' He drew a folded letter from his breast pocket and handed it to her.

She glanced at it, and looked up. 'What can Eveleigh do, from this distance?'

'In all honesty, I don't know. But it's the only thing I can think of.'

She unfolded the paper. In Monsarrat's elegant hand, it read:

Sir,

I have the honour to inform you that your fears have been realised and exceeded in relation to the behaviour of a certain person. I already find myself at a possible impasse in the matter of the murder of Mr Henry Hallward. There are certain permissions – access to sites and people and documents – which I have been denied. In my view, these are essential to the progress of the investigation.

I am aware this was, to some degree, expected. However, due to the importance of my task, and the extreme nature of the obstacles placed in my path, I wonder if I may prevail upon you to remind Colonel Edward Duchamp of the need for his cooperation in reaching a speedy conclusion which is, after all, in the best interest of the colony, and in his best interests as one of its foremost leaders.

I look forward to your response, and remain your most obedient servant,
    Hugh Monsarrat

'I know what your value is to Eveleigh,' she said. 'He can send you into the bushes like a lord sending dogs into a hunt, and he trusts you will come back with a grouse – without having to trouble him.'

'Oh, you're comparing me to a dog now?'

'Mr Monsarrat, this is not like you. You know I am not. I am simply saying, Eveleigh told you this would happen. What can he do?'

'Eveleigh has been sitting in Parramatta like an owl on a roof for years. He knows a lot more than he lets on, I am certain of it, and he may know someone who can intercede on my behalf. In any case, I have a right to his support.'

'No, you don't. Not as far as he sees it,' said Hannah. 'You have a right to nothing, not even your freedom. Eveleigh could have you back in Port Macquarie with a pen stroke. As far as he is concerned, your job is to be useful.' She flipped through her little notebook until she found the word she was looking for. 'Unobtrusively useful.'

Monsarrat stalked over to her and took back the letter. 'I will become obtrusive soon enough if letters travel up the river from Duchamp, gleefully complaining about the time it is taking me to conclude the investigation.'

'Send it, then. But do not be surprised, Mr Monsarrat, if the only letter that comes back is a rebuke to you rather than Duchamp.'

Chapter 3

The *Colonial Flyer* landed on Monsarrat's desk in Parramatta every day. And really he would rather it didn't. He had welcomed the arrival of Hallward's paper, but had borne a grudge against the *Flyer* ever since it had thundered that Grace O'Leary should be executed for a crime she had not committed. Most in the press had been clamouring for her arrest for the murder of the Parramatta Female Factory's odious superintendent, but Mobbs had been particularly vicious, calling her a soulless harpy whose removal from the colony and the world would immediately improve both. Monsarrat had certainly never expected to be standing outside the wooden-gated archway that led into the courtyard of the building where it was published.

Monsarrat had walked here over rutted dirt streets without the neat borders of those near Government House, past low wooden houses in indifferent repair, piles of refuse rotting outside them. Women sat on porches feeding babies or playing with their children, or they stood on the corners touting a less innocent kind of fun. 'Share a dram with a woman, would you?' some called, raising a bottle like a temptation to Monsarrat and any other man who passed. There were no convict work gangs in The Rocks – perhaps the government did not feel the place worthy of a bonded workforce's attention, with its jagged, inhospitable foreshore – but many of them would live here, or try to, once their sentences expired.

Handcarts far outnumbered coaches, and they contained vegetables, rags or wood. Smallholders had set up stalls wherever they felt like it; such a practice was probably against colonial regulations, but no one here seemed to mind. One merchant, however, seemed unsure of what he was selling. The man had a rasping voice and the crooked nose of a boxer. His hair, which had long since deserted his head, might have been red judging by his grey-flecked beard and the remains of old sunburn blisters on his face. 'Jewellery!' he yelled. 'Fine watches! Sidearms! Musket balls!'

Monsarrat was sorely tempted to look at the weapons, perhaps ask a price. But acquiring a gun might lead to him firing it, and his freedom would race away with the shot. In any case, he didn't know how the merchant had come by his odd collection of merchandise, but he probably hadn't done so honestly.

He had similar doubts about the honesty of the man he was about to see. He would very much have liked Mrs Mulrooney's company, but she was otherwise engaged. As they had left Government House that morning, Duchamp's sister had darted across the entrance hall. She had moved at such speed that her skirts, rustling against the marble floor, sounded as though they were urging the partygoers to silence. 'You must walk with me in the new public gardens,' she had said to Mrs Mulrooney. 'They're delightful. Shall we say this afternoon? I always enjoy a stroll after a garden party, especially if I've overindulged in the cakes.' She had smiled, given Mrs Mulrooney's hand a last little pat, and disappeared back into the throng.

So Monsarrat now had an unsavoury prospect ahead of him: meeting alone with the man who had argued for the need to impose state-sanctioned strangulation on the woman Monsarrat hoped to marry.

Through the wooden gates, the courtyard was littered with the usual detritus of industry: carts, buckets, coalscuttles, hay for the horses that delivered the *Flyer*'s brand of morality throughout the colony, and more paper than Monsarrat had ever seen in one place, rolls and rolls of it. He was struck, for a moment, by the power wielded by Gerald Mobbs – the power to decide what truths or lies the blank paper would reflect by tomorrow.

Monsarrat lifted his fist and hammered, a little too loudly, on a small wooden door set into a stone wall. It was opened by a hulking man in shirtsleeves, his index finger stained black. 'Most people know not to knock in the afternoon. Not when we're trying to get the edition together.'

'I won't keep you, then,' said Monsarrat. 'It's been suggested I seek out Gerald Mobbs.'

'Suggested by whom?'

Already irritated by his peremptory treatment at Government House, Monsarrat was stung by this challenge. He drew himself up, staring at the man for a moment in silence. 'Colonel Edward Duchamp, as it happens.'

The name did not inspire the awe he had hoped for, but it did make the man open the door a little wider. 'Mobbs's upstairs – just back from a job, so he says – with cake crumbs on his waistcoat,' the man said, inclining his head towards a rickety set of steps near the corner of the room. 'Don't touch anything on your way through.'

The cavernous room was filled with rows of large, slanted tables, where men were selecting tiny blocks carved with letters and dropping them into frames. Monsarrat leaned over to see if he could discern the story that was being composed for printing, but the man who had opened the door called out, 'You distract these lads, you'll pay for any delays. And it costs.'

An iron press crouched in a corner, silent for now, waiting to be fed.

'An impressive machine,' Monsarrat said.

'Two hundred pages an hour,' the man said proudly. '*Chronicle* can't match it.'

Certainly not now, Monsarrat thought. 'May I ask,' he said to the man, 'after the shooting of Hallward, how were spirits round here?'

'Not much love between those two, but none of us felt any joy at it. No one likes the thought of someone going around shooting newspapermen. Mr Mobbs was very affected by it. Led us in a little prayer, and he's not a praying man.'

Monsarrat made his way through the room towards the stairs to the first storey. They didn't seem as though they'd be up to supporting the weight of a man like the one at the door, but they supported Monsarrat well enough, delivering him into a room full of men scratching at pieces of paper. The air was thick with pipe smoke, and with the noise of men raising their voices to be heard over their work. One of them stopped mid-yell to nod towards the wooden door behind which sat Sydney's only remaining newspaper editor. There was no answer to Monsarrat's knock, so he nudged the door gently with the toe of his shoe, and it opened halfway.

'If you go to the trouble of opening a ruddy door, at least have the sense to open it all the way,' said a rasping voice with a flat, northern English accent.

'Forgive me,' said Monsarrat, doing as he was told. 'I've been sent by –'

The man held up his finger for silence, hastily scribbled something on a piece of paper, then looked up and said, 'Well?'

'Edward Duchamp sent me. Well, his office did, anyhow. On the matter of the murder of Mr Hallward.'

'Ah, yes, I saw you this morning. Duchamp must have whisked you away so quickly we didn't meet. Better come in then, eh.' The man gestured to a rickety chair in front of his desk. Like his staff, he was dressed in shirtsleeves. Unlike them, he wore a neatly tied silk cravat under his topiary of a moustache – a far different proposition than a convict beard that grew through lack of intervention, it spoke of intent and precision, the imposition of will. The rasp in his voice was, in all likelihood, due to the pipe smoke that seemed thicker in this office than in the area outside. 'So what have you to do with Hallward's death?' he asked.

'I'm looking into the matter.'

'You're not a constable.'

'No.'

'So a yard of pump water, dressed as – what, a clerk or a cleric? – walks into my office and tells me he is investigating a murder, in place of the police. At the request of the governor's office. What is to be made of that?'

'I'm sure I couldn't say,' said Monsarrat. Behind the words, he could sense tomorrow's editorial being composed in Mobbs's head.

'You *could*, though. Does the government not trust the constabulary? Is this something a little sensitive, shall we say, that they'd rather be handled discreetly?'

'As far as I'm aware, sir, they simply want to find out who killed him.'

'I'm not that desperate for readers, if that's what you're wondering,' Mobbs said with a smile, perhaps expecting an answering chuckle, which did not come.

'Yet the *Chronicle* has not published an edition since the day of Mr Hallward's murder,' said Monsarrat. 'Whether or not you are desperate for more readers, you must certainly have them now.'

'Not worth it at this cost. No matter how much I disliked the man.'

'Oh really? Professional jealousy?'

Mobbs shook his head, his jaw clenching. 'He was going to bring me down with him!'

'How would he have managed that?'

'He loved stirring hornets' nests. It was a sport to him. And he most enjoyed stirring the governor. Every day he attacked the man – treatment of convicts, land grants, appointment of magistrates. If it rained, it was the governor's fault, and also if it didn't.'

'And how did that make you a target?'

'News must travel slowly up the river,' said Mobbs. 'You've not heard about the licensing, then, in that scab of a town you come from?'

This disdain from a man who had tried to meddle in the affairs of that town – to bring death down on a woman he had never met – sent a pulse of anger through Monsarrat. The shadow in his mind opened an eye. He clenched and unclenched his fists, trying to tamp it down.

'Yes, news can occasionally get stranded on the riverbank before it makes its way into Parramatta. Licensing, you say?'

'Governor Darling wants all newspapers to be licensed by the state. It would make us little more than pamphlets, tracts proclaiming the glory of the Crown and its representative here, interspersed with the occasional notification on changes to regulations and so forth. Not that it would matter – no one will buy newspapers anyway if the governor gets his way.'

'Why not? If you're all struggling under the same conditions.'

'Because the governor also wants to charge four pence duty. You really think someone is going to pay a day's wages for a propaganda sheet?'

'I see.'

Mobbs let out a bitter laugh, stood up and moved over to a grimy window. 'Within half a year. And all because Hallward couldn't help himself. I will never – never – understand why he came all this way to wreck, not to build. I chose this place, Mr Monsarrat. Wanted a chance to be in at the start. God saw I was the man for it. But Hallward collected enemies as easily as this window collects dust – practically anyone with any influence. He worked on the jealous assumption that all wealth and power are ill-gotten, conferred in clandestine meetings, obliging the recipients to favours that work against the good of the people.'

'He believed there was a degree of corruption, then,' Monsarrat said.

'With the fervour of a zealot. He saw it wherever he looked, whether it was there or not.'

'And do you think, on occasion, he was right?'

'Who's to say? But he certainly spent a decent amount of time in prison. On the past few occasions, the jury was dismissed. Couldn't come to an agreement. Odd, given that they were military men, and that the injured party was the governor.'

'The governor?'

'Oh yes. Governor Darling has had a busy few months since he arrived, that fellow. Arrested Hallward over a story on the mistreatment of some soldiers. I was surprised by that, actually, because I'd also criticised Darling for it, just with less poison than Hallward applied.'

'And this last time?'

'Was for an editorial on licensing. The governor doesn't appreciate being called ignorant. No, Hallward was his own worst enemy.'

'Well, that's clearly not the case, as he didn't shoot himself in the head.'

'No, and I wish you the best of luck in trying to identify the gunmen in such a crowded field. I've been going over my own editorials, trying to ascertain whether someone might wish to plant a ball in my own head.' Mobbs shivered, moved quickly away from the window.

'If you fear Hallward may not have been the only editor to anger someone to the point of murder, the news of his death must have been disturbing. May I ask, where were you when it happened?'

'It was – when – around ten in the morning, yes? That morning I was at the Colonial Secretary's Office, talking to a clerk. Boring fellow. Wanted to show me his new file room. I took notes, no intention of doing a story, but couldn't hurt to keep the man on-side. That's where I found out about it. News travels fast in administrative circles. A messenger arrived, blurted the news out to the chief clerk. Well, I raced back here quick as I could.

'If you want me to name the chief targets for the bile that came from the tip of Hallward's pen, half of them were at the garden party: businessmen, pastoralists. Hallward had written that the governor's toadies were being elevated over the competent, and that the colony would ultimately die as a result, murdered by cronyism. Perhaps, Mr Monsarrat, that cronyism began its murder spree with Hallward.'

If that was the case, thought Monsarrat, cronyism must have fired its shot from some height.

～⌒～

Duchamp had shown no inclination to allow Monsarrat to visit the gaol. But the land outside was public property.

The autumn air was still mild, even in the late afternoon, but the chill in the shadow of the gaol walls made Monsarrat glad of his black frock coat, which he would cheerfully have cast aside in the warmer months had propriety allowed it.

The gaol crouched on a patch of land hemmed in by what looked like houses, although they were probably divided into apartments. It seemed unlikely that anyone who could afford a house all to themselves would have risked breathing the same air as the inmates day after day. The prison's sandstone walls, golden in the afternoon sun, concealed a yard where the state – having decided exile was no longer sufficient punishment – squeezed the last breaths from the worst of the prisoners. The stone expanse was only relieved by an arched gate, its dark wood studded with reinforcing nails; it had probably been built by some of those who eventually languished behind it.

The shot must surely have come from one of the nearby houses, although it was impossible to tell which one. Not without standing where Hallward lost his life. The spot was only a few yards away, but it might as well be on the other side of the world.

Monsarrat heard a scrape behind him, and turned to see the gates of the gaol's main entrance opening. Out stepped two women, clothes grey and stained, their unkempt hair hanging unbound from underneath cloth caps which had once been white. The women might have been Monsarrat's age, or Mrs Mulrooney's: the ravages of poverty, which had taken some of their teeth, had granted them a kind of agelessness.

They were accompanied by a rough and unshaven man, but he was clearly not a prisoner. He dropped a few coins into their hands and re-entered the gaol, closing the door behind him as the two women turned and walked towards Monsarrat.

'Pardon me, ladies,' he said as they passed. They stopped, stared as though he had spoken a foreign language. They were very possibly used to being addressed in different terms.

Monsarrat waited for a response. Not getting one, he nervously cleared his throat.

'May I ask, what brought you to the gaol today?'

Silence.

'Only, you see, I have a friend in there. I'm worried for his health, and wanted reassurance he wasn't rotting in muck.'

The two women looked at each other, and began to move off.

'I'm concerned enough to spend a shilling for a report on the conditions in there.'

One of them slowed, turned, but the other grabbed her elbow and hurried her along.

'A shilling – each,' said Monsarrat.

Both of them stopped this time, turning and staring. Monsarrat reached into his breast pocket in hopes of being able to find two shillings. Successful, he held up the two coins, one in each hand. Both of the women put out their palms, and he slowly placed a coin in each.

'So,' he said.

'So,' said one of the women – frizzle-haired, etched skin, probably the older of the two. From Lancashire, he decided, as she continued to speak. 'Whether your friend is in muck or not depends on how much money he has. Them that can pay, they get clean bedding, better food. If they can't – well.'

'The wardens won't be taking as much this week though,' said the other woman. 'On account of everyone having a clean cell at the moment.'

'Really? Why is that?' asked Monsarrat.

'Some lord or whoever. Decided the place needed a good scrub. Wanted it cleaned from end to end.'

'Oh. Why?'

'Couldn't say,' said the older woman. 'Some of that dirt has been there since before I was transported. So your friend will have clean straw even if he hasn't paid for it. For a few days or so, until the rot creeps back in.'

'I see. Well, thank you.'

The older woman shrugged, nodded to her friend. As they moved away, Monsarrat wondered why an administration which was usually happy to let people sit in their own filth suddenly wanted to clean the dirtiest corners of the colony.

Chapter 4

Another starched jacket with a fussy little collar. Another brooch. Hannah would never have bought these clothes without Mr Monsarrat's urging. She could by now have dozens of outfits – the money from the sale of a ruined necklace, given to her by the husband of the woman who had nearly killed her, now sat in a vault at the Bank of New South Wales. But were it up to Hannah she would not have spent a penny of it. It was for her son, Padraig, to set him up in the colonial respectability of his own public house.

In the face of Padraig's silence, however, and Monsarrat's insistence that her housekeeper role would not serve her well in this case, she had relented. Each day, she regretted it more. There was only one small compensation: a purchase she had nipped out to make after Monsarrat had loped away in the direction of the *Colonial Flyer* newsroom.

As the owner of a new fan – albeit one intended mostly for offensive purposes – Hannah felt she would cut quite a fashionable figure in Sydney's ornate gardens.

She had reckoned, though, without Henrietta Duchamp.

The frilly pink parasol that the girl had been swinging around at the party had been temporarily retired from service, along with its matching dress. This afternoon, Henrietta was wearing a pale blue gown, and its companion parasol was made of the same fabric, swagged with blue ribbon.

'You must take better care of your skin in this dreadful climate,' Henrietta exclaimed, as a footman helped Hannah into the coach that had arrived at the boarding house, much to the amazement of Miss Douglas, who had returned from her errands just in time to see it thundering up the road.

'I have a lovely new bonnet,' said Hannah, tugging on the ribbon beneath her chin.

'Rather provincial,' said Henrietta, giving Hannah's hand its first pat of the afternoon. 'Please do not take offence. It's not your fault – it must be difficult to keep abreast of fashions when you live outside Sydney. But now you have me!'

'Yes, how fortunate,' said Hannah, wondering what the refined young ladies of London and Paris would make of Henrietta's assertion that Sydney was a centre of fashion.

'I always bring a spare parasol,' said Henrietta, reaching under the coach's seat. 'Take it, I insist.'

If there was a polite way to refuse, Hannah couldn't think of it. She had been handed a mass of white lace, with ribbons dripping from the edge of the parasol frame. She looked as if she were carrying a cake on a stick. 'How very kind,' she said.

'Think nothing of it! I do believe it's important to help the less fortunate.' As the coach negotiated the streets of the cove's fashionable eastern shore, on its way towards the gardens, Henrietta told Hannah of her charitable works with widows and orphans. 'It can be distasteful work, of course,' she said. 'A lad once coughed blood onto my dress and I had to burn it. But as a Christian woman, I feel I must keep at it.'

Hannah felt a pang of worry for this unknown boy. In the convict huts she had seen orphans abandoned to starvation, disease or abuse. Only luck had prevented a similar fate befalling her Padraig.

'I would be delighted to assist you in your endeavours,' Hannah told Henrietta. 'If you have need of it.'

'That is a generous offer, but really I only go once every few months, and it's rather, well, social. The domain of a certain type of lady. I would hate for you to be uncomfortable.'

'Oh yes,' said Hannah, 'we must not make people uncomfortable.'

'Quite so. Ah – here we are.'

The coach had pulled up at a pair of wrought-iron gates set into sandstone pillars. The gates were open onto a broad pathway that snaked around the harbour.

'You will very much enjoy this, Mrs Mulrooney. It really is the most marvellous place, and everyone will be here on a day like this.'

Hannah could see why. Leaving the coach, they started walking along a path bounded by the glistening water on one side with the scrubby north shore in the distance, and a profusion of trees and flowers on the other. These were interspersed with statues of naked nymphs that were robbed of all salaciousness by their blank stone eyes – clearly a refinement shipped from England. When Hannah had first arrived, the imports were of canvas, cordage, tea and salted meat. What a wonder that the colony had reached a point where they were now importing nymphs.

'I do hope you will not take offence at this, either,' said Henrietta, nodding to a gentleman who was walking in the other direction, 'but I couldn't help detecting a certain lilt in your voice.'

'You have a good ear, Miss Duchamp,' Hannah said, resisting the urge to swat the hand that had snaked its way around her arm.

'You are Church of England, of course,' Henrietta said.

'It's called Church of Ireland there.'

'Oh yes, quite so,' said Henrietta, and Hannah sent up a prayer of thanks to several saints. Letting the girl believe she was a Protestant was one thing, but being forced to overtly disavow her own religion would have cost her more than she was willing to pay.

A group of young women passed by, a knot of silk and whispers, heads bent over a sheet of paper as they walked slowly to avoid tripping on their skirts. Henrietta waggled her fingers at them, and they each bobbed a quick curtsey to her before they continued their stroll.

'Miss Albrecht, this morning,' said Hannah. 'Her lack of deference was quite in contrast to that of those ladies.'

Henrietta frowned. 'To hear her tell it, she is an artist. That type seem to believe different rules apply to them.'

'And I imagine she associates with other unsuitable people,' said Hannah, fully aware that if Henrietta knew the truth, she would consider Hannah to be most unsuitable.

'Well, precisely!' said Henrietta. 'I told you about Hallward, didn't I?'

'Yes, I seem to recall – who is he, again?' said Hannah, sending up another quick prayer, this one of apology for the pretence, and scanning the sky for lightning bolts.

'I thought you'd have known,' said Henrietta. 'He is the man whose murder your nephew is investigating.'

'Ah. An ugly business. I try to stay away from it as much as possible.'

'You're very wise,' said Henrietta. 'There are those who try to stay out of trouble, and those who can't help running towards it – like Hallward. And Miss Albrecht, come to that.' Henrietta leaned closer and whispered conspiratorially, 'Do you know, she plays for *money*? Quite scandalous!'

She's probably rather fond of eating, Hannah thought, while effecting a look of scandalised disbelief. 'Truly! Where on earth would one even do such a thing? Surely not in a public house.'

'Oh, no, not quite that scandalous. She'd never be admitted to Government House if she did. No, she provides entertainment for some of the better households, during parties and so forth. Occasionally she plays at the recital hall not far from here. Not a place I would ever visit, but I suppose it brings music to the masses. A lot of people are charmed by her, saying she is quite the musician, but most of them are men, and I rather think they're dazzled by some of her other attributes.'

'And these other attributes – was Mr Hallward acquainted with them?'

Henrietta chuckled. 'You are a naughty one, Mrs Mulrooney. I've never heard a rumour to that effect. But I've never heard it denied, either. Who knows what happens behind the most respectable of doors, let alone those belonging to the likes of Miss Albrecht?'

Hannah and Henrietta were walking towards a man who stood to the side of the path, distributing sheets of paper – like the one, Hannah realised, the group of girls had been giggling over – from a battered leather satchel. As they were about to pass him, Hannah paused. 'I'll take one of those, please,' she said to him.

Henrietta's eyes narrowed. 'And my brother will take the rest of them,' she said. 'Stay away from that man, Mrs Mulrooney, I beg you, he is peddling lies!'

'Not peddling nothing, miss,' the man said. 'Not charging for these.'

'I will be reporting you, nevertheless,' said Henrietta, turning and walking off.

Hannah raised her eyebrows at the man. He shrugged and handed her a pamphlet, which she folded and slid into her reticule just as Henrietta turned back. 'Do come away, Mrs Mulrooney.'

Several other groups, mostly young ladies interspersed with the occasional couple, greeted Henrietta as they passed.

'You seem to know just about everyone here,' said Hannah.

'Oh, I come here as often as I can. The business of governing is so dreary to observe. Although ... there is one political issue on which I have a strong view.'

Hannah held her breath.

'Our current governor, bless him, has taken remarkable strides in terms of discipline and efficiency – so Edward says, anyway. But Darling was beaten to a very important initiative by his predecessor: the formation of the Sydney Turf Club.'

'I presume you don't mean the kind of turf men cut.'

Henrietta threw back her head and laughed. 'No, of course not! No, I mean racing – horse racing, I hasten to add, not sweaty men pounding around a track. You must come!'

'Well, I don't know the first thing about racing, I'm afraid.'

'As if that matters! Leave that to those men who enjoy it. You should hear them go on about which stallion is out of which mare, and whether they have endurance or speed. Those men pay more attention to horses than they do their wives. But that's not the only attraction of the races – they provide an opportunity to socialise and show off one's new dress. And even for those who care little about horseflesh, the atmosphere can be quite extraordinary if a race is a close-run thing.'

'Well, *atmosphere* – I do understand the importance of that.'

The excitement of the races, though, was the furthest thing from Hannah's mind. She was remembering the sight of twenty thousand people on a hill surrounded by British soldiers, the low Irish sky made lower by the smoke from burning houses. That was what entered her mind whenever she thought of atmosphere, and it would be impossible to replace it with the silly image of horses running around for the entertainment of people who had nothing better to do.

'You must come,' Henrietta insisted breathlessly. 'You must! There is a race meeting on Saturday morning. It would do you the world of good to see it, someone as sheltered as yourself.'

'Of course! Thank you.'

Hannah wondered why Henrietta, who by her own reckoning was vastly socially superior, was so enthusiastic to start a friendship with her. Was she using Hannah to keep track of the movements of Mr Monsarrat? Even if that was the case, Hannah intended to cultivate the woman, and could not fault Henrietta for doing the same.

She also knew well that atmosphere was created by strong emotions – such as excitement or terror – which tended to reveal the truth about people. She would be fascinated to see if anyone allowed their shell to crack at this race meeting.

Chapter 5

'A bit melodramatic, this headline,' said Monsarrat, holding up the pamphlet. '"Sinister Forces at Work". Sounds like something from a play.'

'Before you sniff at it, Mr Monsarrat, perhaps you should read the whole thing,' Mrs Mulrooney said. 'And if the circumstances of Hallward's murder are not sinister, then ...'

'Yes, yes, give me a minute. It does look professionally done, actually – almost like a newspaper.' He squinted at the pamphlet, which was simply a single page, printed on one side with that febrile headline above a few columns of text and without illustration.

> Many of the free occupants of this colony have failed to notice that their rights are under attack. The government is stealing them – not with the direct assault of a highwayman, but with the stealth of a pickpocket.
>
> The owner of one of our two newspapers – a man known for exposing the worst excesses of the administration – has been murdered, leaving only the *Colonial Flyer* in operation. That paper's editor, Mr Gerald Mobbs,

is merely as critical of the administration as he needs to be in order to retain his credibility. More often, he prefers to ignore any issue that casts the government in a negative light.

For instance, Mr Mobbs has not informed his readers of a plan by the governor to license newspapers, meaning that only those who sing the praises of the administration will be allowed to operate. As the government is now rid of its most courageous provocateur, only one voice is left in Sydney. The government will set heaven and hell in motion to ensure it owns that voice.

The pamphlet went on to compare Henry Hallward's editorials to the tepid pronouncements of Mobbs.

'Well?' said Mrs Mulrooney.

'Well, the writing is a little stilted, and that "heaven and hell" idiom is a bit odd –'

'Eejit of a man! I want to know what you think of Vindex's words, not how he is saying them.'

'Vindex?'

Mrs Mulrooney jabbed her finger at the bottom of the page. 'It's signed *Vindex*.'

'*The vindicator*,' said Monsarrat. 'In accusing Mobbs, is the writer after vindication?'

'You don't think Mobbs could be the killer, then?' Hannah asked. 'He told you himself that Hallward was going to destroy his livelihood.'

'He's not as extreme as Hallward, but he doesn't seem to mind upsetting people when he feels it is warranted. And in any case, he was at the Colonial Secretary's Office.'

'Says who?'

'Says Mobbs. It's so easy to confirm, I'm inclined to believe it.' Monsarrat reached across the dining-room table for another slice of the bread which sat on a silver tray next to a plate of cheese, both deposited by Miss Douglas half an hour earlier.

He stopped mid-stretch when he saw Mrs Mulrooney glaring at him. 'Freedom has clearly not improved your manners,' she said, pointedly passing him the platter of bread. 'And Colonel Duchamp was one of Hallward's targets?'

'He seems to have been. But he was reviewing the troops.'

Mrs Mulrooney reached into a pocket, extracted a small, ornate fan, and rapped Mr Monsarrat over the knuckles. 'And how do we know he didn't have help?'

'For God's sake!' said Monsarrat, rubbing his hand. 'You couldn't have purchased a handkerchief?'

'Mr Monsarrat, Colonel Duchamp is controlling the information you receive. You might want to ask yourself again whether you are willing to let him continue to do that.'

'I've sent a note to Jardine on that score, as it happens,' said Monsarrat. 'Duchamp's assistant, you remember. Seems a more reasonable sort. Told him I intend to go to the gaol with or without Duchamp's say-so. Might convince them they're better off helping me than having me haring around unchecked.'

'Perhaps haring around is precisely what you should be doing, Mr Monsarrat. I just hope you make more progress with Duchamp tomorrow. Refusing once to let you meet the warden ... Well, I suppose it can be explained away. If he comes up with another excuse, that will say more than any warden could.'

※

There was no music at Government House the following morning; no rustling silks or glinting jewels. The footman who had admitted Monsarrat yesterday seemed not to remember him and asked for his name again. The man led him to the arched doorway of Duchamp's study, knocked, and stepped back.

'Come in,' Duchamp called. 'We're ready.'

A man was perched on the edge of the seat Monsarrat had occupied the day before. Small and lean, he had thinning hair and wore clothes of the type that would normally only enter Government House on the body of a labourer. For all that, the man sat correctly, shoulders back, gazing past Duchamp towards the portrait of the glowering King.

Duchamp gestured Monsarrat to a small chaise nearby. 'Good of you to come, Mr Monsarrat,' he said, in a tone that suggested he felt it was the least Monsarrat could do. 'May I present David Crowdy. Of the Sydney gaol. You asked for a warden. Here he is.'

Monsarrat hoped the recognition did not show on his face. This was the same fellow who had paid the two women to clean the gaol. He nodded towards the man, who stared steadily back at him. 'I am sorry, sir,' he said to Duchamp, 'but I had rather hoped we would be visiting the gaol. Being at the place itself – measuring footsteps, looking for secret entrances, that sort of thing – can often prove most illuminating.'

'I'm sure it can, Mr Monsarrat,' said Duchamp. 'However, in this case, you will have to rely on Mr Crowdy's observations. There will soon be protesters at the gates of the gaol, you see. We'd hate to have you stuck inside – even though it's a situation with which I understand you're familiar.'

Monsarrat cursed himself. After being forced to pretend to be a free settler during his previous case on Maria Island, he had asked Ralph Eveleigh not to conceal his background again, as the subterfuge had been too draining. Now he wished he hadn't made the request. Duchamp was not the type to approve of former convicts – although he would have had trouble staffing his house and offices without them – and the sudden straightening of Crowdy's spine let Monsarrat know that the warden shared the private secretary's views.

'Very well,' Monsarrat said. 'I will, of course, be permitted to visit at some stage?'

'Oh yes, yes,' said Duchamp. 'Just a matter of finding the right time.'

'And where should Mr Crowdy and I go for our interview?'

'Here is fine,' said Duchamp.

'You will be present? Pardon me, sir, but isn't that irregular?'

'I'll thank you, Mr Monsarrat, not to tell me what is regular. It will come as no surprise to you that bringing order to the colony is one of the governor's priorities, and therefore mine. Why on earth would I not want to hear what Mr Crowdy has to say?'

'As you wish,' said Monsarrat. 'So, Mr Crowdy. You are the head warden?'

'No. That's Mr Gleeson. He's not here,' said Crowdy.

'Well, I can see that.'

'Visiting his sister. Somewhere out west,' said Duchamp.

Monsarrat tried to hide his irritation. 'Were you in daily contact with the victim in the lead-up to his trial?'

'Of course,' Crowdy said. 'We don't tend to leave the prisoners unsupervised. Might have been how it worked in your time, wherever you were. But not now, not here. Oversight is everything.'

'I am glad to hear you say that,' said Monsarrat, 'because there is a point on which I'm hoping to enlighten myself with a visit to the prison. As that's not yet possible, perhaps you can assist me. Where exactly did the shot come from?'

'Couldn't say. I was rather preoccupied with trying to get the prisoner into the cart, to take him to justice.'

'You mean to his trial.'

'Yes. Hard to see how they could have avoided convicting, though. Not this time.'

'You didn't see anyone fleeing the yard?'

Crowdy looked at Monsarrat as if he had lost his wits. 'Had I done so, I would of course have immediately arrested them, despite the fact that there would be some who'd want to congratulate them.'

'And who might they be?'

'Anyone he wrote about.'

'And that wouldn't have included you, of course.'

'Mr Monsarrat,' said Duchamp, 'I will take offence at any attempt to impugn the integrity of an official. Everyone who works for this administration has proven themselves above reproach.'

Monsarrat was not at all sure that was true, but inclined his head in polite apology. Crowdy gave him an unpleasant smirk, showing that the state of the man's teeth likely matched that of many inmates.

'Did you find anything, afterwards,' said Monsarrat, 'on Mr Hallward's person or in his cell? Anything which might illuminate a motive?'

'If I had, I would certainly have produced it. He did leave some papers in his desk, but when I looked later they were gone. I couldn't say where.'

'What papers would those be?'

'Letters, he said. Invoices. His office may've collected them. I heard something about a boy being sent. Whether he arrived or not, I couldn't say.'

'You don't seem to be able to say much, Mr Crowdy,' Monsarrat said. 'Very well. I don't suppose you have any questions of your own, Colonel?'

'I have no intention of doing your work for you, Mr Monsarrat.'

'In that case,' said Monsarrat, 'perhaps you could help me do it for myself. Can I speak with the doctor who examined Hallward's body?'

'He is still unavailable, sadly.'

Monsarrat nodded slowly. 'Well, sir, you clearly have your own work to do, and Mr Crowdy has prisoners to guard. I thank you both for your time.' He rose and bowed stiffly – the growing shadow within would not allow him to make any deeper obeisance – and headed for the door, stopping as he reached it. 'One more thing, Mr Crowdy. Who else was working with you that day?'

'Well, the head warden. Gleeson. I run the prison. He takes the credit. Scares too easily to be in this line of work if I'm honest. Since he trotted off to visit his sister straight after the shooting, there's no one who can tell you more than me about what happened that day. No one at all.'

⁂

Two newsrooms in two days – this was not how Monsarrat had intended to start his investigation. By now, he would have liked to have spoken to the doctor who had examined Hallward's body, paced his way around the prison yard. It did not look as though he would be able to do either this afternoon. But he needed to do something – Duchamp's jab had stung, and any movement was better than none.

This visit could, he hoped, be a great deal better than nothing. He might at least learn who Hallward's true enemies were – he was disinclined to trust entirely the whispers of Duchamp and Mobbs. And he would very much like to know whom Hallward had written about. More to the point, whom he had intended to write about next.

He was also willing to admit to a rising excitement at the prospect of entering the building from which Hallward had praised him, defended Grace O'Leary and chastised the governor as no one else was willing to.

Anyone expecting the *Chronicle*'s offices to look like a palace of free speech, though, would have been disappointed. Hallward's newspaper occupied both floors of a small-windowed building of naked clay brick, not far from the offices of the *Colonial Flyer*. Why newspaper headquarters insisted on always clumping themselves together, Monsarrat would never understand.

The door was opened by a former convict – the scars on the man's wrists told of manacles that had been left on too long, slowly digging furrows into the flesh.

'You a creditor?' he asked, slowly closing the door. 'Can't help you.'

Monsarrat put his hand on the rough wood. 'The governor's office, actually.'

'Oh Jesus, I'm not responsible for anything in the paper,' the man said.

'I'm not here to arrest anyone. Well, not yet. I'm the investigator who's been asked to find out why someone felt it necessary to put a ball in your employer's head.'

'You'd be better off at the gaol, then.'

'Indeed. Off limits today, though.'

'Poke around here if you want to. You probably won't find much – place was looted a few days ago.'

'Looted? What did they take?'

'Nothing much of value to take. Some lead type, maybe to melt down for musket balls. And they caused a fair amount of destruction.'

'Do you think they were looking for something?'

'I couldn't say, sir. Perhaps. Or maybe they just knew the place was empty and thought they'd try their luck.'

The man opened the door and stood aside. Monsarrat stepped into a high-ceilinged composing room similar to the one he had visited the day before, with the same angled tables and frames. Most of the frames were smashed, and the blocks of type were gone. Only one frame remained sufficiently intact to hold blocks, some of which were laid out beside it in no decipherable order.

'I doubt another paper will ever come out of here,' the man said.

'That would be a pity, Mr . . .?'

'Cullen. And not everyone would agree with you.'

'You must have had a fair amount of affection for the place, though. To still be here guarding it.'

'Was paid to the end of the month,' said Cullen.

He has an unusual face, thought Monsarrat. It was grooved by sun and salt water but still open, as though Cullen was forgetting to scowl as most men with similar trenches in their skin did. He had the kind of probing blue eyes Monsarrat saw each day in the head of Mrs Mulrooney. Judging by his accent, he might have come from the same village.

'I do the work I was paid for, no matter how pointless it is,' Cullen said.

'Perhaps less pointless than you thought, if I'm able to find something of use. Where is Hallward's office?'

Cullen showed him to an alcove at the back of the room. Unlike Mobbs's office, it was not cut off from the compositing floor. Its door was useless, as there was no glass in its large frames.

'The journalists sat upstairs, but Mr Hallward always preferred it down here,' said Cullen. 'He liked the sounds, the blocks of type clinking into one another. Said it helped him work.'

Monsarrat stepped through the door, looking at the desk in front of him. Had it not been for the mould growing in a teacup, he could have believed that Hallward had just stepped out for a moment. The desk was utilitarian, the opposite of the ornate one at which Duchamp sat, but handsome all the same. Its inlaid panel of green leather was gouged with indentations where Hallward had pressed his pen too hard. To the side, a rack held past editions of the newspaper, the Gothic lettering of the masthead over the motto: *omnia vincit veritas* – truth conquers all, as Monsarrat knew from his school Latin.

Monsarrat was about to try a drawer when he realised that it did not have a handle.

'Looters were in here, too,' said Cullen. 'Maybe they thought he kept money in his desk. They would have been disappointed – it was just papers. Stories he was working on, that sort of thing. They took them anyway.'

'Did you call the authorities?'

'Why would I do that?'

You wouldn't, thought Monsarrat. Not if you suspected it was the authorities doing the looting.

'Was Hallward arrested here?' he asked, and Cullen nodded. 'Quite upsetting for the staff, I imagine.'

'We were used to it,' said Cullen. 'He came to the door to meet the constables, said good morning, asked if they'd like tea before heading to the prison.'

'I see. And the story he was arrested for – it was published that morning?'

Cullen moved over to the rack, extracted a paper and laid it on the green leather, smoothing it out almost affectionately. 'Third last edition, did we but know it. Two days before he died.' Cullen tapped a fingernail on a story near the top of the page. 'Those are the words that did for him.'

The headline, 'Assault on Liberty', told Monsarrat that the story would be a headlong race to condemnation rather than a gentle rhetorical stroll. It attacked the governor's plan to license and tax newspapers out of existence, predicting the rise of autocracy when the only source of information was owned by the administration. It also listed what Hallward saw as the governor's other failings.

> As readers will know, Governor Darling views the colony as his personal fiefdom. The convicts are his to treat like cattle, the land is his to distribute to his cronies, the plum posts are his in which to install his favourite toadies, while the colony is robbed of the benefit of the skills of more able and progressive men and the energy of smaller, robust landholders.

The articles and letters patent of his appointment give the governor unlimited power, but wiser governors, aware of the growing democratic temper of the colony, have not used the full extent of that power. This governor uses every inch of his. This is an oppressive and tyrannical government which has paralysed the energies of the colony, and readers may soon look forward to the emergence of more evidence of its wrongdoing.

'Yes, well,' said Monsarrat, 'can't imagine Darling being thrilled by that.'

'No,' said Cullen. 'Mr Hallward brought a packed bag in with him that day. He knew what would happen.'

'Ah. A brave man, then.'

'Oh, he didn't mind being arrested. Sometimes he seemed almost to enjoy it. He said it gave him thinking time. And helped him show the governor for what he was. When he wrote a story from gaol, he used the byline *Captivus*.'

'The prisoner,' said Monsarrat. The pseudonyms, it seemed, were piling up. 'Tell me, are you aware of anyone else with a fondness for Latin names?'

'No one else was in prison as much as Hallward was.'

'Do you know if he was working on anything while awaiting his trial? He mentions further evidence.'

'He did that a lot,' said Cullen. 'Liked to tease people. Sometimes he'd publish more stories on it, sometimes not. I wouldn't read too much into it.'

'But if he published from gaol so often, surely during his last two days there he might have worked something up.'

'He did not share his plans with me, sir,' Cullen said, in a cooler tone. 'Now, I'm in the middle of setting to rights the damage from the looting, so if there's nothing else?'

'No, nothing for now, thank you. I may need to come back, though.'

'As you wish, of course,' said Cullen, opening the door.

But when Monsarrat tried to step through it, he found his way blocked by a boy.

He could have been anywhere between eight and twelve: a younger child of the upper classes was often the same size as an older child of the streets. This lad, with his grimy face, seemed to fit into the latter category, so despite his small stature he was probably at the higher end of the range.

The boy opened his mouth to speak, and then closed it, stepping back.

Cullen appeared behind Monsarrat. 'I've told you, we've no bread!' he yelled. 'Never listen, do you? Clear out.'

The boy frowned, as though he hadn't expected this response. Again he looked on the verge of speaking – and decided against it, turned and ran off.

'I am sorry, sir,' said Cullen. 'We get the street lads sniffing around from time to time. Some of them take longer to get the message than others.'

'No apology necessary,' said Monsarrat, wondering if he could prevail upon Mrs Mulrooney to make some shortbread that he could bring for the lad, if Monsarrat was able to find him again. He'd probably disappeared into the crumbling, refuse-hemmed huts of the western shore, unlikely to revisit a place where no bread was to be had.

Monsarrat had just turned a corner when he heard footsteps behind him. Peering back around the corner, he saw that the boy had returned to the newspaper building. He was standing with his head bowed as Cullen ruffled his hair affectionately and handed him a piece of bread.

'It's the damnedest thing. Everyone seems to be concealing something.'

'Ah, Mr Monsarrat, if you expect the majority of people to tell you the truth, you'll be disappointed. Far better to expect everyone to lie and be pleasantly surprised from time to time.'

'Perhaps,' said Monsarrat. He was settled in a chair beside the extinct fire in the boarding house's parlour, a small brandy at his elbow. 'The Duchamps, Mobbs, all accounted for, though, at the time of the murder.'

'If they're to be believed, Mr Monsarrat.'

Mrs Mulrooney sat in the companion chair. A woman dressed like her, a woman of means as she was now, might have been expected to have a sherry on the small polished wooden table beside her, but Mrs Mulrooney had never touched alcohol and said she never would.

'I simply can't credit that Hallward wasn't writing a story while in gaol,' Monsarrat said. 'Crowdy, the warden, said Hallward was working on the accounts. But if the man enjoyed the notoriety of publishing from prison, and with his own livelihood under threat, you'd expect him to be louder than ever.'

'Perhaps he was trying to be,' said Mrs Mulrooney.

'Well, someone may have thought so. The newsroom was looted. Might just have been thieves. Everyone knows by now that the *Chronicle* has closed. But . . .'

'But if you were a thief, would you risk hanging to rob a newspaper? Not known for their riches, are they?'

'Quite. Whereas if you're looking for a story, and can't find it in the man's gaol cell – well, who knows. Hopefully there's something left to discover at the gaol. When the protests die down.'

'You're not telling me you're afraid of wading through some protesters!'

'No, I simply don't wish to carry out my enquiries under the gaze of several dozen of the colony's more outspoken residents.'

'They'll be too busy screaming at the gaol walls to notice you. And if you show up at the prison gates in the middle of a protest, the guards will probably be too distracted to keep a close eye on you while you're there.'

'Hm. Worth considering. In the meantime, I was hoping to ask you a favour. Tomorrow, could you commandeer the kitchen for the purposes of shortbread? There's a young lad who looks as though he could use some – and he just may have some information for us. And have a word to Mr Cullen. It would be useful to find out more about the first story Hallward was arrested for – Mobbs mentioned some soldiers whose treatment seems to have enraged Hallward.'

'Mr Monsarrat, I can honestly say I'd like nothing better – any day on which I can bake shortbread and ask questions is a grand day indeed.'

'I'm surprised, actually, that you're still wearing your respectable clothes.'

Mrs Mulrooney straightened, her nostrils flaring as her eyebrows knitted together. 'My usual clothes are perfectly respectable!'

'Of course, yes, I didn't mean – simply that your usual clothes, much as you love them, would have been unlikely to get you invited to the races by Henrietta Duchamp. But this evening I'm surprised to see you're still in your ... armour, as it were.'

'Well, I thought I'd better stay in costume for a little while longer. Because you and I, Mr Monsarrat, are going to a concert.'

Chapter 6

There were few frilled parasols at the recital hall, a low-ceilinged place, respectable but not opulent. The men and the few women who accompanied them were generally dressed in plain clothes of reasonable quality. For the first time since Monsarrat had arrived in Sydney, he felt he could pass unnoticed, while Mrs Mulrooney's brooch was by far the most extravagant item in the room.

There was no lobby. People milled around the hall, weaving between rows of chairs, greeting friends or calling out good-natured insults. They all quietened down, their chatter ebbing, when a man – tall, thin, simply dressed but still with the silver horseshoe gleaming against his black cravat – stepped up to the podium that stood before the red velvet stage curtains and used his spectacles to rap the lectern. The sound couldn't have travelled more than a few feet, but many of those present had half an eye on him already. He was, it seemed, one to be given silence on demand. His eyes covered the crowd, fixing now and then on a miscreant who coughed or whispered to their neighbour. It was the same stare which had fixed on Monsarrat at yesterday's garden party.

'I suggest,' Albert Bancroft said, 'that everyone takes their seats.'

He was obeyed remarkably quickly, although the lack of a lobby, and therefore liquid refreshment, was perhaps making the audience biddable.

'Now, I assume you have not come here to see me –' Bancroft said.

'So stop talking, Bertie!' yelled someone from the crowd.

Bancroft narrowed his eyes at the audience as though trying to identify the speaker, then cleared his throat. 'In that case, the Royal Colonial Music Appreciation Society presents Miss Carolina Albrecht with Mozart's Piano Concerto No. 21.' He paused, glaring at an unfortunate underling backstage as they jerkily opened the curtain. 'James! Earn your position as deputy president.'

When the sheets of red velvet finally parted, Carolina Albrecht stood with her hand on the piano, staring straight ahead. She did not react as the curtains revealed her, and Monsarrat had the impression she had been standing there for some time, listening to the irascible introduction.

Monsarrat had heard strains from the piano as they drifted through the walls into Duchamp's study during the garden party but had not seen her. Now, he had the uncomfortable sensation that she was staring at him, for all that her eyes were fixed on the back wall. Her gaze was vague but aggressive, a challenge to all comers to try to judge her and see how far they got. A familiar look. Grace O'Leary's look.

Clearly feeling that the back wall had been stared at enough, Carolina moved sedately to the piano stool and took her time settling herself, arranging her skirts and organising her sheet music as though she was alone in a rehearsal room. No one called to her to get on with it. Apart from the occasional clearing of a throat, the room was silent. Then Carolina lifted her fingers, slammed them down onto the keys and dived into the music, summoning strident notes and gentle phrases, and sending them out to weave around the audience.

A hand squeezed Monsarrat's, and when he looked to his side he saw that Mrs Mulrooney's eyes were wet. 'Do you know, Mr Monsarrat,' she said after the noise of applause had died down, 'that this is the first concert I have ever been to?'

'Truly?' said Monsarrat. He had, as a young man and a free one, attended such events when he could, and had also heard his share of bawdy tavern key-bashing.

'When would I have had the opportunity?' Mrs Mulrooney said. 'We sang a lot, as I was growing up. There were fiddles sometimes, bodhrans, tin pipes. But for the past twenty years, all I've heard are laments or drunken songs about unmentionable goings-on.'

'Well, when this is over, we must make up for it,' he said. 'Perhaps start a music society in Parramatta.'

'Where I am sure you will open the curtains more smoothly than was done tonight. But for now, Mr Monsarrat, we have other business. I will go alone, if you've no objection. She strikes me as a bit of a fiery one. Best not give her the chance to eject us because there's a strange man backstage.'

'I wouldn't say strange, but as you wish,' he said. 'I will be here talking to the musical society president – and hoping he doesn't immediately try to get me assigned to one of his properties.'

***

Bancroft was around the side of the stage, smoking a pipe and reading a copy of the *Colonial Flyer*. He stuffed it under his arm when Hannah cleared her throat. 'I am sorry, madam,' he said, 'but this area is not open to the general public.'

'Oh, but I so wanted to thank Miss Albrecht for her performance,' Hannah said, coating her words with what she hoped was just enough wheedling.

'I'm sure she'd appreciate a nice note.'

'I've met her, you see, and I was rather hoping to renew the acquaintance.'

'I believe Miss Albrecht has plenty of acquaintances as it is.'

'Nonsense, Albert,' said a clipped voice with a slight German accent. 'One can never have too many friends.' Carolina stepped from the shadows of the stage. She had changed from her blue gown into a rather severe grey travelling suit.

'As you wish,' Bancroft said. 'I've far better things to do than engage in a debate on the social affairs of women.' He tossed the newspaper aside and stalked away.

'Ah,' Carolina said as she got closer to Hannah, 'you're Henrietta's new friend.'

'Now, I wouldn't put it like that,' said Hannah. 'Given that I've known her the same length of time as I've known you.'

'Really? From the way she was cosseting you, I thought you were her maiden aunt.'

'No. I just found myself conscripted to a garden party while my ... nephew did some business with Colonel Duchamp.'

'I see. Well, while I generally welcome new friends, I prefer not to draw them from the Duchamp circle, so if you'll excuse me ...' She started to walk away.

Hannah realised any claim that she wasn't part of Henrietta's coterie would be disbelieved. 'I was hoping to talk to you about Henry Hallward,' she called out.

Carolina slowly turned back. 'What have you to say about him?'

'I simply wanted to know what he was like. I was a reader of the *Chronicle*.'

'If you were a regular reader, you know very well what he was like. I have no time for curiosity hunters. Goodnight, madam.'

She started to turn again, so Hannah decided to try honesty. 'My ... my nephew is investigating his death. We are concerned about certain things – missing stories, incomplete evidence.

If you wish to see his killer punished, you could do worse than to talk to me.'

Carolina paused, looked at Hannah, then turned again and walked away.

Hannah sighed. It was one thing to take a calculated risk in revealing Mr Monsarrat's role – another to do so without gaining any advantage.

Then Carolina stopped again. 'Madam, I have had a long night of performing. If you wish to talk to me, I suggest you hurry up and follow.'

※

There had been some chitchat, little knots of people asking about each other's children or health, but the hall had emptied fairly quickly and the candles in the sconces were beginning to burn low. It was getting too dim to read Hallward's obituary.

Monsarrat had found the piece in a copy of the *Colonial Flyer* left on a seat. He didn't know whether Mobbs had written it. Whoever had, though, was trying to walk a very fine line between dismissiveness and respect.

> Mr Hallward founded one of the pre-eminent organs of information in this city. His focus on the public good is to be applauded; however, at times his commitment to truth could veer from the path of sober-minded analysis into zealotry.

As Monsarrat folded the newspaper and replaced it on the seat, he noticed the edge of a piece of paper sticking out between the newsprint sheets. He extracted it, to be greeted with the headline 'Sinister Forces at Work'.

Footsteps – he shoved the pamphlet back into the paper, opened it at a random page and pretended to read; sometimes it was best to feign ignorance.

'Mr Monsarrat. I don't usually expect to find musical sensibility in, well, someone like you. I suggest you read somewhere with better light.'

Monsarrat did look up then, to see the tall musical society president – upbraider of audiences and attender of garden parties. 'And I would be delighted to take your advice, sir. However, I am waiting for my aunt. I believe she has gone to pay her respects to Miss Albrecht.'

'Respects are all very well,' said Bancroft, 'but I could have sworn I heard her ask about that slain newspaper editor.'

'That wouldn't surprise me – she's always been interested in current events.'

'I was given to understand you were the investigator, yet you are letting a woman do your work. In any case, one person's current event is another's tragedy. Mr Hallward and Miss Albrecht were close friends. It would be unfortunate to upset her. Another performance tomorrow night, you see. For which she has already been paid.'

'Oh, I'm sure the last thing my aunt would want to do is cause upset. And Miss Albrecht strikes me as the type of woman who is perfectly capable of ending a distressing conversation.'

'Perhaps.'

'I must admit,' said Monsarrat, 'I found Miss Albrecht's performance delightful.'

'Ah, that's right,' said Bancroft. 'Duchamp said you had a certain degree of education. Not enough to keep you out of the hold of a prison ship. Parramatta, was it? I have a property between here and there.'

'A pastoralist. The colony has been good to you, then.'

'Better than the mother country. I would have been lucky to own a smallholding there. Here, I run properties almost as large as my childhood village.'

'The governor must be generous.'

'The governor is canny,' said Bancroft. 'All this land, and all needs farming. He gives it to those who have the mettle.'

'Ah. I was reading Hallward's obituary just then, and I seem to recall a few of his pieces attacking pastoralists over, let's see – the treatment of convicts, was it?'

'You were an admirer of the man, of course,' said Bancroft.

'Not necessarily. I read widely to stay informed.'

'The kind of information Hallward traded in wasn't worthy of the name.'

'I understand you're not the only one of that view,' Monsarrat said. 'Tell me, do you believe that any of those who share your opinion of Hallward could have taken action to, shall we say, address the problem permanently?'

'Certainly not! What a suggestion.'

'I simply ask what others are asking.'

'Others should mind themselves, then,' said Bancroft. 'I must go, but I seek your assurance as a gentleman that you will extract your aunt if the conversation continues beyond the next ten minutes. I do not wish to tire such a pianist.'

Monsarrat nodded, hoping that his lack of a verbal promise would mask his lack of an intention to keep it.

*   *   *

'I knew this would happen,' said Carolina, as she poured sherry for Hannah from a crystal decanter on her dressing table. She nestled the decanter back between brushes and rouged pieces of cloth and pots of mysterious ointments. 'People with Henry's honesty don't generally live to old age.'

'You believe he was killed for his views, then?' Hannah asked. She raised the glass to her lips and lowered it again – a trick she used to make others believe she was imbibing with them. It was the closest she had ever been to sherry. Rum, of course, smelled atrocious, like the brawler's drink it was. She had not expected sherry, in all its gentility, to smell equally bad in its own, cloying way.

'Yes, why not? After what the governor was willing to do to those soldiers – imprisonment, torture to the point of death.'

'Ah, the soldiers,' said Hannah. 'What can you tell me of them?'

'Nothing Henry hasn't already written.'

'Henry, you say. You must have been fond of him.'

Carolina turned away, but not before Hannah noticed her lips suddenly pressing together.

'There is no shame in loving a man,' Hannah said quietly.

Carolina's head whipped back around. 'Of course not!' she snapped. 'Nor is there any shame in keeping your counsel about what form that love takes, even when half of Sydney is gossiping about it. Many loved him, in one way or another. For who he was, what he wrote. And just as many hated him.'

'Do you mean Colonel Duchamp?'

'Oh, it went higher than that. The governor did such disgraceful things to his own troops,' Carolina said, 'so why should he scruple at silencing Henry?'

'Wait. You believe the *governor* killed him?'

'Had him killed. Clearly didn't fire the shot himself.'

'Darling didn't like what Hallward wrote, but having him killed? He could have sent him to a penal colony for hard labour.'

'Where Henry would have found a way to write, and a way to get his writings back to Sydney. In suffering for his honesty, he would have been more powerful than ever. Is the governor's culpability so inconceivable? Or are you afraid that it might be true?'

Hannah pretended to sip at her sherry. She did not want to answer.

'Anyway,' said Carolina, 'this is about more than criticism.' She moved again to her dressing table and began to rub cream into her face. She said nothing for a moment. Hannah did not know whether Carolina was trying to increase the weight of her statement by making Hannah wait for it, but it irritated her. Words were too precious to play games with.

'You might as well tell me,' she said. 'The sooner you do, the sooner I can leave you to your face cream.'

Carolina stopped massaging her face and sighed, perhaps disappointed she had been prevented from playing the scene to its maximum effect. 'Henry was working on a story. Something out of the ordinary, even for him. He said the tremors it would cause would be felt in Whitehall. And that it would make the governor's term the shortest in history. Now tell me, do you think that's worth killing for?'

※

'Then where is it?' Monsarrat asked Mrs Mulrooney, as they walked away from the theatre, using the full moon's light to avoid the worst of the ruts in the road. 'It doesn't surprise me that he was working on something – apparently he relished writing from prison. Crowdy did see papers on the table in Hallward's cell, but he said that later they were gone.'

'And you believe him?' asked Mrs Mulrooney. She skipped to avoid an uneven section of pavement that had only just made itself apparent under a street lamp, and cursed in a most unladylike way. 'These shoes, Mr Monsarrat. Silly little heels. If they were tall enough to help me reach a high shelf, I could forgive them. But all they seem intent on doing is giving me bunions and sending me flat on my face.'

'Your fortitude is appreciated, I can assure you,' said Monsarrat. 'And no, I'm not sure I do believe him. But I can't ask the other warden – apparently he's gone to visit his sister out west.'

'An odd time to do that, don't you think?'

'Yes. You're right. I'll need to go to the gaol again.'

'I daresay you will, while I attend the races with Miss Duchamp. Of course, we must also find out what happened to those soldiers – Carolina mentioned them too. I'd wager the key lies in the story Henry Hallward was working on when he was shot. From what you've told me, there may be a place where we can get answers to both questions at once.'

Chapter 7

Hannah knew what people like Henrietta told themselves about their status as Sydney's social leaders – that they were among the exalted of the world. The equal to their counterparts in London. This was a necessary delusion, allowing them to explain what they were doing down here. The short coach ride east to the racetrack would surely have been uncomfortable for these people, had they any honesty. If they had looked out their coach windows, the view would have proved to them that they were paragons only compared to the world's most wretched.

On this east side of the town – always the favoured side – the elegant buildings were crowded together as though to protect one another from being touched by squalor. They gave way very quickly to dirt streets – neatened by gangs of chained convicts for the benefit of those in the coaches – which sent dust flying into throats and eyes. For the most part, the road gang convicts kept their gaze down. Most overseers were not known for their leniency, and those convicts who had the audacity to soil a fine carriage by putting their eyes on it could expect violent discouragement. In one gang the coach passed, though, a man stared directly at Henrietta and Hannah. He had the reddened eyes of a lime burner, condemned to lose his skin slowly to the caustic substances that were released when he burned oyster shells to extract lime for mortar. His eyes, under their abraded lids, followed the coach. When it was roughly level with him, he spat into the dirt.

Soon the streets were clear of people and lined by ghost gums, interspersed with the occasional shack, until the road widened, the trees fell away, and Hannah found herself looking at a broad, flat expanse of green. The coachman pulled close to a wooden fence, freshly painted and well made but still insubstantial enough to fall to a stampeding horse, should one have had enough of racing. To one side, a roof shaded several rows of seats; many were taken, but some in the middle towards the front remained empty.

As Henrietta led Hannah to the seats, she clamped her hand onto Hannah's elbow, guiding her from one group to the next, introducing her briefly and then falling into conversations about people Hannah didn't know, or prattling about the difficulty in finding a good maid or a decent bolt of silk. Hannah tried to pay attention – people revealed much about themselves when discussing trivialities. But this chitchat, punctuated by laughs that sounded like frenzied horses, was almost enough to rob her of consciousness.

It was just as well that she was not attending to the conversation. Had she been, she might have missed a familiar voice struggling to be heard above the chatter of the crowd. 'Pies! Pies and philosophy – my friends, you will not get a more intoxicating combination. No, not even at a tavern! You will leave here with your stomach full and your education augmented.'

Hannah put a hand on Henrietta's arm, whispering that she would like to go for a stroll. Henrietta nodded distractedly and went back to her conversation about the impossibility of getting roses to grow in such deficient air.

The pie seller was already mobbed. The scent of his wares snaked towards her over the heads of the crowd, and she berated herself for not bringing money now that she had some to bring; she must, she thought, make herself a little purse, perhaps sew it into a pocket of her skirts. But the pies, wonderful as they were, were not what drew her towards the overturned crate and the wiry man who stood on it, shifting from foot to foot as he handed out pies and accepted payment, unable to be still for more than a moment.

Stephen Lethbridge: a man of education and discretion, who also possessed quite an extraordinary facility with pastry. A man who was never happier than when he was trotting with his little hotbox from Sydney to Parramatta and then up into the mountains, unwilling to deprive anyone in the colony of his pies – assuming they could pay, of course.

Mr Monsarrat would not have solved the murder of the Parramatta Female Factory superintendent last year without Lethbridge's help, which had also ensured that Monsarrat was close enough to save Hannah from a fire lit by the murderer. Hannah doubted, though, that Lethbridge would recognise her now. She had seen him sell dozens of pies in Parramatta, and he visited Sydney regularly, probably encountering hundreds of people in the course of each week.

Hannah stood towards the back of the throng, moving forward as it thinned when the pies ran out and all Lethbridge had to offer were his thoughts on some old Roman named Marcus Aurelius. When his eyes swept the dwindling crowd, he saw her, smiled, clapped his hands, jumped down from the box and ran towards her, scattering his few remaining customers. 'Mrs Mulrooney, what a wonderful surprise! I had heard you were in Van Diemen's Land.'

'I was. We were back in Parramatta for all of a few nights before they bundled us away down the river. Thankfully we weren't forced to run here – you are the only person I know who could achieve that. I'm sorry, by the way, for I seem to have lost you your audience.'

'Faithless rogues, the lot of them. Those who stayed were not really listening to my fine words, just in a state of suspension until the race starts. I must say, though ...' He took the hotbox from around his neck, placed it reverentially on the crate, turned and held her hands. 'Well! One hears rumours, including that a certain lady has come into a bit of money. I know of no one more deserving. And I can see, now, that it is true.' He rubbed the fabric of her sleeve between his fingers. 'A very fine cloth, that is. Understated quality. Much like you and me.'

Hannah gave him her first genuine smile of the day.

'And where is your Mr Monsarrat? Not a racing man?'

'Perhaps he would be, had he the leisure,' Hannah said. 'His time is being taken up with the murder of the *Sydney Chronicle* editor.'

'Ah, yes. A great admirer of my pies was Henry Hallward, God rest him. Don't look so surprised – you'd be amazed who I meet through the exchange of pastry for money. I didn't mind the *Chronicle* – at least it attempted independent thought. The *Flyer*, on the other hand, might as well be owned by the governor himself. Only fit to line my hotbox.'

'I shall make sure I send Mr Monsarrat your regards,' said Hannah. 'Are you in Sydney long?'

'I start walking back to Parramatta tomorrow. Those lads working on the new church get restless if I'm not there. The guards asked me not to stay away too long – apparently the pies are better at enforcing order than the soldiers. But, as always, if I can be of any assistance ...'

Hannah realised that the noise of the crowd was dying down. She looked towards the track and saw the horses beginning to line up in the gates. From the stand, Henrietta was scanning the crowd, a look of irritation on her face.

'It was wonderful to see you, Mr Lethbridge,' Hannah said. 'However, I must be getting back to my companion.'

Lethbridge smiled and gave her a low bow.

She had only walked a few paces back towards the stands, when she realised she needed something after all. She turned and called, 'Mr Lethbridge!'

As he slung his hotbox back around his neck, he was constrained from bowing but gave her an encouraging smile.

'You meet almost everyone between here and the mountains, don't you?'

He nodded. 'Sometimes a bit beyond the mountains as well.'

'Mr Monsarrat and I have been a little hampered, you see. Hallward's gaoler – one of only two people who saw the murder – has gone to visit his sister somewhere to the west, in the mountains, so he is out of our reach, together with the story Hallward was very possibly working on. Nothing of it was found, but enough people have mentioned it to give me faith that it may have accompanied this man to the hills.'

'What's the fellow's name?'

'Frank ... somebody.'

Lethbridge smiled again, slapping the side of his hotbox. 'Frank Gleeson, I'd wager! Good fellow. I go by the gaol sometimes, you see. He likes me to save him one or two. And you, my dear, have saved me a trip – I didn't know he was out of town.'

'The timing is a little odd, though,' said Hannah. 'He is a crucial witness, but no one seems to be able to tell us exactly where he is or when he will be back, and I've no idea what his sister's name is – if she exists. Would you mind keeping an eye out, and let us know if you hear anything?'

'It would be my honour. I shall be back in Sydney next Thursday – the Botanic Gardens is a fertile hunting ground for customers. Perhaps you might consider a stroll there?'

Hannah returned his smile. 'I would indeed! Oh, and if I may impose on you one more time?'

'Hardly an imposition from one such as you.'

'My son is droving out west, but he's not answering my letters. Padraig Mulrooney, a young man with red-gold hair. If you were to hear anything –'

'Of course. It is not a name I've heard before, but that means nothing. You know what the life of the drover is like, Mrs Mulrooney – they're always moved around, often spending a month or two without seeing a mail cart. I am certain that nothing has befallen your son, but I shall trot back down the mountain with all due speed should any news arise.'

Hannah took his hand in hers and squeezed it with thanks.

As she walked back to Henrietta, she caught sight of a battered leather satchel. Its owner was trying to interest racegoers in his pamphlets. Many waved them away, but a few people took one, read it where they stood and frowned.

Hannah approached the man. 'Are these your words?' she asked.

He stared at Hannah. 'You were at the gardens the other day.'

'I was, and I took your pamphlet home and read it with interest.'

'I wouldn't say that too loudly, here,' he said. 'And it's not my writing. Me and a few others are paid to hand them out – paid well, given the risk.'

'Paid by whom?'

'We're paid a bit extra not to name a name when someone asks. Come to that, who's asking?' He began to look around him, perhaps fearful that someone with reason to be aggrieved would notice.

'I would like to meet your employer,' Hannah told him, then turned and walked as quickly as she could towards Henrietta in the stands.

The young woman gave her a look of consternation. 'Mrs Mulrooney! You must not wander off like that, a woman as – well, as venerable as yourself. Anything could have befallen you!'

'I am sorry to have concerned you, but I assure you I was perfectly safe. I'm simply enjoying that atmosphere you mentioned.'

'Still, you must promise to stay close to me. You are under my protection, after all.'

'Miss Duchamp, what could I possibly need protection from?'

Henrietta opened her mouth to answer, but stopped when she caught sight of something over Hannah's shoulder. The young woman frowned, then turned back to the track and began an animated conversation with the woman on her other side.

Hannah slowly turned to see what Henrietta had been looking at.

Gerald Mobbs was talking to a man who held a brown leather bag, in far better condition than the pamphleteer's satchel. Hannah noticed that several other men with similar bags were dotted around the course. What were they up to? Mobbs's precise moustache was the only composed part of his face; the discussion was becoming more heated by the minute, and indecipherable snippets made their way towards Hannah on the breeze. Finally, from his brown bag the man took out a piece of paper and handed it to Mobbs, who stalked off so quickly he seemed to be deliberately avoiding the man. When Mobbs passed a man who was reading a pamphlet, he snatched it, threw it to the earth and ground it under his heel.

'There seems to be a great deal of interest in the writings of this Vindex person,' Hannah said to Henrietta.

The young woman's brow clenched with irritation. 'Interest? Outrage, more likely. Some little upstart is trying to cause trouble. These scraps of paper are of no consequence. You should ignore them. The men who hand them out are harassing people, you know. I imagine my brother will seek to have them banned.'

'I see. Will he also ban the men I see here with those brown leather bags? What are they doing?'

'Bookmakers, my dear. Nothing to concern yourself with.'

Hannah frowned, confused. 'But why are they making books at the racecourse?'

'You are priceless,' said Henrietta with a giggle. 'They are taking bets on which horse will win. Something you will find out very soon, if you attend – look, it's about to start.'

A man standing at the side of the track blew into a slightly battered horn. The horses sprang forward, thundering around the track so quickly that Hannah felt a rush of air across her face. It was over in a matter of minutes, one fine black horse crossing the finish line well ahead of the others, its rider standing up in the stirrups and raising his hand in the air.

'I can see the appeal, certainly,' said Hannah. 'Rather exciting.'

'Especially for those who bet on that horse,' said Henrietta, nodding towards two men who were clapping each other on the back and waving paper tickets.

Hannah turned to look for Mobbs's bookmaker; he was now as swamped as Lethbridge had been, but by gamblers surging forward to claim their winnings. Mobbs wasn't among them. She caught sight of him heading towards her and Henrietta. The young woman was looking at him as he drew closer, and Hannah fancied she perceived a delicate shake of Henrietta's head – a movement that may have been a warning.

Mobbs paused. He threw his ticket into the dirt.

'Mr Mobbs seems a little upset,' said Hannah.

'Yes, well, one is going to see that at a racecourse.' Henrietta stood, and without asking Hannah to follow – no doubt assuming she would – began to make her way back to the coach.

Hannah scurried to catch up with Henrietta. When Hannah came alongside her, she said, 'Still, one feels sorry for those who lost their money.'

'For someone to win, someone else must lose.' Henrietta's voice was suddenly lower than her usual girlish trill. 'It's why I stay away from betting, although I know a few ladies who do it in a small way. The excitement of a win makes one silly, while the disappointment of a loss colours the rest of one's day. Best just to enjoy the spectacle.'

This was true, thought Hannah, who enjoyed the spectacle of Henrietta's sly intelligence emerging. The woman was clearly more perceptive than she wanted people to think. Perhaps she did not wish to intimidate potential suitors. And perhaps she had discovered, as Hannah had, that there were significant advantages to being underestimated.

Chapter 8

'I would like to think your presence here would mean I have less work, Mr Monsarrat, not more.' Edward Duchamp did not bother to look up from the papers on his desk. 'You are not here simply to attend garden parties.' He did look up then, staring at Monsarrat over the rim of his spectacles. 'Or recitals, for that matter.'

'With respect, sir, I rather think that what I do with my time in the evenings is my own concern,' Monsarrat risked saying in as calm a voice as he could manage.

'Not when it involves Carolina Albrecht. Whatever the nature of her friendship with Hallward – and I have my own thoughts on that score, let me assure you – she is a woman of questionable morals and even more questionable honesty. Who knows what she is capable of. You should have a care about the company you keep. You are, after all, representing the Crown.'

The same Crown, thought Monsarrat, *which decided I was no longer fit to be a subject. Which felt it necessary to prevent me from ever returning to England.*

'I do assure you, Colonel, that my integrity has not been affected by my listening to a piano concerto.' His reckless shadow twisted and stretched. 'And a very well-played one, at that.'

Duchamp was silent, assessing him. 'Yes, well, the very fact that we are discussing this, rather than the business at hand, is concerning.'

'And it's that business I've come on. I had no intention of providing you with a review of Miss Albrecht's performance. You must know, sir, that unless I am allowed to visit the site of the murder, there are limits to what I can accomplish.'

'I don't see why. Everything is being cleaned up and the protests are ongoing. You've spoken to the warden, and I sent you over to see Mobbs. I might arrange a conversation with Archdeacon Harvey as well – he might have some illuminating things to say: a complaint by him led to one of Mr Hallward's stretches in prison.'

'Nevertheless, I must insist on a visit to the prison yard. Protest or not.'

Duchamp leaned back in his chair. 'Very well,' he said eventually. 'Now that I think of it, perhaps a visit might be beneficial. I should at least appear at the protests. Let these people know the Crown is watching. Symbols are important, you know. No harm in showing them the personification of our efforts to catch their hero's killer.'

Monsarrat had never been in this gaol. In a colony where educated men were scarce, as a convict Monsarrat had immediately been placed in the Colonial Secretary's Office, where his daily duty was to inscribe tickets of leave, conferring freedom on others while remaining a slave himself.

Today, the gaol's gate was concealed behind a mass of bodies, mostly men, with a few dourly dressed women sprinkled between, waving placards and whooping in response to a speech being made by a slight man who stood on a stool. He wore the rough, sturdy brown suit a farmer might choose when visiting town, although this man had added an incongruous scarlet cravat. His dark hair probably sat in a luxuriant wave when brushed, but it was mounting a protest of its own, sticking out at odd angles above a face smattered with freckles. He made no attempt to restrain it, as his hands were too busy gesticulating. He and his audience had not yet noticed Monsarrat and Duchamp watching from their coach.

'Some of you have tickets of leave in your pockets,' the man was saying. His accent had a tinge of Irish to it but oddly elongated vowels, a manner of speaking Monsarrat had first heard only recently. 'Some of you arrived here willingly, removing yourselves from all that was familiar to contribute to the building of a robust, prosperous colony. And what have you found? An administration committed to shepherding this place towards a truly civil society? A governor committed to upholding the rights of the King's subjects, citizens of this extended version of Britain?' The man paused for the jeers and howls he must surely have known were coming. 'No, you have found a man who believes that you are *his* subjects, not the King's. He believes that New South Wales is his own feudal land, and treats Government House as though it is his ancestral seat. And we know, do we not, the best way to deal with such a man?'

'Revolution!' yelled someone in the crowd.

'Now, I must stop you there, my brother,' the speaker said. 'We are not French, after all.'

In the coach, Duchamp shook his head and glanced at Monsarrat. 'My grandfather was French, by the by,' he said. 'And judging by your surname, not all of your forebears came from England either.'

'No. Some were from France,' he said. *Whence they fled to escape persecution for their faith, and would not be happy to see their descendants being persecuted for their class*, he thought.

'Revolution is a blunt instrument, a tide that sweeps away the innocent as well as the guilty,' said the speaker. 'I think we can manage a little more finesse, don't you?'

The crowd laughed, and Monsarrat saw some of them square their shoulders and stand a little taller. They were not, after all, a rabble – they had been given permission to think of themselves as capable of finesse.

'My friends, the best way to deal with tyranny is truth. You may not have the opportunity to vote for the governor, but he cannot hold power if the people of this colony lose faith in him. And if they are acquainted with his perfidy, they will.'

A man near the front yelled, 'They only need to open the windows and stick their heads out to smell the rot on the breeze.'

'Ah, yes, but some of them would rather not,' said the speaker. 'They would prefer not to have to deal with such an uncomfortable reality. Not unless they are forced to. And they *were* forced to.' He paused, lifted his head and shouted into the sky, 'They were forced to by a man who was slain for his honesty, his body hitting the ground not twenty yards from where I stand!'

His audience stamped the ground, rattled their placards, punched their fists into the air. Monsarrat had to restrain himself from getting out and joining them. Protest was for the free, and he hoped that one day he too could indulge his passion for just complaint.

'And where is justice for Henry Hallward? Where is the truth about his death? It lies beside him in the grave!'

In the coach, Duchamp turned to Monsarrat. 'Are you feeling brave this morning?'

'Brave enough, I suppose.'

'Good man. I'm not, but needs must.' Duchamp stepped out of the coach.

The man who had been speaking spotted him immediately. 'Ah! My friends, let no one tell you that protest is meaningless, that you are shouting into the void. Your cries have drawn here no less a person than the governor's private secretary!'

The crowd rushed at the coach, and the guard sitting with the coachman began to shoulder his gun. Duchamp turned to him and shook his head, then walked further from the coach. The crowd was still, silent, gathering around him like a storm.

Damn fool's going to get himself killed, Monsarrat thought, even as his legs disobediently carried him into the crowd behind Duchamp.

The colonel nodded to the speaker. 'Mr Donnelly is quite right,' he said. 'Protest is never useless. While you may not believe it, the governor values the voices of the governed, whether that is through protest or not.'

'The governor values authority,' said Donnelly. 'He values patronage. He values little else. As a beneficiary of that patronage – how many land grants have you received now, Colonel? – you are a hypocrite to suggest anything else.'

Monsarrat held his breath, waited for Duchamp to issue the order to arrest Donnelly, steeled himself to jump in to the protestors' side of the melee should it come to that. But perhaps Duchamp was wiser than Monsarrat had given him credit for. He seemed in no mood to provoke a clash between soldiers and unarmed protestors – an event which, even without Hallward to trumpet it, would likely have resonated all the way back to Whitehall.

'You misjudge the man,' said Duchamp. 'He shares your interest in punishing Mr Hallward's killer. At the time of his death, Mr Hallward was a prisoner of the Crown, and therefore the Crown had responsibility for ensuring his safety. The governor is appalled that we failed to do so, and has authorised me to take all possible steps to identify the guilty. And to that end …' He turned around, took Monsarrat's elbow and urged him forward. 'To that end, we have brought in one of the finest investigators in the colony. A man who has already conducted three highly sensitive and successful investigations, and will now bring his intellectual capacity to bear in this case. Mr Hugh Monsarrat.'

Some in the crowd, Monsarrat noticed, looked bemused. Others looked somewhat disappointed to have their cause for outrage taken away, their temper blunted.

Donnelly, though, was not among them. 'Mr ... Monsarrat, is it?' he said. 'Sir, how can we trust that you will prosecute this matter with vigour, given who is paying your bills? Surely it is in your interest to uphold the current system of authority, a system that resides in the person of Governor Darling?'

Monsarrat inwardly cursed. The whole point of his work was that it should be kept in the shadows. And to have been identified so publicly would give Duchamp a convenient person to blame should Monsarrat's investigation fail. However, since he had been thrust into the public consciousness, he might as well use the opportunity to gain the trust of the people, or at least of those on the margins. And it was on the margins where the truth was often to be found. Wagering that the crowd contained at least a few clerks, he told them, 'You are right, my salary is paid by the Crown. Such as it is – I generally function as a clerk, and I'm sure many here will know that the wages for such a position could not be considered princely.'

The chuckle that rippled through the throng told him he'd been right.

'Surely, though, your sympathy must lie with the administration!' said Donnelly.

'My sympathy lies with the man who was shot here,' Monsarrat said. 'And I can assure you, I am more than capable of looking at the administration objectively.'

'How could you possibly do that?' said Donnelly.

'Well, it helps that I was a convict for nearly ten years, and that my continued freedom depends on justice for Mr Hallward.'

In a place where the minority of people had arrived free, Monsarrat was certainly not the only former convict in the crowd. Nor was he the only one working for the administration – everything would have ground to a halt if a previous conviction was a barrier to current employment. Still, people like him did not generally advertise their past; it tended to make others uncomfortable. And it was making some people in the crowd uncomfortable now. A few – particularly women – stepped back as though they feared that the sedate clerk would transform into a tiger and consume them. Others, though, nodded slowly.

'You don't know me,' said Monsarrat, 'so it's hardly surprising that you don't trust me, particularly in a matter of such importance. I can, though, make you this promise: I will do everything I can to identify Henry Hallward's killer, even if my investigation leads me in directions I would prefer not to go.'

'I suppose we must take you at your word, then,' said Donnelly.

'I don't see that you have any alternative,' said Monsarrat. 'You might even help me.'

'How?'

'Well, sir, I need to get into the gaol. Perhaps you and your supporters could oblige me by getting out of the way.'

Chapter 9

It was marvellous not to be hobbled by whalebone and silk and ridiculous high shoes with fussy little buttons; not to be choked by the gold filigree of a brooch. As soon as Henrietta had deposited Hannah, with a clipped farewell, outside the boarding house, Hannah had raced to her trunk and taken out the black skirt, with its unobtrusive patches, and the white shirt on which no stain would dare to settle.

She had finished changing and was fixing her white cap on her head, tucking away forbidden stray hairs, when she heard a knock.

Carolina was wearing the same dark blue gown she had worn at the party. A sedate dark blue, with a plain collar. A bonnet, simple straw, not overflowing with ribbons like some Hannah had seen in Sydney. And a frown, as though Carolina was surprised to find herself on this doorstep.

'Miss Albrecht! Well, this is –'

'Surprising, yes,' Carolina said. 'As is your attire.'

Henrietta had seemed a bit prissy when she'd corrected Carolina's manners, but Hannah now found herself in sympathy with Henrietta. Directness was an admirable quality, but sometimes Carolina took it too far.

'I prefer comfort over fashion, Miss Albrecht. Now, do you intend to continue commenting on my clothes, or can I help you in some way?'

Carolina frowned. Perhaps, thought Hannah, Carolina only realised how rude she was being when she saw offence. 'I apologise,' Carolina said. 'I was hoping I could come in.'

'Of course,' Hannah said, smiling to show the affront wasn't terminal. 'Tea?' she asked as she settled Carolina at the parlour table.

'Thank you, but no. I cannot stay long.'

Vindex's pamphlet was still on the table, and as Carolina picked it up Hannah chided herself for leaving it lying around. She didn't know where Miss Douglas's sympathies lay, but suspected not with someone like Hallward.

'You agree with this?' Carolina asked.

'I believe in knowing as much as I can, whether I agree with it or not. And my ... my nephew, of course, is investigating Hallward's death. Have you seen these before? Any thoughts as to who is behind them?'

'I am aware of them. I presume that the nameless person who writes them wants to remain so.' She laid the pamphlet down. 'I came not to discuss Vindex, but another chimera. Henrietta Duchamp.'

'That is interesting,' said Hannah, 'as the lady in question believes her brother will try to have these pamphlets banned. You dislike her?'

'Mrs Mulrooney, she and I are here for different reasons.'

'I see,' said Hannah. 'And why are you here?'

'The first governor of this place brought my father here to start a vineyard – he had several in Moselle, you see, in Germany. I came as a child, but he sent me back to Germany for my musical education. I returned as a grown woman.

Many here see this place as an avenue to enrichment, to be plundered and then deserted, discussed at dinner parties in England. I returned voluntarily. I came here to be a member of a new society, one which might avoid the mistakes of the old.'

'And is it succeeding, do you think?'

'Patently not. And there is less chance of it doing so with Henry gone.'

'He was admired by many, your Mr Hallward.'

Carolina looked at her sharply.

'He is not *my* Mr Hallward. Yes, Henry and I were close. But as I've already explained – and shouldn't need to – the nature of that closeness is a matter for ourselves, not for society at large, no matter how much society might disagree.'

'I hope I haven't offended you,' said Hannah.

'I give offence far more easily than I take it.'

'There is nothing wrong with giving offence – not necessarily,' said Hannah. 'Not if you're offending the right people. You are right, it will be harder without Hallward. His was a strong voice. But it is not the only one. Another seems to have picked up the task, this Vindex person. And good luck to him.'

'Indeed. All power to his pen. I imagine he must need to be very careful,' said Carolina.

'I suppose so. Perhaps Mr Hallward should have taken a little more care himself. You talked of a story. A stone he intended to throw in the water here which would send ripples all the way to London. I don't suppose you know anything more about it?'

'Henry and I may have been . . . close,' said Carolina. 'But he told me nothing of this. For a man who made his opinions as public as possible, he was intensely private.'

As are you, thought Hannah. *And I am not at all sure you are telling me everything.*

'Ah, well. We may never know now,' she said.

She leaned across the table, patted Carolina's hand, aware the gesture might offend such a spiky woman. It did not seem to.

Carolina did not snatch her hand away, just stared at Hannah with her disconcertingly frank gaze.

'You will let me know, I hope, if there is any way in which I can be of assistance,' she said, in a conspiratorial whisper which was completely unnecessary as they were alone.

'Assistance with?' asked Carolina.

'Oh, anything really,' Hannah said. 'I simply feel that a chorus makes a better sound than a lone voice. As a woman of such musical talent, I am sure you agree.'

Carolina was silent for a moment. 'I am sometimes to be found at the recital hall, during the day,' she said finally. 'I practise there, for the acoustics. Should you have need of me. This place forces all sorts of unlikely alliances. An association between us would be far from the most outlandish of them.'

If Hannah had not been so preoccupied with Carolina's visit, she would have enjoyed walking down the street dressed in the clothes of a servant. Even if she'd wanted to, though, she would have been ill-advised to wear her finer clothes on her current errand. In this part of Sydney, anything that marked her out as wealthy was inviting trouble.

As she walked, she thought of what Monsarrat had told her about Cullen. An older man with an Irish name, at his post when everyone else had gone. Showing secret kindness to a boy he publicly shunned. Hannah did not hold with gambling, but if she had she would have placed a bet on the supposition that Cullen was protecting the defunct *Sydney Chronicle* out of idealism rather than the obligation conferred by being paid in advance.

She would also have bet that it had been a long time since he'd tasted shortbread. The buttery little squares in her basket were not long out of the oven, and their scent leaked from their canvas wrapping as she walked along. More than once, she had looked around to see a small child following her. This was, in fact, how she knew she was getting close to the newspaper's offices; in the more refined part of town such children would be in their schoolrooms, and never be allowed to follow strange women carrying treats.

Most people in this part of the city surely locked their doors. Hannah assumed that Cullen, if he cared about the *Chronicle*, would do likewise. She had expected the *Chronicle*'s door, then, to bear some evidence of the looters' visit – perhaps a plank nailed to patch a hole, or a wobbly handle. But the door seemed intact. It was covered in peeling blue paint through which she could see the grey knots of the wood. It certainly seemed to be locked now, as there was no answer to her polite knocks. She hoped the visit from Monsarrat hadn't scared the man off.

She had raised her fist to pound on the door when she heard a rustle from the corner of the building – a cat, maybe, or a possum. She walked slowly towards a shrub that grew from the building's foundations, sprouting what looked like tiny posies of colourful flowers. She recalled Padraig, as a boy, trying to pick one for her, and returning with an arm covered in scratches from the plant's prickly stalks. If an animal was in there, it would not want to stay for long; a person, though, might think the concealment worth the discomfort.

She slowed her pace and muffled her footfalls by walking heel-to-toe. When she was within a few yards of the bush, a boy broke from it, belting along the road away from her. Hannah knew she had little hope against a young lad. She would save the chase until she knew whether there was something worth catching.

As she went back to the door, resolving to punish it with her fists for its failure to open, it did exactly that – only a crack, but enough to reveal blue eyes under bushy grey brows.

'I come on behalf of Mr Monsarrat,' she said.

'Then you must go on his behalf, for I know no one of that name,' the man she assumed was Cullen said, in an accent that told her he was from the north, perhaps three or four days' ride from her own town of Enniscorthy.

'Mr Monsarrat was here yesterday,' she said.

'I couldn't say,' said Cullen. 'But I could say that I believe the governor is not above using old women as agents.'

Hannah drew back her shoulders, fixing Cullen with a glare that would have felled Mr Monsarrat. 'Perhaps he's not,' she said, 'but as you can clearly see, there is no old woman here. Stop playing the spalpeen and let me in!' The Irish insult, she hoped, would be more effective than any number of English compliments.

Cullen was silent for a moment, then threw his head back and laughed. 'I've not been called a spalpeen since my grandmother died! Still doesn't prove you're not a woman of the administration.'

'And if I were? You'd truly have aroused my suspicion by now – you wouldn't do any more damage by inviting me in.'

As the door started to close, she prepared herself to stick her foot in it, knowing that if he slammed it she would be hobbling for weeks.

'I have shortbread,' she said. 'Perhaps you would like to share some with your young friend. He looks as though he hasn't seen any for a while.'

The door stopped, then slowly began to open.

※

There had been no resistance as Monsarrat and Duchamp had walked through the crowd to the gaol door. Duchamp pounded it. 'This is the governor's private secretary! Open, please.'

Monsarrat was dreading the creak of the hinges. He knew that Ralph Eveleigh would not want him returned to penal servitude if he was unsuccessful in discovering the murderer, but he doubted those in control of the decision would share Eveleigh's reluctance. To walk willingly into a gaol seemed a little too portentous for comfort.

Monsarrat expected to see Crowdy glaring from the crack in the door as it opened. Perhaps the man wasn't there, because instead Monsarrat and Duchamp were greeted by a snub-nosed lad of no more than nineteen or twenty, whose red hair had induced the sun to punish him even more than most light-skinned people in the colony.

'Do you know who I am?' asked Duchamp.

The boy nodded.

'Well, better let us in then.' Duchamp brushed past him into a cramped entrance room.

It took Monsarrat a moment or two to adjust to the dimness, once the outer door had shut with a *click* that gave him an involuntary chill. The room was small with narrow windows. On top of a wooden desk a register lay open, a pen and plain clay inkpot next to it, looked over by a plain-faced clock.

Duchamp flicked through the register casually. 'I'd appreciate it if you could fetch Mr Crowdy.'

'I'm sorry, sir. Mr Crowdy is not here today. A messenger came, said he was ill.'

'So he left you here alone to deal with the protesters.'

'Not alone, sir. There are a few other wardens about.'

Although, thought Monsarrat, not the only one I want to talk to.

'Perhaps we'll start with you, then,' said Duchamp. 'Your name?'

'Chancel, sir.'

'Did you know Mr Hallward?'

'Everyone knew of him, sir. I brought him meals once or twice. Always very polite, he was. Grateful for food, even though he was ...'

'He was what?' asked Duchamp.

'Even though it was no better than what the other prisoners got,' said Chancel quickly.

'Really? I understood Hallward was not above paying for a few little prison luxuries.'

'I wouldn't know, sir.'

'And how did he occupy his time?' asked Monsarrat.

'Like most of them,' Chancel said. 'Staring at the wall. Keening. Singing, from time to time. Doesn't matter if they're debtors or bushrangers from country roads or pickpockets from town – they all do the same.'

'I see. No writing, then?'

Chancel paused. 'Not a good place for writing,' he said eventually. 'Too much moaning.'

'I see.'

Duchamp looked from Monsarrat to Chancel and back again. Perhaps, thought Monsarrat, he was trying to assess how much damage Monsarrat could do, how much he could discover without Duchamp's supervision. The risk, he must have decided, was low. 'Well, thank you, Chancel,' he said. 'Please show this gentleman to the prison yard. Monsarrat, I'll send the coach back for you – my guard too, just in case that crowd hasn't dispersed.'

'Of course, sir,' said Chancel. But Duchamp had left by the time he finished his sentence.

Chancel looked after him for a moment, then turned back to Monsarrat. 'Would you add your name to the log, sir?' he asked, nodding to the ledger under the clock. 'I would like to make a quick round before I show you the yard – doesn't do to leave them alone for too long. I'll be back shortly.'

Monsarrat took the pen, signed his name, copied the time the clock showed. As well as visitors, the register recorded other information, all crammed into the one book and organised by nothing except the date. New inmates. Dead inmates.

Punishments. The arrival of the gaol cart – the one which was to have taken Hallward to trial on the day he died. This morning, it had arrived at ten o'clock. Yesterday too, and the day before that.

Who had been here the day Hallward was killed, he wondered? He flipped back to the date. No one signed in or out. No new prisoners. But the prison cart had arrived half an hour early, at half past nine.

It was early the day before, too. And for two days after, before resuming its habit of arriving promptly at ten.

Was that, he thought, what Mrs Mulrooney might call a wrinkle?

Chancel's head appeared around the door frame. 'Ready, sir?'

Monsarrat closed the book quickly, as though he had been caught doing something he shouldn't. You are investigating on behalf of the Crown, he told himself. You have every right to look at a gaol register.

'Tell me, Chancel,' he said. 'Is the prison cart often irregular in the time it arrives?'

Chancel shrugged. 'From time to time sir, just like anyone. Begging your pardon but we really should get you out into the yard. I can't leave them alone too long or there might not be a gaol left to guard.'

Chapter 10

Cullen wiped the crumbs from his mouth and smiled at Hannah.

That face, she thought, had spent time under Irish rain as well as colonial sun. It had probably been doing so for about the same amount of time as Hannah's own. It was guarded, but not pinched or cruel; handsome in its craggy way.

Cullen had taken care to spread some old newsprint over Hallward's desk, catching any crumbs. In a place where cupboard doors had been wrenched off their hinges and broken window glass lurked in the corners, such a gesture might have seemed futile to others, but Hannah saw it as a brave last stand against encroaching chaos.

'Why do you stay here?' she said. 'Why not leave this place to crumble, now no one has a use for it?'

'It is all that's left of Henry Hallward, and without him there'd be nothing left of me,' Cullen said, wiping his mouth.

'What did he save you from?'

'Road gang. Before my ticket came through. We'd come out from the barracks, on our way to repair some road or other. He was passing by, and he said, without a word of a lie, "Good morning, gentlemen."'

'I imagine those on a road gang aren't used to that kind of greeting.'

'Most of 'em assumed he was talking to the overseer. They knew, by that point, to keep their eyes down. But I always thought if you're looking at the ground you might as well be in it, so I said good morning back. He smiled and tipped his hat to me. It was worth being hit by the overseer later.'

Hannah nodded. There were two types of convicts who survived the road gangs. The ones who gave up their humanity and became brutes, and the ones who held on to the belief that they were more than animals, even when all evidence suggested otherwise.

'I hope the beating was worth it,' she said.

'The acknowledgement that you are still a soul, still worthy of a good morning? Worth ten beatings. Then he came and found me, in the convict barracks. Said he needed a convict special, for lifting and fetching and carrying and so on. When he found out I had my letters, that he could dictate stories to me, he was delighted. I came here with him that afternoon. And I don't mind if you report on this conversation to Colonel Duchamp.'

'If he wanted something with you, surely he'd have sent soldiers rather than shortbread.'

'I don't know how the man thinks,' said Cullen. 'But I'm inclined to believe you're not in league with him.'

'I'm in league with the fellow who visited you yesterday. Mr Monsarrat.'

'Who's trying to wrap Mr Hallward's death up in a neat little bow.'

'Who's trying to find out what happened. And who noticed your little friend yesterday. Why is the boy taking such pains not to be seen?'

'You'd have to ask him.'

'I'd like to.'

Cullen shook his head. 'He's long gone, missus. Won't be back until tomorrow at least.'

'Who is he?'

'That's not for me to say.'

Hannah was convinced that talking to the boy was important. It would have to wait, though – Cullen wasn't about to rush out and get him.

'I wonder,' she said, 'if you could tell me something else. I keep hearing mention of some soldiers. Some sort of story that got Mr Hallward into trouble. Do you know anything about it?'

'Ah, now that,' said Cullen, 'I can help you with.' He fetched a paper from the rack and laid it on the desk, pulled Hallward's chair out and gestured for Hannah to sit.

'I've rarely seen him so angry,' Cullen said. 'And he was a man given to bursts of rage. Some of them directed at me, and for no good reason.

'I brought him the mail that morning as normal. There had been a lad at the door, with a note. Folded up, nothing on the outside – nothing unusual, Mr Hallward had informers all over the town, one or the other of them would send him snippets of gossip almost every day. When he read this, though, well!'

'It set him off?' asked Hannah.

'He jumped up, pushed his chair over and grabbed me by the neckerchief. Frightened me, I'll be honest. I thought someone had accused me of something.'

'And had they?'

'As it turns out no, thanks be to God. He yelled then. "He's dead, Cullen! Killed by the King himself, or his profane excuse for a representative." He was always referring to the governor like that, you see, missus. I always made a mental note – no one was as good at insults as he was.'

'But who had died?'

'A soldier. A Private Hogg.'

'And murdered by the governor?'

'Mr Hallward liked to exaggerate. But truly, missus, he might as well have been. This place. It makes animals of us. Soldiers, convicts. Doesn't matter. They drain our souls, then feel justified in destroying our bodies.'

He turned to Hannah, blinked a few times. 'Private Hogg and his friend, Private Johnson. Word was they were sick of seeing convicts succeed. People who had come here not to serve their country but to pay for their crime. But neither of those lads were able to leave the army. So they stole a cloak. Their thinking was, get themselves arrested, do their time, and then they'd be at liberty to make their fortune.'

'Seems an odd way to go about it,' Hannah said.

'Best way to get the army to release them,' said Cullen. 'Some convicts, well, they've become rich beyond what a private soldier could ever expect. And they have liberty to go into trade, to increase their wealth, while all a soldier can expect is to be paid whatever His Majesty thinks he's worth until he dies or is no longer up for the job. It would amaze you, missus, the wealth of some of those who came here as convicts.'

'I'm sure it would. You think they were justified in their theft?'

'I can understand it,' said Cullen.

'But why did one of them end up dead?'

'Well, as Mr Hallward said, it was the governor. He viewed the deliberate commission of a crime by a soldier as treason and was determined to stamp it out. Hogg and Johnson were unfortunate enough to commit their crime shortly after Darling arrived. Hogg – he wasn't well at the time. It would have been fine if he'd just been put on a road gang somewhere, but the governor changed their punishment – he had heavy chains specially made for them. They stumbled around under the blazing sun on the road gang. And for Hogg, it was just too much. He didn't last a week.'

'Did the governor relent?'

'Him? No, he made Johnson wear Hogg's chains as well as his own. Only rescinded the order last week. I would like to think Mr Hallward had a hand in that.'

'And that's why he was in gaol, your Mr Hallward?'

'One of the stories got him arrested, yes. He said the governor's actions were illegal. The governor was a murderer. I think if he hadn't been arrested, he would have been disappointed. The constables came the morning this was published. Mr Hallward just stood up and went with them, without even asking their business. They didn't try to restrain him. They'd all done that dance before.'

Cullen tapped the paper he had laid in front of Hannah earlier.

It was a copy of the *Sydney Chronicle*, with a long story underneath the headline 'The Governor's Tyranny'. The first paragraph read: 'It is a sad duty of this journal to inform the residents of this colony that they live not as subjects of the King, but as serfs of a dictator.'

'Did Gerald Mobbs criticise the governor?' asked Hannah.

Cullen went back to the pigeon holes, extracted a newspaper and silently handed it to Hannah. This one bore the masthead of the *Colonial Flyer*. Mobbs had written:

> None of us wishes death on anyone, and the death of Private Hogg is a great pity. But those whose shrill voices are raised in cries of 'murder' should instead be thanking the governor. For it is he who, in making this difficult choice, has ensured no other young men will follow a similar path, and one which might end in their grave.
>
> Those who thunder that the governor's actions were illegal know better – a crime was committed, and it was punished to the fullest extent. There are many in this colony who would understand nothing less.

Hannah was tempted to shred the paper with its sanctimonious defence of torture. Instead she handed it back to Cullen. 'And do you think the governor's a murderer?'

'I've lived under the British yoke. I expect them to treat me like cattle. But when they do that to their own soldiers, how much worse will they do to us?'

Hannah felt a fullness behind her eyes. 'Oh, they are capable of far worse,' she said. 'I have seen it. In Enniscorthy, on Vinegar Hill. At the front door of my father's house.'

Cullen looked at her and slowly nodded. '*Erin go bragh.*'

'*Erin go bragh*,' she repeated quietly.

He patted her hand. 'Come along then, missus. I shouldn't keep you all to myself.'

Monsarrat had seen yards like this before. He had seen people flogged in them, and hanged in them. He had a macabre habit of checking the flagstones for stains, and then talking himself out of believing they were some poor soul's blood.

This yard, though, was a little different. It had the usual stains, high walls and oppressive air. It had two exits: the small door he had just walked through, which for some prisoners led to eternity; and a larger wooden gate, through which a cart could be brought to deliver fresh inmates, or take those already in residence to the judgement of the court. But it also had an audience: the blank windows of several surrounding houses had an excellent view over some parts of the yard.

'Chancel!' he called out.

Judging by the speed of the boy's appearance, he had been waiting just out of sight.

'Where was Hallward killed, exactly?' Monsarrat asked.

'Somewhere in this yard, sir.'

'He was being loaded into the prison cart,' said Monsarrat. 'Where is it normally when receiving a prisoner?'

'Generally right in the middle of the yard, sir.'

'And Hallward would have been facing . . . where?'

'I wouldn't know, sir. I wasn't there.'

'Yes, yes, we've established that. But in the normal run of things.'

'The cart would be brought in through that gate there,' said Chancel, pointing across the yard. 'So he would have walked up to it – well – this way.'

Chancel took a few steps towards the gate, and stopped.

'No one found any musket balls, anything of that nature?' asked Monsarrat. 'It would help us determine what weapon the killer used.'

'No, sir. Whatever killed him probably left the yard in his head.'

'Thank you, Chancel. Oh, the prisoners have recently been afforded the luxury of a clean cell. So I hear, anyway.'

'Well, we did have the place cleaned. It happens, from time to time.'

'And can you remember the last time it happened?'

Chancel was silent.

Monsarrat sighed. 'Very well. Thank you.'

Chancel nodded, scampered off.

Monsarrat paced towards the spot on which Chancel had been standing and looked down. He found himself on top of a large red-brown stain, the ebbing life of Henry Hallward consumed by the porous stone. He stepped back as if bitten.

As much to avoid looking down again as for any other reason, he looked up and found himself staring straight into the dark windows of a row of shuttered attics.

'Never see anyone there,' the woman said. 'And I'm observant.'

The armchair Monsarrat had passed on the way into the house was testament to that. Well upholstered, like its owner, but leaking stuffing. The chair, once a deep red, was also faded from its placement in the sun near a window, from where its occupant could see the comings and goings on the street.

Monsarrat had nearly missed this house and its curious occupant. He had lost track of time, having resumed staring at the stain on the stones, wondering how deeply it seeped between the grains of compressed sand, when Chancel had come into the yard.

'If you've all you need, sir?' he asked, glancing nervously to the gaol door and no doubt thinking of the inmates behind it.

'Yes. I think so. I may call on you again, Chancel, as the investigation unfolds.'

'Yes, sir. With the colonel's permission, of course.'

'Chancel, the colonel brought me here. I think you can assume I have his permission.'

Mrs Selwyn must have seen Monsarrat leaving the gaol, because as soon as he was on the pavement, she was out on her front step, waving to him. As he approached, she called out, 'Do you know anything?'

Monsarrat had a convict's instinctive dislike of the overly curious. Still, when it came to an investigation, the curtain twitcher was a very useful species. This one had told Monsarrat about everyone in the surrounding houses. He'd heard more than he'd ever wanted to know about Mary Lennon's well-deserved gout and Harold Smith's fondness for drink.

There was only one house that so far Mrs Selwyn had failed to enlighten Monsarrat about: the tallest one visible from the gaol yard. One with an attic.

'Odd,' he said, 'that it should just be sitting empty.'

'Not as odd as all that,' she said. 'It belongs to a man who has a property in the west. He's not always in Sydney and doesn't often stay here when he is.'

Monsarrat was on his third cup of tea, and the distillation suffered greatly by comparison to Mrs Mulrooney's brews.

Mrs Selwyn leaned forward, putting a hand over his. 'Although – one hears things. A squeaking hinge, a creak. Ghosts, probably – you do see the occasional shape moving about in there, shadows on the drapes late at night. I don't sleep as well as I once did, not since Mr Selwyn died.' The pressure of her hand on his increased as she leaned further forward. 'I'm a widow.'

Monsarrat cleared his throat, snatching his hand away with a vehemence he hoped wasn't rude. 'I am sorry for your loss, Mrs Selwyn. I'm very grateful to the tea, and your helpful information.'

The woman stood up, smoothing her skirts.

'Oh, you wouldn't happen to know the owner's name?' asked Monsarrat.

Mrs Selwyn scoffed, perhaps offended that anyone would think she could be ignorant of a neighbour's name. 'Bancroft. Albert, I think. Most unfriendly man, but I haven't seen him for quite a time. Gave me a key, though I think I've lost it. Anyhow, he told me not to use it – unless the house was being burgled, in which case I should feel free to stop the thieves. Me! At my own risk!' she said. 'Mr Monsarrat, I would be delighted to assist you further ... in any way you see fit.'

'Exceptionally kind of you, but I'm sure it won't be necessary.' He backed towards the door, turning as he opened it and trying to avoid the impulse to sprint.

Cullen led Hannah through the newspaper office, past the frames – all but one of them smashed. A wooden press sat, hacked and useless, at one end of the room.

'Odd that they left just one frame,' she said.

He glanced towards the intact frame. 'It was hidden in a drawer,' he said. 'I set it here to remind myself what this place is capable of.'

They walked to the back of the building, and Cullen opened a small door with rusted hinges. Hannah stepped into a yard that looked as though it hadn't been maintained since it was built. Voracious weeds sprang through the cobblestones, and a pile of machinery rusted in one corner, next to a stack of broken printers' plates. In another corner, an indistinct lumpen mound was covered by oddly clean canvas.

At the back of the yard was a wooden shed, haphazardly built from mismatched planks, held together with nails that weren't driven all the way in. It did, however, have a door. A closed one.

Cullen made a crescent with his thumb and forefinger, and stuck it in his mouth. A sound like a bird call emerged – the kind of bird she had only ever heard in Ireland, one that did not exist here.

The door was slowly pushed open, its longer boards scraping on the dirt. A grimy face appeared, caught sight of Hannah, and disappeared again. She heard a scrabbling as the door was jerkily pulled closed.

'It's all right, lad,' called Cullen. 'She's a friend.'

There was no response.

'There is shortbread,' Cullen called.

Still nothing.

'Good shortbread. Happy to have it all to myself.'

The door slowly creaked open again. One grimy bare foot emerged, followed by another.

The boy was probably small for his age, although she couldn't tell what age that was. He was dressed in clothes that might once have been decently made, but which were grimy and gaping at some of the seams. His face was narrow and dirty, his sunken eyes gleaming and darting, their brightness intensified by the drabness around them.

Hannah walked forward tentatively, holding out the tray of shortbread. The boy started to back away.

'I'll leave it here, then,' she said, setting it on the ground. 'I'll step away, and I won't move again until you've finished.'

As soon she was out of swatting range, the boy lunged forward and squatted at the tray, shoving squares of shortbread into his mouth with only a cursory effort to chew them.

Cullen was standing next to her at the entrance to the yard. 'His name is Peter. Don't know anything about his father. Mother was a convict. They took him away from her, put him in the orphan school. She was sent out west somewhere, some property or other, and never came back. When he escaped the orphan school they didn't make any effort to reclaim him – they've got enough to worry about.'

'How long has he been living here?' asked Hannah.

'Six months or so. He tried to steal Mr Hallward's pocket watch. The boy thought he was being dragged to the constables but Mr Hallward brought him here, sat the lad at his desk. He was always asking people odd questions, out of nowhere, Mr Hallward was. And he asked this lad, "If you could say one thing to the governor, what would it be?"'

'And Peter's answer?'

'"I am not a dog."'

But you have nearly been reduced to one, you poor boy, thought Hannah. *Eating scraps and living in a kennel.*

'Anyway,' said Cullen, 'Mr Hallward gave him a meal and sent him off, and the lad was back the next day. We arrived to find he'd broken in. He hadn't taken anything, though – he was just staring at the printers' plates, the blocks of type. So Mr Hallward asked him if he'd like to learn the trade, and he's been here ever since.'

'I can't say much for Mr Hallward if he made the boy live in a shed and starve.'

'Oh, he didn't. Peter has a little bed in the attic. One in which he hasn't slept since Mr Hallward died.'

It took only a few minutes for Peter to demolish the shortbread. He stayed crouched, looking at Hannah. She approached him slowly, and crouched herself until her eyes were level with his.

He flinched as though she was going to strike him.

'You'll have to forgive him,' said Cullen. 'Some soldiers tried to take him the other day – just lifted him right up, one by each arm. He struggled and eventually broke free, but not without a few little scrapes and a big scare.'

'Soldiers! Why on earth? Who sent them?'

'No idea, but soldiers tend to take their orders from the governor. Or his pet colonel.'

Hannah looked to the boy. 'I'm not a soldier,' she said quietly. 'I've no intention of taking you anywhere.'

'Why are you here, then?' he said. 'You brought me something, that means you want something.'

What Hannah wanted in that moment was to reach out and smooth the boy's cowlick from his forehead. She knew, though, that she would then lose him. He had spent most of his young life in a world where violence or bribery were the only two possible interactions.

She realised, too, that he was right about her: the shortbread was a form of inducement. 'My friend and I – he was here yesterday, you might have seen him.'

'The thin man,' said Peter.

Hannah smiled. 'Yes, well, he and I, we are trying to find out what befell Mr Hallward. And we're wondering if you can tell us anything that might help.'

'Why would you wonder that?' said Peter.

'You do have a habit of running away. It makes me think there's something you want to avoid talking about. And I'm assuming that your friend brought me out to this yard for a good reason.' She turned around and pierced Cullen with a questioning look.

'I might not have been as forthcoming as I could have been with your friend yesterday, missus,' said Cullen. 'Without Mr Hallward, though, I must look to myself. There is no one to protect me now if I were accused of treason, of sedition, and no one to come for Peter if I'm arrested. It's hard to tell who is working for who these days.' He was silent for a moment. 'Mr Monsarrat asked if Mr Hallward was working on something when he died. Some sort of story. I said I didn't know. Peter, tell the lady what you were doing the day Mr Hallward died.'

'He said one day I could move letters round in those frames,' said Peter. 'But I had to learn how it worked first. He told me I was a copyboy – never had me copy anything, mind, even though I have my letters.'

'What did you do, then, as a copyboy?' asked Hannah.

'Collect things. Drop things off. Make sure Mr Hallward knew where everyone was. And I had to run to the gaol. The day it happened.'

Hannah glared at the man behind her. 'Really, Mr Cullen! No matter how urgent it was, why would you send a young lad to a place like that?'

Cullen looked down. 'Hallward's insistence. As I told Mr Monsarrat, he knew he was going to be arrested. So, before they took him, he told me to send Peter to gaol two days hence, in the morning. Said he'd have something to bring back.'

'The story he was working on,' said Hannah. 'What was it?'

'Don't know,' said Peter, 'but I thought I might have a read of it on the way back.'

'He'd have cuffed your ear had he known,' said Cullen.

'He'd have been in no place to. And I wouldn't have told anyone. But I didn't get to the gaol in time. I heard a shot, and I couldn't hear anything else for a while afterwards, like I'd gone deaf. I ran straight back here.'

'If it deafened you for a little while,' said Hannah, 'it must have been close.'

Peter nodded. 'It was just above me. It came from outside the gaol – from the tallest house I've ever seen.'

※

Monsarrat wished that Mrs Selwyn's hand had belonged to Grace. But he refocused his thoughts back to Hallward's murder, as he forced his feet to carry him back to the gaol. Before he could gain the door, though, a figure stepped out of the shadows.

'I bring greetings to the governor's bloodhound,' said the man, bowing low. When he straightened again, Monsarrat saw the face of the speaker at today's rally: Mr Donnelly.

'The colony's bloodhound is more how I would describe myself,' said Monsarrat. 'But greetings, of course, to you as well.'

'Monsarrat?' the man said.

Monsarrat inclined his head.

'Brendan Donnelly, at your service. Now, Mr Monsarrat, to give you some respite from all of those questions you've no doubt been asking, I have one for you.'

'Very well. I can't guarantee, though, that I'll be able to answer it.'

'I don't think you'll have any trouble with this one,' said Donnelly. 'I was wondering, Mr Monsarrat, do you like fishing?'

Chapter 11

'So Bancroft could be our killer?' asked Mrs Mulrooney.

'Can't say,' said Monsarrat. 'For a start, we must check the records in the Colonial Secretary's Office.'

'Records you've been forbidden from perusing.'

'I might forget that prohibition. Accidentally.'

'Good man. Nothing to be done until tomorrow though. So what can we do on a Sunday to take things forward?' asked Mrs Mulrooney.

'Well, that Donnelly fellow and I are off at dawn in a little rowboat,' Monsarrat said. Just then, Monsarrat and Mrs Mulrooney were most pleasantly diverted by the antics of a family of ducks skimming across one of the ponds that dotted the Botanic Gardens.

Monsarrat suspected that his friend had her own demons she was hoping to leave behind for the duration of their late afternoon stroll. She had told him about her conversations with Henrietta and Carolina. But she seemed most affected by her interaction with Cullen and the boy.

'Oh, now, I nearly forgot to tell you,' she said. 'While we are pining for Parramatta, a little piece of it has found its way to Sydney.' She told Monsarrat about meeting Lethbridge. 'He is rather fond of you, I think,' she added. 'You're the only person who can carry on about Socrates with him without keeling over backwards with boredom.'

Monsarrat chuckled. 'I do enjoy that man's company – and his pies, of course. A cagey one, though. Reserves the right to keep his secrets. I'm fairly certain he will only help us if it suits him to do so.'

It was a mild afternoon, and the calls of the park's birdlife were punctuated by greetings shouted between groups of people. Neither Monsarrat nor Mrs Mulrooney registered their names being called until they heard small staccato footsteps behind them.

'You two! I've been shouting myself hoarse. Anybody would think that you didn't wish to speak to me, Mrs Mulrooney.'

Henrietta was dressed in green, and her parasol was covered in ruching and small green flowers, a matching reticule dangling from her wrist. Several yards away, two other young ladies were scurrying to catch up with her, their skirts lifted slightly off the ground.

'Miss Duchamp,' said Monsarrat, bowing. 'A pleasure to see you.'

'And you, Mr Monsarrat. Mrs Mulrooney, I am pleased to have found you here. You see, I want to ask for your help. I've recently started running a most fascinating enterprise – I mentioned it at the garden party. The Female School of Industry. Stops young girls from sliding into idleness or worse. And it means I can find some decent maids for a change. Something has occurred to me. I would be so grateful for your help in training them. With your common air, I'm sure you would be able to relate to the girls far better than I could.'

Monsarrat noticed Mrs Mulrooney grasp her fan, which had been dangling off her wrist, and begin to raise it. For a moment he feared she would set about Henrietta with it. Instead she emphatically snapped it open and held the stretched and painted silk in front of her face so that her clenched jaw, visible to Monsarrat from the side, would not be noticed by Henrietta.

'Of course,' she said. 'For such a cause, I would be delighted to do all I can.'

'Marvellous! And we shall have tea afterwards – perhaps we can teach them to make it. Monday afternoon, then, after lunch – the large building on Macquarie Street. I would call for you, but I'm afraid I have a prior engagement in the morning.'

The two other young women were beside Henrietta now, their faces shining slightly. They glanced at Monsarrat and Mrs Mulrooney, but made no attempt to introduce themselves. One was quite mousy and perhaps viewed Henrietta as a fashion paragon, as she too was carrying an opulent parasol that matched her dress. 'Dearest,' she said to Henrietta, 'you must see this. He is here, again.' She handed Henrietta a piece of paper.

Henrietta read it, crumpled it and threw it towards the sea wall. She missed by several feet, so that the ball of paper came to rest on the ground in front of some confused seagulls. She did not appear to notice.

'Come now,' said Henrietta's friend, 'an acquaintance of yours desires to speak with you.'

Henrietta smiled at Monsarrat and Mrs Mulrooney, then reached out to pat Mrs Mulrooney's hand yet again. 'Monday, then.' She scuttled off at speed, forcing her friends to lift their skirts again and mince after her as fast as they could.

Mrs Mulrooney slowly lowered her fan, staring at Henrietta through narrowed eyes.

'You mustn't worry,' Monsarrat said. 'She probably tells the governor that he is common too.'

Monsarrat flinched as Mrs Mulrooney's fan connected with his knuckles. 'I can assure you, Mr Monsarrat, these cursed corsets are not so tight that I have suddenly become lightheaded and started caring about people's opinions. But I've had enough of the gardens for one day.' She stalked towards the paper that Henrietta had thrown away, scattering seagulls who had more sense than to impede her. She picked it up and smoothed it out. 'Ah,' she said, 'Vindex has been busy.' She handed the pamphlet to Monsarrat.

'Opinion May Soon Be Illegal,' the headline read.

> We have heard that consideration is being given at the highest levels to banning this publication. We are unsurprised to learn of this, as this administration will stop at nothing to silence dissent. We beg the reader to consider the following question – is it coincidence that one such dissenter was slain in what is supposed to be one of the most secure places in the colony? Especially while in the care of the very administration he criticised.
>
> You will be told, without doubt, that any measures to restrict comment are for the good of the colony, which otherwise will descend into anarchy. But they are not for the good of the colony – they are for the good of the administration, which wishes to continue in its practice of granting favours without scrutiny. And which may have taken certain steps to stop that scrutiny.

Monsarrat handed the pamphlet back to Mrs Mulrooney. 'I had not heard anything about banning this. Mind you, I am not in Duchamp's confidence.'

'No, but Henrietta is. She mentioned it to me at the races. She has probably mentioned it to others. And I wonder … Do you think we have met Vindex?'

'Why do you say that?'

'Did you not notice, Mr Monsarrat, the one intact frame in the office of the *Chronicle*?'

'Yes. Presumably the looters missed it.'

'Or it was hidden. Or it was new. And of all the rubbish left to rust in the *Chronicle*'s yard, one mysterious pile is protected by canvas.'

'You think that Cullen is Vindex?'

'You thought that these pamphlets were not written by a journalist, and Cullen isn't one.'

'I also doubt he's familiar with Latin,' said Monsarrat.

'Who knows what he picked up from Hallward.'

'We should talk to him about this.'

Mrs Mulrooney nodded and began stalking towards the gates. Then she suddenly stopped, turning towards a copse beside the path. When Monsarrat caught up with her and followed her gaze, he saw Henrietta whispering to a man who was no more finely dressed than any of those at Carolina's recital, surely beneath her standards. A man who, nevertheless, clearly paid a great deal of attention to his moustache.

Henrietta turned and caught sight of them. The open face of the shallow young woman had been replaced by an acute stare, along with what appeared to be anger. Mrs Mulrooney returned Henrietta's gaze for a moment, then turned pointedly to the gate and continued walking, far more sedately.

'What on earth could those two have to talk about?' said Monsarrat.

'I've seen her fend off Mobbs twice before. It is easy to believe they met by chance at the garden party and the racetrack, but again here? Do you know, Mr Monsarrat, I believe we have been underestimating that woman.'

Chapter 12

It was just as well that Monsarrat had never liked the low skies of London. He had certainly never liked arriving at his desk at Lincoln's Inn in the dark, only to leave after the sun had completed its short arc above the clouds. Still, he now rather enjoyed getting up in the dark on occasion, here where it had become a novelty. Fishermen went out very early, and Donnelly was no exception.

From Monsarrat's time as a convict clerk in Port Macquarie, he still had some canvas trousers and a simple shirt. They weren't government-issue convict clothes, but rough enough. He had worn them during his confinement in the vastness of the north to go fishing. Since leaving Port Macquarie he had tried to run away from his time as the man in the little hut, who had escaped the work gangs solely because of his intricate handwriting. Its flourishes and evenness had added weight to the requests and recommendations sent to the colonial secretary from Port Macquarie. He had not worn the clothes since he had arrived in Parramatta the previous year. But he kept them with him – a reminder that the rough fabric would claim him again if he did not present his superiors with a murderer.

The clothes felt far rougher than they used to, and he chided himself for getting soft. By the time he had walked to the little steps leading down to the harbour from the Botanic Gardens' gate, he could feel skin beginning to abrade on the inside of his legs.

Donnelly was there already, bobbing up and down in a rowboat tied to a cleat at the bottom of the steps. He startled when Monsarrat appeared, perhaps fearing a convict or navvy had decided to take their chances with the toff in the boat. Donnelly was far too well dressed for a fishing expedition.

When he recognised Monsarrat, he threw back his head and roared, 'Mr Monsarrat! Don't tell me you thought we were actually going to fish?'

'Oddly enough, Mr Donnelly, I did gain that impression from your invitation. Although, I have to say, I apprehended there might be some conversation as well.'

'Ah yes, well ...' Donnelly reached down to pick up a fishing rod. 'We might as well make our trip as plausible as possible.'

The sun was eating away at the night as they rowed away from the gardens, past small tree-covered islands. Monsarrat did not know what the natives called them, but there was one the convicts called Pinchgut; for years, the most refractory prisoners had been dumped there like refuse, and given refuse to eat as well. The island was uninhabited now, but some swore they heard wails skimming across the water on still nights.

As they headed east towards the mouth of the harbour, the structures along the shore thinned out and then disappeared entirely. The rowboat was approaching the two sandstone protrusions that Monsarrat had first passed through in the bowels of a convict ship. The waters of the harbour could occasionally mimic the open ocean, particularly near the heads where the sea rushed in. This morning, though, the water was almost flat, disturbed only by some tiny ridges called forth by a light breeze. Donnelly did not even bother to throw overboard the circular stone tied to a rope that sat in the boat's bow.

When they stopped rowing, Donnelly and Monsarrat craned their necks in all directions, looking for anyone on shore who might notice the odd pairing of a man in a jacket and cravat opposite one in slops. But the only eyes belonged to white birds with violently yellow crests and stubby black beaks, staring down at them from the clifftop trees.

'Rare to see anyone here,' Donnelly said. 'The lookouts of the signal station will be gazing out to sea. Still, as you've gone to such trouble with your attire …' He handed Monsarrat the fishing rod.

The sea was calm enough for Monsarrat to hear the plunk of the sinker as it broke the water's surface. He held the rod but did not expect to feel an answering tug from beneath. As far as he could see, the hook wasn't baited.

'I saw you,' said Donnelly, 'knocking on the doors of the houses near the gaol.'

'Yes, well, they are the only place the shot could have been fired from.'

'Precisely so. Still, I was surprised to see you make the effort.'

'Why? Surely it's the first step a conscientious investigator would take.'

'Yes, a conscientious investigator. I wasn't expecting the government to appoint one of those.'

'Why ever not?'

Donnelly opened his mouth, closed it again, then looked at Monsarrat as though trying to decide whether to trust him. 'Mr Monsarrat, are you aware that I run a small grammar school?'

Monsarrat felt a stab of envy. Running such an enterprise had been his own ambition in England, and if the barristers he'd worked for had agreed to release him, he might yet be sitting by a fire in Exeter with a wife, working on the next day's Latin lesson.

'A rewarding occupation,' he said.

'Particularly, in our case, for a fellow on our Board of Governors: Albert Bancroft. He liked to attend the racecourse on occasion. Was not always judicious in his betting. And some of the school's funds were carried away on the noses of slow horses.'

'Stealing from children takes a particular kind of criminal,' said Monsarrat.

'That it does, and I do hope the fellow doesn't do it again, because he is still on the board.'

'Did you not report him?'

'I most certainly did. The governor's office decided not to involve the constabulary and sent their own man to investigate. Bancroft confessed and offered to pay back the money. And that was good enough. The investigator did not bother to look at the accounts, did not talk to anyone at the racecourse, and did not even interview me, despite my request to see him. He just took Bancroft's word that the money would be paid back. Hallward was wonderful, wrote a thundering editorial about it. But two months later, our school is yet to see a penny.'

'And you believe I intend to operate in a similar fashion?'

'Not since I saw you knocking on those doors. And there's a certain fellow. Known to many in Sydney, whether they like pies or philosophy. I know he spends time in Parramatta as well as here, and he happens to be of the view that you're to be trusted.'

'Well, I'm gratified by your faith in me, and I can assure you that this is no sham investigation. But you could have just asked for a meeting with me.'

'Yes, and wherever that meeting took place, word of it would have likely trickled back up the chain of authority, where I am not the most popular of the King's subjects.'

'I take it the protest at the gaol was not your first, then,' said Monsarrat.

'Not by a mile,' said Donnelly. 'But that is not the administration's chief annoyance with me. I did tend to be a fairly regular correspondent in the pages of the *Chronicle*.'

'Did you indeed? And I'm presuming that you did not write in praise of the governor.'

Donnelly chuckled, reached into his pocket and pulled out a newspaper clipping. 'Read this at your leisure,' he said as he handed it to Monsarrat. 'I know it is still possible that you are the governor's man and that anything I say will carry no weight, but I did want you to be aware of who I am, what my position is, before you accepted my help.'

'And what form will that help take?' asked Monsarrat. He jiggled the line, from habit more than expectation; it remained stubbornly straight and unmoving in the water.

'A little background information. A nudge here or there in the right direction.'

Background information. Nudges. None of it sounded tremendously useful.

'Or what you perceive to be the right direction,' said Monsarrat. 'You are correct in assuming that I'm not conducting this investigation with the governor's agenda in mind – and nor will I let yours guide me.'

Donnelly held up both hands. 'Utterly fair. Reassures me, actually.'

I doubt that, thought Monsarrat. *I wonder if there is more than one person seeking to influence the course of this investigation.*

'As we've taken the trouble to row out here, I presume your guidance will begin now.'

'Yes, well. First, a little background. The governor is not the only one who has taken Mr Hallward to court. Last year, even before Darling's arrival, no less a person than

Archdeacon Harvey, the colony's foremost churchman, tried to sue him for trespass. No doubt at the urging of Alcott – that's the reverend at St James. He worships Harvey far more than he worships God, taking any insult to the archdeacon as a personal affront.'

'Ah. I find it reasonably easy to annoy clergymen. Are you suggesting the clergy had something to do with all this?'

'No ... but Alcott is reputed to be a rather good shot. And during one sermon I sat through, the reverend said that criticism of the clergy is akin to blasphemy and should attract the same penalty as treason.'

'Death, in other words,' said Monsarrat. 'I assume he wasn't speaking generally.'

'No, indeed. The previous day, Hallward had written a story exposing the archdeacon's salary while suggesting his flock was not getting enough value.'

Monsarrat smiled ruefully, shook his head. 'The man seems to have been unable to help himself,' he said.

'No, and thank God for it.'

'I imagine he has run afoul of the magistracy too. Personally, I find that almost as easy as annoying the clergy.'

'It's a little different here in Sydney,' said Donnelly. 'We have fewer of your Parramatta landed gentry. A lot of the magistrates here used to be convicts.'

'Truly?'

'Yes. Although that's not likely to continue now. But there's someone you should meet. Fellow called James Collins – on the bench, but probably not for long.'

'Very well. Should I attend his chambers?'

'Absolutely not! Word'd be back to Duchamp within the hour. May I ask, do you like rum?'

Monsarrat enjoyed the occasional brandy. A glass of claret, if circumstances put one in his path. Rum, though, tasted as though it had been made with the removal of rust or a medical procedure in mind. His stomach still clenched at the memory of one night when he had drunk it to excess, in pursuit of information on a Parramatta murder. If one wished to become intoxicated, there were far more pleasant ways.

'I have no objection to rum,' he said to Donnelly.

'Excellent. Tomorrow afternoon, then? After my classes. At the Sheer Hulk – do you know it? Near Gloucester Street. A little further up the hill from the docks. You'll recognise it by the barber's pole outside.'

'And I presume there's no barbershop in sight?'

'Not a bit of it. Plenty of sly grog, but if anyone there offers you a haircut I would decline. The owner pays off the constables, you see. Most of them are former convicts, so they're happy to turn a blind eye. But just in case somebody further up becomes inconveniently moral and asks them to look into the place, they can say that it has all the hallmarks of a legitimate business. You might find the man on the door a little suspicious of you at first. Just say you're there to see me. My name might not carry much weight at Government House, but in certain other circles it is worth a great deal indeed.'

'Very well. Was Hallward a regular patron?'

'On occasion, though drink was never his vice – causing controversy was far more to his liking. He attracted lawsuits like lint. He was particularly good at annoying self-important beneficiaries of patronage such as Edward Duchamp.'

'But Duchamp hasn't taken legal action against Hallward.'

'True,' said Donnelly. 'Mobbs has, though, perhaps on Duchamp's behalf. Someone broke into the *Chronicle*'s office last month and stole the next day's edition. Mobbs publicly denied the theft, but he boasted enough privately that word got back to Hallward.'

'But it's a crime! Surely Mobbs was arrested?'

'When Hallward went to the constables about it, they seemed singularly uninterested.'

'You think they were instructed by the administration not to investigate?' asked Monsarrat.

'Henry certainly thought so. The following week he published an accusation in the *Chronicle* against Mobbs for the theft, and also against Edward Duchamp for covering it up. So Mobbs sued him.'

'And Duchamp didn't? Surely he wouldn't let it stand?'

'Certainly not. The colonel loves his ceremonies, his symbolism. So he sought a distinctly martial form of redress: he challenged Hallward to a duel.'

'A duel? Good Lord. How did you come to know about it?' asked Monsarrat.

'Because I, Mr Monsarrat, was Henry Hallward's second.'

Donnelly reached inside his jacket, extracted some more newspaper clippings.

'I don't usually hang on to anything from the *Flyer*,' he said, handing the papers to Monsarrat. They did not produce the dry rustle of aged, crackling pages, but they had not been treated gently. A few sheets had obviously been crumpled and then smoothed out. 'Its editor is a lick-arse. Not a very good writer either.'

The first document brought forth a muted leap of recognition in Monsarrat's memory, the *Flyer* being Ralph Eveleigh's paper of choice. Monsarrat had been serving as his clerk at the time, and always looked at the papers after Eveleigh was done with them. The article read:

> An affair of honour has taken place between Colonel Duchamp, private secretary to the governor, and Mr Hallward, editor of the *Sydney Chronicle*, in consequence of a paragraph wherein the colonel's name was coupled with that of Mr Gerald Mobbs in a case of slander.

Monsarrat stopped reading and looked up. 'Mobbs?' he asked. 'Why did he publish a story about a duel to which he was linked?'

Donnelly nodded towards the page.

Mr Hallward, known for his expression of feverish sentiments, suggested that the editor of this very paper, having dosed his pressmen with gin, exhorted them to break into the *Sydney Chronicle*'s offices and slyly procure a copy of that journal the night before its publication. On levelling these charges against Mr Mobbs, Mr Hallward claimed that the alleged break-in had been at the behest of Colonel Duchamp.

Your editor is, unlike his counterpart, a temperate man, and determined to let the issue lie; however, Colonel Duchamp felt honour needed to be addressed and gave Mr Hallward a choice between apologising or duelling. Mr Hallward chose the latter.

Monsarrat's eye snagged on the next paragraph of the article. As he had claimed, Donnelly was indeed Hallward's second. Duchamp's second, as it turned out, was Albert Bancroft.

Two shots had been fired, Monsarrat read, and after each round the seconds had tried to negotiate for an apology. Eventually, they had succeeded – Hallward had agreed to apologise, but only for mentioning Duchamp in connection with the robbery. The story concluded:

We are happy the matter ended without bloodshed and cannot help expressing our regret that two such valuable colonists as the colonel and Mr Hallward should unnecessarily expose themselves to so much danger, on so trivial an occasion.

'So Mobbs had the gall to moralise over the duel when his actions caused it,' said Monsarrat. 'And no bloodshed. Are duels not supposed to have winners?'

'You would think so,' said Donnelly.

'Duchamp's a decent shot, from what I hear,' said Monsarrat. 'Did he not intend to shoot Hallward? Just wanted to send a pistol ball into the air to satisfy honour, that sort of thing?'

'Actually, we heard rumours. He was boasting to cronies, saying all his problems would soon be solved. In the end they weren't. Hallward walked away. But was he supposed to, as far as Duchamp was concerned? I rather think not.'

⁂

'Duels! Little boys playing with dangerous toys. Lucky to make it to old age, most of them,' said Mrs Mulrooney.

'Well, of course some of them don't,' said Monsarrat.

Mrs Mulrooney crossed herself. 'Hallward. Perhaps Mr Cullen can tell us something about it.'

Those who saw her gesture might have assumed she was on her way from church, had anyone been about. But even approaching midday the Sunday streets were almost empty, and they passed only a handful of people on their way to the *Chronicle* offices.

Cullen shook his head when he opened the door to Monsarrat's knock. He turned and went back into the office without waiting for them to follow. When they were inside, he asked, 'What have I done to deserve both of you?'

'Well, if we are a punishment, I'm afraid you're paying for the sins of others,' said Monsarrat. 'Specifically, for the crime of duelling.'

'Ah,' said Cullen. 'I told him not to.'

He dragged some chairs around Hallward's imposing desk, settling Mrs Mulrooney behind it. She gave a brief nod, as though in approval of her superior placement.

'He didn't listen?' she said.

'No. But I'll tell you this. He was a lot more worried afterwards. Said Duchamp was worse than corrupt. Said he was an ideologue – that's the word he used – who believed his corruption was justified. And that he was saved, in some way. He'd written a will, you see. Left it with me. Not that he had much to leave, but he seemed to think it was a real possibility that he wouldn't come back.'

'And the break-in which led to the duel,' asked Monsarrat. 'Any similarities to the looting a little while ago?'

'When they were looking for the next day's edition, they were precise,' said Cullen. 'Nothing else taken, nothing else broken. The looters seemed intent on doing as much damage as possible. On making sure we never published another edition. But the newspaper *was* broken into that night, no doubt about that, and the next day's edition stolen.'

'To what purpose, though?' asked Monsarrat. 'Surely the *Flyer* couldn't have replicated anything in time to go on sale the next day.'

'No. But whether it was the *Flyer* or another culprit, they found out what was going to be in our paper – an editorial in which Mr Hallward accused Colonel Duchamp of abusing his position, getting himself huge grants of land in the Liverpool Plains.'

'How could Duchamp have known this would be in the next day's paper?' Mrs Mulrooney asked.

'Ah, Mr Hallward was not the discreet type. He was always boasting about the paper.'

'Yet nobody knew what he was writing about when he died,' said Monsarrat.

'No,' said Cullen, 'and that would have worried some. He usually couldn't resist bragging, or at least giving little hints. To make him discreet, it must have been a remarkable story.'

Hannah glanced at the slanted tables. One of them bore the remaining intact frame. The letters were no longer in a jumble beside it – some were arranged within it. She walked over. The letters weren't in any discernible order, but some were coated in fresh ink. She turned towards Cullen, raising her eyebrows. 'You know, don't you, that in trying to find out who killed Mr Hallward, we will not falter, even if it leads us straight to the governor.'

'I thought I knew,' said Cullen. 'But then you arrive dressed like a governess, with your footman here.'

'Steady on,' said Monsarrat.

Cullen turned to him, his jaw jutting with barely restrained anger. 'You speak like a toff. In the same voice as Duchamp, and you expect me to believe you're not in league with him?'

'Yes. You can trust me. I was a convict, you see. Twice.'

Cullen paused, then threw back his head and laughed. 'You say I should trust you because you've committed two crimes?' He wiped his eyes. 'Anything interesting?'

'I was sent here for forgery,' Monsarrat said, 'and then lost my ticket of leave for visiting a woman out of my district.'

'Was she worth it?'

'No, as it turns out.'

'There's often a woman involved, I find.'

'And was one involved in your crime, Mr Cullen?' asked Monsarrat.

'Not directly, although the need to feed my sister entered into it. I bled my landlord's cattle – not to death, mind, nor anywhere close. Just enough to make blood cakes. They can keep you alive, mixed with a little oatmeal. But then I was arrested and sent here. A few years ago, the priest sent a letter. My sister had passed away with no one to care for her.'

'I am sorry,' said Monsarrat.

'Sometimes we gaze up at these foreign stars, and it's months before we find that those we love have joined them.'

Hannah felt a little guilty about the action she was about to take. While the men had been talking, she'd moved gradually towards the room's rear entrance. Now, she called out, 'I hope you don't mind, Mr Cullen, but I am just going to get some fresh air.'

'Wait!' he called back, beginning to stride and then run.

By the time he and Monsarrat reached her, she was standing in the backyard, pulling the canvas off the lump in the corner: a large roll of paper.

'There were showers the other day, but this is dry,' Hannah said. 'Almost as though the place is still in use.'

Cullen stared at her, saying nothing.

'Neither Mrs Mulrooney nor I will tell anyone about this,' said Monsarrat. 'But Vindex's latest pamphlet hints at knowledge of the circumstances surrounding Mr Hallward's death. I need to know if it is supposition, or something more.'

'You'd have to ask Vindex,' Cullen said.

'Am I doing so right now?'

Cullen slowly shook his head.

'But you are helping him. You know who he is.'

'And I cannot tell you. Not for any cost.'

'Can you ask him, then? For Mr Hallward's sake. If I leave you the address of my boarding house, will you be able to discreetly let me know if anything else comes to mind?'

'If I can.' Cullen handed Monsarrat a pencil stub and a piece of scrap paper, and Monsarrat scribbled down the address. 'And if I am still at liberty tomorrow morning, I may even begin to trust you.'

Chapter 13

'I'm going to share a secret with you,' said Hannah. 'One which will help you. One which I don't often talk about.'

Some of the ten young women sitting at their desks, those not struggling with Monday afternoon drowsiness, leaned forward. Hannah knew that very few people ever shared anything with them, let alone anything helpful. In her austere, expensive jacket and skirt, with the brooch glittering at her neck, she was by far the most eminent person who had ever given them anything apart from orders.

'Kitchen utensils need to be watched severely,' Hannah said. 'Knives in a drawer go blunt overnight. A skillet will crack just for the sake of it. The bottom will fall out of the kettle. You can't just trust them to go along with it, day after day. You need to check them first thing every morning, make sure they're not up to anything. Give them a good stove and they'll respect you.'

Some of the girls nodded politely, while others looked confused.

'And on the subject of kettles,' Hannah continued, 'I wonder if any of you can tell me how to make tea.'

One girl put up her hand. 'Tis just throwing the leaves in the pot and pouring water over them.'

Hannah gazed at her. 'I knew domestic service required training, but I had no idea how ... deficient your knowledge was.' She regretted the words as soon as they were spoken, and hoped the girls did not feel she was mocking them. In all honesty, she had said it out of pride in the fact that she now knew a word like 'deficient'.

'My ma's always done it like that,' the girl retorted. 'It tastes fine.'

'Young lady ... I'm sorry, what is your name?'

'Susanna,' the girl said, scratching her cheek, which was pitted with the after-effects of smallpox. Her clothes were drab, no doubt thinner than they had once been, but neatly patched, and her cap sat tidily on her brushed, scraped-back hair. 'People call me Suse.'

'You must never allow them to do that, Susanna,' Hannah said. 'Your name is important. If you let people take liberties with it, they will take liberties with you as well. Now, I'm sure your mother is a grand woman, but I'm afraid that tea doesn't taste fine when you scald the poor little leaves. You'll see for yourself. I'm going to make you all a nice cup of tea – you look as though you could use it.'

In the corner of the room, for the purposes of this demonstration, sat a stove of the kind that only existed in grander houses, stoked and ready to educate the colony's future servants. Hannah placed the kettle on top of it, glaring at the wretched thing so it knew that it would fail her at its peril. As she instructed the girls – about warming the teapot, waiting for the water to cool a little before pouring it onto the leaves, turning it round, locking the tea chest securely to stop both moisture and furtive hands getting in – Hannah glanced over her shoulder from time to time to make sure the kettle was still at its work.

'You have to take your time with it,' she said. 'Show it some respect.'

'No one has ever shown us any,' said Susanna, 'but we have to respect tea leaves?'

Hannah suppressed a chuckle. It wouldn't do to reward the lass for cheekiness. Much as she admired it, such a characteristic would not serve Susanna well in the wider world. 'If you want to do the job well.'

'Why should we care?' said Susanna. 'My cousin, now. So happy, she was, when she got a job on the governor's staff. But her mistress still can't remember her name, and sends her out on all sorts of odd errands without so much as a thank you.'

Now this, Hannah thought, was far more interesting than talking to bored girls about tea. 'And who would her mistress be?' she asked Susanna.

'I wouldn't know. One of the women there. Sends her to take messages in the dead of night – into a rough part of town, too.'

'Well,' said Hannah, 'I'm sure those messages are important.'

'They must be, missus, if she wants them delivered so quiet like. You ask me, though, there are easier ways to write to the newspaper.'

⁂

> Here, we all know the common water mole was transferred into the duck-billed platypus, and in some distant emulation of this degeneration, I suppose we are to be favoured with a 'bunyip aristocracy'.

Monsarrat folded the newspaper clipping of Donnelly's article and laid it on the dressing table in his room. His canvas clothes were now folded on the bed, as he shrugged into the black coat that he had worn throughout much of his sentence.

He couldn't fault Donnelly's rhetoric, nor his argument. Donnelly had taken exception to a push to create titled aristocrats in the colony. Monsarrat had never had much sympathy for a system where an accident of birth conferred wealth and social standing, while the intelligent but poor could only hope to empty chamber-pots. And in this place, what would the aristocrats call themselves? Lords of the void? Dukes of the wasteland?

He found himself looking forward to his next meeting with the man.

A letter lay on the table. Judging by the handwriting on the envelope, Eveleigh had not temporarily engaged a replacement clerk. He clearly felt this message was either unimportant or urgent enough to use his own spiky scrawl.

> It is as we suspected. The Reverend Bulmer and Socrates McAllister – as you know, both governors of the Female Factory – engaged the current superintendent. An unimaginative man, by the way, and thankfully that lack of imagination extends to his proclivities and his use of factory labour and funds.
>
> In any case, he was not in a position to resist the Reverend and Mr McAllister when they insisted Grace O'Leary would be best deployed on a property in the far west. Nor did he have any inclination to resist them, the fellow told me. They insisted that such an assignment would provide Miss O'Leary with the space to think about her incendiary ways, while removing her from a large population of inmates whom she could potentially incite to riot. As to where exactly she has been sent, the superintendent either does not know, or will not say.

It was his fault, Monsarrat thought. They had sent Grace to a parched corner of the colony to get her away from him.

She had been starved. Beaten. Her head brutally shaved so that some patches of scalp would remain forever barren. They had tried to kill her in all manner of ways, and failed.

Wherever they had sent her, whatever station she had gone to, it would be run by someone sympathetic to the views of McAllister and Bulmer. Someone who believed all convicts were irreparably damaged, and had been since birth. But perhaps someone who might not see that stain as a barrier to taking the more attractive among the females. The thought made Monsarrat clench his teeth so hard he could hear them grinding, feel a minute part of one of them calving off. He wanted to take the nearest horse – legally or not – and ride west to ...

Where, though? He had no idea where she was, beyond a vague compass point. And he knew that, as frustrating as it was, his surest route to her was to find Hallward's killer and then beg Eveleigh for indulgence. And *that* meant dealing with another member of Reverend Bulmer's cruel fraternity. Another clergyman.

He had arranged to meet Reverend Alcott at St James' Church to, hopefully, learn something of how a newspaper editor came to be accused of trespass by the colony's most eminent cleric. The convicts would have been able to hear the church bells from their third-floor hammocks in the barracks opposite. They would have heard the chatter of the congregation as they gathered for Sunday muster in the gravelled yard, in the shadow of the three-storey sandstone building engraved with the date of its birth and the name of the governor who fathered it.

Monsarrat saw a group of convicts emerging, in jackets the colour of the sea they had crossed and white trousers that would not remain so for long, shuffling off towards a day spent fortifying their ocean-walled prison. He waited for them to pass, then turned towards the church. It was an odd-looking creation from the front – it could have passed for a bathhouse were it not for the tall, angular spire that rose above its arched windows; the copper encasing the spire was probably among the brightest things the convicts in the barracks opposite had ever seen. The church itself was far longer than it was wide, with a columned and porticoed entry leading in to an aisle flanked by the first stained glass used in the colony. Monsarrat reflected that it was little grander than one in a prosperous English town, but here, in the church-starved Antipodes, it might as well have been a cathedral.

The man waiting for him at the end of the aisle seemed drab in comparison to his surroundings. Reverend Alcott wore ballooning white sleeves tied at the wrist with black ribbon, and a white bib that looked almost lawyerly, under a black vest. He watched as Monsarrat walked slowly up the aisle, past the open public pews and the enclosed box pews towards the front. Monsarrat had never sat in a box pew – they were for those who could afford to pay for the privilege of communion with God in privacy.

Reverend Alcott didn't seem to be glaring at him, at least not with the same ferocity that Reverend Bulmer always employed when he saw Monsarrat. Perhaps Alcott was a reasonable churchman. Monsarrat had been assured that such creatures existed, but he suspected they were rarer than Donnelly's bunyips.

It did not take long for Alcott to prove he was no such rare creature. 'I am here as a mark of respect for the governor and for the rule of law,' he said as Monsarrat approached. 'But I urge you not to try my patience.' His voice was deep, quiet but sonorous. The kind that could be raised to great effect in the denunciation of sin as it bounced off stone walls towards the parishioners.

Here we go, thought Monsarrat. *Another churchman who believes he is owed, but that he himself owes nothing.*

'I do appreciate your time, Reverend,' he said. 'There must be many calls on it in a place such as this. Convicts, I am sure, can make challenging parishioners.'

'Oh, they go to St Philip's. I don't concern myself with the fallen.'

Of course not. Why minister to those in most need of it?

'I do not know how much assistance I can give you,' Alcott continued. 'I have not seen or spoken to Hallward since the business in March.'

'I do not expect you to give me information about his murder,' said Monsarrat. 'I'm simply trying to build a picture of the man. There is a chance that understanding him might help me understand what happened to him. And, so far, those I have met seem to view him either as the guardian of free speech or a cynical provocateur.'

'Hallward was a treacherous, mendacious agent of chaos, and I've never respected the law more than when it enabled us to hold him to account for wrecking our service.'

'And how exactly did he accomplish that?'

'By insisting on sitting near respectable people, some of the most high-ranking officials in the land, who had absolutely no wish to be near him. By airing his grievances in public. By refusing to bow to authority, even that of God. In other words, by being himself.'

A housekeeper had appeared as Alcott led Monsarrat into the presbytery, a plain room with a writing desk in one corner but dominated by a large wooden table, surrounded by spindly but sturdy wooden chairs. Alcott had waved the woman away.

'I cannot spare you much time, and nor do I wish to,' he said. 'But if I must talk about that man, I would rather do so away from any parishioners who might come in seeking succour.'

Alcott gestured to a seat and took one himself.

'So, Reverend,' asked Monsarrat, 'what did Mr Hallward do to earn your low opinion of him? Make too much noise during service?'

'No, the man bought a box pew.'

'Oh. And why was that a concern? Shows piety, I would have thought.'

'Piety!' Alcott rose, began pacing the length of the table. 'Let me tell you, Mr Monsarrat, that man never did anything for pure reasons. He leased a very specific box pew. The one right behind the governor's! Wanted to make the man uncomfortable, I can only assume. Perhaps overhear what he could. When the governor found out, he was furious.'

'Why did you let the pew to him, then?'

'An oversight by a deacon. When I discovered, I had only one possible course of action. You understand.'

Monsarrat was not sure that he did. 'And that action was?' he asked.

'Well, I had to nail it shut, of course.'

'Of course. Hallward can't have been happy the following Sunday.'

Alcott flopped heavily back into his seat. 'No, of course he wasn't. He was angry because, as he put it, we had taken his money for nothing, and he simply wanted to – how did he put it? – commune with the Almighty in a degree of comfort. Ridiculous. He didn't want to pray, he wanted to protest!

'Then the governor said he could not concentrate on his own worship with such a man nearby. He might have gone to St Philip's! And of course everyone would have followed, and the generosity which has supported this church since it was built would have gone with them.'

Ah, thought Monsarrat. Even in the house of the Lord, it comes down to money. 'What did Hallward do?' he asked. 'When he found his box pew was no longer his?'

'Hoisted himself up, climbed in over the top! His feet profaning the carvings! Everyone was staring, and quite a few seemed upset.'

'At a man entering a pew he had paid for?'

'At a man causing a scene in a church! It was too late for me to do anything that day so I had workmen come in during the week and nail some boards to the top of that pew.'

'You were reasonably certain he would be back, then,' said Monsarrat.

'Yes. The following week he was apoplectic when he saw the planks on top of the box.'

'Did he tear them off?'

'No. He sat in the aisle. People had to walk around him – thankfully the governor was away that week. I asked Hallward afterwards for an assurance that he would not cause any further disruption, and he refused to give it. Of course. And then ...' Alcott reached into a pocket and pulled out a newspaper article. Did half the men in Sydney have snippets of Hallward in their pockets? The reverend handed it to Monsarrat. 'Proof.' He waited, clearly expecting Monsarrat to read it on the spot.

While Hallward's article did indeed attack the archdeacon, its first target was Gerald Mobbs.

> The *Colonial Flyer* has been pleased to pass a high eulogium on the Venerable Archdeacon Harvey. As we differ somewhat from the editor on this subject, and as his panegyrics will go to refresh our memories on certain points of the public character of the archdeacon, we will here quote them piecemeal, and make our remarks thereon.
>
> The *Flyer* tells us: 'No Church dignitary that ever breathed could have been more zealously, faithfully, and ably employed in advancing the morality and piety of a country than the present archdeacon of New South Wales, since his acceptance of an office which is no less irksome and responsible, than it is useful and important.'

Monsarrat looked up at Alcott. 'Mr Mobbs is clearly an admirer of the archdeacon.'

'A good man, that one – for a journalist. He would certainly never do anything as base as revealing, and commenting on, a man's pay.'

Monsarrat looked back down at Hallward's article.

> How far three thousand pounds a year is irksome to receive, we cannot form a judgement, never having had the good luck to receive so goodly an income. If it be irksome to the archdeacon to receive it, we can only say that we think it a very extraordinary trait in his character. We never knew but one or two instances of the clergy feeling it irksome to receive a good stipend.

Monsarrat handed the article back to the reverend. 'A little indelicate, perhaps, but do you really believe it rises to the level of treason?'

'Mr Monsarrat, there are far more convicts than free citizens here. The only reason we are not overrun is the respect commanded by our institutions, including the church. Hallward was chipping away at that.'

'You must be relieved he is dead,' said Monsarrat.

'I have made no such statement.'

Nor have you repudiated it.

Monsarrat rose to take his leave. 'How well do you know Mr Mobbs?'

'Socially,' the reverend said. 'We have been on some outings together with Colonel Duchamp and his sister.'

'Oh? Picnics? Strolls in the gardens?'

'Shooting parties, largely. Not that Mobbs ever managed to fell anything. The colonel – now he is an excellent marksman. And while his sister demurred from taking part in such an activity, I gather she is such an excellent shot that the army must bemoan the unfortunate fact of her gender.'

The girls hung up their starched pinafores on pegs near the door. Hannah knew that any school run by Henrietta would never allow such creatures to take these pristine garments home with them into their impure lives.

When Hannah noticed Susanna folding and stroking her apron before hanging it up, she put a hand on the girl's shoulder. Susanna started and wheeled around, eyes wide, and Hannah felt a pang of guilt. What did a hand on the shoulder signify in this girl's world? Hannah suspected she had just forced Susanna to confront something she'd rather forget.

'Thank you,' Hannah said softly, 'for taking such good care of that pinafore.'

Susanna shrugged as she hung it on the peg. 'Might as well be convict canvas and have a broad arrow on it, missus,' she said. 'It marks me out as inferior every bit as much as convicts' slops would.'

'Ah, you must never think that. If you wish, you can see it as a symbol of hard work rather than servitude. And don't you dare let me hear you say you're inferior again – plenty outside of these walls to do it, you don't need to add to their voices.'

'A fine idea,' said Susanna, 'but you've never had to tell yourself over and over that you're a person, just to keep yourself believing it while others act as though you're an animal. I wouldn't expect a lady like you to understand.' The girl's words were not accusatory – she was merely stating a fact.

Hannah looked at her for a moment, knowing it would be a risk to talk about her own past. She, of course, did not feel her actions had been criminal, but the British justice system disagreed. And while Henrietta was perfectly happy to give some of her exalted time to a middle-class woman, Hannah doubted she would feel the same about a housekeeper with a ticket of leave in her pocket.

Hannah tried to convince herself that what she was about to do was a mark of trust, a proof to Susanna that in Hannah's eyes, at least, the girl was far from inferior. She tried to ignore the other reason to make this revelation: because Susanna had a family member on the governor's staff, she could be useful.

Hannah took a deep breath, put her hand on Susanna's shoulder as the other girls filed out. 'And now for my second secret of the day.'

Susanna, who had begun ambling towards the door, turned around. She stood politely at attention, a neutral expression on her face.

'I understand very well,' Hannah said, 'because I have been a convict.'

Susanna shook her head slowly. 'You don't seem like a bad sort, missus, but you mustn't play around with me like that. Don't claim kinship where none exists.'

'I assure you, I'm not. I came here before you were born, got my ticket when you were still just a child. But the ticket exists. I came to this colony in the hull of a prison ship.'

Susanna's cautious eyes widened. 'I'd like to believe you, missus. But why would you admit it to me when you don't have to?'

'Because I was lower then than you are now. You are a currency lass, yes? A child of convicts, but never convicted of a crime yourself. I haven't had the easiest time of it, but since I got my ticket I have not been without food, have not wanted for work. I've been comfortable. Happy, for the most part. And you, you've no criminal stain. You can have all that, too. Food, for yourself, for your family. A life away from the cliff's edge.'

Susanna was silent, frowning in thought.

'For now, though, Susanna, I was hoping you'd agree to do something for me.'

The girl nodded cautiously.

Hannah opened her mouth, drew in a breath and –

'There you are!' Henrietta's voice rang out behind Hannah. 'My dear Mrs Mulrooney, I do applaud your commitment, but please don't forget that you and I have an appointment for afternoon tea.'

'Do forgive me, Miss Duchamp,' said Hannah, smiling. 'You were, though, bemoaning the scarcity of good servants. This girl here shows promise – if you've no objection, I'd like to give her some additional lessons.'

'I don't see why not,' said Henrietta. 'If you're willing, of course, to donate your time.'

What have I been doing all afternoon?

'Of course, I can think of no better cause,' Hannah said. 'Although I wonder – no, no, it's too radical a solution.'

The spark of intelligence behind Henrietta's eyes asserted itself. 'Do continue. I would not like to dismiss an idea without hearing it.'

'Young Susanna has a kinswoman who is in service. Doing quite well, by all accounts. It might be beneficial to the young ladies here to see what a real servant looks like. Even if they cannot meet the standard, they will at least know what that standard is.'

'I see no harm in that,' said Henrietta. 'We must not let it keep us from our tea, though. I wonder, as she is doing so well, whether your protégée might make it for us.'

Chapter 14

Hannah had to admit she was impressed with Susanna's tea. Not as good a brew as Hannah would have made, of course, but then she'd had far more time to practise. The tea was perhaps a little over-steeped, but only the most discerning drinker would have noticed. The service had clattered slightly as Susanna set it down a bit too hard, as though afraid the cups would run away if they weren't put in their place, but this kind of wrinkle could be smoothed away with time.

Other wrinkles, though, were far more concerning. Chief among them: why had Henrietta been deep in conversation with Mobbs? In order to avoid spooking the young woman, Hannah knew she must take an indirect approach.

'You do seem to like your walks in the gardens,' she said, unable to resist mimicking Henrietta's habit of holding her little finger out as she raised the cup.

'Yes, well, it's not Kew Gardens, but what is?' Henrietta allowed some delicate giggles to escape. 'You must forgive me – you've probably never had the pleasure.'

'I'm afraid not, but then there are gardens in Ireland too.'

'Indeed! You surely have visited Powerscourt, an extraordinary property! And that channel they dug so the servants can move between the house and outbuildings without anyone having to be bothered by the sight of them – quite ingenious.'

Hannah clasped her hands in front of her, otherwise she feared one of them would deliver the slap Henrietta deserved. 'It is interesting you say that,' she said. 'You're clearly an admirer of ingenuity.'

'When it increases one's own comfort.'

Hannah stood and wandered over to a side table where the *Colonial Flyer* sat alone on the polished wood. She picked it up. 'I particularly admire the ingenuity behind producing a newspaper,' she said. 'Haven't the faintest clue how they do it, of course. But to get so many copies out so quickly, bearing news of events that happened only yesterday – it is truly miraculous.'

Henrietta frowned, only for a moment, but long enough to warn Hannah to be careful. Hannah laid the paper back on the table and took her seat next to Henrietta. 'Conversation is a much better way to find out what is going on, isn't it? Being able to look at someone's face when you're talking to them tells you so much more.'

Henrietta was still suddenly. 'Yes, you are right, of course.' Her voice had none of its usual girlish lilt; it seemed to have deepened as her eyes probed Hannah's face. 'Gives you a sense, I think, of whether people are really what they seem.'

Interesting, thought Hannah. She had a choice now: maintain the fiction and get nowhere, or gamble on some judicious honesty in the hopes of forming an alliance, in a move that would risk alienating Henrietta if even one note was imperfect. She sighed, leaning back in her chair. 'We all present a façade, don't we?' she said, letting her accent stretch and spring back into its original shape. 'We tell stories to others about who we are. Not from dishonesty, but for survival. And,

Miss Duchamp, I am well aware that women of your station need to stage a play every day of your lives. It must be exhausting. But perhaps a little less so if you can confide in someone who understands.'

'Yes,' said Henrietta, 'a confidante is a wonderful thing. One must, though, take care to choose the right person. Otherwise one might find oneself conversing with a phantom.'

* * *

Monsarrat heard the Sheer Hulk before he saw it: singing, yelling, brawling. Just about any noise a human throat could make was being made, especially those called forth by drunkenness. The sun was beginning its descent to the horizon but, even so, those in such a state at this hour must have had rum for breakfast. As he approached, a constable standing serenely in his blue coat with its red collar nodded at him, seemingly oblivious to the clamour.

From the scuttling and smashing Monsarrat heard inside, he guessed that broken earthenware was a regular feature of nights at the public house. The barber's pole, though, was pristine – perhaps the clientele believed it had the power of a talisman.

He heard a metal bar being lifted from the inside when he knocked on the door, which opened a crack. A large man came up behind him, with no jacket and his shirt open almost to his waist. 'Let me in, damn you, Arthur!' the man bellowed.

'It's who'll come in after you that I worry about,' the mysterious Arthur said from the other side of the door. 'If this fella identifies himself satisfactorily, I'll let you both in. Otherwise you can dispose of him before you cross the threshold.'

'I'm here for Donnelly,' said Monsarrat.

He heard the bar lifting again. 'All right, in with both of you,' said Arthur, who turned out to be a small, wiry man with strands of grey hair trickling from an almost bald dome.

'Gaffney, I don't need to ask you to behave yourself. I know you won't. Mr – whoever you are, I hope you know how to handle yourself among beasts such as these.'

'I suppose we will find out, won't we?' said Monsarrat.

The room was dimly lit, with a fireplace at one end and candles set at seemingly random intervals on the shelf that ran around the length of it. Below the shelf, benches jutted out from the walls, with mean tables at each. At one, a group of constables toasted the landlord when a serving woman brought them more rum; at another, a dice game was in progress. A glazed-looking man in a soldier's uniform sat near the fire. And near him, in the corner, a table was distinguished by the fact that no one there was yelling or fighting.

'Mr Monsarrat,' Donnelly said, standing and waving, 'you had better come join us. It is foolish to go unclaimed here.' One other man was at the table, dressed soberly in the manner of a lower functionary rather than a navvy. 'Collins, this is Mr Monsarrat. He has been engaged by Colonel Duchamp to identify the murderer of dear Henry.'

'Are you sure it's wise, Donnelly, to bring an administration man to us?'

'I am fairly certain, James, that Mr Monsarrat can be trusted. And if it turns out he can't be trusted, you can make sure we get a light sentence.'

'If I'm still on the bench by then,' Collins said.

'You'll have to forgive James,' Donnelly said to Monsarrat. 'Governor Brisbane had no problem appointing former convicts as magistrates, but as I told you, that has changed.'

'Yes, passing a counterfeit promissory note apparently compromises you so completely that you can't be trusted to utter an honest word the rest of your days,' Collins said. 'So the governor and his lapdog believe, anyway. There's a rumour that he will cut the bench, remove all the former convicts and replace us with people like Albert Bancroft, who will no doubt dole out a sentence of several hundred lashes – or death by torture, as it should be known.'

A serving woman came to the table and put a cup of rum in front of Monsarrat. He lifted it, smelled it and had to stop himself recoiling. It was probably diluted, but it was rough all the same. 'Could I trouble you for some brandy?' he asked the woman.

The men laughed.

'You come for rum, or you don't come at all,' said the woman. 'One shilling.'

After Monsarrat had paid her and she'd wandered off, he lifted the cup. He tried to let as little liquid as possible past his lips. He was the only one not enthusiastically imbibing, but he did not want that to be a cause for mistrust.

'So,' said Donnelly, 'as I said, James, I believe Mr Monsarrat can be trusted. I also believe it is in our interests to help him – I would be amazed if a successful investigation didn't damage the administration, perhaps give them the jolt they need. And I believe that someone, somewhere has to know something that will help catch Henry's killer, whether they realise it or not.'

'Do you suspect anyone in particular?' Collins asked Monsarrat.

'Hallward annoyed a lot of people. What have you heard?'

'What haven't I?' said Collins, taking a long draw from his cup. 'A jealous lover, the government, the King, leprechauns, demons. Everyone has a motive and an opinion.'

'And are some more frequently stated than others?' said Monsarrat.

'Albert Bancroft's name has come up more than once. I must caution you, though – he is not a well-liked man, particularly not among those who have in the past been assigned to one of his properties, so the rumours about him could be wishful thinking. But I gather he owns a house opposite the gaol.'

'Are you not aware of anything more specific?'

'Not at this stage, I'm afraid,' said Collins. 'I'll send word to Donnelly if anything comes to light.'

'I may well see Bancroft later tonight, actually,' said Monsarrat.

Collins frowned and made to stand, but Donnelly dragged him back down. 'He's going to the musical society, you fool. Isn't that right, Mr Monsarrat?'

Monsarrat nodded. 'Mr Collins, I too am a former convict. I have met men like Bancroft before, and bear them no love.'

Collins slowly sat back down. 'Worth it, I suppose, to hear the wondrous Miss Albrecht play. She is very brave to keep on with it.'

'Brave?'

'Well, you must've heard – she and Henry were . . . sweet.'

'I had heard, yes.'

'If you find the culprit,' said Collins, 'the worst punishment would be to let Miss Albrecht loose on him. She told me she would . . . What's that phrase she uses, Donnelly?'

'Ah, yes. The English translation of the German phrase about moving heaven and earth.'

'That's right,' said Collins, 'she told me she would set heaven and hell in motion to see Hallward's killer suffer.'

Collins took one last pull of rum from his cup, put it down and stood. 'I wish you both the best, gentlemen, but it is time I was off. I prefer not to breathe fumes over those who come before my bench – undermines my authority.'

'Bancroft is not the only person who interests me,' Monsarrat said after Collins had left. 'What do you know of Gerald Mobbs?'

'Mobbs has been the administration's lackey since the day Duchamp stepped off the boat. He hated the fact that the *Chronicle* outsold the *Flyer*,' said Donnelly.

'Well, to hear him tell it, the *Flyer* was making money hand over fist, and the only risk to its continued profitability would have been in the *Chronicle* goading the government into imposing a licence or a tax.'

'Mobbs has a habit of saying whatever is convenient and convincing himself it's true, so those who don't know better tend to find him quite believable.'

'Still, he has an alibi. And he is hardly the only one who had reason to resent Hallward,' Monsarrat said. 'The man seemed to enjoy making enemies.'

Donnelly smiled. 'Do you know, I think he did. If they hated him, at least they were noticing him – for Henry, being ignored, irrelevant, was a kind of death.'

'My ability to identify the person who caused his actual death is now somewhat more constrained than it was.'

'Yes, I'm surprised Duchamp hasn't dismissed you already. It's one thing to be a former convict – many are, including our friend Collins, of course – but the intimation of plotting, scheming, an ability to carry on a prolonged deception ... well. Unwelcome, I'm sure.'

'Yes, and I'm rather less comfortable than your friend was with the attention. As for why Duchamp hasn't dismissed me, I haven't given him the chance. I've steered clear of Government House today. If he means to send me back to Parramatta, he will find an opportunity eventually. Until then, I'll do whatever I can to discover the truth.'

'If I can help, of course –'

'Thank you, and I accept your kind invitation to the site of the duel between Hallward and Duchamp.'

Donnelly frowned. 'I made no such invitation, and I don't understand what the point would be.'

'Nor do I, yet. But the administration fears whatever Hallward was working on when he died, and the line between Hallward and Duchamp runs right through Mobbs. A duel between two of them, caused by a third, well, it merits looking into. Even if looking into it brings me no closer to the truth, it might yield something almost as valuable.'

'And what might that be?'

'Leverage, Mr Donnelly. My ability to continue with this investigation rests with Duchamp. If this duel runs deeper than two men shooting into the air so that they could tell themselves honour had been satisfied, I may yet be able to convince him it is not yet time for me to sail up the river.'

Chapter 15

'You are under no obligation to go, of course,' Monsarrat said to Mrs Mulrooney, back in the boarding house parlour. He was standing in front of the mirror above the mantelpiece, fiddling with his cravat. It had come askew at the Sheer Hulk, as though breathing the air of the place resulted in instant dishevelment. 'If you're tired.'

'The elderly get tired of an evening, Mr Monsarrat. You're not suggesting that I am among their number, I hope.'

'I would not dare. Especially not since you have the fan. What is it – wood? Ivory?'

'Which is harder?' asked Mrs Mulrooney. 'If it is not the kind I have, I'll be sure to get it. Now, you won't stop me from coming tonight. We need to speak to that Bancroft fellow.'

'And try not to scare him in the process,' said Monsarrat. 'I'd rather he not know that I'm aware of the ownership of that house. As it is, making another appearance at the music society after being warned off by both Duchamp and Bancroft – it's a declaration of sorts. What I don't know is whether it will serve to flush out information or send people to ground. We have to try, though.'

'It's just that we are attempting a fair bit of flushing, at the moment,' said Mrs Mulrooney. 'Between Bancroft and Henrietta, not to mention our friend Vindex.'

'Yes. Not only is Miss Duchamp somehow connected to Mobbs, but whoever hit Hallward in the forehead from such a distance would need to be a good shot, and according to Reverend Alcott she is. Along with the colonel and any number of other men, of course.'

'Did Alcott talk about Mobbs's shooting prowess?'

'Hopeless, apparently.'

'And his own?'

'Hm. No, actually.'

'It's interesting that he chose not to, given he seems to believe Hallward was intent on bringing down the government. And that he bore a personal grudge against the man.'

'The problem is,' said Monsarrat, patting his cravat, 'we have too many possibilities, and the weather vane seems to be pointing to them each in turn.'

'Yes, everything is wrinkly,' said Hannah. 'It could just be minding its own wrinkly business, or it could all be connected somehow – the house, the grudges, the guns.'

Monsarrat had been worrying away at his own wrinkle: the German expression James Collins had used, the one that Miss Albrecht often said. There was a faint tinge of familiarity to the phrase.

'Well, hopefully we'll get some answers tonight. At the very least, I want to know how somebody who has the rank of colonel managed to miss twice at ten paces.'

─────

On the stage was a woman in her thirties, her hair decorated with long scarlet feathers held in place by glittering clips, her over-rouged cheeks quivering as her voice tried and failed to take flight, to do what the aria she was singing demanded.

Mrs Mulrooney leaned towards Monsarrat. 'The sacrifices I make for you,' she said.

'Yes, you're a very good auntie.' He smiled, flinching at the thought that the fan might materialise.

Before it could, the woman finished her song to a smattering of polite applause. It was the most courtesy anyone in the hall had shown her all evening; a number of unabashed conversations had been taking place, and very few eyes had been on the singer.

These included Bancroft's – he had been surreptitiously glancing at Monsarrat and Mrs Mulrooney all evening. And after Bancroft shook a few hands, clapped a few gentlemen on the back and bowed to a few ladies, he made his way towards the newcomers. 'What on earth are you doing here?' he said. 'Not busy enough?'

'Forgive me, sir,' said Monsarrat. 'We were hoping to hear Miss Albrecht.'

'Who was far better than that little dumpling tonight,' said Mrs Mulrooney.

Bancroft pursed his lips and glared at her. 'She happens to be my niece.'

'You should talk to her parents, then,' said Mrs Mulrooney. 'See if they can guide her towards a more suitable occupation.'

Monsarrat shot Mrs Mulrooney a warning look. She frowned at him but went silent, at least for now.

'Forgive my aunt,' he said to Bancroft. 'Charming as your niece is, we are also here to see you.'

'I've already made it clear that I wish to limit our association,' said Bancroft.

'Your wishes will be respected, naturally,' said Monsarrat. 'I do, however, have a question that you are in a unique position to answer. You were a military man at one point – I can tell from your bearing.'

'Mr Monsarrat, I doubt you know the first thing about me, or anyone like me. Men of honour who came by their fortunes honestly.'

Monsarrat inhaled, clenched his fists.

'Mr Monsarrat has no fortune, but I assure you he is acquainted with honest work,' Mrs Mulrooney said quickly. 'No, marksmanship is an interest of ours. In fact, am I right in thinking that Duchamp is a fine shot? What about you? Were you the best marksman in your regiment?'

Bancroft glared at her. 'Why?' he asked. 'Do you have something you wish disposed of?'

'Oh no,' said Mrs Mulrooney. 'When I have something I wish disposed of, I do the disposing myself.'

She smiled sweetly at Bancroft, and Monsarrat resolved to talk to her later, no matter how many thrashings with the fan he earned himself. She was, he thought, perhaps feeling emboldened by her newfound wealth and its outward manifestations. She was becoming somewhat reckless. A little bit, he had to admit, like him.

'So why is that any business of yours? Unless you want me to bag you a magpie for your supper.'

'Do you know, I don't think it's important enough to take up any more of your time,' said Monsarrat. 'You're a pastoralist, I understand. I'm sure you have a long way to travel tonight. Unless you have a place to stay in Sydney?'

'Which would be none of your concern either.'

'I see. Well, thank you for obliging us.'

'I'm afraid I can't oblige you any further. If either of you ever comes here again, I shall ask you to leave in the most public and embarrassing fashion possible. The request to leave – that I would have done anyway. But the embarrassment – that, dear lady,' he bowed stiffly to Mrs Mulrooney, 'is for my niece.'

'I know it's tempting to bait a man like Bancroft, but you must try to fight the urge,' Monsarrat said to her as they walked back to the boarding house.

'Haven't I been controlling myself for twenty years? I now have enough money to buy my father's farm fifty times over – more money than I really understood existed before. Does that not buy me the right to a few honest statements?'

'In this investigation, I very much fear it doesn't.'

'Then whether I am a servant or a wealthy dowager, I am equally voiceless.'

An infuriating woman, sometimes, Monsarrat thought. But deserving of a voice, more than most.

'I know you find it frustrating. I assure you it's not forever.'

'Nothing is, Mr Monsarrat. And I confess to finding everything frustrating at the moment.'

'I see,' he said. 'No word, then, from Parramatta?'

'Young Henson has written. He tells me that Helen is taking good care of the cottage. He says she knows how important it is to send word if any letter arrives.'

'But none has.'

'No.' Mrs Mulrooney stopped suddenly and took a deep, juddering breath, gazing up at the moon. 'Is Padraig looking up somewhere too, Mr Monsarrat, like his old mother? Or will he never look up again? And if he has died, will I ever know where he lies?'

Monsarrat felt suddenly unmoored. His friend's fierce practicality and genial irascibility had always seemed to him as immutable as the moon she was gazing at.

'I am sure your son's yet above the ground,' he said. 'When this is over, I promise you I will bend all of my efforts to finding your Padraig.'

She smiled quickly at him. 'You're kind, Mr Monsarrat – don't look surprised,' she said as he raised his eyebrows. 'You're still an eejit of a man half the time, but you're a long way from the worst of them. You'll want to be putting some effort into looking for your Grace, too.'

Monsarrat's step faltered. 'I will. I know Ralph Eveleigh, though. He's sympathetic, certainly, but he believes I was put on this earth to clean the more inconvenient messes, not to look for a convict. For him to help me – and for him to retain his position – I must solve this case and write it up in my finest copperplate hand.'

Chapter 16

Monsarrat's companion was not providing him with any distraction from the constant jolting. This road between Sydney and the marsh where the duel had taken place was one of the worst he had encountered in a colony of ruts and muddy holes, grabbing the coach wheels and pointing them in a direction the coachman had not intended.

He had dragged Donnelly from his breakfast. Now Monsarrat wished he had thought to bring some bread, perhaps cheese. As it was, Donnelly mostly showed Monsarrat the back of his head as he pointedly looked at the passing scenery.

'Care for a stroll?' Monsarrat asked when the coach pulled over to spell the horses.

'I'd care for a little food. As I've been denied it, you can stroll on your own.'

A quick stab of resentment. A pulse from the shadow. For a moment, Monsarrat felt some sympathy with those who resented the Donnellys of the colony, born of convicts but removed from the more visceral aspects of their parents' past lives. Monsarrat would bet the elder Donnellys would have been delighted if their biggest problem was an early start to the day and a lack of immediate breakfast.

'Not his usual sparkling self today, I notice,' said the coachman as Monsarrat unfolded himself from the coach.

'No. You know him?'

'Oh yes.' The coachman strapped a feedbag to the bridle of the dark brown horse that had been pulling them along. 'Suits him to have a conveyance handy. He pays well, and I wait at the fringes of his protests so he can duck off quickly if things get out of hand.'

'Risky work, Mr . . .'

'McCarthy.' The man extended his hand. 'Yes, it is. Profitable, though. And I happen to believe in what he's doing. We're treated as serfs while the land beneath our feet is carved up and doled out like slices of cake.'

'And if you were to be arrested?'

'Sally's a fast one,' said McCarthy, patting the horse's flank. 'She's not much for conversation, though, and neither is our friend at the moment. If you care to sit up front with me, you'll get some fresh air and a bit of talk, and the trip will pass quicker for both of us.'

By the time they arrived, Monsarrat was intimately acquainted with Sally's pedigree and with the goings-on of those rich enough to rent McCarthy's coach. Monsarrat was clearly not among their number, but the man insisted on providing his address anyway, just in case.

The scrub here stopped a long way from the water's edge, and the soil was dense, wet. Monsarrat had to work his fingers back and forth to scoop up a clod.

'Don't get it close to your waistcoat,' said Donnelly, whose temper had been improved by a nap on the second leg of the journey. 'It stains, that stuff. I've never been a man of fashion, but a rusty streak of dirt across one's clothes is below even my standards.'

Monsarrat squeezed the small sod, and water dribbled down his hand. 'I imagine you had greater concerns the last time you were here.'

'Yes. Specifically, trying to discourage Henry from participating. Colonel Duchamp has a reputation as a decent marksman.'

'And yet he missed.'

'Oddly, yes. Twice. I've no doubt he wanted to kill Henry. That much was apparent from the look on his face, as well as the boasting he'd been doing about being rid of his problems. He may have been worried about civil unrest, of course. The public were already upset about those two soldiers the governor had mistreated, especially the one who died in those chains. The colonel's dispatch of a man some saw as a hero would not have made things any better. I would have had no problems at all drawing people out in their thousands to protest such an outrage, and Duchamp knew it. He may have feared it would even turn into a riot.'

'So the colonel was – where?'

Donnelly paced towards a tree that faced west, towards the interior where Grace O'Leary laboured on an unknown property.

'And presumably Hallward was directly facing him?' said Monsarrat, going to stand a few yards away from Donnelly, looking towards the sea. 'Round about here?' He put a hand to his eyes to shield them from the glare of the sun across the water.

Donnelly nodded.

'And this was early in the morning?'

'Yes. We had set out in the dark. But I can see your concern, Mr Monsarrat – the sun was in Henry's face.'

'How did you allow yourself to be given such a disadvantageous position?'

'Duchamp insisted on a coin toss. He won, so he chose the positions.'

'Not very sporting.'

'Well, I don't think he knew whether Henry intended to shoot to kill. And Henry – good man, as I told you – couldn't resist a jab now and then. Even if Duchamp did not want him dead at the beginning of the process, I'd wager he did afterwards.'

'Why is that?'

'Duchamp had wanted the duel in order to keep his honour intact. Henry was hell-bent on making sure it was in tatters.'

'I gave the command to fire,' said Donnelly. They were sitting, now, on twin rocks which had partially sunk into the soft mud, looking at some magpies wheeling against the morning sky. 'Duchamp, God rot him, is quick. As soon as the word was out of my mouth he whipped around, had his pistol aimed at Henry's chest before Henry had even raised his own weapon.'

'So why didn't Hallward die there and then?' asked Monsarrat.

'Well, he certainly didn't seem to be doing anything to prevent Duchamp from killing him. He turned to me and said, "Did you say fire?" Then he aimed his pistol straight up. Hit a tree branch, scared some cockatoos. They made a devil of a racket, and one of them decided to leave a calling card on Duchamp's shoulder as it flew over.'

'He would not have liked that,' said Monsarrat.

'No, indeed.' Donnelly shook his head and chuckled. 'Especially not when Henry told him that even the cockatoos had educated opinions. Then he said no one need worry because he had been given a clean bill of spiritual health that morning, since he always told the truth. It seemed to make Duchamp even angrier. He said he wasn't surprised to hear Henry joke about the state of his soul, that everything was a joke to him and the colony could crumble as long as there was enough printer's ink for Henry to make snide comments.

'And did he?' asked Monsarrat. 'Hallward? See everything as a joke?'

'Oh, no, Far from it. He believed Duchamp would not stop until he had a servile press. He said as much, there and then. So Duchamp aimed his pistol again. Stared at Henry so hard I thought Henry might die from the hatred in the man's eyes before the ball had a chance to reach him.'

'But he didn't. Either from the look, or the ball,' said Monsarrat.

'No. Henry Hallward may well be the only man in the colony to have had his life saved by a lizard.'

'I'm sorry, a lizard?'

'The kind with those long, whippy tails, crests on their heads and stripes on their backs. See them sometimes by the harbour, pretending to be statues. Water dragons, I think they're called. They behave very familiarly, even with gentlemen, and this one – three feet or so, no word of a lie – scurried out of the bush and ran over Duchamp's feet. It startled him – he looked away for a moment as he fired, and the ball went wide. Wound up in the mud.' He nodded towards a rust-stained patch some distance away.

Monsarrat stood, paced towards it. 'That must be thirty yards,' he said. 'Quite a distance for a duelling pistol.'

'Not these ones,' said Donnelly. 'These ones were rifled.'

'Truly? I thought all duelling pistols had smooth bores.'

'Rifling's common on the continent, but considered unsporting here and in England. Increases accuracy, you see. Not to mention range. Duchamp was very fond of them. He smiled when Bancroft opened the box they were in, picked one up and stroked it. Said it felt like an extension of his arm. That it set him apart. Honour demanded that he had to offer Henry its twin, of course. And when Henry picked it up, Duchamp told him that one way or another, he was holding his own doom in his hands.'

'So, Duchamp had the deadliest duelling pistols he could find,' said Monsarrat.

'Yes. And he barely took his eyes off Henry as he reloaded. I whispered to Henry, then. Said I'd never seen someone look so murderous. That perhaps a strategic retreat might be in order.'

'And what did Hallward say?'

'He didn't have a chance to say anything. Bancroft could see the way things were going too. Probably didn't want to give me a chance to foment rebellion. He stepped forward and said honour had been satisfied.'

'And that was enough for both of them?'

'Well, Henry could never resist a parting shot – a rhetorical one, at least. When Duchamp refused to shake the hand he offered, Henry suggested a letter to the editor next time Duchamp was upset. He said he would publish it with minor corrections to spelling and grammar.'

'He was certainly good at getting a rise.'

'Oh, yes. Anyway, Duchamp decided to stay behind. Said he wanted to be alone with his thoughts. Henry approached him. He said while Duchamp clearly believed Henry himself was the greatest threat to Duchamp's good name, it was the governor's actions, and those of others close to him, that would cause Duchamp's downfall.'

'I doubt Duchamp would have given that credence for a minute,' Monsarrat said.

'Maybe, maybe not,' said Donnelly. 'But he said he intended to make sure that those who had laid traps on the road were no longer able to do so.'

'Was that a threat?' asked Monsarrat.

'Duchamp was forever threatening Henry,' said Donnelly. 'Not to put anything past him, mind, but Henry would have been dead a lot earlier if Duchamp had made good on his promises.'

'And why did he stay behind?' asked Monsarrat. 'He does not seem the kind of man who frequently indulges in reflection.'

'I suppose not,' said Donnelly. 'Decent place for reflection, though. Nothing here but some irascible cockatoos, and a few balls in the ground.'

⁓

'I fear I have been felled by a head cold – most inconvenient,' the note read. 'I wonder, my dear Mrs Mulrooney, might I prevail on you to attend to the girls at the School of Industry alone?'

Hannah folded the scented paper with its fussy handwriting littered with almost too many loops and flourishes for legibility. The real art, she thought, was to make handwriting beautiful yet readable, like Mr Monsarrat's. The legibility of her own hand was improving; the beauty was a long way off.

She looked up at the footman who had delivered the note, and who was now standing to attention on the boarding house doorstep, waiting for a response.

'Kindly tell Miss Duchamp I'd be delighted to help,' she said, 'after I run an errand which can't be avoided.'

The footman nodded and turned away.

'Oh – before you go,' she called, and he stopped. He said nothing, but he made no attempt to disguise his irritation at being called back. 'Should I need to communicate with Miss Duchamp during the course of the day, I presume I could find her at home?'

'The lady's whereabouts are no concern of yours,' he said, turning back to the gate.

Hannah watched him go and then moved towards the door, unbuttoning her expensive jacket as she did so. Henrietta's illness could not have been better timed. It would allow Hannah to interview Susanna's cousin without interference, of course, but there was another benefit. With Henrietta absent, there was nothing to stop Hannah from changing out of these torturous clothes and into her black-patched armour, her preference for the morning's first battle.

⁓⁓

'You're all staring,' Hannah said to the young women sitting in the classroom of the School of Industry. 'I don't mind, but many would. They like you to keep your eyes down. I suggest you practise now.'

The girls bowed their heads. Hannah felt a little bad for berating them. 'I am fully aware that I am not dressed as I was when you first saw me,' she said. 'This is deliberate. I have spent some time in service. And I can assure you that the right clothes, and the ability to look after them, will make your lives easier.'

When the classroom door opened, the girls forgot all about looking down, snapping their heads around. It was as though a swan had landed in the middle of a flock of seagulls.

The girl who tentatively peered around the door was not ostentatiously dressed – far from it. But her dress was a fine wool, her collar was intricate lace, and her cap was a translucent white linen. She was, very simply, the ideal servant. Or at least, she looked it.

Susanna was smiling at the girl, and the girl was smiling back.

'Susanna,' said Hannah, 'is this your cousin?'

Susanna turned to meet Hannah's eyes, before remembering herself and lowering her own. 'Yes, missus.'

'Perhaps you'd like to present her to the class, then.'

'This is my cousin –'

Hannah sighed. Her motives for being there had little to do with the training of servants, but she wanted to impart some knowledge on her way through. 'Susanna, start by saying, "May I present –"'

The girl clearly wasn't sure if she should still be looking down, at the class, at her cousin or at Hannah, so she glanced around the room and mumbled her way through the introduction. 'May I present my cousin, Emily.'

'It is very nice to meet you, Emily,' said Hannah, 'and good of you to come. Your mistress was able to spare you today?'

'Yes, ma'am.' Emily bobbed a quick curtsey. 'She gave me a few errands and then told me to have the rest of the day to myself, as she is intending to be out until late evening.'

'A busy lady, then. Emily, please come up the front so that everyone can see you.'

Emily walked over to Hannah, then turned and smiled at the girls with none of Susanna's self-consciousness.

Hannah had never expected to be extolling the values of a life in service. She knew that she would have been miserable as a servant in a large household, somewhere where bowing and scraping was required. It would have made her sick, after a while, continually debasing herself to someone who had the means to employ her simply because of an accident of birth.

These girls in front of her, though . . . If they weren't pouring someone's tea or emptying someone's chamber-pots, what would they be doing? She feared she knew the answer – if a local girl didn't become a servant, there were very few ways she could feed herself apart from thieving, or transacting business on a street corner.

'I wanted you all to see,' Hannah told them, 'what it means to work in a grand house. How you present yourself. How you carry yourself. And what to watch out for. Because I can guarantee to all of you that there will be surprises when you find employment.' She looked at Emily expectantly.

The girl nodded. 'We did not use forks when I was growing up – mostly ate with our hands. At Government House they have three different forks at meals, and one especially for fish!

And they only explain things to you once – which fork goes where. Have to make sure you listen.'

Emily spoke for half an hour, with minimal prompting from Hannah, about everything from laying out dresses to lighting fires to putting a plate down from the correct side. Some of the girls were transfixed, some a little disbelieving – and some looked terrified.

When Emily had finished, a girl towards the back raised her hand. 'What if we can't remember it all? What if we make a mistake and we're dismissed?'

'If that happens, this school has failed,' said Hannah. 'It exists to ensure you can remember everything, and that you make as few mistakes as possible.'

As the rest of the girls filed out, Susanna and Emily remained, chatting quietly in the corner of the room.

'Thank you, Emily,' Hannah said when the room had emptied. 'You've given them a lot to think about.'

The girl smiled, bobbing again with such fluency that Hannah had no doubt the movement had been performed hundreds of times.

'I wish we'd had more time to talk about your duties as a lady's maid,' Hannah said. 'You serve the governor's ... wife, is it?' Hannah was reasonably certain she knew who Emily worked for, but had no intention of showing any interest in Henrietta Duchamp to the girl who was most probably her maid.

'No, not his wife,' said Emily. 'His private secretary's sister, Miss Henrietta Duchamp. She keeps me busy. Everything has to match exactly, you see, and if I can't tell the difference between the duck-egg blue parasol and the powder-blue one, I catch hell for it. Laying out her clothes is like doing a different puzzle each morning.'

'That solves the mystery of how you found your way here so quickly,' Hannah said. 'Your mistress is patron of this school, is she not?'

'Yes, ma'am.'

'Earlier you mentioned running errands – I imagine they were for this very place.'

'Begging your pardon, ma'am, but no. I wish they had been. She had me bring a message to someone in a far worse part of town. A house just opposite the gaol.' Emily shivered. 'And for a while I was bringing food to the same place. Almost too much to carry. I had to leave it on the porch, which was odd because it wouldn't have lasted long in that part of town. I hate spending any time near the gaol.'

Food, thought Hannah. Henrietta had been spending enough time there to need to eat. And if there was so much Emily could barely carry it, she probably wasn't eating alone. It would have been more discreet not to use a servant, but Hannah could not imagine Henrietta procuring her own food.

'Well, I can understand why, with that awful murder there recently. Must have been a shock for you and your mistress.'

'Yes. She came home from her morning visits and took straight to her bed.'

'Visits? She wasn't working here?'

'No,' said Susanna. 'She wasn't here that day. She cancelled all the classes, said she was too busy with her visits. She asked me to get word to as many of the girls as I could.'

'Oh, and who was she visiting?' Hannah asked Emily.

'I wouldn't know, ma'am. She didn't bring me along. She said true good works were best done in private.'

Chapter 17

Duchamp was sitting at his desk with his hands clasped. 'I must say, Mr Monsarrat, I hoped you would come with more definitive news. I thought that as you and that aunt of yours had time to enquire after my marksmanship – yes, Bancroft told me everything – the official part of your duties must be more or less complete.'

The colonel turned to Lieutenant Jardine, who was motionless behind him. 'Have you ever heard such a thing, Lieutenant? Would you not think our recidivist friend here would have better things to do?'

'I couldn't say, sir.'

Monsarrat schooled his expression into a mask of servile neutrality. 'I fear my enquiries have not yet reached a conclusion, sir,' he said. 'Not, that is, if you want me to submit a report that meets all the administrative requirements. Of course, I could simply find that Mr Hallward's death was a result of a stray projectile. Perhaps one discharged during the course of a duel.'

Duchamp narrowed his eyes, stood up from his desk and wandered over to the far wall, where a portrait of the governor hung. He stared at it. 'Even without Hallward to accuse the administration of everything from satanic rituals to eating our young, undoubtedly trouble-makers like that dreadful Donnelly would use such a finding to foment an uprising.'

'All the more reason, sir, to reach a conclusion quickly. An interview with the medical examiner who examined Hallward's body would be extraordinarily illuminating, I feel.'

'As I've told you before, Dr Merrick is essential to the functioning of the colony and is likely to be far too busy.'

'I beg your pardon, sir,' said Jardine. 'Perhaps if I accompany Mr Monsarrat to this interview, I can ensure he doesn't take too much of the doctor's time.'

Duchamp shot Jardine a poisonous look, but the soldier had resumed his habit of standing ramrod straight and staring into the middle distance. He must realise, Monsarrat thought, that he had put his superior in a position that meant Duchamp had no choice but to agree.

'Very well,' Duchamp said, probably grasping for a way to save face. 'I suppose it'll look good in the report. Not too long, though, Jardine – I need you here.'

'I would also like to revisit the gaol,' said Monsarrat. Of course he could simply march up to it and bang on the gates, yelling out to speak to that odious Crowdy. But that approach would give Monsarrat nothing – not, at least, without the private secretary's approval.

'Absolutely not, Mr Monsarrat,' said Duchamp. 'If you forgot to ask some relevant questions when you were last there, that is hardly my concern.'

'I asked all the questions I could have at the time. But the man I most need to talk to, Gleeson, wasn't there – visiting his sister, apparently. He might have returned by now. People will pick holes in any investigation that doesn't involve interviewing the last man to see Hallward alive.'

'The head warden is not back, so I can save you a trip,' Duchamp said.

'Really? You're an extraordinary administrator, sir, to know of the comings and goings of a warden.'

Duchamp glared at him. 'I consider it my duty to know everything about the colony. Including, Mr Monsarrat, the backgrounds of all former convicts who work for the administration. I heard you were a very good advocate – argued eloquently before the bench, for a range of clients who were delighted with you. Until you were revealed as a fraud.'

It still rankled: his years working for lawyers half as bright as him, men who thought nothing of getting him to write their briefs and claim the work as their own. His short, blissful time as a respected member of the Exeter legal fraternity. The shame of capture, the terror of death, and the sentence that had sent him tumbling down to the other side of the world.

He wondered what response Duchamp was hoping for. Embarrassment, perhaps. A shudder as his past clawed its way to the surface. But whatever the colonel was after, he would not get it. The shadow within Monsarrat wouldn't allow it.

'All the more reason for the investigation and its procedures to be above reproach, wouldn't you say?' he said. 'You've known of my background since I got here. And as you know, others in the administration must know too. If they dislike the eventual outcome of this case, they won't hesitate to use my past to throw suspicion on it.'

Duchamp looked at the ceiling, let out a bitter laugh. 'You are right, there may well be those who don't like your eventual findings, both here and in England. And if they don't, do not think for a moment that it will be me who bears the blame.'

'Good of you to accompany me, Lieutenant.'

'Some people were made for an office ...' He inclined his head towards Monsarrat. 'But I am not one of them. I am grateful for the opportunity to use my legs for the purpose for which they were made.'

'And to keep an eye on the twice-over felon,' said Monsarrat.

'Mr Monsarrat,' said Jardine, 'I will carry out all lawful commands, but I don't happen to share my superior officer's view that all convicts are a rotten branch. I do, however, subscribe to your view that this investigation needs to be untainted.'

'That's very . . . un-martial of you.'

'We need to keep order. If there was any implication that the search for Mr Hallward's killer had not been carried out with all due haste, that the government had not bent resources towards it, there would be unrest. Perhaps riots. I will shoot at a man across a battlefield, but I would prefer not to shoot at one who is unarmed in a crowd of protestors.'

The hospital had nothing in common with the exterior splendour of its London counterparts, crenellated like palaces despite the horrors they concealed.

On the verge of a nearby road sat small knots of Aboriginals. Groups of women, some nursing babies, others restraining toddlers from bolting out in front of coaches; a few men standing, talking or watching the women. One man was wearing a soldier's old coat he'd got from God knows where.

Jardine followed Monsarrat's eyes. 'They come here in hope of treatment,' he said. 'Including from diseases we gave them.'

In Port Macquarie, Monsarrat had enjoyed an easy friendship with Bangar, a Birpai tribesman. His people had treated the interlopers with far more kindness than they deserved. The Birpai had saved convicts from drowning and returned escapees who'd chanced the bush. They were rewarded with the gratitude of the commandant, slop canvas clothes and rum. The administration here would never know what benefits could be had from a relationship with the natives. In Sydney, as in Parramatta, those whose ancestors had owned this country had been moved off it.

'Yet we believe we are the civilised ones,' Monsarrat said, knowing as he spoke that the words would mark him out as an irredeemable heretic to many.

'Well,' Jardine said. 'It's necessary, the governor would say.'

'And you?'

'The governor does not seek my views on such matters.'

'If I may say so, Lieutenant, you seem, well, perhaps a different sort of soldier from the colonel.'

'There is only one sort of soldier, Mr Monsarrat. The sort who follows orders.'

'Even dishonourable orders?' asked Monsarrat.

'Well. The field of battle can do odd things to a man's character. But no, Mr Monsarrat, I have never received such an order. Should that ever occur, I will have a choice to make.'

The building they were approaching had three sections, but the two wings were blank-windowed, and one was encased in a cocoon of scaffolding that seemed to be the only force holding it up. The central section, though, was still larger than the two-storey slab that passed for a hospital in Parramatta. Inside, the runner sent by the duty clerk to fetch Dr Merrick took some time to do so, returning without the doctor but with an invitation to the man's office.

'I'll wait here, Mr Monsarrat,' said Jardine.

The office of Monsarrat's friend in Parramatta, Dr Homer Preston, boasted a rough table, stacks of documents, grimy windows and a curmudgeonly feline. Dr Merrick's office would probably be seen as an exemplar of colonial squalor by his colleagues on Harley Street, but compared to Homer's it was positively refined. A polished desk bore rows of handsome ink pots and a bronze sculpture of a rearing horse. There were shelves full of books, all of which were standing to attention neatly rather than jostling one another like the medical texts that crammed Homer's shelves. In the corner, hanging from a stand, were the bones of some indigent or pauper, transformed by death into a teaching aid.

Dr Merrick stood as Monsarrat entered, but made no attempt to greet him or wave him to a chair.

'Colonel Duchamp approved my visit, doctor,' Monsarrat said.

'Fine,' said Merrick, 'but I'm not sure how much I can tell you. Cause of death is fairly obvious. Have you ever seen a pie that has been dropped on the ground? That's what Hallward's forehead looked like.'

'I see. And did you extract the projectile?'

'Yes.'

Monsarrat waited a moment for Merrick to supply the information the man must know he was after, but the doctor had already started shuffling papers on his desk. Monsarrat cleared his throat. 'And the projectile was from – what? A rifle? A musket?'

'How am I to know that, man? Do I look like a soldier?'

You look like someone who doesn't want to answer my question, Monsarrat thought.

'And may I see it, this projectile?'

Merrick sighed. 'If you must, but I doubt it has become any more probative for having sat in a cupboard.' He brushed past Monsarrat, opened the door which led from his office, and leaned around it. 'Ainsley! Fetch the Hallward ball.'

Monsarrat heard a mumbled acknowledgement and receding footsteps.

Merrick went back to his desk, sat down and picked up some papers, shuffling them and peering through his wire bifocals as Monsarrat watched. He had the uncomfortable feeling that something was rising inside him, something that cared nothing for propriety and convention.

After a moment, Merrick looked up. 'I am tolerating you because you tell me you have the colonel's blessing. Although *blessing* is probably too strong a word – I rather have the impression he resents your presence here.'

'Your resentment, or his, are of no consequence,' said Monsarrat, remembering belatedly to take the heat out of the words with a slight bow. 'All due respect, of course.'

'You are a former convict, yes? Twice over, from what I understand. Oh, don't you worry, I have my friends in the Colonial Secretary's Office. Files can be found in very short order, if people are motivated. So, given your history, I doubt you have much familiarity with the concept of respect.'

Monsarrat clenched and unclenched his hands, trying to stop one of them from balling into a fist and aiming at the doctor. 'You are right, I am one of the fallen – as are most people here. But those who fall can rise.'

'A convenient fiction, something we tell our wives and children so they don't gibber with terror at the prospect of living among you. But I'm a man of science, Mr Monsarrat, and phrenology is an interest of mine. I suppose you don't know what that is.'

'The notion that the shape of one's skull provides insight into one's character,' said Monsarrat. 'You talk of fiction, you should start with phrenology.'

'You fancy yourself an educated man,' the doctor said, going back to his papers. 'I can tell. The accent, for example – no doubt deliberately acquired, rather than conferred by the circumstances of your birth. I wonder what you sounded like as a child? Dropped consonants must have littered your nursery floor.' He chuckled quietly, no doubt congratulating himself on his wit. 'If you were truly educated, you would not question what is proven science. Particularly when you're lucky enough to hear about it from the lips of one of your betters.'

'Am I to understand,' said Monsarrat, 'that there is some sort of link between phrenology and my permanently fallen status?'

'Criminals like yourself tend to have certain similarities in the shape of their skulls. I wonder, for instance, if you have a saddle-like depression at the top of your head. That's the area, you see, which governs morality. If it is undeveloped in your brain, your skull will tell the story. You can possess the world's greatest intellect, or the most extraordinary artistic ability, and still be condemned by your cerebral physiology to be a criminal.' He looked up again. 'Not your fault, really. You were simply born defective. I wonder, actually ... Would you consent to an examination?'

Monsarrat opened his mouth but had no idea what to say. Although expletives crowded in his throat, he had no intention of releasing them – that would support the man's point. He was grateful to the orderly for choosing that moment to knock on the office door. 'Come,' said Merrick. The man who entered looked oddly familiar: a broken nose, bald and burnt head, and a face brutalised by the sun. It wasn't until he spoke in a dry, rasping voice, though, that Monsarrat recognised the merchant he had seen in the streets near the *Flyer*'s offices.

'Begging your pardon, doctor,' the man said. 'The ball that killed Hallward ... I'm afraid it seems to have disappeared.'

Monsarrat had never been a gambler, but he was willing to bet that Dr Merrick's orderly Ainsley was a former convict. If he'd worked for the man for any length of time, Ainsley couldn't have helped overhearing some of Merrick's views on the nature of criminality. Perhaps he'd even allowed Merrick to palpate his cranium.

Some convicts, Monsarrat knew, had been hollowed out by days of casual abuse and nights keening for loved ones across the seas, wondering if wives or husbands had remarried, if children still lived. They entered a fog from which they never again emerged, where remembered horrors were amplified within their skulls but present terrors couldn't penetrate. These convicts, he knew, would simply stare at the ground or, at the most, nod if someone told them they had been born deficient. Someone with enough guile to sell goods of dubious origin by the side of the road, though, had probably not sunk too deeply into the mist.

Monsarrat waited until close to dusk before getting to The Rocks, by which time he knew Ainsley would have been dismissed from Merrick's rooms, and would have had time to set up his other means of earning a living.

Ainsley's wares, judging by his shouting, had changed a little. 'Fine lace collars! Fans! Ivory curios!'

Monsarrat had no idea what the citizens of this part of Sydney would do with an ivory curio. 'I was after something a little more martial,' he said, as he strolled up to the man's stall.

Ainsley started talking before he looked up. 'You'll have to be more specific, sir, and I'm sure we can ... You were in the office today?'

'I was,' said Monsarrat. 'I doubt I will be admitted again.'

'Looking for the bullet which killed himself in the gaol.'

'Indeed. Seems it didn't stop moving when it hit him, though, as it's left your custody.'

Ainsley looked to the side. 'That it has.'

'And you wouldn't have had anything to do with that? Only, I did hear you a few days ago, talking about your wares. And you weren't mentioning fans or ivory.'

'What you heard is no concern of mine,' said Ainsley.

'Let me make one thing very clear,' said Monsarrat. 'I am not interested in informing on you for any activities which might be, shall we say, legally questionable. I simply wish to know what happened to the slug.'

'I don't know anything about that.'

'If you say so. Do you know what? Perhaps if I gave all of my superiors gifts, they might be more inclined to reward me with their credibility. Fans for their wives and daughters, of course, and lace collars. And what gentleman would not want an ivory curio sitting on his desk? Dr Merrick, for example, seems the kind of man who'd appreciate such a thing. Although I imagine he would check against the register of possessions of the recently deceased, those who had come under his knife.'

Ainsley rolled his lips together, his eyes darting up and down the street. 'It's not as though they miss them.'

'Of course not,' said Monsarrat. 'No harm done. And if a particular item happened to be inside a victim, it's not as though you're stealing it. He never owned it in the first place.'

'Ammunition is expensive,' said Ainsley. 'It's a public service, so it is.'

'Quite. So the ball that was found in Hallward's brain – it was among those you were selling last week?'

Ainsley was silent.

'Look, all I want to know is what Merrick dug out of Henry Hallward's skull,' said Monsarrat. 'Was it a bullet? From a rifle, a Baker rifle perhaps?'

'Not from any rifle. It was a ball. The kind you'd find in a pistol.'

Chapter 18

'Not the sort of weapon you'd normally choose. Not if you want accuracy and range,' Monsarrat said.

'It's an odd choice, there's no doubt. But at least we know more about the murder weapon now. Now, is it safe to defy Duchamp, do you think?'

'Probably not, but I don't see an alternative,' Monsarrat said, trying to quash his nerves. He had picked up the newspaper several times this morning, reading a sentence or two, laying it down and immediately forgetting what he had read. 'Anyway, if they're going to treat me like some sort of scientific specimen, I certainly won't be following orders about avoiding gaols – they think I belong there anyway. And I won't be staying away from the Colonial Secretary's Office, either.'

'Neither should you, Mr Monsarrat. We need to be sure that Bancroft really owns that house,' said Mrs Mulrooney.

'Though he's far from our only prospect, of course. There has to be a reason Henrietta lied about where she was when Hallward was shot.'

'Perhaps there's some connection? Henrietta's maid was bringing food to that house Bancroft supposedly owns.'

'Yes, that's certainly interesting. They don't seem to socialise, except at dos like the garden party, and Henrietta is vastly disapproving of the recital hall. It's . . .'

'Wrinkly?'

'Wrinkly in the extreme, Mr Monsarrat.'

As the two of them mulled on this, there was a knock at the door. Mrs Mulrooney hurried to answer it and found Cullen standing there, the morning sun shining on his face, the grooves in his weathered skin serving as conduits for tears to run from his eyes and splash onto the ground. 'Begging your pardon for bothering you, Mr Monsarrat,' he said in a choked voice. 'Missus. But it's Peter. He's been taken, and I've not the first idea where to.'

If ever there was a time for strong tea, this was it. Hannah tried to be quiet, but Miss Douglas had the ears of a bat; the discreet clatter of a cup on a saucer was enough to draw her into the kitchen. 'We have had this conversation before, Mrs Mulrooney. The kitchen is off limits to my guests.'

Hannah tried to draw her mouth into a sheepish smile. Miss Douglas's other strict rule was that no guests were to entertain anyone – and in the parlour, a rough-looking Cullen was noisily emptying the contents of his nose into one of Mr Monsarrat's handkerchiefs.

'So you did, Miss Douglas,' Hannah said, 'and I do apologise for disturbing you. I wanted to avoid that. But my nephew – he is on the governor's staff, I may have mentioned – has a very important job, and requires tea to settle his mind before he starts the day. With your permission I'd like to make some for him, as I know just how he likes it.'

Miss Douglas stared at her for another long moment, then nodded. 'See to it that you clean up after yourself.'

'I will ensure you find it as you left it,' said Hannah. *Better, actually*. She would never have allowed dust to colonise the corner of the sideboard the way this woman had.

After Miss Douglas had minced back to her quarters, Hannah carried a tea tray into the parlour.

'You gentlemen need to be quiet,' she said, 'or we risk a dragon invasion.'

Monsarrat nodded. He knew better than to start asking for details without her, and it was clear that he'd been sitting in silence, keeping Cullen company as he dried his tears.

'Peter has been taken, you say,' she said to Cullen. 'By whom?'

'The constables. They pounded on the door about an hour ago. I pretended not to be there, and I didn't know whether Peter was – he comes and goes. But then they broke down the door, you see. I thought they were going to arrest me, but they pushed right past me, went into the yard. When I followed them I saw they had Peter. One on each side of him, dragging him by the arms – as though he was a six-foot-tall navvy, not a skinny little boy.'

'Did they say anything?'

'Only that they were arresting him for distributing pamphlets. And thieving. They wouldn't tell me where he was to be taken.'

Hannah put a hand on Cullen's arm. 'I must ask,' she said, 'could there be any truth in what they said about thieving? I'm not saying it's right to drag a lad away like that, but he wouldn't be the first boy to pick up an unattended apple from a cart.'

Cullen shook his head vigorously. 'He's a good lad, and I've done everything I can to make sure he stays that way – I know, missus, what can happen to boys like him. The government expects them to live on air, and then gets surprised when they're found with a stolen crust of bread. But I take my meals at the *Chronicle* and make sure he gets half so he doesn't need to thieve. And he's seen what happens to them that do. A smart lad.'

'And the pamphlets?' Hannah asked.

Cullen nodded. 'I warned him against it, but he said it might help Mr Hallward's soul rest. And he's rather taken with Ca... with Vindex.'

'What did you say?' asked Monsarrat. He slapped the table. 'Mrs Mulrooney, you have my permission to flay me with that fan of yours. I am, as you continually say, an idiot of a man!'

'Well, yes. Is there any particular idiocy you're thinking of?'

'I know who Vindex is! Something about a German phrase I was told she uses.' He turned to Cullen. 'It is Carolina Albrecht, is it not?'

Cullen nodded hesitantly.

'But that's wonderful!' Hannah said. 'If Peter was arrested on her behalf, perhaps she would be willing to speak for him.'

'Whether or not the authorities know who Vindex is, it wouldn't take much imagination for them to suspect the pamphlets are being printed from the *Chronicle*'s offices. Yet I am unmolested, and none of the others who hand them out have been arrested, as far as I've heard,' Cullen said.

'Is there another reason why, then?' said Monsarrat. 'From what I know of constables, they're not in the habit of breaking down a door at the crack of dawn in pursuit of a crust of bread that is already being digested.'

'No,' said Cullen. 'They've far better things to do, particularly in that part of town. I do have a notion of why they have taken him. But I pray that I'm wrong.'

Hannah shivered. She too had an inkling of what might be behind the arrest and if she was right, she feared Peter would become another lost boy whose face would haunt her.

'No one seems to know what Mr Hallward was working on when he was killed,' she said. 'But I imagine some are anxious to find out.'

'What if,' Cullen said, 'someone believes that Peter was able to collect the story before Hallward was murdered?'

'Then we must find him,' said Hannah. 'Because if someone believes he knows where the story is, he is in a very great deal of peril.'

The schoolroom was at the back of the baker's shop, and given the scrawny appearance of most of the children, the smell must have driven them insane with hunger.

The baker grunted and indicated the back of the shop with his head when Monsarrat enquired. 'Crawling with currency children,' he said.

This, Monsarrat knew, was not intended as a compliment. The currency lads and lasses, born in this place impossibly distant from the birthplace of their parents, had been nicknamed after the pound currency used in Sydney; this, in the view of the ruling classes, was far inferior to the pound sterling used in the mother country, though most of those in Donnelly's schoolroom would have been overjoyed to see a pound of either description.

The youngest of the children sitting at the indifferently constructed wooden desks was about five years old; the oldest perhaps twelve. But they were all learning the same thing – today it was the alphabet. Donnelly stood at the front, inscribing letters onto a slate, holding them up and asking the children to copy, which they did with varying levels of skill.

Monsarrat envied Donnelly for – well, just about everything. The ability the man had to speak his mind without having a ticket of leave to lose. The schoolroom with children bent over their slates. Monsarrat had no idea whether they liked their schoolmaster, but what mattered was that they learned from him; even the youngest were frowning in concentration, trying to form the letters that would separate them from workgang louts.

Donnelly was guiding the hand of a young boy, helping him form an H, when Monsarrat cleared his throat. 'Continue,' he said to the class, walking to the door and shaking Monsarrat's hand. 'I'm afraid I can't spare you much time, Mr Monsarrat. As you can see ...'

'I wouldn't dream of keeping you from your class, Mr Donnelly, but I have some urgent news.'

Even after Donnelly pulled the door closed behind them, Monsarrat could hear the whispering of the children, sounds that reverberated off the corridor walls as though they had soaked into the ground and were now blooming.

'There's a boy – Peter. He works as a copyboy at the *Chronicle*, or did.'

'Ah, Peter FitzGerald. I taught him to read, at Henry's request. He wanted to give the boy a job, and it would have been difficult for him to deliver parcels without being able to read the addresses.'

'And do you know anything of his current whereabouts?'

'At the *Chronicle*, I imagine. I believe he is in the care of old Cullen, who is refusing to vacate the offices. He'll have to eventually, of course. It's kind of you to be concerned for Peter, but I assure you that if the opportunity presents itself, I'll do what I can to find him a position. I'd hate to see him steal food and end up in gaol.'

'I very much fear he already has,' said Monsarrat. 'He's been arrested. Cullen does not know where he was taken, and he fears there is a connection with the fact that Peter was on his way to collect Hallward's last story when the shot was fired.'

Donnelly's face drained of colour, and he stared at Monsarrat in seeming incomprehension before shaking his head. 'They think he might have succeeded in collecting the story, then. They think he might have read it, might know what was in it.'

'That is Cullen's fear, yes. But the document itself has disappeared, along with the head warden.'

'Frank's gone? I hadn't heard. That is disturbing. He and Henry had an arrangement – Henry couldn't have edited the *Chronicle* from prison without him.'

'So there is every possibility that wherever this man is, he has the story with him.'

'Perhaps, Mr Monsarrat,' said Donnelly. 'There's one thing I'm certain of, though: Duchamp and his cronies know Henry was planning something exceptionally damaging, but they don't know what it was. And they will not believe Peter when he says he doesn't either. That lad's fate rests on one thing – you need to find that story, and you need to do it quickly.'

Carolina's angular face seemed rounder somehow, softer, blurred by the music. The stiffness in her jaw, present whenever she played in front of others, had disappeared now that she thought she was alone. It was a notion Hannah would have to disabuse her of. She disliked interrupting the woman's practice at the recital hall, but Peter's safety justified the invasion. Finding Hallward's story might save him, but Hannah had no intention of trusting his life to that eventuality.

Standing at the back of the hall, Hannah loudly cleared her throat. Carolina either did not hear or ignored her, so Hannah stamped a foot – still no reaction. She inhaled deeply. 'Miss Albrecht!' she yelled. Her voice was louder than she had intended, particularly the last syllable after the notes from the piano trailed off.

Carolina set her jaw, standing as she smoothed down her day dress. 'When I invited you to call on me here, madam, I did not think you would be impolite enough to interrupt my practice.'

Hannah strode towards her, talking as she went. 'And I would never do anything so rude, except in the most extreme circumstances.'

'And your circumstances are extreme?'

'Possibly. Yours may be too. But at the moment, a certain young boy is likely to be in more extreme circumstances than all of us.'

'Perhaps this is no conversation for a concert hall with good resonance. Come.' Carolina turned and walked, without waiting to be followed, towards her dressing-room. 'You mentioned a boy,' she said, as she closed the door behind them.

'Yes. Mr Hallward's copyboy, Peter, has been taken off by the constables.'

'Whatever for?'

'They say he was distributing your pamphlets. That's their excuse, at least. Complete rubbish, of course.'

Carolina stared, then shook her head. 'You must be mistaken, madam. I have no pamphlets. And while it is regrettable that the young boy has been taken, it is no concern of mine.'

Hannah felt a growing, rushing anger. Her son, for all she knew, was lost to her. She would not let another boy go. But she knew that if she unleashed her emotions, any possibility of civil conversation would disappear. She would give Carolina a final chance.

'Miss Albrecht, I know you are Vindex. It is a marvellous thing, providing an independent voice. Tyranny is not absolute as long as one person is willing to speak. But surely you must think of those you have been speaking to, and speaking for. People like Peter with no voice of their own. He was arrested for your sake. That was the excuse, anyway, although we believe those who have taken him think he has Henry Hallward's last story. I am told you cared for Hallward.'

Carolina turned away. 'I did.'

'You seem melancholy but not consumed by grief.'

'I have become adept, Mrs Mulrooney, at reinforcing my interior scaffolding so that my exterior doesn't collapse in on the emptiness. My grief would provide entertainment for Colonel Duchamp and his sister, and I will not dishonour Henry's memory in that way.'

'Yet you would dishonour his memory by allowing a lad he cared for to suffer, or worse. Who knows what Peter is enduring right now? And he is there, at least partly, because of you! If you tell the authorities he had no part in it . . . maybe offer yourself in exchange for him . . .'

'What am I to do about it?' Carolina asked, raising her voice. 'Present myself as the publisher of illegal pamphlets? They would then have reason to arrest my associates. Mr Cullen would soon find himself in a cell next to Peter – another voice silenced.'

'You will not help, then?'

'I cannot! I would be unable to do any good and could do a great deal of harm. You said yourself that this colony needs independent voices. What is the fate of one boy against that of a whole society?'

Hannah stood slowly and spoke quietly, knowing that if she allowed herself to start yelling, she would not stop. 'The fate of one boy, *madam*, is everything,' she said. 'A society that weighs out the value of one life against another like flour in a market – or worse, one life against a principle – has already lost its soul. You do not wish to dishonour Mr Hallward? You have. And your gender. And no amount of perfumed music will cover the stench.'

Hannah turned and yanked open the dressing-room door, letting it bang flat against the wall, and strode away towards the doors of the recital hall.

Chapter 19

Hannah didn't blame Emily for baulking at carrying messages for her mistress to this part of town. Hannah was not fond of the gaol either. Its outer walls seemed to be encroaching onto the pavement with each passing hour and she had the uncomfortable sense that if she stood here long enough, they would eventually reach her and keep moving until she was on the other side of them.

But it wasn't the gaol she was here for. Everything seemed to centre on that cursed house. If Peter wasn't being held behind those looming walls, she thought, it was more than possible he was being held there.

Hannah realised she was probably wealthy enough to have a carriage at her disposal, but acquiring one had never occurred to her. She thanked God she was wearing her servant's attire, rather than the stuffy jacket and skirts of a woman of means. Not only would they have been dreadfully hot, but a woman tearing through the streets in a lace collar and a brooch would have drawn all sorts of notice. However, the sight of a servant rushing around was not unknown. A woman dressed as a domestic had perhaps fought with her husband or been caught in a minor act of theft, or was on an urgent errand.

As Hannah walked past the houses opposite the gaol, approaching the one Monsarrat had told her about she saw a lace curtain twitch. It had to be the widow, Mrs Selwyn, who was convinced that ghosts were responsible for the strange noises at the residence next door. *Might as well be hung for a sheep as a lamb*, Hannah thought. She turned up the path and knocked on the door.

The woman who answered might have been around Hannah's age, but it was hard to tell. The lines around her mouth spoke of a lifetime of pouting. She couldn't decide where to fix her eyes, peering behind Hannah as though afraid she might have brought an army of ghosts. Hannah waited for Mrs Selwyn to say something – perhaps ask what she was doing here or who she was. But the woman said nothing, just continued to probe the space around Hannah with those frenetic eyes.

'My employer, Mr Monsarrat, sent me,' Hannah said eventually. 'He told me about the ghosts.'

Mrs Selwyn inhaled sharply, as though she had been holding her breath since Hannah knocked on the door.

'Nice man,' she said, 'with a nice voice. All the voices around here are rough – they don't caress you the way that man's voice does.'

Hannah cleared her throat, tried to keep the impatience out of her voice. 'He is also very generous. He wanted me to reward you for your help.' She lowered her voice. 'This is not a place to be flaunting anything valuable, not in the street. May I please come in?'

Mrs Selwyn stood aside, and Hannah walked into a dim parlour. Mrs Selwyn slumped into the armchair facing the window and gestured Hannah towards a rocking chair opposite it. Hannah sat carefully, hoping it would support her weight.

'You mentioned valuables,' Mrs Selwyn said.

Hannah felt in the coin pouch she'd sewn into her skirts. 'My employer suggested flowers,' she said, withdrawing three shillings from the pouch and holding them out to Mrs Selwyn. 'But you and I know that flowers do not fill a belly – or buy a woman the comfort of a dram of gin at the end of the day.'

Mrs Selwyn's eyes widened, and she reached out for the coins.

Hannah snapped her hand shut. 'Mr Monsarrat told me about ghosts.'

'Probably laughing as he did so,' said Mrs Selwyn. 'I do not think he is a believer.'

'You can hear my accent – you know that where I am from, ghosts are commonplace, and it can take a whole conversation to decide whether a figure you meet is of this earth. He may not be a believer, but I most certainly am. It's a fascination of mine. I wonder – if I were to add another shilling to this pile, might I occupy the chair that you are currently sitting in? You see, it has such an excellent view of the house you told him has the ghosts. I will not disturb you, and I'm sure you've better things to do than keep me company. But it is an opportunity I do not wish to pass up – hauntings are rarer than you think, even in Ireland.' Hannah opened her palm again, drew another coin from her pocket and dropped it onto the others. She held her hand out, open and flat as though she was feeding an apple to a horse.

Mrs Selwyn snatched the coins, stood up and, with a ridiculous flourish, gestured Hannah to the chair. She sat there, hoping she was the only living thing between the two armrests. Even through the lace curtain, she did have a good view of the front of the house. If she stayed alert long enough, she could hardly fail to miss anyone arriving or exiting.

'I'll leave you to it, then,' said Mrs Selwyn. 'Although if you stay beyond sunset, it'll be another shilling.'

'Which I shall pay happily. Oh, and may I ask, have you by any chance seen a child nearby in the past few hours?'

'Not a place for children,' Mrs Selwyn said.

I fear others might disagree with you, thought Hannah as Mrs Selwyn scuttled out of the room. After a minute Hannah could hear liquid being poured into a glass.

─⌇∽⌇─

The screech of rusted metal drew Hannah out of her lurid waking nightmares about Peter's fate. The noise sounded as though it was coming from the ghost house. Hannah crept as close as she dared to the window. If Henrietta did have a reason to visit this house, she was by no means stupid, and a disturbance of the lace curtains could be noticed by her as it had been by Hannah.

But Henrietta wasn't there. Instead, a man stood just outside the house's gate, staring over at the gaol. He had, perhaps, opened the gate and then closed it after him, and Hannah thanked it silently for making such a fuss and waking her. He had his back to her. He wore shirtsleeves with a loosely tied cravat. Mr Monsarrat, Hannah thought, would never allow himself out in public looking like that.

The man suddenly turned towards the ghost house as the door opened, and Hannah caught a glimpse of a precisely clipped moustache. He walked up the path towards the house. The lace through which Hannah was looking did nothing to dim the effect of the pink silk gown, reticule and parasol worn by the woman who stepped out to greet him at the door. The man bent over her hand and kissed it.

They were both turning to go inside, when the woman stopped sharply. She was frowning and staring through a crack between the lace curtains, directly at Hannah.

─⌇∽⌇─

The streets were quiet, which was hardly a surprise. The slanted light told of an afternoon drawing to a close; Monsarrat supposed it was not a fertile time for stallholders. And, of course, one of those stallholders was otherwise engaged at present. With Donnelly at his schoolroom, there would be no need to wade through protestors before pounding on the gaol doors and demanding admission. Monsarrat was not sure what he would find, but a surprise arrival might unearth all sorts of interesting information. Now that Chancel knew him, Monsarrat might be admitted a little more easily, and be given the chance to form a view based on a visit which hadn't been curated by Duchamp.

Monsarrat did not, however, get that far. As he was passing the houses opposite the gaol's high walls, a hand descended on his shoulder.

'Eejit of a man! Anyone can see you. Get out of sight, now!'

He turned and felt a momentary sense of dislocation – Mrs Mulrooney, where she shouldn't have been, and dressed in the clothes she loved but had needed to forswear. She was tugging him towards a narrow gap between two houses. 'I'd thought I was doing a good enough job of leaving unseen,' she said. 'And then you came striding along, you big black-and-white streak. Why don't you beat a drum, do a proper job of it!' Her eyebrows were drawn together by a thunderous brow. 'Close your mouth before something flies into it. Jesus, you look like you've seen a ghost! But then so have I, after a fashion.'

'Would you care to explain to me what you're doing near the gaol?' asked Monsarrat.

'Trying to get away from it. As you should be – for now.'

'Trying to ... But why would I? I need to find out whether Peter is there.'

'If he's not, then you've just annoyed Duchamp. If he is, the wardens are not likely to tell you. Did you think that Crowdy fella would open the door and say, "Of course, right this way, Mr Monsarrat, we'll take you to the cell where we're holding the boy"?' She shook her head, and Monsarrat hoped the students of the Female School of Industry never had cause to feel the weight of her disappointment. 'Mr Monsarrat, if you'd think, just for a minute. We're as sure as we can be that Peter wasn't arrested for pickpocketing – that he was taken by somebody who had cause to fear what Hallward had written. The best way to find him is to find that.'

'Yes, well, I agree with you, dear lady, except that is no simple matter.'

'Isn't it? I have some information on that score to share with you back at the boarding house, but let's not just go meandering down the street, though thankfully I doubt anybody's home, except that superstitious busybody, and Henrietta and Gerald Mobbs – who, it seems, are in Bancroft's house.'

'Henrietta and Mobbs? Together?'

'Oh yes, very much so. I saw them not half an hour ago. And she may have seen me. We'll need to go behind the houses. A few brambles, nothing you're not equal to. As long as you can break your usual habit and try, just for once, not crash around like a tethered bull.'

'Mrs Mulrooney, so far in the past couple of days, I've been referred to as defective, told that my only value is as an exemplar of phrenology, and compared to livestock. Do you think that for a few minutes you might refrain from insulting me?'

'That entirely depends, Mr Monsarrat, on whether you intend to behave yourself. Now come on, and quickly. I don't think Henrietta has left yet, but she could at any moment – and if she sees us, getting into the gaol will be the least of your problems.'

❦

'She looked right at me,' Mrs Mulrooney told Monsarrat. 'Whether she recognised me, I couldn't say.'

Mrs Mulrooney had given a shilling to Miss Douglas, asking her to go for a walk and allow them time alone in the kitchen.

She was in the process of brewing tea, something Monsarrat suspected she needed at the moment as much as he did.

'Hopefully not,' he said. 'She was not expecting to see you there, and people tend to dismiss and ignore things that they're not expecting.'

'That one, I think she probably expects anything,' said Mrs Mulrooney. 'Far more cunning than she lets on. Pretending to be sick so she can visit a man is one thing, but sending me to the School of Industry is another – she intended to keep me occupied.'

Mrs Mulrooney set a cup of tea in front of Monsarrat and sat down opposite him. 'Why was Gerald Mobbs calling at the house? He has an alibi for the time of the murder, and he's hardly the kind of man I'd imagine her associating with. I see her on the arm of an officer whose chest is so heavy with medals he can barely stand up.'

'I don't know. It's all very suggestive, but we can't assume anything except that they were at that house. I didn't know either of them were that tight with Albert Bancroft, though – assuming he does own the house.'

'Does he, though? Houses change hands, Mr Monsarrat.' Mrs Mulrooney always seemed to think best on her feet, and now she sprang up and prowled around the table as though guarding it. 'We are making assumptions. We are presuming Hallward's death was an attempt to prevent him from publishing his story. What if it's beyond that, though?'

'You had better tell me what you mean, dear lady.'

'The governor wants to license the media and impose a tax – this wouldn't just affect the *Chronicle*, would it?'

'No. As we've discussed, Mobbs would be out of business too.'

'Ah,' said Mrs Mulrooney, 'but if the thorn was removed – if Hallward was no longer there to nibble at the administration, to raise cries of cronyism and corruption, and if all that was left was one, well-behaved newspaper – there would be no need for taxes and licensing.'

'If you're right –'

'If I'm right, you will never be allowed back in that gaol except as an inmate. But in a way, it doesn't matter. Because we still need to find Hallward's final story so we can free that boy.'

Chapter 20

The mirror in the parlour was placed so that it absorbed the morning sun, sending blinding glints back to those unfortunate enough to be looking into it. Especially, thought Hannah, those who had been up all night plotting and fretting about a lost boy.

Glare and exhaustion made doing up the catch of that blasted brooch more difficult; Hannah had been fiddling with it for a full five minutes. And she had far more important tasks at hand – starting with another visit to the School of Industry. She hoped Henrietta would be sufficiently recovered from her false illness to be in attendance today. Hannah intended to march in, express surprise and joy at the young woman's quick recovery, and watch her face for any signs that she had seen Hannah peering through Mrs Selwyn's lace curtains. There was always something – a blink, a purse of the lips. Henrietta might be cunning, but she was only human.

'I very much fear, my friend,' said Monsarrat from behind her, 'that you were right.'

She had been so intent on the brooch that she hadn't heard him approaching, big-footed lummox that he was. She must not let that happen again – the next person to approach her might not be so benign.

'I usually am,' she said. 'You usually tell me I'm not. What has changed your mind?'

'This.' Monsarrat laid a copy of the *Colonial Flyer* on the table.

Monsarrat had taught Hannah to read, and she often looked at the newspapers which he invariably left lying around their parlour in Parramatta. Really, they left a lot to be desired: uniform columns, tiny headlines or none at all, just screeds of type going from one column to the next, with little to distinguish them. It wouldn't hurt journalists, she'd always thought, to make the headings a little larger.

Gerald Mobbs, it seemed, had unknowingly taken her advice. At the top of the first column, in big bold type, was the headline 'Investigation tarnished'.

> The investigation into the death of Henry Hallward, editor of the now-defunct *Sydney Chronicle*, has been compromised to the point of untenability by the character of the man leading it. In the absence of the governor, an unnamed authority has foisted on Ralph Darling's long-suffering private secretary a man whose background must call into question every word he utters.

Hannah's stomach clenched. The story seemed to be following a very short and straight path. She hoped she was wrong about where it was leading.

When she read the next paragraph, she wished she wasn't so often right.

> Hugh Llewelyn Monsarrat, who is currently barging his way into drawing rooms and prisons and, of all places, musical societies in what he says is the pursuit of justice, has himself been on the receiving end of our justice system.

Occupying a position that requires unimpeachable integrity, Mr Monsarrat first came to these shores having been convicted of forgery. Did he forge letters, perhaps? Promissory notes? No, his perfidy went beyond even these serious offences. He fabricated no less than a call to the bar, a qualification which enabled him to practise as a lawyer, representing unwitting clients in the courtrooms of Exeter. His crime, then, is doubly deplorable, as these good people paid for the representation of a qualified lawyer, and all the money he earned while plying his illegitimate trade can be considered to have been stolen.

Nor was Mr Monsarrat rehabilitated by his seven-year sentence – a risibly lenient decision of the court, which would have been justified in hanging him. On being granted his ticket of leave, Mr Monsarrat almost immediately breached its conditions, finding himself transported to Port Macquarie, a penal settlement where the most refractory are gathered and no doubt teach each other yet more imaginative ways to contravene the law.

This is the calibre of the man who has been charged with solving this most appalling slaying. The *Flyer* does not know what was behind the decision to appoint Mr Monsarrat. We do, though, submit this incontrovertible truth for our readers' consideration – that any assertions he makes, any findings of his investigation, must be treated with the greatest suspicion.

Hannah wanted to spit on the newspaper. She wanted to trample it beneath her feet and tear it to shreds. She settled, though, on throwing it into the parlour fire, where it browned and curled and sent up smoke she was afraid to breathe in, so noxious were the words.

Monsarrat took a poker and stirred the paper's ashes. 'I do wish that would help. Satisfying as it is, though, that was by no means the only copy of this morning's *Flyer*.' He tossed the poker aside, and it landed with a clang, breaking one of the flower-painted tiles that surrounded the fireplace.

'Miss Douglas will not be happy,' Hannah said.

Monsarrat whirled around to face her. The sudden movement from someone usually so precise, so deliberate, was jarring. 'Miss Douglas can go to the devil!' he roared. 'Along with Gerald Mobbs and Edward Duchamp and everyone else who sees me as damaged beyond repair!'

Hannah started. She had rarely heard his voice at such volume. 'It's unfair, and it's upsetting, but I am not your enemy. If you'd stop screaming, we can decide what to do.'

'What to do? What can I do? Everything Mobbs has written is true! I was relieved, after the pretence on Maria Island, that those in power knew I used to be a convict. But this! It impugns my integrity. Makes me look calculating. A creator of illusions. It's one thing for people to know I did not come here free. Another for them to have a slanted view of the crimes which brought me here fed to them with their breakfast. I will never, no matter how many murderers you and I bring to justice, be allowed to forget my past. They will disregard it when it suits them and smother me with it when I become a problem. Good God, why can't I be a simple clerk or a schoolmaster like Donnelly?'

'Now you'll stop that, Mr Monsarrat. Might as well ask why you weren't born a duke or an earl – or an Irish farmer. You don't deserve this, but Mr Hallward did not deserve to die. We can bring him justice, and we can save that lad – but only if you stop bleating about this and bend yourself to solving this murder. You must get justice for a brave man, and rescue a small boy.'

'I can do neither if I'm dismissed because of this slander,' said Monsarrat.

'Well, even if you are dismissed, it's not your fault if you don't know about it. Continue on. If you meet a closed door, go to the next one. But you will not go to Government House, and you will not be home to receive letters, so unless Duchamp comes looking for you, you've no reason to abandon your post. Even more reason to stick at it. Someone fears you are nearing the truth. Someone who knows all about your past.'

'You mean Duchamp? It's true that if the man is guilty and there needs to be an investigation, best it be conducted by someone who is easy to undermine.' Monsarrat shook his head and took a sip of tea. 'But we have so many other possibilities. Mobbs, of course – he's bound to know people who could find my convict records, without Duchamp's involvement. Albert Bancroft. Henrietta. Even Reverend Alcott.'

'Well, you'd better get started,' said Hannah, 'before too many people read the paper. Yes, the *Flyer* has attacked your integrity; yes, Sydney's finest drawing rooms are closed to you, but certain people – some of whom might have more information than we know – will view a denouncement from the *Flyer* as a stronger reason to trust you than a visit from the Archangel Gabriel.'

⁂

Hannah paused in front of the doors of the Female School of Industry. In her woollen truss, she believed that she looked fierce and severe. She was grateful for this, as it disguised the creeping nervousness that clenched and slithered inside her.

She could have sworn her eyes had connected with Henrietta's through the curtain. That she'd seen a flicker of recognition. But the lace had made everything hazy, and Henrietta had stopped only for a moment before turning towards the door. Perhaps she had simply seen a movement of the curtain and a dark shape behind it, and cursed the neighbour's curiosity.

The worst thing, Hannah told herself, would be to have gone undetected and then give herself away through nerves. Although, of course, this wasn't the worst thing. Because if Henrietta had seen her, had recognised her, then she had turned swiftly away to sow doubt in Hannah's mind. That would make Henrietta dangerous.

Hannah inhaled, squared her shoulders, smoothed down her jacket and stepped inside.

Henrietta was in the small office next to the classroom, writing quickly but without obvious haste. 'Miss Duchamp,' Hannah said. Henrietta did not look up, holding her left index finger in the air to ask Hannah to wait as she continued writing.

After a moment, she blotted the document, slowly folded it, set it aside and looked up. 'Mrs Mulrooney,' she said, smiling. 'I am surprised to see you, I must say.'

'I was sorry to hear of your illness. I am pleased to see you seem much recovered.'

'Yes. Some indispositions fell one like a tree but soon pass over. I feel quite myself this morning. Now, can I help you?'

'As a matter of fact, I had presumed that I would be the one doing the helping,' said Hannah. 'Not knowing how ill you were, I assumed there might be need of me here.'

Henrietta stood up. 'You are kind. But as you can see, I am perfectly capable of taking back the reins. Do allow me to walk you out, though.' There was no hand-patting now, no gentle touch on the elbow – Henrietta simply swept ahead of Hannah and expected to be followed. 'I understand it was a rather interesting lesson yesterday,' Henrietta said as they breached the door. 'I had to discipline my lady's maid for deserting her post. Not that I needed her, of course – I was in bed, resting. But she really must not leave without permission. If you are using her to set an example for the girls, I think it was a poor one.'

'I do apologise,' said Hannah. 'It was very thoughtless of me to take your maid away with you ill.'

'Don't worry about it for another moment,' said Henrietta, sure-footed as she descended the stairs to the front door. 'Although of course you'll ask next time, won't you? If you want something belonging to me.'

'Of course.'

'I do like you, you know. I knew about your nephew's past – well, Edward told me. I don't hold you responsible. It's not as though you're the convict.'

Did she know the truth, and was simply batting Hannah back and forth between her paws for amusement?

'A word of advice,' Henrietta said, opening the door to the street, 'from an experienced city woman to a neophyte.'

Hannah nodded, all respect and rapt attention.

'One hears so many rumours in Sydney. Intentions can so easily be misread that a simple mistake – yes, my dear, I'm sure it was a mistake – might come across as an act of malice. You will bear that in mind, won't you?'

'I will, and again I apologise,' said Hannah, but the door had closed.

Monsarrat pounded on the door of the *Flyer*'s office with such force that he had to pick a splinter from his hand. The man seemed to be connected to every aspect of this business, from the Duchamps to the duel. Monsarrat also wanted the editor to see the breathing man he had turned into a paper monster.

The door was dragged open by the same fellow who had admitted Monsarrat the other day. When he saw who was standing there, he smiled nastily. 'Your morning paper spoiled your breakfast, did it?'

'It did make it a little harder for me to choke down my egg. So I thought I'd return the favour to your proprietor. Is he in?'

'It is not usually our practice to admit irate people who have been the subject of this newspaper's attention,' the man said, beginning to close the door.

He stopped when a northern-accented voice behind him called out, 'For God's sake, let him in. He is not dangerous – the worst injury I'll sustain is a headache from his incessant talking.'

The man shrugged, opened the door and gestured Monsarrat inside.

Mobbs was standing at the bottom of the staircase that led up to his office. He beamed at Monsarrat as though at an old friend. 'Please do come up, Mr Monsarrat. No need to keep these men from their work.'

By the time Mobbs's office door closed behind him, Monsarrat's anger was beginning to flag. Until he saw the smirk on Mobbs's face as he settled behind the desk.

'Anyone,' Monsarrat said, 'would think that you do not want Hallward's killer apprehended.'

'I find that an odd interpretation of this morning's editorial,' said Mobbs. 'Obviously I would very much like to see the killer of a newspaper proprietor apprehended. All I did was question if you are the right man to do it.'

'You could have done that without slandering me.'

Mobbs extracted a copy of that morning's paper from his desk drawer, then set it between them so the story about Monsarrat was clearly visible. 'Do me a courtesy, if you would, Mr Monsarrat. Point to the section of this article that isn't true.'

'Why, it's all true, damn you, but painted a very unflattering shade.'

'There would be nothing to paint if you had not committed two crimes, Mr Monsarrat. Here in this colony, more than anywhere else, vigilant press is required to make sure the stains brought by criminals like you do not leak out and pollute the whole society.'

'If you were truly interested in a press that held wrongdoers to account, you would be supporting me in my attempts to identify Hallward's assassin.'

Mobbs's eyes turned furious in an instant. He stood up and thumped his fist on the table. 'I am sick to death of hearing about Hallward!' he yelled. 'The man has become a saint to some in death, and I assure you he never was one in life.

He has been praised as the guardian of the truth, voice of the voiceless, while those of us with more moderate views – which are no less important, I'll have you understand – are drowned out. No more, Mr Monsarrat! Now that Hallward is no longer frothing at the mouth in print every second day, there is room for other voices, those of us who guard the real truth – that this colony will only survive if the authority of the administration is not undermined. With Hallward no longer yelling in every ear, the voice of reason – *my* voice – will finally be heard!'

'It was heard loudly enough when you broke into Hallward's newsroom.'

'The accusations of involvement in the break-in are completely unfounded. That's why we went to the trouble of fighting a duel over them.'

'And does not your particular brand of pollution spread all the way to Government House? To the colonel's family? To his sister?'

Mobbs rounded the desk, grabbed Monsarrat by the lapels of his jacket and pulled him, so that Monsarrat could feel the man's spittle as he spoke.

'You will not, *sir*, presume to make any assumptions on that score. Should you decide to concern yourself with such matters, you will find I jealously defend my interests. And I might, Mr Monsarrat, be tempted to use more than a pen to do it.'

Mobb's veiled threat of violence distressed Monsarrat. Not for his own sake – violent men were a part of life in the colony. But this man might have Peter. And Monsarrat did not know whether consideration of the lad's tender years would be enough to prevent Mobbs using any means possible to extract Peter's secrets.

'I don't know what you expect to find, Mr Monsarrat,' said Mrs Mulrooney. 'Months ago, wasn't it? And, in any case, the duel was reported in the *Flyer*. It's not as though anyone was trying to conceal anything, to deny that it happened.'

'Reported in the *Flyer*, as you say,' said Monsarrat. 'Reported by Mobbs. You'll forgive me for being ill disposed towards anything that man writes.'

'I don't think it's a sin that requires forgiveness,' said Mrs Mulrooney.

She was almost running to keep up with Monsarrat's long strides, and seemed happy to do so, if it meant they could keep the appointment she had made the week before with Stephen Lethbridge.

'Hopefully Lethbridge has something. Did he tell you where in the gardens he would be? Our friend has a habit of collecting the most remarkable information, which people hand over with their payment for a pie,' said Monsarrat.

'Or they pay to make him stop talking about the Greeks and Romans,' said Mrs Mulrooney.

'My dear lady, I doubt such a thing is possible.'

Lethbridge had positioned himself directly inside the gardens' gates, where everyone entering and leaving could see him and inhale the scent that escaped his hotbox. Monsarrat and Mrs Mulrooney stood to the side while he served his last few customers, and those who had been clamouring for his pies lost interest in his discussion of the relative merits of Platonic and Aristotelian philosophy.

When the crowd dwindled Lethbridge jumped off his crate and bounded over to Monsarrat and Mrs Mulrooney, not stopping until Monsarrat's hand was in his. He pumped it up and down as though hoping to draw water. 'My dear fellow! Wonderful to see you. Parramatta is missing a dash of intellect. Do you know, I believe you're the only man in the entire town who reads Catullus in the original?'

Monsarrat smiled in spite of himself, clapped Lethbridge on the shoulder. 'And you, Mr Lethbridge. Odd as it is to see you out of your natural habitat.'

'Oh, I don't have one, Mr Monsarrat. Although I suppose you could say the road is where I actually belong.'

'And that road may have taken you to the door of somebody we are very interested in speaking to?'

Lethbridge gestured them over to a nearby bench. 'I hope you don't mind if I stand,' he said. 'My legs seize up if they're not constantly used, you see. And yes, Frank Gleeson – visiting his sister somewhere to the west, so Mrs Mulrooney told me.'

Monsarrat nodded. 'So the governor's private secretary said. But I would not necessarily set great store by his honesty.'

'Very wise, Mr Monsarrat, and I am about to prove you correct. Frank Gleeson, you see, does not have a sister.'

'How on earth would you know?'

'He told me. Just this week.'

'Extraordinary fellow you are,' said Mrs Mulrooney, 'to find him so quickly.'

'I actually found him a few weeks ago, only I didn't realise it. There's a house – well, it's more hole than wood – on the road to Blackheath. I have wagered with myself for quite a while now how long it would be before I scampered past to find it collapsed in on itself. But a few weeks ago I saw a man outside the place. Hammering new planks above the old, he was. My first thought was, *You won't be there long*. If he was intending to live in it, he'd have to tear it down and start again. The repairs he was making, they were enough to keep out the rain – the worst of it, anyhow. Why anyone would want to live there, though, I couldn't guess.'

'Your first thought,' said Mrs Mulrooney. 'There will be a second thought, then.'

'Ah, you're right, my lady. My second thought was that, at least from behind, the man doing all that hammering looked an awful lot like Frankie Gleeson. As he was in Sydney, though – or so I thought – I presumed it was a passing similarity.'

'But you went back there this week,' said Monsarrat.

'Yes – well, I had been given the task by this lady here,' said Lethbridge. 'And I know better than to deny her. And when I knocked on the door – not too hard, mind, didn't want to send the place crashing down – Gleeson answered.'

'Happy to see you, was he?' asked Monsarrat.

'Hardly. Tried to close the door again. But wardens don't make that much money, particularly when they have deserted their posts and are not being paid, so the offer of a few free pies was enough to get me in there.'

'What was he doing there in the first place, though?' Monsarrat asked. 'And what did he tell you?'

'Not a lot,' said Lethbridge. 'I have to say, the man seemed frightened. And miserable – getting cold at night now in mountains, and he only had a bedroll and a little fire. He was cooking a bandicoot over it when I arrived. Not terribly good eating, those creatures – not all the pastry and gravy in the world could disguise their stringiness. Believe me, I tried.'

'Do you think we'd have any luck if we went out to see him?' Monsarrat asked. 'Or would that send him further into his burrow?'

'I can't answer that. Nor will I need to – he will be here this afternoon.'

'Why on earth would he come back to Sydney if he is so frightened?'

'I think he is beginning to fear starvation more. And I did tell him that I would conceal his return. Gave him the address of an inn near Camperdown. Told him that you will have paid his lodging by the time he arrives, so you'd best hurry.'

Mrs Mulrooney gave Lethbridge a loud kiss on the cheek. He blushed, rubbing the spot. 'Very forward of you, Mrs Mulrooney.'

She laughed, but the sound faded quickly. 'You've ... you've no news of my Padraig?'

Lethbridge frowned. 'I'm sorry, no. You mustn't assume anything, though – my range only extends so far.'

For a moment, Mrs Mulrooney looked on the brink of tears. Then she swallowed, straightened.

'May I ask,' said Lethbridge, 'how you are getting on with Miss Henrietta Duchamp?'

'How am I ... an odd question.'

'Allow me to explain. The staff at Government House are not immune to the charms of my pies, although woefully ignorant of philosophy. I let it be known that you are well regarded among the Irish aristocracy. That despite your humble pretensions you are a wealthy woman, much sought after for your wisdom. Thought it might help, and I hope it has.'

Mrs Mulrooney seemed to be struggling to suppress a smile.

'And you'll be taking something for your trouble,' she said.

'I certainly wouldn't reject it. An offer to pay for the pies I gave Frank would be met with acceptance as well. That's the only problem shared by pies and philosophy – there's not a lot of money in either of them.'

Chapter 21

'I was rather surprised to receive your letter of the third instant,' Eveleigh had written in a hand which bore none of Monsarrat's curlicues or flourishes. It was practical but unadorned, like the owner of the hand it had come from.

> I know you are keenly aware of the condition attached to your continued freedom – the discreet investigation of matters of sensitivity. I know you appreciate that this investigation has to occur at arm's length from myself and this office.
> You were also warned, as I recall, to expect obstacles, and that there would be little I could do to intervene. I have faith that you will find a way through your current difficulties and bring this matter to an acceptable end, and I look forward to hearing of your success.

There were none of the usual niceties. In the world in which Eveleigh moved, it was highly irregular to begin a letter without a flowery declaration that the writer was honoured. And the fact that this letter was signed only with the initials R. E. told

Monsarrat more about the fastidious Eveleigh's irritation than any words could have.

Monsarrat looked over the top of the letter and across the table towards Mrs Mulrooney.

'From himself?' she asked.

'Yes, as it happens. We are on our own.'

'When have we not been? The rest of the colony need not know that, though. As far as everyone else is concerned, you have the colonel's blessing to carry out this investigation in whatever way you see fit. If one were, say, one of the colony's administrators, one would be used to keeping secrets – and flattered to be trusted to do so.'

'I suppose, but who are you –'

It made Monsarrat slightly nervous that Mrs Mulrooney never allowed her fan to stray too far from her. It sat on the breakfast table at her elbow now, and she snatched it up quickly and administered a sharp rap to his knuckles.

'Honestly,' he said, rubbing his hand, 'I feel as though I'm back in the schoolroom.'

'Perhaps you should be, Mr Monsarrat. Perhaps then, you'd remember to think. You would also remember a certain gentleman we met at the garden party. One who is a great admirer of your hand, and one who can give you access to more documents than anyone else in the colony. At least he may if he hasn't read this morning's *Flyer*.'

───※───

The Colonial Secretary's Office was housed in one of the colony's finer buildings. Its striated sandstone blocks were all completely flat where other buildings bore the protrusions and chisel marks of those who had taken the rocks from the earth.

Inside, a clerk sat at a desk, a large ledger open in front of him. 'Sir, I am sorry but nobody can be seen without an appointment,' he said when Monsarrat confessed that Alexander Hawley was not expecting him.

'You may find he's willing to make an exception on my behalf. We met at Government House.'

The clerk paused. Hawley no doubt mentioned his invitation there at every opportunity. 'It is most irregular,' the clerk said, 'but I shall ask him, if you care to wait.'

He was back within a few minutes, with Hawley beetling along in his slipstream. 'Mr Monsarrat!' The chief clerk grabbed his hand, shaking it vigorously. 'I was telling Thompkins about you – wasn't I, Thompkins?' The junior clerk looked up, gave a tight smile, and fixed his eyes back on the letter in front of him. 'Wonderful for someone like him to know that it's possible to rise from a mere desk clerk to working at the highest levels, doing ... what is it that you're doing, actually, Mr Monsarrat?'

Monsarrat allowed himself to exhale slowly. Either Hawley had not seen the paper, or it didn't matter to him, or, better yet and as Mrs Mulrooney had suggested, it burnished the position he already held in this man's eyes.

'It's on that point I've come to see you, Mr Hawley.'

Hawley smiled expectantly.

'I'm afraid that as it's a matter of state, we will need to have this discussion somewhere more private.'

'Of course, of course!' said Hawley. 'Right this way. Hold the fort there, Thompkins. You heard Mr Monsarrat – I have affairs of state to attend to.'

'It's of the utmost importance that you don't speak about this to anyone,' said Monsarrat. 'Even Colonel Duchamp would deny knowledge if you asked about it – while marking you down as someone who can't be trusted. Discretion is rewarded.'

Hawley was nodding so quickly that his spectacles threatened to slide off the end of his nose. Monsarrat shifted uncomfortably in the small chair he had been offered. Hawley's office was small, and overrun by journals, ledgers, and sheets of yellowing paper rolled up and bound with red ribbon. There was barely room for a second chair, and Monsarrat's knees were pressed uncomfortably against Hawley's desk.

'I wonder, Mr Hawley – given your knowledge of the place, you're probably the only person who can help me. Could you tell me where I might find land grants? And house deeds.'

'No trouble at all, though it would help if you could tell me which land grant or deed you're looking for.'

'I would if I were able to. But I'm afraid I'm not at liberty to give out that information.' In a way, it was true: he was not authorised to be having this conversation at all.

Half an hour later, Monsarrat was sitting at a small table among rows of shelves, hemmed in by a fortress of ledgers. Hawley had given a tour, telling him where the information was filed. It was a convoluted filing system, though, and he would have dearly loved to tell Hawley precisely what he was looking for. That, of course, was impossible, so he had to flick through hundreds of lists of names.

It seemed Hallward had been right in criticising the administration for patronage. Three times since he'd taken office, the governor had made substantial grants of land to Duchamp – enough to make the man rich, if he had any facility at all with agriculture, or the sense to hire someone who did. It was pleasing to have the information, but not really revelatory – Monsarrat had believed Hallward's writings on the subject. He knew that the colony, so distant from its mother, operated like this.

It was when he turned the page of the ledger of title deeds, though, that he knew his trip had been worthwhile. It turned out that Albert Bancroft had sold the house opposite the gaol three months earlier. And in the column next to the address, a clerk had written the name of the new owner: Gerald Mobbs.

Emerging from the room, rubbing his eyes, he did not immediately notice Hawley was standing right near the door.

'Has that effect on me too,' Hawley said. 'There's only so long one can stare at writing on a page, no matter how fascinating one finds it.'

'Fascinating, but sadly not fruitful in this case,' Monsarrat said. 'However, I did think of a question I wanted to ask you. Gerald Mobbs. You know him?'

'Ah, yes, the editor. The only one now. He was at the garden party, of course. Very interested in my file room. Can't say I blame him.'

'No, indeed. So he was here on the day Henry Hallward was killed?'

'Quite. He wanted to fossick around – among the property titles actually, same as yourself. Only, he didn't get much of a chance. He needed a bit of a rest when he got here. He arrived in a lather, as though he'd run all the way. And he left as soon as the word of Mr Hallward's murder came.'

'So what time did Mr Mobbs arrive? Must have been late morning – I believe the murder occurred around ten?'

'Ten? Oh, I don't think so. It's only five minutes quick walk from the gaol and our messenger was here with news of the shooting just after Mobbs arrived. That was a little after half past ten.'

'Well, various sources have said Hallward was shot around ten,' Monsarrat said, puzzled. 'Mr Hawley, are you sure?'

Hawley pointed to a clock on the room's mantelpiece. 'You can rest assured that this is one of the most accurate clocks in the colony. I checked the time that day so I could enter the events in my log.'

Monsarrat thought of the clock in the gaol, and felt something flop over in the pit of his stomach. Hawley trusted his clock, Monsarrat thought. Just as those at the gaol had trusted theirs.

Taking his hat from the table where he had laid it, he bowed to Hawley and strode to the door, breaking into a run the instant it closed behind him.

He had no memory of most of the journey and did not slow as he approached the gaol, almost slamming into the door, raising his fist to hammer on it. It occurred to him he must be the only former convict trying to get in rather than out.

The door was cautiously opened by Chancel.

'I won't take much of your time,' Monsarrat said, pushing past him.

Chancel followed him into the entrance room. 'I can't let you go any further,' he said.

'Fine,' said Monsarrat. He stared at the clock, then opened the register underneath it, turning to the page which recorded the gaol's comings and goings. 'Chancel, look here.' He tapped his finger on the time of the arrival of the prison cart. 'The cart was early that day. And the few days around it. Why?'

'Oh, it wasn't, although the driver caught an earful from Mr Crowdy at the time,' said Chancel.

'He wasn't early?'

'No, sir. Not as it turned out. A few days later, you see, the surgeon came. Got out his pocket watch. Showed it to me. The clock was half an hour slow. I changed it back immediately, sir.'

<hr />

'So Mobbs owns the house from which the murder was committed, and arrived at the Colonial Secretary's Office flustered and bothered only a short time after we now think the murder happened,' Hannah said. 'No mistake in Hawley's clock, I'm sure.'

'None at all,' said Monsarrat. He was in the same state Mobbs was on the day of the murder, having run to the boarding house to find Mrs Mulrooney. 'Chancel said that when Duchamp inspected the gaol, he took an interest in everything, including the clock. But if we act now, the colonel could have us both in gaol with a nod of his head, and Peter would likely be lost forever. All we have is a slow clock, an exerted newspaper editor and the deed to a house. Even though Mobbs owns it, we could not irrefutably prove he's been staying there, much less shooting people from the attic. We need incontrovertible evidence. Frank Gleeson might be able to give it to us.'

'Well, someone lives there, or at least is there at night,' said Hannah. 'And Emily was delivering food. Who was it for, if not Mobbs and Henrietta?'

'We should visit the house on the way back from seeing Gleeson,' Monsarrat said.

'And I might be able to make another small expenditure on behalf of the investigation,' said Hannah. 'Mobbs and Henrietta would expect us to travel on foot, or perhaps in a small cart. If they saw a coach and wondered at its occupants, the last people they would think of would be us.' She reached into a pocket and pulled out a small cloth bag that jingled as it moved. She pressed it into his hand. 'Mr Monsarrat, I have an errand for you. Go out and rent a coach. A good one, but not ...' She held up a finger, extracted her little book from the other pocket, and flipped through the pages. 'Ostentatious – yes, I think that will do very nicely. Off you go, Mr Monsarrat.'

'Very well,' he said, standing. 'I believe I know just the man to help us.'

McCarthy's coach was perfect, declared so by Mrs Mulrooney. It was a demure dowager, so comfortable in its standing that it didn't need to display itself by decking itself with baubles. The coach was black, with gold pinstripes around the doors, the paint unchipped and the seats inside comfortably stuffed. Monsarrat worried, though, that even an understated vehicle might find itself an object of interest in the part of town he had visited earlier that day to pay in advance for the room where Frank Gleeson was hopefully waiting for them.

It was early evening when they arrived in Camperdown. The sky looked like slate, and it would be dark by the time they emerged. Monsarrat got out and offered his hand to Mrs Mulrooney, who ignored it and jumped lightly down to the pavement.

'I'm not sure how long we'll be,' Monsarrat said to McCarthy. 'Will you be all right here?'

'You needn't worry about me – it's not my first time in this part of town,' McCarthy said, opening his jacket.

Monsarrat could see a pistol in his belt. 'Does everyone in Sydney own a gun?'

'Only the intelligent ones.'

The oldest of Sydney's buildings had been constructed when Monsarrat was a child. After arriving from England he had missed, at first, walking through squares and doors that had stood for centuries, or down corridors in the Temples by the Thames whose walls had absorbed the whispered conversations of Tudor courtiers. This was, of course, the least of his worries at the time, and not something he had thought about for over a decade.

The building they entered now, though, looked as though it had been standing for a century or more – and didn't appear to be in a fit state to last much longer. Its roof bowed alarmingly in the middle, and Monsarrat saw a few broken shingles, no longer able to hold on to the steep slope, littering the pavement. The place didn't appear to have been painted since it was built, with large patches of raw wood showing through a colour that was probably once white. Windowpanes that had been broken – perhaps by weather, but more likely with the assistance of locals – had not been replaced, and planks had been nailed across the openings. A parlour of sorts was downstairs, with an extinct fire and a grate out of which ashes were raining onto the floor.

Monsarrat turned to Mrs Mulrooney. 'I know what you're thinking, and we don't have time.'

'If I can find a brush, I can at least deal with those smuts.' She nodded at the fire.

'And they'll be back by next week,' said Monsarrat. 'Come along. McCarthy may have a gun, but I'd rather he not have to use it.'

The stairs were uneven, covered with a torn rug that seemed designed to trap an unwary toe. At the top of the stairs, two doors faced each other. A small amount of light was leaking from beneath one of them.

Monsarrat looked at Mrs Mulrooney, raised his eyebrows and knocked. 'Frank Gleeson?' No one answered, but Monsarrat heard the creaking of bed springs as somebody shifted around. 'It's Hugh Monsarrat,' he called.

'And Hannah Mulrooney,' Mrs Mulrooney said. 'Stephen Lethbridge's friends.'

More creaking, and the door was opened by a man in shirtsleeves, without a cravat. 'You were followed?' he said, peering around the door as though anticipating an ambush.

'No. Would you expect us to be?'

'I don't know what to expect now. You could have tried to be a bit more discreet, though.' He inclined his head towards the window.

Monsarrat walked over and saw McCarthy still sitting on his seat, hand near his pistol.

'Who do you think would be following you, sir?' asked Mrs Mulrooney. 'Oh, by the way, may I sit down?' The room, in addition to a bare mattress on the rusted base, contained a small table with one rickety chair.

'By all means,' said Gleeson. 'Although I can't vouch for the stability of the chair.' He took another glance out of the window. 'I'm only here because of Lethbridge. That man is a keeper of secrets. Can't get him to shut up about Socrates, but whatever you pour into his ear will not come out of his mouth, not if you ask him to keep silent.'

'Yes,' said Monsarrat, 'he's trustworthy – in that way, at least. He explained what we're doing here?'

'Yes. And as you're working for the colonel, I very nearly stayed in the mountains. Lethbridge says the man doesn't know, though.'

'The colonel will not be informed of this meeting, or your location,' said Monsarrat. 'In any case, you may be worrying for nothing – Duchamp is not aware you are not simply visiting your sister.'

'Oh, he's aware. That much I guarantee you. Lethbridge agreed to do me a great service – I asked him to go to my cottage in The Rocks today, see if everything was secure or if anyone odd was hanging about.'

'And what did he find?'

'A mess,' said Gleeson. 'Door hanging off the hinges. Furniture overturned. Someone had taken a knife to my armchair, and my mattress. And the sideboard had been taken to pieces – the drawers pulled out, torn apart.' He turned to Mrs Mulrooney. 'My mother gave me that sideboard, missus.'

'I'm sure she'd care far more about your safety than that of the sideboard,' Mrs Mulrooney said.

'It doesn't matter, and I doubt I'll be going back there.'

'Why not?' asked Monsarrat. 'When this is over?'

'It may not ever be over,' said Gleeson. 'If certain secrets remain that way, the colonel will never stop looking for me. And if they come out – this administration is not likely to reward me by allowing me to resume my post.'

'When you speak of secrets . . . ?' asked Monsarrat.

'Those which Henry Hallward uncovered. Those which, as night follows day, he was killed for.'

'We believe that the young copyboy, Peter, has been taken perhaps because someone thinks he has Hallward's final story,' Mrs Mulrooney said.

'It would make sense,' Gleeson said. 'Peter was on his way to collect the story when Hallward was shot. But they are wasting their time.'

'And why is that?'

'Because that boy doesn't have the story. I do.'

He stood, reached underneath the mattress, extracted some papers and spread them on the table. He seemed unwilling to dislodge Mrs Mulrooney from her chair, so he kneeled beside her as they both scanned them.

This newspaper has uncovered a conspiracy so vile, and so vast, that it threatens the soul of the colony. Regular readers will know that this newspaper has often brought to light instances of nepotism, favouritism and patronage. Many of these surround the governor's principal private secretary, Colonel Edward Duchamp.

What they will not be aware of, as very few people are, is that this largesse extends to exclusive contracts for the transport of grain from the interior to Sydney to a company owned by Colonel Duchamp. This means the colonel will profit from every bite of bread eaten in this town.

Lest we be accused of an undue focus on the governor's staff, we beg to note that his generosity extends beyond those who work for him. Mr Gerald Mobbs, editor and proprietor of the *Colonial Flyer*, has recently found himself enriched by the gift of a property opposite the gaol from whence this article is being written. The previous owner of the property? Albert Bancroft, the colonel's great friend, his second in at least one duel. We also have it on good authority that Mr Mobbs's company is about to be granted the exclusive contract for government printing.

The governor is no friend of the press, you may say, especially if you learned in these pages that he was considering a tax on newspapers and a licensing regime that would limit our ability to report the truth. So why would he be extending such kindness to one of the town's two newspaper proprietors?

Those of you who have lived in Sydney for any length of time, or recall it before the foundation of the *Chronicle*, know that in its early years the *Flyer* was simply an unabashed mouthpiece for the government. Its contents were limited to government announcements, reports on courts and crops and weather. But there was no criticism, no investigation, no opinion. The newspaper simply printed what the government wanted it to.

I opened the *Chronicle* because I had trouble believing the government was perfect – and because history has told us that those administrations which try to present themselves as the most virtuous are, quite often, the least. Since then, of course, my suspicions have been confirmed many times over. The reporting in these pages has met with the approval of many in Sydney, to the extent that the *Flyer* had to take a more independent stance in order not to lose all of its readers, because who would pay to be lied to?

But this did not suit Mr Mobbs. He yearned for the time when he could pour platitudes and lies onto the page, spread them out like butter on bread, and charge for them. And the administration longed for the days, banished under the previous governor, when those in government chose what facts were presented to the public, when those who contributed to the colony through hard work and noble endeavour were rewarded with pap. Of course, that tyranny of information left many hungry, and not everyone believed they were receiving the truth about their government, but they had no recourse, no source of truth.

We are now on the cusp of returning to those grim days. Why? Because a conspiracy exists between Mr Gerald

Mobbs, Colonel Edward Duchamp and his sister Miss Henrietta Duchamp, to bring about the destruction of the *Chronicle* – and, with it, any hope of appropriate scrutiny on the actions of the administration.

As I previously mentioned, I am writing this article from prison, and will this very day face court on a charge of criminal libel over my exposure of the governor's grants to his toady in chief. So, a reader might ask, do I not have an interest in denigrating both my competitor and the administration that continually arrests me? Can anything I write be trusted, particularly an accusation of this nature?

But proof exists, in the form of letters between Mobbs and Duchamp, intercepted by me and published in full in these pages. It is my fervent hope that thanks to these disclosures, I will leave prison and step into a colony where the rights of all are respected, and where those whose only aim is to fearlessly report the facts are not continually incarcerated for doing so.

Monsarrat had not realised he had been gaping, until he felt the dryness inside his mouth. 'This is . . . This is . . .'

'Astounding,' said Mrs Mulrooney.

'And dangerous,' said Gleeson.

'How did it come to be in your possession?' asked Monsarrat.

'I tucked it into my shirt as soon he had finished writing it. My deputy at the gaol, Crowdy, was not nearly so well disposed towards Mr Hallward. Crowdy could not be allowed to see it, even though he knew Hallward and I had what we will call "an arrangement".'

'And this arrangement included access to paper and ink, and the ability to get documents out of the gaol?'

'Yes. Among other comforts, which had very little bearing on his ability to write a story or otherwise.'

'Did anyone come looking for the story?'

'I wouldn't know, Mr Monsarrat,' said Gleeson. 'Hallward told me a lad was to collect the story, but I didn't know when he'd arrive, and even if he had come he wouldn't have been given it. I was at sixes and sevens after the shooting, and I felt I had no choice but to take it with me. When I read it, I ran.'

'Why?'

'They would be sure to find out. Crowdy would tell them I was helping Hallward. He's been wanting to be rid of me for years, says I'm too kind to certain of the prisoners. He would be only too happy to let them know I was taking money from a prisoner in exchange for favours. The fact that it was *that* prisoner – well, they would assume I knew what the story said. And mine would be the next head with a ball in it.'

'Why not hand it in then?'

Gleeson stood and walked over to the window, looking down at the coachman. He turned back into the room. 'Still no one there, thank God,' he said. 'You mustn't think much of my principles, Mr Monsarrat – taking bribes from a prisoner and so on.'

'Your principles aren't the ones at issue here, Mr Gleeson.'

'It might surprise you to know,' he said, 'but I believed in Hallward. In what he was doing. Yes, I was happy to profit from him. The risks I took deserved some compensation. But nothing could induce me to take those risks in the first place if I did not think that a rot was growing, and that Hallward was able to expose it, perhaps fix it. I would never have handed in those pages, Mr Monsarrat. My friend died for them.'

Monsarrat looked at Gleeson for a moment, and nodded. 'And those letters he mentioned. The proof.'

'From what I understand, they are in the custody of a man who was braver than I am – a man who stayed at his post even as I deserted mine. If the governor's men haven't got to the letters already, you'll find them in the possession of Mr Cullen, at the offices of the *Chronicle*.'

Chapter 22

The coach came to a stop a small distance away from the house opposite the gaol, but the argument within it continued. The windows, thankfully, were closed. There was little wind, and at this time of night no noises to conceal a conversation. A stray, starved dog wandered past, sniffed at the coach wheels and then scuttled away when the horse snorted.

'It is too dangerous!' said Monsarrat. 'Henrietta may already be aware that you are suspicious.'

'Mr Monsarrat, as dangerous as it is for us, it's even more so for young Peter. His only hope of survival, if he is still alive, is if they believe he has the story and is refusing to tell them. And of course he has a story of his own now, doesn't he? So we must get to him before anything comes out.'

Monsarrat shook his head. 'Very well. I'll go and see what I can find.'

'You're never going by yourself, Mr Monsarrat. Without me to look after you, you might be in all sorts of trouble.'

He slapped his hand on his thigh in frustration. 'You are ... *the* most infuriating ... woman in creation.'

'And I'm ... coming ... with you.' She smiled to take the sting out of the mimicry.

'If I have to lock you in this coach –'

'I'll find a way out, and I'll be on my own for a time until I find you, which will put me in more danger. You cannot prevent me coming with you, and I might get hurt if you try.'

'All right, then. You must promise me, though – the first sign of trouble, you'll be back to the coach.'

Again, he offered her his hand to help her down, and again she ignored it and jumped quietly onto the cobbles.

'I wonder,' Monsarrat said to McCarthy, 'if I might ask you a favour.'

'For an additional fee, you can ask whatever you like.'

'Can you warn us if you see someone coming?'

McCarthy pulled back on Sally's reins, and the horse whinnied. 'How's that? She never does it otherwise, not unless there's a trough nearby.'

Monsarrat nodded, handed over a coin, and silently gestured Mrs Mulrooney towards the house. She whispered, 'There is a lane at the side. Might be wise to start there.'

'The lane sounds like an excellent idea,' said Monsarrat. They did their best to stay in the pools of darkness created by the shadows of overhanging branches and walls. It became harder, though, as they approached the house. Lamplight in the windows – somebody was home.

The front windows, as it turned out, were not the only ones lit. In the darkness, they could see light coming from the side of the house, close to the ground.

'I didn't notice it there before,' said Mrs Mulrooney. 'Wouldn't have noticed it now, if not for the light. A cellar?'

Monsarrat shrank down and crept closer, with Mrs Mulrooney beside him. The light was coming from a grated aperture, too small to be called a window. When he looked in, he had to clasp his hand over his mouth to stop a gasp.

He glanced up and saw Mrs Mulrooney, stricken, biting her knuckle in a similar effort to remain silent.

The aperture was the only opening in the room, apart from a closed door. The cellar itself was made of rough stone, with a wooden floor from which a few planks were missing. A dish encrusted with food, hours if not days old, sat by the door. The only furniture was a small, bare mattress. On it was the curled, emaciated form of a boy, facing the wall.

Peter wasn't moving. He might be alive, Monsarrat thought, but the leftover food by the door clearly wasn't fresh.

Then the boy stirred, turned around and opened his eyes.

Mrs Mulrooney gasped, and the sound flew into the cellar on the still air. Peter looked up at the window, saw her and started to cry silently.

'Hush-hush-hush, lamb,' whispered Mrs Mulrooney. 'I think that someone is in the house with you. Just nod if that's true, don't speak.'

Peter nodded.

'Have they beaten you, hurt you?'

He shook his head, and Mrs Mulrooney exhaled slowly. 'But you want to go, and they won't let you. Because they think you know something, and they don't believe you when you say you don't.'

Peter nodded again, and his lower lip began to quiver.

'Now I want you to be very brave,' Mrs Mulrooney said. 'It will be over soon. My friend Mr Monsarrat and I are coming to save you. But we cannot do it now, because someone is there. First thing in the morning, though, we will be back and you will be free. But you have to pretend we were not here, otherwise they might take you somewhere else and we won't be able to find you.'

Peter nodded, but then gasped as the door to his cell began to open. Monsarrat and Mrs Mulrooney flattened themselves against either side of the window.

They heard footsteps, light ones. They did not dare look, and as it turned out they didn't need to, because Henrietta had the kind of voice that carried well. 'Do I hear voices?'

'Just humming, Miss Duchamp,' Peter said. His voice was surprisingly steady.

'Hm. And you have not changed your mind? Decided to be honest?'

'I am honest.'

There was a silence.

'You know, don't you, that we mean you no harm?' Henrietta said quietly. 'When this is over, we will find you a position. A good one. The stables of Government House, perhaps? Would you like that?'

'Yes, miss.'

'But first you need to help us. You can't possibly understand, a child of your age, what will happen if you don't. You can't know anything of revolt. And I do not want you to. I am trying to protect you, everyone, from a future of chaos.'

'I told you all I know, miss.'

'So you keep saying. I would like to believe you.' She sighed heavily. 'Very well, this is tiresome for both of us. I will give you the rest of the evening to think about it. And I mean truly think about it, Peter. The people who could get hurt. Unrest in the colony. And you – you're the only one who can do something about it.'

Footsteps sounded again. When Henrietta next spoke, her voice was closer to the window. 'I want to be your friend, Peter. I want to help you, but you need to help me. I will bring down some soup shortly. And after that, the next time I enter this room, I do hope we'll have a change of heart.' A few more footsteps, and the door creaked. 'Say your prayers now, and get some sleep, there's a good boy.'

After they heard the door closing, Mrs Mulrooney peered in

through the window again. She did not dare risk speaking, but gave Peter a reassuring smile.

From the street, a horse whinnied. Mrs Mulrooney grabbed Monsarrat's arm, dragged him to his feet with surprising strength and motioned towards the back of the house. A proud householder might have created a garden, but here there was only scrubby dirt. No hiding places.

From around the corner, they heard the rustle of footsteps, slowly making their way down the side of the house. Then Henrietta's voice again, this time closer. 'Good to see you kneeling, Peter,' she called out, probably speaking to him through the window. Then more rustling, as Henrietta's silk gown dragged along the ground.

Monsarrat and Mrs Mulrooney huddled in the darkest corner of the backyard. He was not at all confident of escaping detection, but there was no better hiding place to be found.

The horse whinnied again, and the footsteps stopped and began to recede. They heard a quiet conversation in the distance.

Eventually, the talking stopped, and they heard what sounded like the front door closing. Monsarrat, uncomfortably crouched in a pool of darkness, made to stand, but Mrs Mulrooney pulled him down. 'Not yet,' she whispered. 'She's crafty.'

Five minutes later, the front door of the house opened again and did not close for some minutes. When it did, Mrs Mulrooney led Monsarrat up the other side of the house, where they could reach their coach without passing the front door. Monsarrat did not wait, this time, for Mrs Mulrooney to ignore his offer of help – he grasped her around the waist and lifted her into the coach, diving in after her.

He rapped on the front window of the coach. 'The *Chronicle*,' he whispered.

Once they had turned the corner and left the gaol behind, together with the house that had become another gaol, Mrs Mulrooney leaned forward and gave Monsarrat a hard rap on the knuckles with her fan. 'You will not treat me like a sack of potatoes again, Mr Monsarrat. I am perfectly capable of getting into a coach at speed. Do not forget what I have been through, and the resilience it has given me.'

'I do apologise – you're absolutely right.'

'And we're to go to the *Chronicle* now, are we?' she said, her arms crossed.

'Well, yes, do you disagree? We can always –'

'Of course I agree, eejit of a man. We must get those letters, and Cullen's probably out of his mind with worry by now. And after that, Mr Monsarrat, we will be getting that boy, and they will find out what former convicts are really capable of.'

~~~

The little coin purse Hannah carried was getting light. It was made lighter still when a few more shillings were passed over to McCarthy.

'What did herself say to you?' Hannah asked McCarthy as they pulled up outside the peeling door of the *Chronicle*.

'Asked me what I was doing there,' said the coachman. 'Told her I was waiting to collect somebody. She asked who, I told her it was none of her business.'

'Very good of you,' said Monsarrat. He clapped McCarthy on the shoulder. 'I do appreciate it.'

McCarthy flicked the reins, began to move off. 'Behave yourselves now,' he called over his shoulder. 'I'll fish you out of trouble if I have to, but I'm far too lazy to enjoy it.'

Monsarrat rapped quietly on the door of the *Chronicle* offices. After a few moments, he and Hannah looked at each other, and she gestured towards a larger arched gate. Perhaps, she thought, they could find something thin, like a piece of bark, and use it to lift the latch.

But then the door slowly opened.

'Have you found him?' asked Cullen, peering around to see if Peter was waiting behind them.

'Yes,' said Hannah. 'We don't have him, not yet,' she added hastily, when a smile began to form on Cullen's face. 'We will, but we need your help.'

He nodded, gesturing them inside. 'I haven't seen my cottage in days. I've been sleeping here since Peter disappeared. In case he comes back. I didn't want him to be locked out – it's the only home he has.'

'And he will have again, if that is what he wants,' said Hannah. 'First though, I want to tell you a story. If we are correct, it is a story you already know.'

'It wasn't looters, of course,' said Cullen when Hannah had finished talking. He had settled her behind Hallward's desk, and she did feel it suited her. 'I can't prove it – I wasn't here – but not enough was taken. They could have melted down the type blocks, for instance, but they just smashed the frames. And Mr Hallward's purse was still in his desk, even though the drawers were pulled out. If he'd been keeping the letters anywhere in the building, they would have found them.'

'But Gleeson said you had them,' Hannah said.

'Mr Hallward may well have told him that, for the purposes of secrecy. He wasn't above a little misinformation when it suited him.'

'But they must exist,' Hannah said. 'Hallward surely would have kept them somewhere safe.'

Cullen frowned. He reached for a piece of paper and a pencil stub, then scribbled something and handed it to Hannah. It was an address. One to the east of the harbour.

'There is only one place I can think of,' Cullen said. 'But I can't go myself. It is not appropriate to call on a lady so late at night – unless you're another lady.'

※

The cottage was small, but where many front yards were scrub or bare earth, this one had a path bordered in carefully placed flowerbeds. Some sprouted roses of the kind that were hard to coax along in this salt-soaked air.

Monsarrat had insisted on coming with Hannah in the coach, staying hidden as she went in but ready to help if help was needed. They both knew that Carolina would never answer her door to a man.

A dim light shone from between the not-quite-closed curtains. Hannah knocked. Waited. Knocked again.

Carolina opened the door. She was wrapped in a brocade robe, a late-night scowl on her face.

'Miss Albrecht, I apologise for calling on you so late. May I come in? It is a matter of some urgency.'

'Your urgency may not be mine. Have you come to remind me what a disgrace I am?'

'I have come to beg for your help.'

'You should beg elsewhere.'

'I gave you an opportunity once before to help a boy. What I am about to ask might help him too – but it might also help you. Help all of us. Help everyone understand why Henry Hallward was killed, and to appreciate the consequences of leaving that crime unpunished.'

※

In the backyard of the *Chronicle*'s offices, Cullen opened the door to the shed where Peter had been sleeping, then picked up a stick that was lying nearby. He looked at Hannah. 'Which board did Miss Albrecht say?' he asked.

'Third from the right.'

'And what will we find?' asked Monsarrat.

'Letters,' said Hannah. 'That's all I know. It's all she knows, so she says. Hallward told her where they are, told her the administration would be concerned to know he had them, but didn't say what was in them.'

Cullen levered up a floorboard. He extracted a packet wrapped in oilcloth and handed it to Hannah. 'Are you sure you want these? Perhaps they draw trouble to them.'

'How do you think Mr Hallward came by them?' asked Hannah.

'There were payments, to various clerks,' said Cullen. 'Generous ones. They would receive money every month, whether they were able to procure any information or not, on the condition that they pass on anything related to Mr Hallward or the newspaper. He must've been paying them for some time, and all they were able to find was the occasional letter from Duchamp to a friend, complaining about Hallward's editorials. But then one of them did find something a little more interesting.'

'What?'

'You will see. It was only one letter, but it started everything. And then Hallward turned to Peter. I begged him not to – but given the lad's skill as a pickpocket, Hallward thought an occasional raid on the mail cart might prove fruitful. And it did. They must have eventually realised that letters were going missing. They dried up, were probably being privately delivered. But by then Mr Hallward had enough to be going on with. Please, be careful. Both of you.' He turned to Hannah. 'You especially, missus.'

'We will,' she said. 'By the time they know we have them, it will be too late for them to do anything about it.'

There were four letters, and three of those were merely notes, cryptic and seemingly innocent unless one knew the context. Late into the night Monsarrat and Mrs Mulrooney pored over them at the small table in the boarding house parlour, while Miss Douglas paced in her room on the floor above, clearly not trusting her guests to douse the fire before bed. Whenever her foot hit a particularly noisy floorboard, Monsarrat started. 'Cullen has me believing these letters have the power of attraction – soldiers at the door, that kind of thing,' he said.

'If you ever accuse me of superstition again …' said Mrs Mulrooney. 'We are perfectly safe.' She paused. 'Unless someone was watching the newspaper. Or the coachman informed on us.'

'Or Peter slipped up, the poor boy. Let something out, made Miss Duchamp suspicious. Or Lethbridge said something.'

'I'm reasonably confident of him.'

'As am I, but I see shadows everywhere now, and one cannot always rely on people's good nature.'

She stared at him, and while he was used to seeing her irritated, what he saw moving across her face now disorientated him, as though someone other than his friend was in control of her muscles. 'Don't you think I know that, Mr Monsarrat?' she said. 'I got a glimpse of the good nature of your countrymen when they piked my father through.'

'My dear lady, I do apologise. Of course, you're right.'

She shook her head. 'It's all right, Mr Monsarrat, I'm just tired. And feeling the silence coming from Padraig.' She shuffled papers in front of her, then held one up. 'Scented paper – the same stationery Henrietta used to send me a note telling me she was ill.' Hannah looked down. 'It's addressed to someone known as Dearest G. Urging him to keep faith. Reminding him of his obligation to support the governor. It says, "I know you understand the importance of our cause, and that you can be relied on to assist in it, keenly aware as you are of the consequences of failure and the rewards of success – the end of the *Chronicle* and the supremacy of the *Flyer*." A threat, perhaps?'

'I don't know. Mobbs seems fairly committed. I think this is from him.' Monsarrat held up a note in a cramped hand, which simply read:

> Errand unsuccessful, I'm afraid. However, I do hope you enjoy your copy of this morning's newspaper. I know you like to stay informed.

'That would be the break-in, I suppose,' said Monsarrat. 'The one they fought the duel over.'

The most revealing letters were those in rounded, sloped handwriting – the kind that Monsarrat had seen on Duchamp's desk. One said:

> I trust you received the deeds to the house. I do, of course, wish you to enjoy this property, but must remind you of the purpose for which it was given. Our mutual friend will be visiting frequently to assist with preparations.

The other, also addressed to Mobbs, attached a clipping from the *Chronicle*: the editorial in which Hallward had decried the governor's treatment of the two soldiers. Duchamp had written:

> The damage this man is doing to the stability of the colony is incalculable. I believe he sees it as an amusement, his own form of bearbaiting, perhaps. He cares little for the consequences. But if he continues unchecked, he will undermine faith in the administration, and I hardly need outline for you what that means. The reversion of this colony to a state of equilibrium depends on public trust in government. You will, of course, need to be occasionally critical, so that when

the *Chronicle* closes there is no outcry, no perception that freedom of speech is being curtailed. And thereafter I look forward to the business of government being communicated without theatrics: soberly, fairly, and for the good of all of those in the colony.

Monsarrat read the passage to Mrs Mulrooney.

'You can't just march up to Duchamp and challenge him, though,' she said. 'You would not return from that meeting. And don't forget why we're here. Yes, it seems as though they all had some involvement in the murder. But there is still no proof.'

'No, we don't even know for sure what kind of firearm was used. We think it was a pistol, but thanks to Dr Merrick's orderly, there is no longer even a ...'

Monsarrat stopped talking, his mouth hanging open, a frown gathering.

'A what?'

'My dear lady, I am a fool.'

'Not all the time.'

'It was a pistol ball that killed Hallward.'

'Yes, so you've said.'

'And Donnelly told me Duchamp was practically in love with his pistols. I bet he would have liked nothing better than to kill Hallward with the pistol he had intended to use to dispatch him at the duel.'

Mrs Mulrooney stood and walked to the window. 'How would that have been possible?'

'Donnelly explained to me that Duchamp's duelling pistol was rifled – giving it increased accuracy and range. Not as good as a Baker rifle, but, still, not bad – especially if there was some kind of sight fitted.'

'But Duchamp has an alibi – didn't you tell me he was busy at the time of the murder?'

'Yes. Inspecting the troops – I checked. It wouldn't stop him from giving the pistol to someone else, of course.'

'Henrietta? We know she wasn't where she said she was. Or Mobbs? How can you prove it, though?'

Monsarrat sighed. 'I can't. There's his debunked alibi, although that in itself isn't proof. And it's almost certain it was Duchamp who changed the clock at the gaol – he was there at the time. But is it completely incontrovertible proof? No.'

'Unless …' Mrs Mulrooney walked over to the table and picked up the letters. 'Perhaps you won't have these tomorrow. Perhaps you will have already sent them somewhere else – pretend you have, at least. Somewhere beyond the colonel's reach, his influence. *The Times* of London? Would that be a sufficiently fearsome prospect?'

'Perhaps – although even if it is, it's hard to see how that would induce him to confess to a murder.'

'Oh, he'll never confess to it. Especially if he wasn't the one who pulled the trigger. But if there's one thing I've learned, Mr Monsarrat, it is that some people will happily sacrifice others when it's convenient. And Duchamp strikes me as just the type.'

Chapter 23

'I'm paying you good money, and I won't do it for substandard tea!'

Monsarrat had rarely heard Mrs Mulrooney use such a tone with anyone apart from himself.

They had gone to bed only a few hours before, after Monsarrat had made two fair copies of the letters and Hallward's story; the originals would soon be out of Duchamp's reach. For Monsarrat, the night had been more a series of consecutive dozes, his mind unable to rest as it absorbed the contents of the letters. It seemed his friend hadn't fared much better. She had barely nodded at him when she walked into the parlour.

'And it's not the leaves' fault,' she called back to Miss Douglas. 'You simply don't let them steep long enough. It's like drinking from a forest floor puddle. My friend and I have –'

'Your *friend*?' said Miss Douglas.

'My nephew, I should say, and I have need for sustenance today.'

Monsarrat smiled kindly at Mrs Mulrooney. 'I take it you had a restless night too,' he said.

'Doesn't deserve the name "night".'

'At least we know what we must do. Straight to the house as soon as I've spoken to Duchamp.'

'Yes, but I think we need to change the plan.'

'We went over this endlessly last night, my dear lady. If we start changing things, introduce uncertainty, we increase our peril, and Peter's.'

'I'm thinking of Peter. Once Duchamp knows what we have, what's to stop them sending someone on a fast horse to make sure the lad can never talk about his incarceration?' said Mrs Mulrooney.

'My bet is the colonel will be distracted by his need to send someone to the dock when I tell him the letters are already on board a ship waiting to sail. If there is a full-scale search of departing ships, we will know we have hit a nerve. While Peter ... well, as far as Duchamp knows, he isn't going anywhere. He doesn't know we know Peter's location. It is a risk, but one I don't see a way around.'

She didn't respond; she did, though, set down a cup of tea in front of Monsarrat, fragrant and sweet.

'I swear, this stuff has probably saved my life on numerous occasions,' Monsarrat said. He put his hand on hers. 'We may save quite a few other lives today. Peter, in the immediate term. But who knows how many people will perish if the government decides to take a more authoritarian bent?'

Mrs Mulrooney nodded. 'I know, I know, Mr Monsarrat. Let's make sure you are not among them. I ask only one thing.'

'Of course. Anything.'

'At least let's tell Cullen our plans. The poor man is out of his mind with worry.'

'He won't be any less worried when he hears what we intend to do,' said Monsarrat.

'Perhaps not, but he will have the truth. We can give him that, even if we can't give him anything else. I could leave when you leave to meet Duchamp. I'd see Cullen, then join you at Government House.'

'You take the coach, then.'

'No, Mr Monsarrat, you have a task to entrust Mr McCarthy with. It's important that you arrive in a manner befitting a man of your standing – Duchamp notices these things. I will be fine – I'm known in that area now. And as you can see, I don't intend to dress like a candidate for pickpocketing.' She stood up and smoothed down her black servant's skirt.

'I don't like it, but what chance have I of talking you out of it?'

'None, as you very well know,' she said. 'Now let's get you something to eat – you're going to need it. I know how vague you get on an empty stomach.'

<hr />

Hannah stood at the door of the boarding house, watching the coach move off. She took a heavy cloak from a peg inside the guesthouse door, wrapped herself in it and moved in the other direction.

Fifteen minutes later she was hammering on the *Chronicle*'s door. It was opened almost instantly by a red-eyed Cullen.

'You've slept no better than me, by the looks of it,' she said.

'Today might be the last for all of us. You. Mr Monsarrat. Peter. Me. I didn't want to close my eyes when I might soon be closing them forever.'

'Well, it's not my first last day,' she said. 'Mr Monsarrat is on his way to confront the colonel.'

'*What?* Then he's signing Peter's death warrant!'

'No, we won't allow that to happen. If you let me in, I can explain – probably not the wisest for me to be seen on the street passing time with you. And I have something just as valuable as information.' She held up a small cloth drawstring bag and opened it; Cullen peered inside as the fragrance of tea wafted up to meet him.

He smiled. 'A small pool of light in the darkness. You, as well as the tea. Mrs Mulrooney, it has never given me greater pleasure to invite someone into this newspaper office.' He opened the door fully, stood aside, and gave her his estimation of a courtly bow as she entered.

―⁂―

It wasn't until Monsarrat was close to his destination that he wondered about Mrs Mulrooney's insistence he take the coach. His appearance without an appointment or an invitation would seem odd enough, particularly to the protocol-obsessed colonel. If Monsarrat arrived in a coach when they were used to him arriving on foot, the addition of another unexpected element might be enough to spook them.

But really, there was no choice, because McCarthy and Sally had a job to do.

Monsarrat rode up the front until they were just out of sight of Government House. He handed McCarthy a packet and a small pouch of coins. 'You're sure you know where to go?'

'I do, and Sally does too,' McCarthy said. 'Those roads, they're not easy to travel on at speed in a coach. I have a saddle in the back, I'll pull away and unhook the old girl, and we'll be off. If anything happens to the coach ...'

'Mrs Mulrooney has agreed to pay for it to be fixed,' said Monsarrat, hoping this wouldn't be necessary. 'And if you have to drag him from his dinner ...'

'I will, Mr Monsarrat. I understand what's at stake. Now, into the back with you, next to the saddle. We're nearly there.'

A few minutes later, the coach was pulling up beside Government House. When one of the soldiers on duty saw who was emerging, he knocked into the other and then scurried off.

'Best pull around the side,' Monsarrat said to McCarthy.

By the time Jardine arrived, Monsarrat was standing alone in the driveway.

'Do come up here, Mr Monsarrat, I detest shouting.'

Monsarrat climbed the few steps between them.

'You are irregular on a few points,' Jardine told him. 'You don't have an appointment, and I understand you recently found a more comfortable means of conveyance.'

Monsarrat smiled at him.

'Surely you have better things to do, Lieutenant, than concern yourself with how I move around.'

Jardine glanced to the side, where some younger soldiers were standing guard, watching the exchange. He seemed to stand straighter, if that were possible.

'Quite. And yet I have abandoned these urgent tasks to come see you, Mr Monsarrat, so if you would be kind enough to let me know what precisely it is you want, I'd be most grateful.'

Monsarrat was a little surprised by Jardine's waspishness. Although Monsarrat would never have allowed himself to think of the lieutenant as an ally, given the identity of the man's commanding officer, neither had he seemed completely lacking in sympathy.

'I need to see the colonel,' said Monsarrat, 'on a matter of the utmost importance.'

'Perhaps you could tell me what that matter is.'

'Well, it is confidential. But I believe he will find it well and truly worth his time.'

※

'It seems to me your plan relies on an awful lot of luck,' Cullen said. His shoulders were slumped and he hauled them back with what seemed like some effort, shaking his head roughly to keep himself awake. 'What if there's a roadblock? What if Mr Monsarrat is arrested? And the colonel has soldiers at his disposal – he could easily send some to the docks and to Peter at the same time.'

'I hope Peter is beyond his reach today. I know it's far from perfect, Mr Cullen,' Hannah said, tucking a last few strands of hair into her cap. 'If Duchamp arrests Mr Monsarrat, we have a packet of letters that will ensure his freedom, which are being taken to a place beyond Duchamp's reach. As to a roadblock, I suppose there is nothing we can . . .'

I am a stupid woman, she thought. *I have seen British regiments stopped in their tracks on the streets of Wexford, and I still didn't think of this until now.*

'Mr Cullen, do you have a pen and paper? And without Peter, have you a means of getting a message to someone, quickly and quietly?'

Cullen went to the door, opened it and whistled outside. 'Someone will be here soon enough,' he said to Hannah. 'They know that particular whistle means there will be payment.'

Within a few minutes, the dirty face of a young boy appeared around the door.

Hannah blotted the letter she had hastily written, handed it to him and asked, 'Have you your letters?'

'Yes, from Mr Donnelly.'

'Good lad. So you know where he is to be found, then.'

The boy nodded.

Hannah drew out some pennies and pressed them into his hand. 'The same again when you get back,' she said. 'But you must come back with a reply. Even better, with the man himself. Ask for Mr Cullen. By the time you return, he will be the only one here.'

'Complete fabrications!' fumed Duchamp. 'Monsarrat, I'm appalled that a man of supposed intellect like yourself could be taken in so easily.'

'As am I, Colonel. The thought that I was duped for so long, having hoped a man in your position would never act with such dishonour, saddens me.'

'But these letters are not even in my hand!' Duchamp said, tossing them back across his desk at Monsarrat so that the pages scattered. One landed in Monsarrat's lap; others drifted down by his feet.

'No, sir,' said Monsarrat. 'They are in mine.'

'You see? Forgery! The same crime for which you were transported to these shores!'

'They are copies, not forgeries,' said Monsarrat. 'The originals are elsewhere, and very clearly written by your hand, Colonel.'

'Produce them then.'

'I cannot, sir.'

'And you are under arrest! Forgery as well as ... let's see, seditious libel? That would be fitting.' He nodded to Jardine, who moved forward. Monsarrat liked the man, and believed the amity was returned. But Jardine was a soldier. He would arrest anyone on the order of his superior.

Monsarrat had been arrested before. Twice. He had known that should it happen now, his first instinct would be to bolt from the room. He also knew he would not get far – at best, other soldiers would quickly descend; at worst, a lead ball would find its way to the back of his head. So he forced himself to remain seated, still and calm, wondering why his skin wasn't splitting from the pressure of containing his terror. 'I think you might find, sir, that arresting me would be a tactical error.'

'Tactical ... How dare you employ the language of the battlefield, you who have never been on one! And in this case, there is no such thing as an error. This is my colony. I own the tactics, I own the strategy, I own the terms of engagement.'

'What you don't own, sir, is a packet of documents that has been taken to the dock. There's a ship leaving tomorrow for England, I understand. The letters will be on it, addressed to *The Times*. There's another letter with them that explains my intention to confront you, and provides the reader with some guidance as to what it would mean if I were to be arrested or disappear from view.'

Duchamp nodded to Jardine. 'Send someone to search the ships, there's a good man,' he said.

Jardine saluted, turned and left the room, perhaps with a little less speed than the circumstances called for.

'Mr Monsarrat, you may rest assured that the originals will be in my possession within the hour,' Duchamp said.

'Oh, I do apologise, I should have said – the letters being sent to London are copies as well. No point sending the originals, as no one up there is familiar with your handwriting anyway. But some of those in the colony are.'

'And most of them work for me,' said Duchamp.

'Yes, although some have expressed a degree of concern as to the direction you are taking. I understand that one man in particular has corresponded with you on the issue, and that a number of terse notes made their way upriver. Ones that you didn't bother to dictate. Ones that mean Ralph Eveleigh would recognise your handwriting. And I informed Mr Eveleigh of the possibility of my arrest or disappearance.'

Duchamp shook his head. 'That damned Eveleigh. He sent me a demon. Oh, you look gentlemanly, but you have deployed low cunning in this case! But know this, Mr Monsarrat. I am the governor's man. Everything I have done – and I am not saying that I have done what you accuse me of – has been in his interests. That will not be forgotten, no matter what some secretary in an outpost says. I am loyal to the governor, and he is loyal to me.'

'I'm sure that's true – until you cause him more trouble than you're worth. Perhaps then Eveleigh might find himself sailing down the river on a more permanent basis.'

Duchamp glowered at Monsarrat then sat back down behind the desk. 'Mr Monsarrat, you'll never prove that I killed Henry Hallward, for the simple reason that I didn't.'

'I know that, sir. Gerald Mobbs did – with the pistol you gave him. One that you used in the duel against Hallward. You do like your... elegant solutions.'

'And do you know, I just thought of another one.' Duchamp smiled suddenly in a way that made Monsarrat nervous.

The colonel stood again, and Monsarrat did likewise, uncomfortable at the thought of Duchamp looming over him.

Duchamp walked around the desk, not stopping until his nose was inches from Monsarrat's face. 'Hugh Lewelyn Monsarrat,' he said, 'I challenge you to a duel.'

Chapter 24

Hannah, of course, had no intention of waiting for Monsarrat before attempting to free Peter. She had promised the lad she would be back first thing in the morning, and she never broke promises to children.

She ran all the way to Mobbs's house from the *Chronicle*'s offices and propped herself up against the wall of a nearby house, getting her breath back while watching Mobbs's place for signs of life. There were none. Mobbs could be expected to be in his office at this time on a weekday morning, and it was Henrietta's day at the School of Industry – Hannah imagined that a bright woman would realise that now, more than ever, she should follow her routine.

There was always the possibility that Monsarrat's visit to Government House had caused a disturbance, that a messenger had been sent to the conspirators, that they were on their way here. For now, though, all seemed quiet.

She crept towards the house next door, seeing the twitch of the lace curtain. The front door had opened before she had a chance to knock; Mrs Selwyn stared at her silently.

'You were absolutely right,' Hannah said. 'There is something very suspicious going on in that house. I intend to find out what it is, but I need your help. I believe you have access to a key?'

'If I do, why should I give it to you?'

'I will tell you everything I know, straight afterwards,' said Hannah. 'Before anyone else has a chance to read it in the newspapers.' *If any newspapers are left after this.*

Mrs Selwyn pursed her lips, probably rolling around in her mind the value of knowing information before anyone else, being able to impart it breathlessly to those who would marvel at her connections.

'And, of course, there's this.' Hannah handed over a few shillings. She had been chipping into Padraig's inheritance far more than she would like to. She did hope Ralph Eveleigh appreciated everything, when it was all done.

Mrs Selwyn pocketed the money, then led Hannah through to the backyard and handed her a shovel that had been propped against the side of the door. 'I can barely remember where I buried it. To the right, I think,' she said. 'You'll have to dig down.' She went back inside, closing the door firmly behind her.

'I suppose you'll have to ride with them, Private. Will your horse take two?'

Jardine was holding Monsarrat's upper arm, perhaps less tightly than he could. 'You're lucky it's house arrest and not the gaol,' he said, more loudly than necessary, possibly for the benefit of the soldiers at his command. 'The colonel has his own ways of dealing with inconvenient people.'

The colonel, thought Monsarrat, *is looking for a palatable way to kill me.*

He'd been momentarily shocked into silence when Duchamp had suggested a duel. Then he'd managed to say, 'Colonel, as you pointed out several times, I'm a ticket-of-leave man. If I participate and you are injured –'

'If you do not participate, I will make sure you're hanged, and be certain no one will rise up to protest your death as they would have done for Hallward. Duels are typically at dawn, so we will keep you under guard at your lodgings until then. As the wronged party, I will choose the positions. You, Mr Monsarrat, will face east.'

Into the rising sun, Monsarrat thought. 'There is one other issue,' he said. 'I do not possess a pistol.'

'I think we can find one for you,' said Duchamp.

Monsarrat was sure a pistol could be found for him – it just probably wouldn't contain a ball. He now faced the choice between certain death on the gallows and probable death near a swampy waterway.

He bowed to Duchamp. 'I look forward to seeing you at dawn.'

'Oh, so do I, Monsarrat. You have no idea how much.'

Now, as the soldiers bickered over who would have to take Monsarrat on the horse, a carriage pulled up to the portico. The door slammed flat against its side, and Henrietta Duchamp jumped out, a whirl of green taffeta, her agitation betrayed by the fact she had left the matching parasol in the carriage. She approached Jardine with a haste Monsarrat wouldn't have thought possible in such a dress. 'What has happened? A messenger from my brother came to the school, blathering about some kind of fight.' She turned to Monsarrat, frowning at the sight of Jardine's hand restraining him. 'What on earth is he doing here?' she asked Jardine.

'Making some accusations against the colonel, Miss Duchamp.'

'There are accusations to be made against you too, Miss Duchamp,' Monsarrat said. 'But I was unable to get around to them before your brother challenged me to a duel.'

Henrietta stared at him, then turned to Jardine. 'And the other one – that odious little dumpling of a woman. Where is she?'

Monsarrat could feel his shadow roaring forth – attacks on his friend always made it happen. His shadow had a habit of hurling words like weapons, without any thought for the consequences. He forced it back down. He wanted Jardine focused on him, on searching the ships, not on finding Mrs Mulrooney.

'His aunt?' asked Jardine.

'Do you really think that's what she is? When did you last meet an Englishman with an aunt who sounds as if she came from a peat bog? For all the rumours I heard – that she is seen in the better circles in Ireland as some sort of female Solomon – I didn't credit them.'

The shadow gave a final flex and unfurled, rising through his throat. He had no way of controlling what was about to emerge.

'Better to rise from a peat bog than descend into a sewer,' he said.

Henrietta gasped, turning to him. 'I did not give you permission to speak!'

'Yes, permission to speak. Something you've been after since you and your brother started that conspiracy with Mobbs. You could do better, by the way – not a man I would have thought you'd take as a lover, but then of course love has nothing to do with it. It's hard to convince a man to take a life unless he is looking so hard at the benefits of a liaison with a beautiful and well-connected woman that he almost doesn't notice his hand on the trigger.'

'How dare you suggest – ?' Henrietta started.

'Oh, I suggest nothing. There is proof, I assure you, mixed in with the letters bound for London, and the others that will no doubt be read avidly by Ralph Eveleigh in Parramatta. But if you are concerned for your reputation, I wouldn't be worried about an affair. You can't be imprisoned or hanged for that. Kidnapping, though – that's a rather more serious matter.'

Henrietta walked slowly up to him, looked him up and down then spat in his face, with a scowl more appropriate to a brawler at the Sheer Hulk than a finely dressed colonial princess. Jardine stepped back, dragging Monsarrat with him.

Monsarrat felt the moisture running down his cheek – and his shadow couldn't have asked for anything more. 'The point is, Miss Duchamp, I do not recognise your authority to permit me to speak or otherwise. You are every bit as grubby as Mobbs and your brother. There is a stain that no amount of silk can cover and a stink that no amount of scented stationery can remove. Your own speech will soon be taken up with protesting your innocence at trial.'

Monsarrat heard the words being injected into the air from his throat, in his voice, while his rational mind could merely stand back and listen. It was very unlikely, of course, that someone like Henrietta would face a trial – those were reserved for odious little dumplings like Mrs Mulrooney. But Henrietta's pause, her frown, told him that she did not see the prospect as completely impossible, and his shadow rejoiced.

'You, Mr Monsarrat, will be lucky to see a trial,' she said. 'All sorts of unfortunate things happen to the prisoners at Sydney's gaol.'

Monsarrat shrugged. 'You would know.'

Jardine cleared his throat. 'Actually, Miss Duchamp, the prisoner is not headed for the gaol. Your brother has given orders that he be placed under house arrest, pending tomorrow morning's duel.'

Henrietta clapped her hands. 'Oh, Eddie is clever, isn't he? That is perfect! Do you know, Mr Monsarrat, my brother is one of the best shots in the colony? He only misses when he intends to. Edward will be very contrite, of course, and explain that honour gave him no choice. The governor will be cross, but no more. And a duel is much quicker than a trial. Best get him on his way, Jardine – I'm sure he has some farewell letters to write, that sort of thing. I have business elsewhere.'

She turned, lifted her skirts and took tiny, swift steps down the portico stairs. As she was getting into the carriage, she called out to the driver, 'Sydney gaol!'

As Monsarrat was marched back onto the driveway, he stared after Henrietta. He was not much for prayer, not to a God represented by the likes of Reverend Alcott and Horace Bulmer. But he did pray, then. That Mrs Mulrooney and Peter were safe. That Henrietta was not making her way back to his friend.

Then the soldier on horseback reared up at an obstruction in his path – a blockage that had also brought Henrietta's carriage to a standstill.

A group of protesters was standing around fifteen yards away, just on the other side of the open gate that led to the grounds. They were blocking the road to the gaol.

Standing in front of them, his arms folded, was Donnelly. Next to him, some of the larger men in the group – probably chosen to be at the front – held placards proclaiming a desire for free speech and honest government.

Donnelly looked up towards Monsarrat. 'Lovely day for it,' he called. 'A shame you're detained at present. You owe me a fishing trip.'

Monsarrat laughed.

'You are disturbing the peace, and will disperse immediately,' Jardine called to Donnelly.

'I'm afraid we can't oblige you there,' Donnelly replied calmly. 'We are exercising our right to peaceful assembly.'

'You have no such right on private land,' Jardine called.

Laughter rippled through the crowd.

'Private land, is it?' said Donnelly. 'Who owns it then? The colonel?'

Jardine was silent.

'Or is it the Crown? Which would make it public land.'

'You still have no right to be here,' said Jardine. 'It's in the governor's domain.'

'Actually, you're half right,' said Donnelly. 'We're an inch outside the governor's domain. Of course there's probably some regulation or other about preventing ingress and egress, I forgot to check. We shall wait patiently while you get someone to look it up.'

'You'll do no such thing – you'll move on.' Jardine shouldered his musket and aimed it, and the other soldiers did likewise.

'Donnelly, don't be a fool,' said Monsarrat. 'Move on before they shoot you!'

'Not a bit of it, Mr Monsarrat,' called Donnelly cheerfully. 'We are simply standing here. Lieutenant Jardine knows what would happen if he fired on a group of people standing peacefully on public lands, whose only offence was to hold up signs he didn't like. Of course, in Sydney there are no independent journalists, but the news would still travel. Fancy a court martial, Lieutenant?'

The soldiers stared at the protesters, waiting for Jardine's signal to fire; the protesters stared back, waiting for Donnelly's signal to flee.

Henrietta's voice rang out from the carriage. 'Oh for goodness sake!' She leaped out and ran to a soldier's horse, which had been left to its own devices when its rider had dismounted to deal with the protesters. The soldier heard the horse whinny, turned, shouted and started running towards her, but she vaulted onto the animal in an arc of green fabric. Monsarrat could see shock on Jardine's face as Henrietta spurred it towards the protesters. When they didn't move, she pulled back on the reins, and the horse reared. She looked down at Donnelly from the saddle. 'If you don't get out of the way, you filthy little man, I'll trample your friends.'

Monsarrat was fairly sure she would make good on her threat.

Donnelly obviously agreed; he turned around and spoke to the group. 'Best make way. I don't think this lady cares much for the regulations.' The protesters parted, leaving a gap just wide enough for Henrietta and the horse to get through. She kicked its sides far harder than was necessary and galloped off towards the gaol.

Jardine turned to the soldier whose horse Henrietta had taken. 'You'll stay here, Watkins, and take the names of this lot – serves you right for being so careless with your horse. The rest of you, off we go. And as we are now short of mounts, Mr Monsarrat, you will go on foot.'

'That package you are waiting on, Mr Monsarrat,' Donnelly called out, 'your friend has gone to collect it. Where would you like it delivered?'

Monsarrat should have known. Mrs Mulrooney had gone alone to retrieve Peter. He hoped Donnelly's little ploy had given her enough time to get away.

'Perhaps best to take it back where it came from,' said Monsarrat, hoping Donnelly understood he meant the *Chronicle* offices. 'It seems we will have company at our boarding house. House arrest, you see, until tomorrow – the colonel's challenged me to a duel at dawn.'

Donnelly frowned, nodding. 'Very well, Mr Monsarrat. I wish you the best of luck.'

'What's this package?' Jardine asked.

'Oh, some writing implements,' said Monsarrat. 'My pens are heavily used and don't last as long as I'd like. Although by the looks of things, I shan't need them.'

'Well, I must say I hope you do – hard to find good clerks,' said Jardine, but then he nudged Monsarrat in the back gently, urging him towards the boarding house and its parlour. Monsarrat realised it would probably be the last room he would ever see.

Hannah had climbed over the fence, not wanting to risk the noisy rust of the gate. The small click the key made as it unlocked the door seemed impossibly loud in the still morning, and she half expected a detachment of guards to run out of the gaol to investigate.

She opened the front door only as far as she needed to, in order to slip through – she did not want to risk it being as talkative as the gate was. Standing just inside, she listened for movement, trying to feel any disturbance in the air. There was none.

The entrance hall was dusty, with long-abandoned cobwebs in the corner of the ceiling. To the right, the dining room looked equally so: a large empty table that had lost its sheen, surrounded by mismatched chairs. On her left, though, was a room that had been in more frequent use; a small parlour with two chairs faced a fire that smelled of fresh woodsmoke.

Hannah hoped the front-door key would also work on the cellar door – searching the place would take an unacceptably long time. She quietly made her way downstairs to the cellar. Naturally it was locked, and the key had no effect. She swore, and reprimanded herself for doing so; this investigation was turning her into a foul-mouthed harridan.

'Mr Cullen told me not to use that word,' said a small voice from the other side of the door.

'Peter! You are unharmed?'

'Yes.'

Hannah exhaled noisily in relief. 'Peter, I can't open the door. Do you know where the key is kept?'

'Have you a hairpin, missus?'

'What?'

'A hairpin. My mother used to have one before . . .'

'Oh. Yes, of course.' Hannah slid her fingers under her cap, extracted one of the pins and pushed it under the door.

After a moment, she heard metal disagreeing with metal. The lock clicked, and the door opened. Peter stood staring at her.

'Oh my Lord, look at the pallor on you! Well, there will have to be shortbread when it's all over.'

Peter looked at her, then closed the last few steps between them and threw his arms around her waist, his head side-on, nestling into her stomach.

She stroked his hair. 'There will be hugs later, too, if you want them, Peter. For now, though, there is no time. Tell me, do you think you can still run?'

He nodded vigorously.

'All right, then. So you and I are going to the front door – very quickly, but very quietly. When we get outside, we'll run as fast as we can. And then you will be safe.'

Peter nodded again. Hannah took his hand, and they began their way up the stairs.

Perhaps if Hannah had not had to spend time convincing Mrs Selwyn to hand over the key, things would have been different. Or if she had found its burial place more quickly. Or if the key had worked in the cellar lock.

As it was, when they got to the top of the stairs and walked towards the front door, it opened. Henrietta stood there, her face pink, her hair messy, a stain on her skirt. But her hands were steady. Hannah could tell, because the hand pointing the pistol at her was not trembling in the slightest.

Chapter 25

'I thought I was hiring rooms to respectable people!' Miss Douglas said, glaring at Jardine and the two soldiers with him. 'What will everyone say when they see *them* at my door?'

'They will say that you are a good woman, helping the colony,' said Jardine. 'Mr Monsarrat here is under house arrest, and this is the closest thing he has to a house.'

'His aunt has taken over my kitchen, you know!' Miss Douglas said.

'Yes, I'm sure that's very ... inconvenient.' Jardine failed to mask his lack of interest. 'But I promise you, you will never have to see either of them again after tomorrow. We will simply need to impose on you until dawn, when Mr Monsarrat has an appointment.'

'Dawn, then,' Miss Douglas said. 'And if you or any of your soldiers trample my flowerbeds, you will be paying for them.'

Jardine bowed slightly. 'I will be here with Mr Monsarrat. I wonder, actually, if there's a chance of a cup of tea?'

'No,' said Miss Douglas, 'there is not,' and she flounced out of the room.

Jardine and Monsarrat stood in the parlour, staring at each other.

'You might as well sit down, Lieutenant,' Monsarrat said. 'It's many hours until dawn.'

'You just want me to sit down so that you can.'

Monsarrat shrugged. 'It doesn't matter to me whether I sit or stand. I would not be doing either for long, in all likelihood.'

Jardine lowered himself into a seat at the parlour table, laying his musket across his lap so that the bayonet and barrel were pointing in Monsarrat's direction. 'I must say, you seem quite sanguine about the whole situation.'

'Sanguine or not, it will happen anyway,' said Monsarrat. 'Might as well meet it well. An easier death than hanging, especially as I suspect the colonel would request a long rope.'

Jardine gave a short bark of laughter. Monsarrat had the impression that it was precisely calibrated to convey grudging amusement, but not to invite familiarity.

Monsarrat managed a small smile. He had been close to death before. He had lain in a cell in Exeter, howling into the stones after a judge had placed a square of black cloth on his wig and said that Hugh Llewelyn Monsarrat was to be hanged by the neck until dead. And he knew there were those in Parramatta who would be delighted to see that sentence carried out. His railing against fate, his sobbing in that faraway cell had helped Monsarrat stand straight as he walked to what he thought was the gallows. But he found he had instead been walking towards his death as an Englishman, sent to the colony with no possibility of return. He could not now, though, wring his hands, kick the wall, keen for himself. So he relinquished control to the shadow, which knew all about bravado and bluster but nothing about mortality. If the documents had reached Eveleigh in time, mortality was something he might not have to confront just yet.

The shadow, as it turned out, had some rather interesting things to say. 'I suppose the colonel will have to explain to my employer why he is now without a clerk.'

'I imagine he'll dictate something, yes,' said Jardine.

'I wonder if he'll help Eveleigh find a replacement. The streets of Parramatta are not fertile hunting grounds when one is looking for a copperplate hand.'

'Nevertheless, I think Eveleigh will have to make do with what can be found there,' said Jardine. 'The colonel would like nothing better than to see Eveleigh have to transcribe his own letters.'

'Yes, he does rather seem to have taken a set against my employer. I wonder why. Eveleigh is an inoffensive enough man.'

'Not to the colonel, he's not,' said Jardine. 'For a start, he foisted you on this investigation. And he tried to tell Duchamp how to run things. Gives him advice about the kind of reports to be sent back to the Home Office. It is not appreciated. The colonel has said he knows best how to serve the governor, as he did in Mauritius. He said Eveleigh had probably never picked up anything sharper than a pen.'

Monsarrat thought for a moment, remembering what Eveleigh had told him. 'Probably not, but it's a weapon he is very skilled in wielding. The colonel, though, seems almost to believe he has some sort of ownership over the governor.'

'I wouldn't go that far,' said Jardine. 'He does like to make sure that all important information comes to the governor through him, but that's what a private secretary should do, I imagine. Make sure the message is accurate – and make sure it's heard.'

Monsarrat began pacing around the room, more out of habit than anything else. 'Yes,' he said. 'And only room for one messenger. Must be frustrating.'

'How so?'

'A man of your ability – and your age – I'd expect you to be a captain by now. Perhaps the colonel wishes to be the only senior officer around the governor.'

Jardine laughed. 'I see what you're doing, Mr Monsarrat. Very clever of you, I must say. You use your words every bit as effectively as I would use musket balls. But no, I'm afraid my loyalty is to God, the King and my commanding officer, and that will not change. Oh, could you stop pacing? It's very distracting.'

Monsarrat stopped and inclined his head in acknowledgement. 'Your fidelity is admirable. Unshaken by your commanding officer's involvement in conspiracy to murder.'

'You are very amusing, Mr Monsarrat, truly,' Jardine said. 'But the man doesn't have it in him.'

'Your faith in him does you credit, Lieutenant,' said Monsarrat. 'I do hope you don't have cause to regret your service to him.'

'I won't. Now, do you think your landlady has a chess set? For all your crimes, all your dissent, I still enjoy the way your mind works, Mr Monsarrat. The colonel may have challenged you to a duel, but I'm challenging you to a game.'

The pistol had a mother-of-pearl grip, the green and blue glints complementing Henrietta's dress. 'Tell me,' she said, 'I'm curious. What's your real name?'

'You know my real name,' Hannah said.

'But I presume that there is no Mulrooney blood in Mr Monsarrat's veins.'

'You are correct. He is my employer, my friend. He is not my nephew.' As Hannah spoke, she eased Peter behind her.

'Oh, don't worry about the safety of the boy you're about to kidnap. I won't harm him.'

'I'm freeing him. And what assurance do I have that you won't?'

Henrietta cocked her head to the side and pursed her lips as though considering the question. 'Well, none,' she said. 'Best step away from him, though. It's a small pistol, I know, and rather pretty, but it's still capable of forcing a ball through you both.'

A few months before, Hannah had sat across a table from another privileged woman who was intent on her destruction. Rebecca Nelson, though, had been mad, while Henrietta Duchamp seemed in cold command of all her faculties. Utterly sane, if amoral. Capable of helping develop a conspiracy that would have delivered her the entire colony, no doubt wrapped in a bow that matched her parasol. She had clearly decided that the main impediment to her claiming the prize was Hannah.

While Rebecca and Henrietta were different, they were equally deadly. And the fear that Hannah had struggled to tamp down when Rebecca had locked her in a burning house, the terror she knew would rob her of the ability to escape, rose again now.

I will not have this, she thought. *You will not shoot me.*

She wasn't sure, though, what she could do to prevent it. Her only hope was to delay Henrietta long enough to think of a way out.

'You've been remarkably clever,' Hannah said, 'and you like things tidy. So why put yourself to the trouble of having a dead body to deal with? Surely you'd rather not answer questions about how I got that way. Especially when I'm no threat to you alive.'

'No threat? Are you not standing here, with the boy?'

'And you think they will believe me, over you?' Hannah asked.

'I would rather not find out. I was not made to be a convict.'

Of course you weren't. While the rest of us chose it. Begged for it.

'But what have you done, really?' Hannah said. 'What can you be accused of? Meeting with a newspaper editor? Taking a young orphan from the street and feeding him? That's what

Peter will say when they ask.' She turned to the boy, who was standing very still, breathing heavily, his eyes fixed on the gun. 'That *is* what you will say, isn't it, Peter? That you spent a lot of time here with Miss Duchamp, eating more than you have in a year.'

He nodded slowly.

Hannah addressed Henrietta again. 'After all, it isn't as though you pulled the trigger of the gun that killed Mr Hallward.'

Henrietta said nothing. Hannah would have loved to see some faltering of her arm, some shaking of the hand that held the pistol, but it was as steady as ever.

She still wasn't talking, though. Simply staring.

She is calculating. Assessing her options.

'Well, you cannot be held responsible for the actions of a man.'

'Mobbs – a common little journalist. A man who, at his trial, would say I gave him his instructions,' said Henrietta. 'That I cut a groove for the pistol in the windowsill, so all he had to do was pull the trigger. That I drilled him, day after day. That we wanted to use the same weapon with which my brother should have dispatched the man.'

'Let him! No one believes journalists.'

Henrietta laughed softly, then raised the gun so that it was pointing at Hannah's forehead. 'My dear, if that were true, I wouldn't have gone to all this trouble.'

You must not let her confess anything else to you.

'And what trouble have you gone to?' Hannah asked. 'Trying to introduce the poor man to a bit of culture? A lost cause, probably, but not against the law as far as I'm aware. Shooting me, though, would be. At worst it could see you hanged, while at best it would be an inconvenience. What would you do with my body, bury it? Blood and soil, they tend to stain. Your dress would be ruined.'

Henrietta glanced down briefly. 'Very well. Perhaps it might be something of an error.'

'I knew you were an intelligent woman. You'll let me take the boy, now, yes? Look after him? I don't believe hurting a child was part of your plans.'

'Many things weren't that have since had to be enacted,' said Henrietta. 'No, I don't wish to hurt the boy. I probably would have sent him back to the orphan school, where he would have been whipped for telling tales. But you are not a child, Mrs Mulrooney. You will for the present share Peter's confinement. Things are unsettled now. Your path might end in gaol – it would be no trouble at all to find one of my necklaces in your pocket – or it might end in the cellar. Either way, that is where it is taking you for the moment.'

Perhaps McCarthy was in Parramatta by now, standing by as Ralph Eveleigh read the packet he had been sent and wondered if Monsarrat was more trouble than he was worth. Perhaps Mrs Mulrooney had succeeded in getting Peter out, and was sitting in his little shed with him, feeding him spoonfuls of tea. Or perhaps McCarthy had been intercepted and strung up from a tree, and Mrs Mulrooney was in chains or worse.

Monsarrat wished his imagination was normally as good as it was now. He could feel the violent jerk as Sally was whipped, bolting away from under McCarthy and his noose. The fists as they landed on Mrs Mulrooney, the chains around her wrists. All with no way of knowing whether his thoughts were self-torture or preparation.

Whatever the case, they were certainly having an effect on his chess game. Their two-person tournament was now in its fifth hour. Plates of congealing gravy, deposited with bad grace hours ago by Miss Douglas before she stomped to bed, were at their elbows.

'No one ever falls for the Spanish Opening!' crowed Jardine as Monsarrat laid his king on its side in a gesture of surrender. 'Especially not twice in a row. You could be doing a little more to make this entertaining, Monsarrat.'

'I do apologise, Lieutenant. I find myself somewhat distracted.'

'Understandable, I suppose. Do try to concentrate harder, though. I will let you be white again, if it means that there will be some semblance of a challenge.'

Jardine was so busy rearranging the pieces he didn't immediately notice one of his men walk in, his hand extended, a note pinched between his fingers.

The private cleared his throat. 'From the docks, sir.'

Jardine took the note without looking up, then laid it to the side of the board. 'Are you still there, Private?' he said after a moment.

'I thought you might wish to send a reply, sir.'

'Hard to do that when I haven't read the damn thing yet. Dismissed. I'll call if I need you.'

After the soldier had left the room, Jardine said, 'I find that everyone from the lowliest private would try to impose their own priorities on you, if you let them.' He finished placing the last pawn before unfolding the note. 'Nothing found in any of the ships going to England. Makes me wonder if you were bluffing about writing to Eveleigh as well.'

'I most assuredly wasn't. Did they tip out every barrel of meal? Unroll every bolt of silk? Search the passengers?'

Jardine paused as he studied Monsarrat. 'Why couldn't you have just found it was Albert Bancroft? Or the husband of some fictional lover? Or someone Hallward beat at dice five years ago? You'd be home by now. Things were certainly not meant to unfold like this.'

Monsarrat gave him a sharp look. 'Do you mean to tell me there was a plan for how things were meant to go?'

Jardine bent over the board again, suddenly fascinated by the arrangement of the pieces.

'Did you – did you have a part in this?' Monsarrat asked him.

'No. Nor did I want one. And I don't know much. Snippets. Overheard whispers.'

He looked up, his face drawn. 'My duty is all I have, and it binds me as surely as a priest is bound by the seal of the confessional.'

'By this time tomorrow, I will be dead,' Monsarrat said, and the weight of the statement hit him with such force that had he been standing, he would have stumbled. 'I would rather not go to my grave without knowing precisely what I had been part of. You are loyal, I know. It is a characteristic I admire, even though I believe your loyalty to be misplaced. You would never speak against your commander.'

'No, God help me.'

'But this is the last conversation I will have. So it would not be unexpected if I were to muse a little on my fate, and what led to it.'

'I'm not sure I follow.'

'I'll probably start rambling,' said Monsarrat. 'Make all kinds of suggestions, articulate all sorts of ridiculous ideas. And, of course, you will tell me they are ridiculous. If they are.'

Jardine was staring at him now.

'Consider it the last request of a dying man,' said Monsarrat.

'Very well. I will do that much.'

Monsarrat stood and walked over to put his elbow on the mantelpiece. He dislodged a vase from its place, but did not bother to set it to rights. 'If he was so displeased about my assignment to the case, why didn't Duchamp simply send me away again and put one of his own men on to the matter; have them discreetly say it couldn't be solved – leave it at that?'

'I couldn't possibly say, Mr Monsarrat.'

'The governor, I know, likes things to be orderly – that's his reputation, anyway. Perhaps the protests were rattling the colonel. He didn't want the governor to come back from Norfolk Island into a sea of screaming people.'

'One does not want one's superior to develop an unfavourable view,' said Jardine. 'I'm speaking in generalities, of course.'

'Of course. So you make sure that you wade into a crowd of protesters with a man who has been brought in from the outside. Someone independent. Someone to quiet the throng.' Monsarrat glanced up and saw that Jardine had gone back to staring at the board. 'Why would he take that risk, though? He might have believed – hoped – I would settle on someone else. But he couldn't know, not for certain.'

'There you are,' said Jardine. 'Simple statement of fact.'

'So I don't understand . . . Ah! Unless – oh, that is clever. If I'm right, that is very clever indeed.'

'There is no fear of me saying the wrong thing in response to that statement. I've no idea what you're talking about.'

'He couldn't lose! Either way, he would get something he wanted!' said Monsarrat, slapping his hand on the mantelpiece.

Jardine looked up, smiling. 'You do seem rather pleased with yourself, Mr Monsarrat,' he said. 'You seem to believe your path is becoming clearer. Just make sure not to take that vase with you when you go down it – your landlady would object, I fear.'

'If the colonel decided he didn't like where my investigation was heading, all he had to do was discredit me,' Monsarrat said. 'I do have two convictions, so it wouldn't be terribly hard. Particularly if one has an unusual degree of influence over the editor of the town's only newspaper. If my assertions were not to his liking, he need only portray them as the ramblings of a criminal mind.'

'I suppose that's an explanation,' said Jardine. 'Not saying it's a truth, mind.'

'Of course not, Lieutenant. No one could accuse you of adding any certainty to this. And – and! Another benefit to the colonel: if I am discredited, so is Eveleigh. Duchamp can place his own man in Parramatta and effectively control the two seats of power.'

'If one had a particularly Machiavellian mind, one might see things that way,' said Jardine.

'And are you an admirer of Machiavelli, Lieutenant?' asked Monsarrat.

'I might be. Colonel Duchamp certainly is.'

'Well, I must thank you.' Monsarrat sat down opposite Jardine. 'If I am to be sent to my grave, at least I will know why.'

'Will you, Mr Monsarrat? I couldn't say – I've just been making the occasional polite comment as you ramble. Really, I was hardly listening. I was planning my strategy for the next game, actually.'

The door opened again, and the same private walked in and saluted.

'I told you I would inform you if I wished to respond to the intelligence from the dock,' said Jardine. 'At this point, I do not.'

'I do beg your pardon, sir, but that is not why I have intruded. You asked me to inform you at this hour. It is time.'

Chapter 26

Hannah suspected that Peter didn't often cry. Boys who cried in his world would have been considered impossibly weak, the tears an invitation to a beating. But the prospect of freedom so abruptly denied had worn him down. After Henrietta clicked the lock behind them, he went over to the mattress on which he'd spent these past couple of nights, sat down and silently tears began to leak from his eyes. He did not embrace them, not as Hannah might have done. He did not suck down air so that he could put more force behind his sobs, let them shake his body until he couldn't breathe. He was simply too worn out to stop the tears, so they escaped, finding their own path down his face and falling where they may.

Hannah sat down on the mattress beside him. She had once been used to the smell of confined humanity; she had barely noticed the stink of the sweat and the urine and the fouler substances the convicts emitted. Their betters produced the same substances, of course – they were simply more skilled at covering the smell, and had the resources to do so.

The comfortable cottage in Parramatta smelled of lye and wood smoke and brewing tea. Without her noticing, it had supplanted those memories of the baser odours. But the memories came back now, all the stronger for having been banished for so long. Called to the surface by the bucket in the corner, which surely hadn't been emptied for the whole time Peter had been here, and was in danger of overflowing. And by the sweat that had soaked into the mattress, no less pungent for having come from a little boy rather than a grown man.

She did not know whether he would welcome an embrace. He might prefer her to ignore his tears. So she sat silently, within reach but not reaching. After a few minutes, however, it was more than she could bear. She was not sure whether it was for his sake or hers, but she reached for him and drew his head onto her shoulder. He allowed it, and after a minute of stillness allowed his little arms to extend like vines around her neck.

'I am sorry,' she said. 'That you're back in here.'

'I suppose I'll go to hell now,' he said.

'What nonsense. You're not going to hell. Who told you that?'

'Miss Duchamp,' said Peter. 'She said if I didn't tell her things, I would go to hell. The archdeacon told her, and he knows because he talks to God all the time.'

Hannah leaned back, taking Peter gently by the shoulders. 'I want you to look at me.'

His head remained bowed.

'You don't need to hide your tears from me,' she said.

'Boys aren't supposed to cry.'

'Peter, grown men would cry in your situation, and if any of them tell you anything different then they're lying. And they wouldn't be sitting there quietly, either – they'd be rolling around on the floor and gibbering.'

Peter gave a small laugh.

'You need to listen to me, because I tell the truth, and Miss Duchamp does not. Children do not go to hell.'

'Yes, they do. The matron at the orphan school was always telling us we were bound there.'

'Then she's a liar as well. Sometimes people like to threaten hell to make children behave. Even priests – especially priests, actually. And matrons, and scheming little madams who would rather send others wading through the mud on their behalf than get their own skirts dirty. But I would not be surprised if many of those who threaten hell wind up there themselves one day. God does not punish children. The Blessed Virgin wouldn't allow it, I can tell you. And He will not punish you, or I'll deal with Him.' She crossed herself at the blasphemy. *I hope You understand*, she prayed silently. *I'm just trying to calm the lad down. It's what You would want, I'm sure of it, and if I'm not mistaken there's very little of what You want getting done these days.*

She taught him his catechism to pass the time. She didn't even know if he was Catholic but there were worse things to be learning in this situation. Then she taught him every song she remembered from her childhood, particularly the rebellious ones. She told him stories of spirits and sprites and fairies. Peter slept then, and she must have as well. No one, of course, had lit the lamp by the door, and she opened her eyes to a blackness so deep she might as well have kept them closed. She wasn't sure what had woken her. A rustle? A rat, perhaps, scurrying across the floor. Or the quiet little voice.

'Do you think she'll come back soon?' Peter whispered.

'Perhaps. It's not likely though. She has a fair few things to be going on with. Someone else might come.'

'Not the man. I hope not.'

'The one with the silly moustache that goes all the way to his ears?'

Peter nodded. 'She left me alone with him once. I coughed and he heard. He came down and hit me.'

I hope he hangs for it.

'Not him, at least I don't think so,' Hannah said. 'No, someone you know rather better. Someone who knows where I am.'

'I hope he hurries,' said Peter.

'He will, don't worry.'

But after another half-hour had passed, she wondered if he would. Perhaps there had been a raid on the *Chronicle*'s offices; perhaps he had been arrested.

When she heard movement outside the door, she braced herself. Once it opened, it might reveal the last person she would ever see before a shot from a pretty little gun sent her to be punished for her earlier blasphemy. Henrietta, though, would surely not need to bang so loudly at the door, with such force. She would just use the key.

Whatever was making all that noise, the door didn't seem as though it could stand up to it for long. After several more blows it splintered and buckled, the latch slipping out.

Cullen, holding a mallet, stood behind it. 'What's the point of spending all that money on a few little locks,' he said, 'when a couple of decent blows with a hammer does the job?'

Peter ran to him, and Cullen bent over and picked the boy up, wheeling him around and setting him on his feet outside the door.

Cullen turned to Hannah. 'Are you coming, missus? Only it seems we've a bit to do, and not much time to do it in. And, it turns out, we're expecting a visitor.'

※

There was no coach for Monsarrat this time, but he did get his own horse, hemmed in by Jardine on one side and a soldier on the other, with a third riding in front through the pre-dawn gloom.

In the boarding house parlour it had felt almost as though he and Jardine were closed in a box around which the world was moving without the slightest regard for them. But Jardine's easy manner, enhanced by hours together with Monsarrat in the room, nothing to do but talk and play chess, disappeared as soon as they stepped through the door. Now, he was the martinet again, the guardian of efficiency, the barker of orders. Now, he referred to Monsarrat as 'the prisoner'.

On the road they were passed by a comfortable coach that did not slow for them. It did not need to – Jardine and the others clearly recognised it, and scrambled to the sides of the road to allow it to pass. As it did, Monsarrat saw Duchamp's sharp profile in the back, with Albert Bancroft, probably reprising the role of second, beside him.

'I do not have a second,' Monsarrat said quietly to Jardine once they were back on the road.

'You won't need one.'

The vegetation was scrubby; stunted, gnarled bushes with the occasional eucalypt sentinel. None of it provided cover from the rising sun, by now just high enough to be blinding for anyone who faced east. Monsarrat kept his eyes trained on the shadows, blinking and trying to resist the urge to rub them, blocking out the voice which told him his exhaustion might fatally slow him. On the deep green of the waxed, stubby leaves being slowly revealed by the lightening sky. A grey-furred creature returning from its night-time forage. And beyond, the sloshing water that glinted in the low rays of the sun. Above him, flying foxes returned to their trees; when the sky darkened again and they flew back, it was likely Monsarrat's eyes would be permanently closed.

Duchamp was already there, in full uniform and with his ceremonial sword at his waist. He had already taken up his position to the east, and was laughing with Bancroft. The men stopped talking as Monsarrat passed them to assume his sun-seared position to the west. Duchamp nodded to Bancroft, who went to the coach and returned with a polished wooden box. Duchamp said, 'I have chosen the positions, as you see.'

'Yes,' said Monsarrat. 'I'm surprised, actually. Given your reputation, I would have thought firing into the rising sun wouldn't present a problem.'

'If we weren't already here, I would challenge you. I am an honourable man, Mr Monsarrat. That is why I will allow you first choice of weapons.'

Bancroft stepped forward and opened the box. Inside blue velvet lining, two ornately engraved duelling pistols glinted at Monsarrat.

I suspected it would be a rope, he thought. *A knife at night. Maybe a fall from a horse. I never for a moment thought it would be a pistol with flowers scratched into it.*

He reached over and took the furthest gun, hefting it. Perhaps Duchamp thought Monsarrat was getting a feel for the balance of the weapon, its shape, the way its grip fitted his hand. In truth, he had rarely held a gun. He had no idea what to feel for. He was using the charade to buy a few extra breaths. Pretending to play Duchamp's game.

What if he refused? If he simply declined to follow the expected rules, the accepted procedure?

Duchamp cleared his throat. 'I know you don't have anywhere to be, Monsarrat, but I have a colony to run, so if you wouldn't mind getting on with it?'

Monsarrat looked up at him and nodded. 'Yes, getting on with it is a good idea.'

They turned their backs on each other, then walked in opposite directions while Bancroft counted to ten. *All of the steps*, Monsarrat thought, *that I took without a thought. The ones that led me to Exeter, into the courtroom, onto the boat. And they end with a stroll through a swamp.* He waited, his back turned, for the command to fire.

When it came, he turned to see Duchamp whirling around, his arm outstretched. Monsarrat had no doubt the gun would be aimed at his forehead.

The baker's shop was closed and shuttered. Baking was an early-morning business, so it was odd to find the shop completely abandoned at this hour, Hannah thought. Not that the shop was where they were heading. Cullen led Hannah and Peter around to the back, unlocking the door to Donnelly's schoolroom and bustling them in.

'The *Chronicle* offices aren't safe,' Cullen said. 'Your boarding house neither. And probably not here, not for long. Best I could think of at short notice. Now, I want you to sit, both of you.'

'I'm not much for sitting,' said Hannah. 'More of a pacer.'

'Missus, you can pace to your heart's content when this is over. But now I need you to sit.' He bowed. 'If you would do me the honour.' He pulled a chair from behind Donnelly's desk and gestured her to it.

'I can't promise I'll stay still,' she said as she sat. 'The letters, the ones going to London – did they find them?'

'No. Mr Donnelly paid a sailor to conceal them on his person. Miss Duchamp won't stop looking, though. She'll have plenty of time on the way to England.'

'She's never going to England!'

'Oh, she is. She booked herself a passage, leaving tomorrow. Probably wants to be in London when the letters arrive, see if there's any hope of intercepting them.'

I was transported for stealing butter, Hannah thought. *But if you have a pretty dress and the right accent, kidnap and conspiracy get you a first-class cabin.*

Peter climbed onto her lap with all the assumed ownership that Padraig had displayed at the same age. She put her arms around him, and he rested his head on her shoulder. She could see dark specks moving in his fair hair, but stroked it anyway; if there ever came a day when lice were the worst she had to contend with, she'd be delighted.

It occurred to her, suddenly, that she might be a grandmother. She knew what drovers did when they got to town. Padraig might not even know. She imagined a child with red-gold hair, trailing after its mother as she hung washing or peeled potatoes. Growing up without knowing about blood and bravery on the other side of the world, the pride and the pain that it brought.

Hannah only realised she was crying when a teardrop landed on Peter's hair.

Cullen dragged a chair over from one of the children's desks and placed it next to her. Sitting on it, he only came up to her waist, and could easily rest his chin on his knees if he wanted to. She smiled at him, but his look of concern did not flicker.

He took her hand in his. An intimate gesture, one she knew he would not have chanced unless he thought there was a need for it. 'You've heard, then. About Mr Monsarrat.'

Hannah swayed in her chair, enough to make Cullen brace himself against her to stop her toppling to the ground with Peter in her arms.

She should never have let Monsarrat go alone. For such an intelligent man, he was awful at navigating the world, avoiding the rutted parts of the road. Sometimes she suspected he enjoyed the occasional bump. Some bumps, though, were lethal. Had they shot him? Was he now awaiting trial on some obscure charge that came with a death sentence?

Monsarrat had rescued her from the shapeless days as a servant, the ones that slid into each other, melded together in their uniformity so you didn't notice them sneaking past two or three at a time, until so many had escaped that your son was suddenly a grown man.

'Is he . . . ?' she whispered.

'Not yet,' said Cullen. 'At least, well, I don't think so. But Donnelly's been flitting about these past few hours, and he told me the colonel has challenged Mr Monsarrat to a duel. One he has no hope of surviving.'

'Do we have time to try to save him?'

Cullen was shaking his head. 'The duel is at dawn. An hour or so from now.'

'But, but then ...' She lifted Peter from her lap, gently put him on the floor and started for the door. 'We must go now, Mr Cullen. If there is to be any hope at all.'

Cullen strode to the door and stood in front of it. 'I can't let you, missus. It's too dangerous. And anyway, things are already in hand.'

'Not in mine!'

'But in the hands of others. Mr Donnelly and our visitor will follow Mr Monsarrat.'

'Oh yes – the visitor. Who is it?'

'Not sure, but Donnelly was watching the road to your boarding house in case someone came looking – and someone did. Donnelly didn't tell me who. But he said he was confident this person could save Mr Monsarrat's life.'

Hannah was still for a moment, then jinked around Cullen and made for the door.

'I beg you, don't follow them!' Cullen called.

'I've no intention of doing that. Just as I've no intention of allowing that minx to sail away to England without cleaning up her mess.'

Chapter 27

Monsarrat did not answer Duchamp's gesture. His arm stayed dangling at his side. He loosened his fingers. The gun fell to the ground.

Duchamp frowned. 'I can't very well shoot you while you're standing there unarmed, can I?'

'I don't see why not,' said Monsarrat. 'Of course, it's not exactly honourable but perhaps your definition of honour is flexible enough to allow it.'

'Pick up your weapon, man. Don't die a coward.'

'No intention of dying a coward. Or a criminal. I am a ticket-of-leave man, Colonel. Even if I were to survive, I would be quickly hanged if I injured you. So if I'm to leave this place in the back of a cart, or draped over a horse, I would rather not enter eternity with a fresh crime to my account.'

Duchamp lowered his gun slightly, shaking his head. He turned to Jardine. 'Make him pick up the gun, Lieutenant. Tie his hand around it, if you have to.' Duchamp turned back to Monsarrat, bending his elbow to aim at the sky. It would be the work of half a moment, of course, to straighten it again when Monsarrat was appropriately armed.

'I will not, sir,' said Jardine.

Duchamp stalked up to him and grabbed him by the shoulder. 'That is a direct order, Lieutenant!'

'I have never disobeyed a direct order in my life, sir. But this order, I cannot comply with. You are asking me to force this man to wield a weapon. I will not.'

'Then I will shoot you as well!' Duchamp screeched.

Bancroft stepped forward. 'Colonel, before you do, may I suggest you wait until you know who is approaching?'

'Don't be ridiculous, we are undisturbed – that's why I chose this place.'

'Yes, but listen,' said Bancroft.

Duchamp did. So did Monsarrat. Hoof beats, getting louder.

'They will surely pass by,' Bancroft said. 'But best not to alert them with the sound of a shot.'

So they waited as the hoof beats grew louder, until there was a rustling in the trees around the clearing, and the sound of whinnying.

'Best lower the weapon for now, sir,' said Bancroft quietly. 'There's no need for them to know what we are about.'

'I'd say it's perfectly obvious what you're about,' said Donnelly, stepping into the clearing. 'You do have rather a taste for duels, Colonel.'

'Perhaps you and I had better have one,' Duchamp suggested, 'after I dispatch Mr Monsarrat.'

'I'll thank you not to do that,' said a voice from the trees.

To Monsarrat, the voice was jarringly out of place – he had only ever heard it within the confines of a small office.

'Far more difficult than you'd think to find good clerks here. The government doesn't transport nearly enough of them,' said Ralph Eveleigh, stepping up behind Donnelly, a dusty travelling cloak around his shoulders. 'Were it not for his copperplate hand, I'd say you can do what you like with the devil. But really, his loss would make my job much harder.

Yours too, before you shoot him to spite me. Destruction of government property – something I never would have thought you capable of, until I read certain letters.'

※

Hannah had not reached the docks as quickly as she would have liked. Peter had made a sound that called her back, the wail of a boy who could not accept another loss.

She had gone to him, kneeled, hugged him. 'You are the bravest boy I've ever met.'

'I don't want to be brave.'

'Ah, but you can't help it, you see? It's like your big toe – you might not notice it, or think about it very often, unless you stub it, but it is always there, and you can't separate it from yourself.'

'You should stay here. Like Mr Cullen says.'

'You and Mr Cullen will stay here, Peter. Look, you can practise your writing. Do me a drawing on the board – I will look forward to seeing it when I get back. And I will be back. But your captor is about to escape, and I can't let her.' Hannah released him then, stood up and looked at Cullen. 'I have to do this,' she said. 'What they did to us – they called it justice. And if we deserve justice, so does she. I cannot continue to breathe the air of a world that would allow her to go unpunished.'

Cullen took her hand again. Looked down at it, as though trying to read a hidden message in the calluses of her palm. 'I will not be able to stop you. Not without resorting to actions I'm not willing to take. Not without you hating me.'

Hannah smiled, shaking her head.

'Off with you then,' he said. 'Give her the thrashing she deserves. And then come back. That drawing will be waiting for you.'

'I promise.' Without meaning to, she reached up and gave him a peck on the cheek. 'You're not the worst of them,

Mr Cullen.' She turned once more to him as she left. He was smiling vaguely, rubbing his cheek, while Peter looked up at him, frowning.

The sight had helped her forget her exhaustion as she ran to the docks. But now, faced with a collection of ships of various sizes, all of them being loaded and unloaded by yelling men, she faltered. A dockworker came up behind her with a cart, nearly knocking her into the water. 'No place for women, this,' he called over his shoulder as he passed. 'You need to be out of the way. Work being done here.'

She was tempted to whack him, but such an action might end with her in the water anyway. 'I do beg pardon, sir, I'll be more careful. I wonder, do you know which ships are bound for England?'

'Do I look like the harbourmaster?'

'I couldn't tell you, as I've never met the man. Perhaps you could tell me where he is, though.'

'Still home with his wife, most likely. Early, isn't it? He doesn't get here until the hands of his pocket watch tell him it's seven. Leaves the rest of us to do the real work.' He trundled on, barking at other workers to get out of his way, not slowing for anyone. Including a young servant who had just come down a gangplank and was nearly knocked off her feet by the cart.

Hannah walked slowly closer, looking around. Where the servant was, the mistress might not be far away. She nearly walked past the girl, who was still brushing down her skirts. Hannah stopped, gasped and turned. 'Emily! How wonderful to see you! I had hoped you would be the one here.'

Emily bobbed down, her eyes darting around in case any other carts were plunging towards her. 'Yes, missus,' she said. She seemed ill at ease: perhaps it was the prospect – sprung on her – of leaving the familiar, or a recent dressing-down by Henrietta for some small infraction.

'You needn't curtsey to me,' said Hannah. 'I'm here as a servant today, not a mistress.'

'Who are you serving?' asked Emily.

Hannah paused, wondering if this was worth the risk. If Henrietta was aboard and saw her from the deck, Hannah might end up entering the water and never coming out. But Henrietta would surely not involve herself in the tedious business of stocking her cabin for a long voyage. She would likely arrive in state just before sailing.

'The same person as you,' Hannah said to Emily. 'You're making everything ready for the sailing?'

'Yes. The mistress trusts only me with it, you see.'

'And how exciting that you are also going! To see the country where your parents were born – very few get that opportunity.'

Another risk. But having heard Henrietta complain about the tediousness of training servants, she doubted the young lady would want to spend her time in England training another one.

'And you know it's a terribly long, tiring journey,' Hannah said.

Emily nodded. Her eyes shone a little in the growing light.

'Your mistress understands this. It's a journey she has made herself, of course, and she knows about the importance of saying goodbye. She suggested I come and talk to you.'

'But how could she? She is in her cabin.'

Already, thought Hannah.

'Ah, this was a few days ago.'

Emily nodded.

'And she knew that you'd be sad to leave your family, that you might appreciate the opportunity to bid them farewell. She's asked me, you see, to come and finish the work of getting ready to sail.'

'But she said I was the only one –'

'It just shows the regard in which she holds you. She wants you to have this time. There will be precious little once you're under way, I assure you. I'm surprised she didn't mention it – is she a bit distracted, I wonder?'

Emily leaned in, employing the whisper of a servant gossiping about her mistress. 'She hasn't been herself, no.'

'It's disconcerting on the eve of a journey,' said Hannah. 'So much to prepare, and the worries about squalls and storms and God knows what else. But if you hurry, you can say goodbye to Susanna and your parents, and be back here in plenty of time.'

'Perhaps I should ask her,' said Emily. 'I'd hate her to think I was deserting –'

'You could,' said Hannah, 'but you said yourself, she is in a bit of a mood. She might change her mind.'

'And you'll thank her for me?' said Emily, and Hannah nodded reassuringly. 'I'll be back soon, and she can send to me in the meantime if she needs anything.'

Hannah smiled, squeezing Emily's shoulder. 'Of course. I'd be happy to.'

Emily glanced up at the ship once more, as though expecting to see Henrietta on the deck. She bobbed another curtsey to Hannah, then walked up the dock as fast as her skirts would allow her. Hannah looked up at the ship, wondering how difficult it would be to find Henrietta's cabin. Two young sailors were making their way down the gangplank, jostling each other and laughing, perhaps intending one last visit to a Sydney whorehouse.

'You lads planning on having a good morning?' she said as they passed.

They stopped, staring at her. The kind of men who had no place in their world for a woman of Hannah's age, unless it was their mother.

'You'd like a bit more money to spend, perhaps,' she said.

'And why would you give us some?' said one of the sailors.

'I've a message I need delivered. Before you get up to whatever you're going to get up to, go to the schoolhouse behind the baker's. Tell the man there that his friend is in the cabin, keeping a young lady company, and won't leave until someone arrives to escort them safely.'

The sailor held out his hand. She extracted a shilling from the little pouch. She was about to put it on his outstretched palm when she snatched it back. 'Now, how can I know that this is not just going to be spent, that you'll deliver the message?'

'Perhaps you'll pay us more when we come back,' the sailor said.

'Oh yes, happy to provide another shilling if you can come back with proof you've delivered the message. But I should also let you know, I'm here on behalf of the government.' Not actually a lie – the government had paid her passage to Sydney – but she was getting a little concerned by how easily these half-truths slid off her tongue. 'I'm taking care of a woman who is very close to the governor. It is imperative for her safety that this message gets through. If it doesn't, there will be consequences for those charged with delivering it.'

'Well, you can rely on us,' said the sailor. 'We best go do it now. We might be a bit more forgetful later.'

Hannah nodded. 'A fine idea. Bright lads the both of you, I can tell. Off with you now. Don't get into any fights.'

The sailor chuckled and clapped his friend on the back, and they walked up a dock that had seen its share of staggering sailors returning to their ships.

The last time Hannah had been on a ship this size, she had been in its hold. She breathed in and steadied herself, not knowing how she would feel if she saw redcoats on the deck. This was a merchant ship, though – no military. Just gruff and often toothless men tightening this and checking that.

The third one she asked jerked his thumb towards the rear of the boat. Expecting the cabin door to be locked, she was not quite prepared for the creak as it swung open. She closed it behind her and stood in front of it.

Henrietta was sitting with her back to the door, writing at a tiny desk under the cabin's open hatch. 'You have the ink, I hope,' she said without looking up. 'I must have enough for the voyage. God knows what the quality is of the stuff they have on board, if they even have it. Oh, and my quilt needs mending. There's a tiny tear, it'll drive me mad if it's not fixed.'

'Yes, you do like things just so, don't you?' Hannah said. 'Whether it's a quilt or a colony.'

Henrietta spun around. 'Where's Emily?'

'Gone.'

'You wouldn't! You don't have it in you. Don't have the courage.'

'Courage enough to escape from that little room. Why would you assume I'd done something to her? No, she is gone to see her family.'

'She would never desert her post.'

'She would if I told her that you'd offered her the opportunity to say goodbye.'

'Why on earth would she believe something so ridiculous?'

'Perhaps because she is under the mistaken impression that you view her as something more than a tool.'

Henrietta stood. 'Kindly get out of my way.'

'I'm quite comfortable here, thank you.'

Henrietta grabbed Hannah's shoulders, trying to drag her from the door. Hannah calmly ground her heel into Henrietta's foot.

'Guards!' Henrietta yelled. 'Guards, I'm being attacked!'

Hannah laughed. 'No guards here. Everyone's getting the ship ready. And when they burst in and see me? Do you know what I will say?' She deliberately thickened her Irish accent, pruning away the flat r's and the clipped words and the tone that contained no music. 'We're sorry to have disturbed you, sir,' Hannah said, talking to an imaginary guard over Henrietta's shoulder. 'My mistress – she has a nervous complaint, you see. Few people know of it, and I'd appreciate it if you could keep it that way. It's just that sometimes she, well,' Hannah leaned forward and whispered, 'sees things that aren't there.'

'They would never believe you. I am known for my efficiency, my organisation.'

'Not a bit of it. Very few on the lower rungs of society have cause to think much of either you or your brother. I will be believed, because they'll want to believe me. By all means, let's test it out.' Hannah lifted a fist to rap on the door behind her shoulder. 'Guards!' she yelled.

Both women were still and silent for a moment.

'No one coming,' said Hannah. 'No thundering feet dashing down to rescue you. And in truth, you don't need rescuing. I'm not here to harm you – I'm here to talk.'

'I find myself not in the mood for conversation,' said Henrietta.

'Yes, well, I found myself not in the mood to be locked in a cellar and threatened with a gun, but none of us have what we want all the time, do we?'

Henrietta opened the small drawer in her desk – it had been too much to hope that she'd left her mother-of-pearl pistol behind. She pointed it at Hannah. Suddenly the licking fear was back; it tried to crawl up from Hannah's stomach and squeeze her mind until she could no longer think. She rammed it down, hoping it would stay there, and took a shuddering breath. 'Probably not even loaded,' she said, managing to keep her voice from shaking. 'Your brother is widely acknowledged to be one of the best marksmen in Australia, and I know you've done your share of shooting too – enough to understand the folly of keeping a loaded gun in a desk drawer where seas can get rough. But while an accidental shot would be hard to explain, it would be even harder to account for a dead woman bleeding all over your nice cabin. And I told you, I mean no harm.'

'You break into my cabin yet mean no harm?'

'On the contrary, I come with a gift.' Hannah inhaled, hoping Monsarrat would forgive her. It just did not seem as crucial for the letters to reach London as it had yesterday. Either things would be resolved to the point where nobody would need the endorsement of *The Times* of London to believe it, or the Duchamps would prevail, in which case Hannah would likely end up dead. 'I will give you the location of that packet of letters you and your brother are so desperately seeking.'

'They were never on a ship,' said Henrietta. 'We would have found them.'

'Did you search every sailor and make them turn out their pockets?'

Henrietta slowly put down the gun. 'Very well, then, where are they?'

'First, we talk. Let's start with why you did what you did. Why you felt you had the right.'

Henrietta laughed. 'That's it? You've gone to all this trouble because you want to explore my motivations? I'm happy to enlighten you on that score, Mrs Mulrooney – you need only have asked.'

'I am asking now.'

'The last two governors were good men, so everyone says. I disagree. They exercised lax discipline in the hope of redeeming those who are beyond redemption. Is it any wonder soldiers were committing crimes because they believed they were better off as convicts?'

'Until the current governor sent one of them to the grave,' Hannah said.

'Exactly! An example had to be made. Many examples before people learn.'

'And if a young man dies after being forced to work in the blazing sun in impossibly heavy chains – a young man who voluntarily left his country to serve its people out here – that's a price worth paying?'

'Regrettably, sacrifices must be made.'

'So the value of a life is determined by social status, the ability to contribute?'

Henrietta sighed. 'India was a gold mine for people like us,' she said. 'The daughters of officers who had been stationed there would swan around at home, exotic silks and the money to pay for a seamstress. Me, well, let's just say blue muslin can get tiresome. Especially when it draws sneers from idiot girls who can have a different dress every day.'

'Well, I think I've yet to see you in the same outfit.'

'Oh yes, we are on our way. If I'd left it to Eddie, he would have increased our fortunes by finding a rich man for me to marry. But I will not be sold off, especially not to a man who has far less wit than I do. Those ones who simper after me at garden parties.'

'So you have made your own way,' Hannah said.

'Shipping, sealing, skins, tea. Farming, of course. If we capture this ground, people will be paying me court, bringing me petitions.'

Henrietta lifted her chin, lengthened her neck, as though she was already considering the request of a petitioner.

'At the cost of a life,' said Hannah.

'It's easy to go a bit soft in your later years, I know. Nothing to be ashamed of – you're not the first woman I've met who has no appetite for the task of building a colony and claiming one's place among its leaders. But someone needs to, Mrs Mulrooney. Someone needs to recognise that the world runs more smoothly when the right people are in charge. If you are in a coach, would you want a skilled coachman or someone who's just having a turn in the name of fairness? Some people are simply superior to others, and they should have the reins. It's better for everyone, otherwise the whole thing goes off the road and we end up in a ditch.'

'Ah. So it's better for the convicts, and the underclass, to have you sitting in Government House and ordering your dresses from London.'

'It is. And enough insolence about the dresses, thank you. You wouldn't begrudge a soldier his uniform. As for the convicts, have you read Dr Merrick's papers? I have. He says they are born deficient. That they need their betters to guide them, to feed them, and to make sure buildings are built and farms are farmed.'

And who's building the buildings and farming the farms?

'So you never associate with convicts or former convicts,' Hannah said.

'Not if I can avoid it. Your Monsarrat, I had to make an exception for him. Would have been rude not to. Politeness, Mrs Mulrooney, sets us apart from them. He seems to have more wit than most.'

'Oh, he does.' Hannah silently prayed that the present tense was correct. 'He's a highly intelligent man. No one is born deficient, Miss Duchamp.'

'Leading such a sheltered life, you wouldn't have had much experience with convicts, so how could you know? For all that you insist on dressing up as a servant from time to time.' Henrietta ran her eyes up and down Hannah's working clothes.

Here we go, thought Hannah. *For better or worse.*

'How could I know about convicts?' she said. 'I used to be one. I committed my crime to prevent the death of my child, and I would do it again tomorrow.'

Henrietta gaped at her. 'I should have suspected. I knew there was something dreadfully common about you.'

'And yet, I am not less than human. I was not born with a lust for theft – I've taken nothing that is not mine since I arrived here twenty years ago. I have committed fewer crimes than you have, and less serious ones.'

Henrietta smiled, shook her head and reached for the pistol.

'None of this changes anything, Miss Duchamp,' said Hannah. 'The presence of a hole in me would be very difficult to explain away.'

'Not if the ball is at the bottom of the harbour, along with the rest of you,' Henrietta said. 'We are on a boat, yes? You couldn't have planned it better for me, so I thank you.' She smiled, raised the pistol and fired.

Chapter 28

Monsarrat was grateful to be inside the coach for this journey. Had things gone differently, he wouldn't have been surprised if Duchamp had dragged him along behind it.

Jardine had been denied admittance, as had Donnelly and Bancroft. 'Administrative matters, I'm afraid, gentlemen,' Eveleigh said. 'There are plenty of horses – take your pick.'

'You have more advice for me, then, on how to report the wheat yield?' Duchamp asked as they bounced along past dark gaps between looming white trees. 'Or are you just interfering for amusement this time?'

'I assure you I wouldn't have found it at all amusing had I lost my best clerk. It would be very tiresome to train someone else, and in the meantime I would have had to do all the work myself. Imagine if Jardine was suddenly taken from you – most inconvenient.'

Duchamp inclined his head in acknowledgement. Monsarrat wasn't surprised that Duchamp was more than happy to discuss him as though he were a bale of cloth at a market. That Eveleigh seemed willing to do likewise was more of a concern. Monsarrat hopefully ascribed his superior's seeming indifference to the need to lull Duchamp into thinking he had a sympathetic ear.

Any hopes Duchamp might have had of sympathy, though, were shattered in the next instant.

'I don't find this grubby little conspiracy of yours particularly amusing either,' Eveleigh said.

'Oh? You would rather have let Hallward destroy the authority we need to govern?'

'As far as authority goes, I've always felt it incumbent on us to earn it. By behaving appropriately. By leading. By not murdering those we govern.'

'I did no such thing,' said Duchamp. 'But the only reason you don't see Hallward as a problem is that he is not *your* problem. He was whining in print every day about land grants and the treatment of convicts, especially those who used to be soldiers. You, Mr Eveleigh, were not one of his favourite targets – I was. Puts rather a different complexion on things.'

Monsarrat's shadow – it, too, responded to the idea of impunity when it came to punishing one's tormentors, although it did draw the line at murder.

'I was on the receiving end of the occasional barb, when Hallward bothered to turn his eyes westward,' said Eveleigh. 'But you're right, he did not pillory me about land grants, almost certainly because I haven't been given any.'

Duchamp leaned forward. 'That can change, Eveleigh. Lovely farmland out around Rose Hill, I understand.'

Eveleigh clapped his hands and rubbed them together, and for a second Monsarrat feared he had been misjudging the man, mistaking practicality for moral rigour.

He needn't have worried.

'Oh, how fascinating. A bribe!' Eveleigh said. 'I fear I must decline, though.'

'I am not bribing you, Eveleigh. I haven't done anything wrong to make such an action necessary. I simply seek to elevate your station – however, if you have no wish to be elevated, it's probably all for the best.'

'Done nothing wrong? I would be most grateful if you could explain to me how you came to that conclusion.'

'You're not in the governor's confidence,' said Duchamp, 'so you might not be aware of the plans to license newspapers. All in response to Hallward, of course. Mobbs is a solid fellow, but the *Flyer* would have been hit as well – can't apply it to one and not another. They both would have needed government permission to operate. The licence would be withheld if we felt that a particular paper was being regularly used to peddle sedition.'

'And there's a matter of tax, I understand,' said Eveleigh.

'Yes, four pence.'

'No one is going to spend so much on a newspaper, are they?' said Eveleigh. 'Even if it's your friend's.'

'They won't have to now, that's the point. The governor does not have to resort to regulation now that the only newspaper in Sydney is run by a responsible man, a fellow who understands what a misplaced word can unleash. I might remind you that my attempts to discourage Mr Hallward did not at any time amount to a breach of the law.'

'Perhaps not,' said Eveleigh. 'Oh, except the murder. That, I am fairly certain, could be described as a breach of the law.'

'A murder I had nothing to do with.'

Monsarrat had been holding his tongue, knowing that Eveleigh liked to talk uninterrupted. He had been doing a first-rate job of silently chipping away at Duchamp. But there hadn't yet been time for Monsarrat to tell Eveleigh everything he knew. And Duchamp liked drama – an unexpected interjection would land between them far more devastatingly than one that had been discussed in whispers beforehand.

'What did you think Mobbs would do with the pistol you gave him?' Monsarrat asked.

Duchamp glared at him, then turned to Eveleigh. 'For God's sake, keep your man under control. His ramblings are interfering with our business.'

'Yes, he does ramble. But sometimes he rambles to interesting places. I would like to see where he is bound right now.'

Monsarrat briefly bowed his head to Eveleigh, before turning to Duchamp and pointedly failing to repeat the gesture. 'You gave the pistol you fired at Hallward during your duel to Mobbs so he could help it complete its task.'

'I did no such thing.'

'Odd, then, that the ball in Hallward's forehead came from a pistol. Likely a duelling pistol. And you are in possession of some of the very few scratch-rifled pistols in the colony. The only ones capable of a hit at that range.'

'How did you . . . Dr Merrick would never –'

'Merrick didn't,' said Monsarrat. 'But, of course, he is not the only person with access to the effects of the deceased.'

'Be careful, Mr Monsarrat,' said Duchamp. 'I could have you charged for obstructing the investigation. If that's not already an offence, I'll make sure it becomes one.'

'Obstructing the investigation? Obstructing myself?'

Unexpectedly, the ridiculousness of the situation enfolded Monsarrat, and he began to laugh. One of the first genuine laughs he had ever emitted in Sydney. He looked across at Eveleigh, who was keeping a straight face.

'The only obstruction, Colonel,' Monsarrat said, 'was from you. Oh, and that helpful piece Mobbs wrote about my criminal past, his analysis of my character.'

'And yet,' said Eveleigh, 'despite such a vicious attack from a member of the press, Monsarrat somehow refrained from entering into a conspiracy to kill the journalist. So you see, it can be done.'

He is enjoying this, thought Monsarrat. *Ralph Eveleigh, who hoards smiles as though they were money, is enjoying himself.*

Duchamp, though, clearly was not. 'Who do you think the governor will believe? A felon twice over, and the man who thought such a person was an appropriate representative of the governor – or someone he has been under fire with?'

Eveleigh leaned forward. 'Colonel, I feel I can say without any doubt that the governor will believe what it suits him to believe. Of course, if it also suits us, what is the harm?'

'You and I have rather different objectives, Eveleigh,' said Duchamp.

'Do we? I wonder. Let's set those objectives out, shall we? See if there's any area where they, if you'll excuse me, bleed together.'

Hannah's life was saved by the British guns that had been fired at her more than a quarter of a century ago. She had practised with her fiancé Colm before the old uprising. Ducking, running. Sensing danger and dropping before it could be carried to them on a musket ball. They didn't dive to the ground; it was quicker, Colm had told her, just to let things go, let all the intention out of your muscles so that they no longer allowed you to remain upright. If you simply crumpled, you dropped out of sight for an instant – and sometimes an instant was all you needed.

With a gun again aimed at her, and no child in need of protection, Hannah dropped.

She felt the air disturbed by the shot as it whizzed over her head, the vibration of the door as its timber splintered.

And on the other side of it she heard the yelp, the thud.

She looked up. Henrietta was staring at her pistol with a frown, as though wondering why it had failed to hit Hannah.

The young lady and the pistol could have all the time they wanted together, thought Hannah. On the other side of the door, however, it was likely someone was badly hurt. She had to pull it a few times to get it open, as the shock of the impact had warped it.

Sitting with his back against the bulkhead was a young sailor. He wore the sparse whiskers of the newly grown. He was wide-eyed, sweating and panting, and blood was pouring from a wound in his shoulder.

Hannah kneeled next to him. 'Settle down now, *a buachaill*, there's a boy. I am looking after you now. You're going to keep your eyes open, is what you're going to do, and keep talking to me. And we will fetch the ship's surgeon, and you'll be back on the rigging before you know it. You look like a tough one – not going to let yourself be dispatched by a shoulder wound, I'm sure. What's your name?'

'Jack,' the boy whispered.

'Jack, my boy, you're going to have a wonderful story to tell those old sods in the galley tonight. Bet half of them haven't been shot, no matter what they tell you. And right now my friend is going to . . .' She turned around. Henrietta was standing in the doorway, the pistol still at her side. 'Have you a scarf? A shawl?'

Henrietta kept staring.

Hannah stood, took her by the shoulders and hissed in her ear. 'For God's sake, do you want this boy's murder on your soul?'

Henrietta darted back into her cabin, fetched a shawl and handed it to Hannah.

'Now go fetch the surgeon,' Hannah said.

'What are we . . . What are you going to say?' Henrietta asked.

'Depends on whether you bring the surgeon back in time. Off with you!'

It was probably the first command Henrietta had ever obeyed, particularly from a social inferior. She lifted her skirts and ran up the corridor.

Hannah crumpled the shawl and pressed it against the wound. 'Now, Jack, do you have a sweetheart? Handsome lad like you, you must do. You don't seem like the kind of sailor who goes to whorehouses. I want you to tell me about the colour of her eyes . . .'

Monsarrat had seen Jardine stand preternaturally still. Now, though, that ability seemed to have deserted the man. He stood, walked to the window. Sat. Stood again. Monsarrat, an inveterate pacer himself, found himself feeling increasingly sympathetic to Mrs Mulrooney. Entering its second hour, Jardine's ovoid path around the rug in the outer office was beginning to grate.

'You might as well sit,' Monsarrat said. 'There's nothing either of us can do. Did you know? Any of it?'

'I knew he hated Hallward, which put him on a par with half of the officers and administrators and pastoralists and clergy in the colony,' said Jardine. 'And I knew there were discussions about licensing newspapers and so on, but Mobbs rarely visited – certainly no more than you'd expect.' Jardine sat down. There were several sumptuously upholstered chairs to choose from, but the lieutenant chose a spindly wooden one against the wall, resting his head on the flocked wallpaper. 'Perhaps I should have seen it. But you know how men like the colonel carry on, blustering and ranting at the latest person who has displeased them.' He rubbed his eyes. 'Forgive me. It has been sometime since I slept, being too busy guarding you. I have not yet begun to grieve for the colonel.'

Monsarrat found himself stifling an impolite yawn, blinked in the hope that the sleep-fogged world he and Jardine now inhabited would become clearer, brighter.

'You very well may not have to. Highly likely nothing will happen to him,' he said.

'But something already has. The man who convinced me to leave England behind, it's him I grieve for. Do you know, Mr Monsarrat, I was on the verge of leaving the army? Thought I'd get into farming. Comfortable cottage near a lake, pretty wife, that sort of thing. But the way he spoke about this place – he said we had an opportunity to construct a society as it should be done. We wouldn't need to weave the old evils into the fabric – we could make whatever pattern we wanted. And we would do it through courage, honour, honesty. That man knew what he was about and went about it publicly with direct, decisive action. This skulking about, these secret deals, the splitting of hairs over whether providing someone with ammunition makes you a murderer – that is not a man I recognise.'

The door to the office opened, and Ralph Eveleigh stepped out. 'Gentlemen!' he said, as though they were old friends who had arrived unexpectedly. 'I think you had both better come in.'

'Young Jack will be back on his feet in a few days, thanks to you staunching the wound,' the surgeon said. 'You will not be short-handed for long, Captain Hart.'

Hannah smiled. Her insistence on seeking out Henrietta had nearly killed this boy, and she had no wish to see another young man fall to an English weapon.

'I would very much like to know exactly what transpired to put that lead in him,' said the captain.

They were seated in the map room, around a table littered with papers that had been hastily abandoned when the captain had heard the shot.

Hannah had not been listening as carefully as she should have to his name. He had the kind of northern English accent Hannah tended to associate with the relentlessly practical.

He was looking at Henrietta.

She said, 'I shall return to my brother, the governor's private secretary. He will attend to the matter.'

'I will attend to the matter,' said the captain. 'This is not a navy vessel, madam. I am responsible for its safety, and that of its crew, and I answer to the East India Company, not to the governor.' He leaned back, eyeing her. 'You will be leaving the ship,' he said. 'And if your brother wasn't your brother, he would no doubt be sending a detachment down here to arrest you. Now, I ask you again – what happened?'

Henrietta glared at him silently.

He turned to Hannah. 'And you – do you have anything to say?'

'I begged her not to take the pistol. But a woman travelling alone – she said she wouldn't feel safe without it. And then – she is a little clumsy. Has a problem with her nerves.'

If I am going to have to lie for you, Hannah thought, *I might as well enjoy it.*

'You wouldn't credit it, sir,' she continued. 'I found her screaming last week, because she had seen a fly on a rose petal. So, well, she found a ship full of sailors disconcerting, especially for a woman in such a ...' Hannah leaned forward and put on a conspiratorial whisper. 'Such a delicate mental condition. Anyway, she heard some sort of splash outside. Might have thought it was a sea monster. Startled her, poor lamb, and she dropped the pistol. It went off, and poor Jack has paid the price for her skittishness.'

'And,' the captain said, 'Jack happened to be lying on the floor to catch a ball from a pistol that went off when it hit the ground?'

'I think it might have hit at an angle,' Hannah said. 'Must've done. Only explanation.'

'Very well. As Jack will recover, I won't be pursuing the matter, but pistol-wielding women are not welcome aboard. You will see to it that she vacates this vessel immediately.'

'Of course.' Hannah rose, went over and put her hand under Henrietta's shoulder, helping her to her feet as though she was an invalid. 'Come along, my dear. We'll get you home and tucked into bed with a nice cup of tea, and then the doctor will give you some of that special medicine you like.'

Henrietta was too smart to rebuke Hannah for the picture she had drawn. But Hannah tried not to imagine what kind of revenge the woman would seek were she ever in a position to do so.

Chapter 29

'You shouldn't need to take more than two or three men,' Duchamp said to Jardine. 'Mobbs won't expect to be arrested, so by the time he realises what's happening, hopefully you'll have him in irons.'

Jardine nodded. 'Yes, sir. And on my return I will be resigning my commission.'

Duchamp leaned back in his chair, staring at Jardine. 'You'll do no such thing,' he said. 'You will be punished for insubordination.'

'As you wish, sir,' said Jardine through barely open lips. He saluted, turned and left.

'No, he won't,' said Monsarrat.

Eveleigh and Duchamp both turned to him, astounded in the face of such a reversal of nature: a convict giving an order to the private secretary.

Monsarrat was not sure that what he was about to say was a good idea. Jardine had treated him decently, but unless Eveleigh backed Monsarrat, he could very well end up in gaol with Mobbs. Although that would almost be worth it, he thought. Anything to salvage something good out of this distasteful bargain that Eveleigh and Duchamp had struck.

The Duchamps' part in the conspiracy – and the existence of the conspiracy itself – would be buried. After all, what they really needed was a killer. And they had a killer. All they had to do was introduce him to the public. If Mobbs started talking about the colonel or his sister, he would be dismissed as raving, or mendacious, making up stories to avoid punishment for his crime. If anyone asked Monsarrat or Jardine, they were both informed that they would be arrested if they answered.

Monsarrat now understood how Jardine had felt when he mourned the superior he thought he knew. Monsarrat himself, when he had leisure, would silently keen for Ralph Eveleigh.

'You are asking the lieutenant to swallow his principles,' said Monsarrat. 'And you will not punish him for refusing.'

'Will I not?' said Duchamp. 'Perhaps the two of you can discuss it when you're in the guardhouse together.'

'Yes, certainly. That will give us leisure to read *The Times* when it arrives.'

'I don't believe you ever put those papers on a boat bound for England.'

'I suppose you'll find out in due course,' said Monsarrat. 'The ship has not left yet, by the way. I have until the morning to retrieve them – might be a little difficult, from the guardhouse. However, I will happily run there now, at all speed, if you agree to my terms.'

'I am not giving you money, Mr Monsarrat.'

'That's fortunate, as I don't want any. No, you've done quite well out of those land grants from the governor. You will share his largesse. I happen to believe that Mr Jardine – as he will be soon – would make quite a fine farmer. You will transfer to him a sizeable amount of land – good land, mind – and organise his honourable discharge.'

Duchamp turned to Eveleigh. 'This is why I don't hire former convicts. You must bear some blame, of course, for not doing more to keep him under control. But honestly, this is the end. Leave him with me, if you please, and I will make sure he learns some discipline.'

Monsarrat held Eveleigh's eyes. He did not know how severely he had misjudged the man. All Eveleigh would need to do was nod and Monsarrat would descend into a confinement from which there would be no release.

Eveleigh gave a long, hard stare. 'Do you know, Monsarrat, you are an extremely useful man, but sometimes you're more trouble than you're worth.' He turned to Duchamp. 'Mr Monsarrat will be returning to Parramatta with me, Colonel. He will not be threatened, pursued, incarcerated, or anything else. I do hope there is time to get those papers from the ship, but other copies exist, and I will not hesitate to make use of them if I have to.'

Duchamp stood up and kicked his chair. 'You two deserve each other.'

Eveleigh shrugged. 'Perhaps we do. I'll take it as a compliment. Oh, and please don't forget the rest of our bargain. I will be authorised to take on a second clerk, and confirmed as private secretary for Parramatta.'

'Go to the devil.'

'Not the assurance I was expecting, Colonel. Perhaps you'd like to try again?'

Duchamp put his palms on the desk, pressing down. 'I am sorely tempted, Eveleigh, to admit everything just for the pleasure of seeing you sacked and your lackey hanged.'

'Except you might hang with him,' said Eveleigh. 'And you may not be the only one.'

'Henrietta? She's on her way to England. No one's arm is that long.'

So, there really were no plans to punish the Duchamps, thought Monsarrat. Mobbs would bear the guilt for the three of them, while the brother and sister would still be hosting parties long after the last editions of the *Chronicle* had yellowed. But because Mrs Mulrooney had needed to feed her infant son, she had been ripped from her home. Eveleigh's bargain was not one Monsarrat would have made; it was not one he felt he could support. But he hadn't been in the room when it had been hammered out. It had involved, no doubt, the trading of influence, some chest beating and bluster, and threats both veiled and naked.

Perhaps Monsarrat could convince Eveleigh to do something – anything – to cause even minor discomfort for the Duchamps. Some sort of signal to them that shooting people and kidnapping children had consequences.

But Eveleigh was stubborn. Once something was agreed, he would not unpick it without the most compelling reasons. And his time, it turned out, was short.

'Well, Duchamp,' he said, standing, 'I wish you the best of luck, particularly without Jardine. Man of honour, by the looks of it. And those letters – they're not at my home, nor my office, in case you are intending to send someone to check. For all the good it'd do searching for them, they might as well be at the bottom of the ocean.'

'And I wish you were with them,' said Duchamp. 'I shan't bother wishing you a pleasant journey.'

'Never mind, we shall have one anyway,' said Eveleigh. 'I have arranged for a little cutter to take us up the river tomorrow morning. There is a lot for us to do, including the engagement of the second clerk who will free Mr Monsarrat to concentrate on more unconventional duties.'

Monsarrat and Eveleigh stood at the front of the house. Monsarrat could almost feel the colonel's brooding intent like heat from a fire, as he sat in his office and no doubt tried to convince himself he had outsmarted the men from the west.

'Sir,' said Monsarrat to Eveleigh, 'Mobbs deserves punishment, no question, but he is not the only –'

'I'm going to stop you there, Monsarrat. This decision isn't yours, and has been made.'

'But –'

'In any case,' said Eveleigh, 'I am well acquainted with your housekeeper's, shall we say, intractable character, and she will be most displeased with you if you don't greet her.'

'But she's –'

'Coming up the drive,' said Eveleigh. 'With an intriguing entourage.'

Monsarrat turned. A cart, of the kind that would normally transport grain or lumber, was rolling up towards them. Next to the driver sat a man dressed in the uniform of a merchant captain. Next to him was Henrietta Duchamp, wearing a look of such anger that Monsarrat half expected trees to ignite as she passed.

In the back of the cart, seemingly unconcerned by the judders that must have been travelling up through the wheels to the flatbed, sat Mrs Mulrooney. Monsarrat stared, and then began to chuckle.

'I will wager that is by far the humblest conveyance Miss Henrietta Duchamp has ever travelled in,' said Eveleigh. 'And to be accompanied by a servant and a seaman – well, all I can say is I can't wait to hear the story behind it all.'

Eveleigh did not have to wait long. When the cart was still rolling to a stop, Henrietta jumped down, all high dudgeon and blue silk, and stormed up to the guard at the Government House door. 'Arrest this woman!' she said, pulling her arm backwards to point at Mrs Mulrooney, who looked not the least bit worried. 'And him, while you're about it,' she said, nodding towards Monsarrat.

Eveleigh gave a courtly bow. 'Miss Duchamp,' he said. 'Ralph Eveleigh, your brother's Parramatta counterpart. I don't believe we've met.'

'I doubt you are in any way comparable to my brother. And you appear to be leaving, Mr Eveleigh, which is all to the good.' She turned back to the soldier. 'Well?'

Eveleigh glanced over at the soldier, shaking his head. 'I'm afraid I can't allow that, madam. These two people have, you see, committed no crime that has gone unpunished. Unlike some here.'

By now, the seaman was approaching, and Mrs Mulrooney had slid off the back of the cart and was brushing down her skirts. She looked up, saw Monsarrat, clapped her hands together and beamed.

'I can't say who needs arresting and who doesn't,' the seaman said to Eveleigh. 'But this woman wounded one of my crew and damaged my ship. I would like to talk with whoever can make recompense.'

'Oh dear, I am sorry for any inconvenience you have been caused,' said Eveleigh. 'Allow me to conduct you to the lady's brother – who, as it turns out, is the only one who can order an arrest.'

As Eveleigh and the merchant captain went inside, with Henrietta stalking after them, Mrs Mulrooney raced up the steps towards Monsarrat, barrelling into him and trying to get her arms all the way around his back. It was the first time Mrs Mulrooney had ever embraced him. He was surprised by the gesture, a little shocked and very, very pleased.

'Eejit of a man, I feared you dead!'

'Well, it seems you will need to deal with my idiocy for a while longer.'

'Monsarrat!' Eveleigh had returned and was standing, arms folded, at the door. 'A clerk might be of use in here.'

'Mr Eveleigh!' called Mrs Mulrooney. 'Can I tempt you with some shortbread when this is over?'

He gave her a rare smile. 'My dear, you are the only lady in the colony who knows my true weakness. For now, though, I must relieve you of your nanny duty and deprive you of your charge. I have a task for him.'

'Off with you, then, Mr Monsarrat,' she said. 'There are some other lads I need to sort out.'

⁂

'It is only because she is your sister that she is not in my brig. That, and she seems a little simple.'

Henrietta glared at Captain Hart and opened her mouth, then shut it again after a warning look from her brother.

'All I know is she nearly came to harm on your ship, Captain,' said Duchamp. 'Why should I not have you prosecuted?'

'If anyone should be prosecuted –'

'Do you really want to pursue this, against the sister of the governor's secretary?' Duchamp asked.

Hart said something under his breath. It sounded, to Monsarrat, a lot like a word he had heard other sailors employ in extremis. Hart added, in a louder voice, 'Clearly I do not, sir, which is why she is here and not below decks on my ship.'

'And you brought her here like a sack of grain in a cart.'

'You, sir, should be thanking me. I have a young sailor lying wounded. I have a ship full of cargo that has missed the tide. And I have an owner to write to. Perhaps I should tell him that we are delayed due to weather. Or perhaps I should recommend he seek compensation for the late sailing – from you, personally. The contents of my letter will depend on your next action.'

Duchamp stood slowly, clearing his throat. 'I thank you, Captain, for delivering my sister safely home. As I'm aware you are unable to reassign her cabin at short notice, I would like you to keep the cost of her passage. I suggest you return to your ship and make ready to sail at the earliest opportunity.'

Hart nodded, bowing slightly.

'But my luggage!' screeched Henrietta. 'My pistol!'

'Your luggage awaits you on the dock,' said Hart. 'As for your pistol, I do not believe you should be in possession of such an item. I have confiscated it, and it is now in the hands of someone who can be trusted to make sure it doesn't, well, misfire.'

―☙―

The pistol felt heavy in Hannah's pocket. It had no ball or powder in it now; it was merely a relic, a beautiful but meaningless object. She had no intention of reloading it, now or ever. And she certainly had no intention of reuniting it with its owner. She was grateful to the ship's captain for disarming Henrietta, but suspected the woman wouldn't remain disarmed for long.

The lads didn't see her at first when she looked into the schoolroom. Cullen had Peter in his lap. The boy had dozed off, slumped against Cullen's chest, as Cullen listened to Donnelly, who was cross-legged on top of his desk.

'We had no idea whether we would be there in time,' Donnelly was saying. 'We kept listening for shots – ah! There she is!' He jumped off the desk.

Cullen beamed. Peter stirred and woke.

'Our heroine,' said Donnelly.

'Stop that blathering,' Hannah said.

'Oh, I'm not the only one who thinks so – look.' He pointed to the board. A child's drawing showed a woman wearing a white blob of a servant's hat. She was holding a sword, and facing a creature that might have been a dragon.

'Did you do this, Peter?' Hannah asked.

The boy nodded, still a little groggy from his sleep.

'It is by far the best drawing I have ever seen,' she said.

'That's what I told him,' said Cullen. He deposited Peter on the floor, went to Hannah and took her hand. 'Are you unharmed? Did you find Miss Duchamp?'

'Yes,' said Hannah. 'I doubt there'll be any consequences for her, though. Perhaps not for any of them.'

'Ah, well, you might be wrong there,' said Donnelly. 'I heard Mobbs was arrested earlier. How true it is, I don't know.'

'Nothing would surprise me, not with that one and her brother. But for now,' Hannah kneeled down, taking Peter by the shoulders, 'I thought you might like to come back to the boarding house and eat shortbread and sleep in a feather bed for the night. *After* a wash. There's a dragon who lives there – she looks a lot like a woman – but we just ignore her and she goes away after a while.' Hannah looked up at Cullen. 'Will you be all right without the lad?'

Cullen smiled. 'If I know you're the one taking care of him. You probably don't believe it, but I have a cottage. Haven't always lived at the *Chronicle*. Just enough room for a little bed near the hearth, when you've finished ruining the boy. For as long as we stay there, anyway.'

'You're moving on?'

'I seem to be out of a job. But I hear there are more opportunities to the west. I wonder, if I find myself passing through Parramatta, would you have any objection to a caller?'

⁓

Eveleigh and Monsarrat were standing outside Government House, looking down across the green slope towards the dazzling harbour.

'And are we to leave tomorrow?' asked Monsarrat. 'I can't help feeling as though the job isn't done.'

Eveleigh glanced sideways at him. 'Mr Monsarrat, have you something to say to me?'

Monsarrat paused. Eveleigh was not the worst of them, not by a long way. But very bound up in structure, in hierarchy, in the respect due to his office. Criticism from a clerk may not be taken well. Still, the man had invited him to speak, and the shadow had not yet receded far enough to allow him to hold his tongue.

'I took you, sir, for a believer in justice. How is this outcome just?' asked Monsarrat. Judging by the shock on his face, Eveleigh was as surprised by the challenge as Monsarrat was himself. Perhaps, thought Monsarrat, his own respect for authority was not as robust as it was when he arrived in Sydney.

'Yes, Mobbs will be punished, deserves to be,' he continued. 'But what about Duchamp and his sister? They conspired to kill a man and enslave a colony, yet there is to be no consequence?'

'No, there is not.'

'And does it not enrage you?'

'Mr Monsarrat, I do not get enraged. But I am not happy about it. You are right, they deserve punishment. But you and I do not live in a world of ideals. We cannot afford to. Don't forget that Duchamp was probably acting on the governor's orders, or at least with his knowledge, and even if he's not, they are brothers in arms and the governor has shown an inclination to give favours to those he is close to. If I were to push for a trial, I would get nowhere. Everything would be swept under the rug, and I would find myself reassigned to Van Diemen's Land. Unless they were able to find a credible complaint against me, so that I could vault the chasm and join the ranks of convicts.'

'You are silent from fear?'

'I am silent from practicality. At least this way, Mr Monsarrat, someone pays – someone who deserves to. But if payment is to be extracted from Duchamp or his sister, it will occur in the afterlife.'

'So, expediency and connections are more valuable than justice.'

'They shouldn't be, but they are,' said Eveleigh. 'Come on, Mr Monsarrat, you know this! You have lived through its consequences. I took no joy in negotiating away the just punishment for the Duchamps. But I would do it again, because it was the only way.'

'And you get another clerk out of it.'

'This should please you, Mr Monsarrat,' Eveleigh said.

'Well, it doesn't displease me.'

'Ah, your reaction is far too muted. And I am intimately familiar with muted reactions, so I know what I am speaking of. Because with another clerk, I might be able to allow you some time to search in the west for a certain female convict.'

Chapter 30

Two months later

Gerald James Mobbs, former editor of this newspaper, has been placed at the bar to receive sentence following his confession to the wilful murder of Henry Thomas Hallward, the editor of the now defunct *Sydney Chronicle*.

His Honour, after much deliberation, passed the sentence of death. Having consideration for Mr Mobbs's contribution to the colony over many years, the sentence was commuted to life.

Monsarrat folded the *Colonial Flyer* and laid it on the table in his parlour – his own parlour, thankfully, in his little cottage in Parramatta, with no one to scold him for getting newsprint on the tablecloth.

'If you smudge that, you'll be washing it.'

'I do apologise,' he said, putting the paper under his arm and looking up at Mrs Mulrooney. 'It's happened just like Eveleigh said. They'll probably tuck him away in some quiet penal settlement – can't see him on a chain gang.'

Mrs Mulrooney sat opposite him. 'It's been a month. You must stop picking at it.'

'But look! Look at this.' He handed her the newspaper. 'Bottom of the page.'

He waited as she read, squinting a little as the lamp on the table battled with the dusk. The words, contained in a border due to the importance of the news, notified the reader that Miss Henrietta Duchamp was to marry some baronet from Hertfordshire.

'Duchamp probably needed to get her out of the way. But still, hardly a just punishment,' Monsarrat said.

'She will make her own prison, Mr Monsarrat, and you must leave her to it. Ah, Helen, let me help with that.' Mrs Mulrooney walked to the parlour door and held it open for the young convict who had been assigned to them as a servant.

Helen had to turn sideways, and probably inhale, to get both herself and the tea tray through the door. 'You should sit, missus,' she said. 'I cannot be a servant if you will not allow me to serve.'

Mrs Mulrooney laughed and did as she was told. The girl who had come to them from the Female Factory, with a daughter conceived through unwilling congress with the superintendent, had been quiet, watchful; the young woman who was now emerging was quick witted, efficient and just a little bold.

Helen was followed into the room by Eliza in her nightdress, the little girl dragging a doll as she trotted up to the table and climbed without invitation into Mrs Mulrooney's lap. Helen put her tray on the table, and Mrs Mulrooney started feeding Eliza morsels of shortbread. She seemed to care far less about the crumbs on the tablecloth than she had about the newsprint.

'Have you washed the windows?' she asked Helen.

'I have. Yesterday, too, and I'll be happy to do them again tomorrow if you like. But you know that he's not coming for the windows.' She smiled and laid an affectionate hand on Mrs Mulrooney's shoulder, who put up her own hand to squeeze it.

'You seem to be more excited at the prospect of my assistant clerk than I am,' Monsarrat said.

'Mr Cullen will make an excellent clerk, Mr Monsarrat. And I can try to put some fat on to young Peter.' To Helen, she said, 'It's good of you to take on another one. Peter won't mind where he sleeps, but I'd rather him here than in the Prancing Stag with Mr Cullen, at least until they find more permanent lodgings.'

'It's no trouble, missus,' said Helen. 'Now, if you feel she's had enough shortbread, I'd better get Eliza into . . . Oh, I'll answer it.'

The knock was not the tentative tap of someone sorry to rouse a household as night drew in; nor was it the hammering of someone to whom knocking was a prelude to breaking down a door. It was polite but forceful.

'Nonsense, off you go, Helen,' said Mrs Mulrooney. 'Mr Monsarrat will get the door and I'll take care of the tray.'

The man at the door looked rough. Dirty. Judging by the lathered state of the horse tied to the fence behind him, he had ridden for some time to get here. Monsarrat might have been alarmed, but the fellow's darting blue eyes were familiar. He was young, but it was hard to tell how young, as his lower face was obscured by a beard – red-gold, like his hair.

'You must be Mr Monsarrat,' he said, in an accent Monsarrat had heard with increasing frequency lately, unique to this place, with its far more elongated vowels and far less crisp consonants. 'May I . . . may I come in? I'm –'

Monsarrat heard a shriek behind him, and the clatter of a dropped tray. He was nearly knocked off his feet as a blur dashed past him, and then Mrs Mulrooney was sobbing, reaching up, flinging her arms around the fellow's neck, dragging his head down so his cheek could be kissed, and kissed again.

Monsarrat smiled, stood aside and gestured for the man to enter. 'I presume,' he said, 'that I have the honour of addressing Padraig Mulrooney.'

※

Padraig was having to eat one-handed. His other hand was being held by his mother. In the past half-hour he had been hugged, kissed, wept on, cuffed on the ear, told he was an eejit of a boy, sent to wash his face at the pump behind the house, and ordered to get a bucket of water for 'that darling horse that brought you safely', which was now standing near the pump sampling the greenery.

Padraig was still in his travelling clothes and doing his best not to dirty the tablecloth, but a few stray smears of road dust had found their way onto the pristine white. Mrs Mulrooney did not seem to mind. 'I will have your hide if you go silent again for so long,' she said, kissing his hand.

'I am sorry, Ma, I knew you would worry but I've been on my way back to you all this time, working eastwards. I gave the odd letter to the driver of the mail cart, hoping he would ignore the fact that I couldn't pay. I suppose he didn't.'

'I thought you were dead!'

'If you haven't killed me, no one can.' He ducked to avoid the cuff he knew would come, then turned to Monsarrat. 'Thank you, sir, for looking after her. Keeping her safe.'

'You are most welcome,' said Monsarrat, 'but it has been rather the other way around.'

'Padraig, you can stop here as long as you wish,' Mrs Mulrooney said. 'It might be a little crowded but we will all squeeze in – won't we, Mr Monsarrat?'

'Of course, and I am more than happy to sleep at the office – I suspect Eveleigh would approve.'

'You'll do no such thing. We will manage.'

Padraig sighed. 'I am sorry, Ma, truly. But I won't be able to stay for more than a few days. I've been sent on an errand.'

'To fetch what?' said Mrs Mulrooney.

'The both of you, if you'd consider a journey west.'

Monsarrat smiled. 'I had been considering such a journey in any case,' he said. 'But may I ask why?'

'My mother has written to me of your success. Two murderers identified, against the most challenging of odds.'

'Four, now,' said Mrs Mulrooney. 'Well, six really, but that's a story for the journey.'

Padraig turned to his mother. 'I boasted about you to the overseer, to the other drovers. The last property I was droving on, I was there for a few weeks. They had plenty of time to hear the stories, so when it started happening, they sent me to get you.'

'When what started happening?' asked Mrs Mulrooney.

'Convicts. Dying. Killed by the same hand, probably, but in different ways. Imaginative ways – ways that match their crimes. An embezzler had promissory notes stuffed into his mouth until he choked. A man who'd stolen an expensive necklace was strangled with a cheap one. A seditious priest was ... well, crucified. No one knows who's next, or if the killer will stop at convicts, but everyone agrees on one thing. They want someone to come, and quickly. They want the best. And that, everyone says, is the pair of you.'

Authors' Note

Attempts by governments to discredit or stifle the media are dangerous, but they are a long way from new.

In New South Wales in the mid- to late 1820s, Governor Ralph Darling was a frequent target of two newspapermen in particular. His responses nearly cost the colony an independent press.

This is the environment in which *The Ink Stain* is set. We wrote it because we thought it was a good story, and we intend it to be enjoyed as just that – a story, not a manifesto. But we also wrote it because in the current climate it bears repeating that a free and fearless press is one of the most precious products of democratic societies. It's also important to remember how quickly such freedoms can be taken away.

While this is a work of fiction, we are now well and truly in the habit of basing the situations and people Monsarrat and Mrs Mulrooney encounter on real people and events, and here we lay out what is fact and what is fabrication.

Many of the fictional events based on real situations occur out of order, or earlier than they actually did. We have compressed the timeline in some instances, to account for the fact that this book is set early in the term of Governor Darling.

Edward Smith Hall and Dr Robert Wardell

Henry Hallward is an amalgamation (as is his surname) of two newspaper editors working in Sydney at the time this story is set, and events from both of their lives have been fictionalised in Hallward's.

Edward Smith Hall, who also holds the distinction of founding the New South Wales Benevolent Society, was editor of the *Monitor*, and arguably Ralph Darling's chief antagonist. Darling described him as 'a fellow without principles, an apostate missionary', and a 'revolutionary scribbler'.

Hall was a frequent critic of Darling and his administration. He was vehemently opposed to the mistreatment of convicts, regularly called for civilian juries at a time when military juries were the norm, and often criticised the decisions of magistrates and what he saw as Darling's draconian approach to governing the colony. Many of his attacks centred on Darling's practice of giving land grants and other favours to friends and family, and Hall decried the nepotism and cronyism which he saw as a hallmark of Darling's governorship. Hall was arrested seven times for criminal libel and, like the fictional Hallward, often continued to edit his newspaper from prison.

Governor Darling was not Hall's only target. Hall wrote a satirical piece on the income of Archdeacon Thomas Hobbes Scott of St James' Church (which still stands, in King Street, Sydney, and is still operating as a church). He also criticised Scott for his involvement in politics, and one of his criminal libel charges relates to his writings about Scott (he was the first person in the colony to be convicted of this particular crime). Hallward's fictional piece in this novel includes phrases directly lifted from one of Hall's articles.

Like Hallward, Hall was also involved in a long-running dispute with the church over a box pew at St James' Church. Hall, a widower with eight children, had leased a pew for £4 a year. One morning in 1828, as he led his family in to worship, he found his name removed from it, on the pretext that it was needed for public officials, an excuse Hall did not believe. He refused an offer of an inferior pew in a draughty part of the church.

The next Sunday, on finding the door to the pew locked, he vaulted over its walls and forced the lock so his children could enter. The Sunday after that, finding a roof had been nailed onto the pew, he and his family sat on the chancel steps. After several other disputes and incursions on the pew, some involving constables, Hall was summonsed for trespass, and sued Archdeacon Scott for trespass on his rights as a tenant. The cases dragged on for two years. In the first matter, Hall was found guilty of trespass – and ordered to pay one shilling. In the second, the court found in favour of Hall and ordered the Archdeacon to pay £25.

Dr Robert Wardell was another frequent critic of the administration. A barrister, and a former editor of the *Statesman* in London, he started the *Australian* newspaper (not connected to the modern newspaper of the same name) with friend and fellow barrister William Charles Wentworth.

The *Australian* was very clear on its views on press freedom. Its first editorial read: 'A free press is the most legitimate, and at the same time the most powerful weapon that can be employed to annihilate influence, frustrate the designs of tyranny, and restrain the arm of oppression.'

Dr Wardell had a habit of writing satirically, and one story in particular enraged the establishment. Entitled 'How-e to Live by Plunder', the story accused Robert Howe, editor of the *Sydney Gazette*, of stealing a story from the *Australian*'s offices and publishing it. Wardell, in his editorial, also accused Colonel Henry Dumaresq, the governor's brother-in-law and private secretary, of involvement.

Dumaresq challenged Wardell to a duel, which took place near what is now the suburb of Homebush. After trying and failing to shoot each other, Wardell agreed to make a verbal apology and honour was declared satisfied.

By the way, Gerald Mobbs is not based on Robert Howe, although the *Sydney Gazette*, like the fictional *Colonial Flyer*, was more pro-government than either the *Australian* or the *Monitor*, and operated as the administration's official organ. Colonel Edward Duchamp is only very loosely inspired by Colonel Dumaresq.

While we're on the subject, Henrietta Duchamp is a complete fabrication; however, the Female School of Industry existed and was founded by Governor Ralph Darling's wife, Eliza. It was on Macquarie Street, close to where the Mitchell Library now stands.

Brendan Donnelly is loosely based on Daniel Deniehy, whose remarks about the bunyip aristocracy have been put in Donnelly's mouth.

The Sudds and Thompson affair

The epicentre of the acrimony between the governor and the press was the treatment of two soldiers, Patrick Thompson and Joseph Sudds of the 57th Regiment.

Sudds and Thompson were among those who believed that convicts, once their sentence was served, had more opportunities in the colony than soldiers who had never committed a crime. They, and others, watched former convicts grow into prosperous merchants and traders. They were not the only ones to believe that those who arrived free were often at a disadvantage, particularly if they wore a uniform.

Thinking to serve the sentence of the court and then better themselves once in possession of a ticket of leave, the pair committed a very visible theft of a bolt of fabric from a store in Sydney's York Street, dressed in their uniforms. They were sentenced to seven years.

Their timing, however, could not have been worse. Governor Darling decided to make an example of the two men. He commuted their sentence from transportation to seven years on a road gang in leg irons (despite lacking the legal authority to do so). He ordered special chains made, which ran from the leg irons to a custom-made collar, festooned with spikes so that the men could not lie down. At a ceremony ordered by Darling, the pair were stripped of their soldiers' uniforms, put into yellow convict clothes, and had their irons riveted on under the gaze of their former comrades.

Sudds, already in poor health, died shortly afterwards. Thompson was then forced to wear Sudds' chains as well as his own.

Darling was excoriated by both Hall at the *Monitor* and Wardell and Wentworth at the *Australian*.

Darling strikes back

In response to continued press attacks, Governor Darling proposed a licensing regime for the colony's newspapers. In effect, this would have required newspapers to seek annual permission to continue publishing. He also tried to institute a 4d stamp duty, which would have put newspapers out of reach of all but the wealthiest.

In essence, this would have resulted in a state-run media, had it not been for the intervention of Sir Francis Forbes, the first Chief Justice of the Supreme Court of New South Wales. Chief Justice Forbes ultimately overturned both measures, saying in relation to the licensing scheme: 'So far as (publishing) becomes an instrument of communicating intelligence and expressing opinion, it is considered a constitutional right, and is now too well established to admit of question that it is one of the privileges of a British subject.'

Darling, of course, was a more nuanced man than can be conveyed in this brief note. There is no doubt, however, that he was far stricter than his predecessors Lachlan Macquarie and Thomas Brisbane. He seems to have had a rigid, militaristic approach to the punishment of convicts which bordered on the inhumane and in some cases, such as that of Sudds and Thompson, overstepped that line. He was of the view that educated convicts were particularly culpable, as their intelligence and learning gave them advantages which 'common' criminals lacked. Our friend Monsarrat will collide with this attitude when he and Mrs Mulrooney return in *The Valley of the Swells*.

One last note: the gaol in this book is called Sydney Gaol, but is fictional and only very loosely based on the real gaol of the same name.

For those interested in further reading, the books and papers we relied on in writing this novel include:

A History of the Criminal Law in NSW 1788–1900, G. D. Woods, Federation Press, 2002

Early Struggles of the Australian Press, James Bonwick, Ulan Press, 1890

Ralph Darling – A Governor Maligned, Brian H. Fletcher, Oxford University Press, 1984

Edward Smith Hall and the Sydney Monitor, Erin Ihde, Australian Scholarly Publishing, 2004

The Wentworths, Father and Son, John Ritchie, Melbourne University Press, 1997

Settlers and Convicts, or, Recollections of Sixteen Years' Labour in the Australian Backwoods, Alexander Harris, C. Cox, London, 1847

'Defamation Law and the Emergence of a Free Press in Colonial NSW', Brendan Edgeworth, *Australian Journal of Law and Society*, Vol. 6, 1990

'The Origins of a Free Press', Jack Herman, *Press Council News*, Vol. 15, No. 1, February 2003

'Believers in Court: Sydney Anglicans Going to Law', Cable Lecture, Justice Keith Mason, 9 September 2005

'The Politics of the Pew: Faith, Liberty, and Authority in a Sydney Church in 1828', Matthew Allen, *Journal of Religious History*, Vol. 42, No. 1, March 2018

'Newspaper Acts Opinion', C. J. Forbes, April 1827, Supreme Court of New South Wales

Acknowledgements

As this book was being edited, Tom underwent a traumatic but necessary surgical procedure. He's recovering well and wants to send his thanks – to which I wholeheartedly add my own – to everyone who has sent kind wishes, and embraced Monsarrat and Mrs M.

As always, my thanks and gratitude go to my family. Craig, Rory and Alex, thank you for putting up with the stress and deadlines, the half-drunk cups of coffee and demands for hugs and chocolate. I love you.

Tom and I both wish to thank my remarkable mother, Judy, who does so much for everyone and makes it look easy. She is one of the strongest women I have ever met and was integral to getting this book onto the page.

We owe a great debt of gratitude to my aunt, Jane Hall Keneally, to whom this book is dedicated. She was an incredible support to Tom, Judy and the rest of our family in the aftermath of Tom's surgery, and we can't thank her enough.

Editors are the unsung heroes of the publishing industry, and I'd like to thank two of the best, Catherine Hill and

Kate Goldsworthy, who put so much work into this manuscript and left it a lot better than they found it.

And finally, I owe more than I can repay to my father, without whom Monsarrat and Mrs M would not exist. Tommy, thank you for taking me along for the ride.

Meg Keneally
December 2018